The Helmet and the Cross

By the same author
Non-fiction
A Creel of Willow
A Snowdon Stream

Fiction
The Ring-Givers
The Seal
Sammy Going South
The Hunter and the Horns
My Feet Upon a Rock
Crows in a Green Tree
The Grey Seas of Jutland
The Mules of Borgo San Marco
A Moral Obligation
A Declaration of Independence
Harry Doing Good
Glory of the Sea
The Willow-Pattern War
The Solid Gold Buddha

THE HELMET AND THE CROSS

W. H. Canaway

C

CENTURY

LONDON   MELBOURNE   AUCKLAND   JOHANNESBURG

First published in Great Britain in 1986 by
Century Hutchinson Ltd
Brookmount House, 62–65 Chandos Place, London WC2N 4NW

Century Hutchinson Group (Australia) Pty Ltd
16–22 Church Street, Hawthorn, Melbourne, Victoria 3122

Century Hutchinson Group (NZ) Ltd
PO Box 40-086, 32–34 View Road, Glenfield, Auckland 10

Century Hutchinson Group (SA) Ltd
PO Box 337, Bergvlei 2012, South Africa

ISBN 0 7126 9512 5

Set by Input Typesetting Ltd, London

Printed and bound in Great Britain by Anchor Brendon Ltd, Tiptree, Essex

For Pam

ACKNOWLEDGMENTS

The author's thanks are due to the following persons and institutions:

The British Army; East Midlands Arts; Peter Knight; the late Archimandrite Kyriakos; Richard Parris; Paul Sidey; the *Sunday Express* (which published the germ of this novel as my short story); Thorn EMI and Colin Woodley; the Revd H. L. H. Townsend (who first introduced me to the work of Josephus many years ago).

W.H.C.

And the Gentiles shall come to thy light, and kings to the brightness of thy rising.

Isaiah 60,3

SOME CITIES OF SYRIA PALAESTINA

Antioch

Damascus

ABILENE

Sidon

PHOENICIA

Tyre

Caesaráea
Philippi

ITURAEA

Gischala

R. Jordon

Ptolemais

TRACHONITIS

Capernaum Julias

GALILEE

Sea
of
Galilee

Magdala Hippos Dion
Tarikheae

Jotapata Gamala

Tiberias Gadara Capitolias

Sepphoris

Caesarea

DECAPOLIS

Scythopolis Gerasa

SAMARIA Sebaste Pella

Apollonia R. Jabbok

Antipatris PERAEA

Joppa

Jericho

Jerusalem

JUDAEA Philadelphia
(Amman)

Herodeion

Askelon Dead
Sea FtMachaerus

Agrippeion

Ft Masada

IDUMAEA
(Edom)

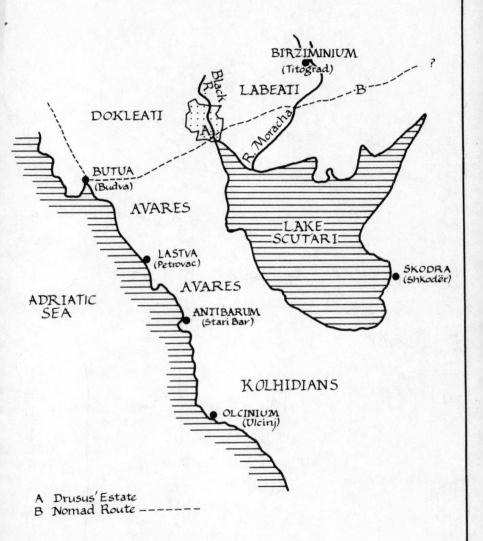

A PART OF SOUTHERN ILLYRIA

BIRZIMINIUM
(Titograd)

LABEATI

Black R.

DOKLEATI

R. Moracha

B

?

BUTUA
(Budva)

AVARES

LAKE
SCUTARI

LASTVA
(Petrovac)

AVARES

SKODRA
(Shkodër)

ADRIATIC
SEA

ANTIBARUM
(Stari Bar)

KOLHIDIANS

OLCINIUM
(Ulcinj)

A Drusus' Estate
B Nomad Route -------

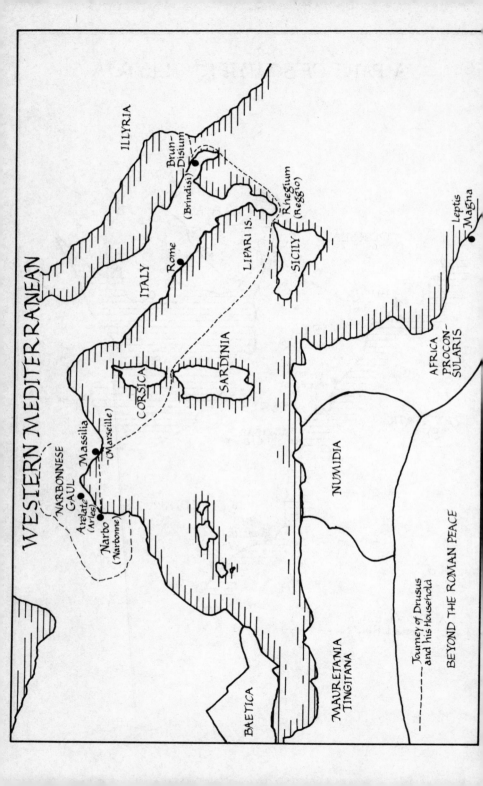

WESTERN MEDITERRANEAN

ILLYRIA

Brun-
Disium
(Brindisi)

ITALY

Rome

LIPARI IS.

Rhegium
(Reggio)

SICILY

CORSICA

SARDINIA

NARBONESE
GAUL

Massilia
(Marseille)

Arelate
(Arles)

Narbo
(Narbonne)

NUMIDIA

AFRICA
PROCON-
SULARIS

Leptis
Magna

BAETICA

MAURETANIA
TINGITANA

------- Journey of Drusus
and his Household

BEYOND THE ROMAN PEACE

BOOK ONE

The Helmet

Greek and barbarian, with his property or without it, can go with ease wherever he likes, just as though going from one homeland to another. The Cilician Gates hold no terror, nor the narrow and desert approaches from Arabia to Egypt, nor inaccessible mountains nor uncrossed expanses of rivers, nor tribes inhospitable to the stranger: for safety it is enough to be a Roman.

— Aelius Aristides (in *The Romans*, by R.H. Barrow, Pelican Books, 1949, p.127).

ANTE SCRIPTUM

Professor John Potts strolled along a mosaic path on the campus of the new Jerusalem University. It was late afternoon in high summer, but the heat bothered Potts not at all. He had spent too long in hot climates to be affected by the weather, and was at that time holder of a chair in Semitic languages at a university in Southern California. Potts was thirty-nine years old, a Cambridge graduate with higher degrees from the Sorbonne and Brandeis. He had brought over a group of students on a study tour of the Holy Land. Potts himself had visited Jerusalem on many study trips, mostly at the Archeological Museum. He was tough and stocky, with a deep chest and a black-shadowed chin. After a classical education at Repton he had specialized first in proto-Hebraic and then in Aramaic. Some of his recreations – caving and rock-climbing – were relevant to his academic work. At that moment he was ambling along with a slight smile on his face, relaxed and happy. Professor Potts was playing hookey.

He and his students had spent the day at the university, and the group had begun the afternoon at the photographic library. After a couple of hours Potts had handed them over to one of the archivists. He walked through a rear entrance into the Shrine of the Book, which they had visited that morning; he threaded his way among the tourists crowding the rotunda where scrolls and their jars were on display. Then he walked out into the tunnel of geodesic arches symbolizing the caves where many of the 'Dead Sea' scrolls were discovered. Potts lifted a finger to one of the security

3

guards – who by then knew his face – as he emerged into the dazzle of light. Like a rebirth, he thought as he went down the white steps. Not a student of his in sight!

Half an hour later he was sitting on his hotel terrace on the Mount of Olives, sipping iced orange juice and at peace with the world. He told himself that he owed it to his students as well as to himself to get away from them for a while. They were energetic, eager to learn . . . and so young. At his university the greater part of his time was taken up with research and administration; he had only six hours of lectures and seminars with the occasional public lecture. Here he was seldom free of undergraduate company. From time to time it struck him forcibly how much they had to learn of things which he took for granted.

He was reminded of an example from a couple of days earlier. One of his students had been listening to a conversation in Hebrew, and had told Potts enthusiastically how exciting she had thought it, to be listening to the very language spoken in those streets two thousand years before.

Potts had said, 'You aren't. Hebrew was used only ceremonially. You'd have been hearing Aramaic – if you hadn't been hearing Greek.'

The young fresh face fell in disappointment.

Potts felt a twinge of regret and said. 'Sorry if I gave you a let-down. But the truth is what's important.'

'So what's the truth?'

Potts said wryly, 'Someone else asked the same question in this town, once.'

His student nodded and smiled, her mood lifting again. The sombre wall of forty years was confronting Potts, and now and then a valedictory fugue oppressed him: it threatened now as he observed the moods of youth, as evanescent as the patterns of a breeze on the surface of a lake, but so sharply felt for all that.

'But then in a way, could be I was right to imagine myself hearing Hebrew centuries ago? Like we know the Nativity wasn't December twenty-fifth, but that's been Christmas so many centuries it's become right?'

Potts grinned and said, '*Touché*. I am decapitated.'

*

4

He collected the students and took them to a vacant seminar room. When they were seated he looked round the puzzled faces, and the hum of conversation died away.

Potts said, 'I've been talking with Ann, and it's occurred to me that there are holes to fill. The lecturer you heard on the flight out concentrated on Judæa, on the Jews and the Jewish Christians.'

He switched on an overhead projector and took up a felt pen, beginning to sketch.

'Let me draw a map while I talk,' he continued. 'The Holy Land was part of Roman Syria, which stretched from Antioch in the north to Agrippeion in the south, and the Jews formed perhaps seven per cent of the total population.'

Potts smiled as someone gasped.

'Yes, Reuben,' he said, still sketching. 'But they kicked up a fuss out of all proportion to their numbers. . . . Now then. The country was different from what we see today. There were many more trees, for one thing, and that means a moister climate and bigger areas of fertile land. There was jungle in places along the banks of the Jordan north of Jericho, and there were lions still in the country before the Romans cleared them out for their circuses.

'But it was a land of cities too, a land with a population of somewhere between five and a half and seven million.'

Under his pen the city names grew on the projector sheet: Sidon, Damascus, Tyre – familiar enough names – but then lesser known ones began to appear among the familiar: Gischala, Julias, Capernaum, Tarikhæa, Tiberias, Gamala, Jotapata. . . .

'The thing to remember is that most of the cities were hellenized, and the common tongue was Greek, though now we're working down into Judæa and the proportion of Jews increases, Aramaic would be heard more frequently. But it's a good bet that the conversation between Jesus and Pilate took place in Greek. And although Judæa wasn't incorporated as an Imperial province until 6 A.D., there had been a Roman presence since the time of Herod the Great's father. The *Gentiles Keep Out!* sign on a wall of the Jerusalem Temple was written in Greek, Latin and Hebrew. The Temple itself was a masterpiece of Greek architecture. And the carpenter's shop where Jesus worked was only four miles from the big Greek city of Sepphoris, which comparatively few people have heard of, though everyone knows of the small town of Nazareth. Sepphoris was just a stroll down the road. So now you know it's no accident that the Fourth Gospel was written in Greek. And that's all we have time for now.'

So, sitting on the terrace with his orange juice before dinner, Potts contemplated the shark's teeth skyline of the Judæan wilderness. The group was due to visit Qumran next day; and before recalling that conversation and the discourse that had followed it, he had decided to spend all day at the beach. Now he was not so sure. Ann's insight had embodied an artistic rather than a spiritual truth, he considered on reflection; but the end result was the same, and the source of his uncertainty. He had been growing weary of the group's constant proximity, but how had its members been feeling about him? Potts' attempt to distance himself had brought him to the verge of professional negligence, just going through the motions. It would not do.

Professor Potts shook his head, and went in to dinner. By the time he had finished the meal his mind was made up, and he called for brandy with his coffee. Recalled to a sense of his responsibilities, he raised the brandy glass in a silent toast to his students. He was a scholar in the field of the scrolls, had done important work on one of them. Next day during the visit to Qumran he would take the group into one of the caves where scrolls had been found, and make the subject come alive.

He stood glumly outside the ruined monastery of Qumran, the ancient Secacah, some miles to the south of Jericho and a lot higher up. He had his back to the roofless masonry pit of the Scriptorium, where his six students listened to the exposition of their learned guide in the place where the Essene monks had sat at their stone benches inscribing on cleaned skins and creating the documents which – two thousand years later – would become known as the Dead Sea scrolls. To Potts it was a wordless buzz. That ceased, and the guide led his party over to the Hall of Congregation. Potts took no notice; he was too angry with himself. His hands in the trouser pockets of his safari suit, he stood at the head of a glacis which sloped down to a fearsome plateau, an abomination of desolation in tune with his mood. The plateau was reddish brown, featureless except for a litter of rocks and boulders dancing in mirage under a dreadful sun. Far away on the left the Mountains of Moab lumped up through the heat haze like bunloaves; to the right lay the tawny hills through which the Jericho road wound from Jerusalem.

Potts was furious with himself because he could not put into effect his plan to take the group into a cave, for the reason that their insurance expressly forbade such activity, along with all kinds of flying except by scheduled flights; scuba-diving and mountaineering. Potts grunted with annoyance, feeling that he could do nothing right.

He strolled down the glacis to the plateau. Immediately to his left cliffs fell away to the Dead Sea shore in a long sweep. Toward their tops the cliffs bulged out in horizontally banded formations like weathered turrets plunging on for another couple of hundred feet. On the turrets the black mouths of caves could be seen. Perhaps he could describe a typical interior adequately to the students? They would be engrossed for an hour or so yet.

He picked his way along the cliff edge. It was just after two-thirty in the July afternoon, the sun still high in a sky of molten mercury. Potts looked down at the Dead Sea as he walked: boiling pewter in swirling mists far below. For the first time an incongruity stuck him. The Dead Sea was one thousand three hundred feet below sea level. Potts had always thought of the plateau as high ground, but he now realised that it too might be below sea level. He glanced down once more at the Dead Sea, making a mental note to consult a good map back at the hotel. Then something closer caught his eye. It was a tiny glint in a crevice perhaps sixty feet below him. He moved six inches to the right; the glint was gone. He found it again, moved fractionally to the left, and it vanished at once. Again Potts relocated it, catching his breath. By being in one place within a few inches, at a

7

certain time, with the sun at one particular angle . . . The odds against catching that scintilla of reflection were enormous.

He fixed the position of the crevice carefully and climbed down. For all his bulk Potts moved lightly and precisely, picking his footholds with care and noting handholds as he went; he was not going to hold onto the blistering rock unless he had to in emergency. He reached the crevice and peered inside with growing excitement. He saw a small gold box, and beyond it a battered Roman helmet, its crest long gone, with a dark scorpion sitting on the rim. There was a scatter of bones beyond, but the light was dim in the farther reaches of the fissure.

Potts picked up a stone and dropped it with a clatter; he missed the helmet but the scorpion retreated inside it, and that was enough for Potts. He leaned in and snatched the box at the extremity of his reach, scratching his knuckles on the rock.

He sucked his hand, then buttoned the box into his jacket pocket before climbing back to the plateau.

It was a small, heavy gold box, about six inches long, four wide and an inch and a half deep, abraded here and there, but not badly damaged. He inserted the blade of his penknife and then very gingerly lifted up the lid.

There were documents inside. Very gently Potts took them out. One was a much-folded skin, not to be tampered with at all, but left to an expert. The other, topmost document was of newer parchment, better preserved and folded only once, with writing on the inner surface. It had been damaged by time, but not so severely as to preclude reconstruction. Eaten by curiosity, Potts opened the fold as far as he dared. He read:

—––S TIB A D XIX KA– JA–

It was a military order written in the reign of Tiberius Cæsar, commanding the centurion

M –RUS–– –CIPI–

8

(M. Drusus Scipio, that must have been, whose bones, helmet and other hidden impedimenta lay in that fissure.) Comanding him to do what A. D. XIX KAL JAN? That was ANTE DIEM UNDEVICESIMUM KALENDAS JANUARIAS, the nineteenth day before the Kalends of January. Potts would no doubt find out more in the end, but in the meantime he had to report the find to the proper authorities: the box and contents belonged to the Department of Antiquities. Potts could begin with the guide, who was a senior member of the Museum staff.

The box in his hand, Potts glanced at his digital watch, wondering what time it was in California. He was bursting to tell his wife about the extraordinary manner of his find. She worked for an academic publishing house in downtown Los Angeles and so had been unable to accompany him, but he would call her as soon as he could.

As he started back to the ruins of the monastery, Potts remembered Helen's quoting Castaneda to the effect that no series of events may be called random: if the observer is in the right place at the right time, then a causality will be seen. But for one decision of conscience Potts would have been sitting at the beach. He had determined to do the best he could for his students, and had been balked. Out of pique he had taken a walk, and found himself in time and place able to intercept that wink of gold like a signal across almost two thousand years of time.

Professor Potts shook his head, then sucked his hand again as he walked, wondering who M. Drusus Scipio had been, and how he had met what must have been a most unpleasant death.

I

Herod the Great had many things wrong with him during his last year of life. But he began to feel really ill after a group of young men tried to dismantle a huge golden eagle which he had put up above the Great Gate of the sanctuary: an image that defiled the holy place, and a symbol of Rome to boot.

When he had executed those concerned, his illnesses increased in severity: a constant slight temperature, pains in the stomach and bowels; gangrenous genitals. He went to Callirhoë on the eastern shore of the Dead Sea, where there were hot baths from natural springs of sweet water. As part of his course of treatment the doctors lowered him into a bath full of hot oil. He fainted at once, and when he came again to his senses he had become convinced he was going to die. He sent to Sebaste for his favourite Greek physician, however, then set about sending some more precursors to Hades.

He had already framed his wife's grandfather Hyrcanus and had him put to death. He had drowned her brother Jonathan. He had made his sons Aristobulus and Alexander kings, then had them throttled to death at Sebaste. When the Greek arrived Herod was at Jericho, in his palace there. He had just sent the guard to slaughter his eldest and sole surviving son, Antipater, then had every village headman in Judæa rounded up and imprisoned.

Herod's orders were that his own death must be the signal for theirs: if Judæa would not lament his own passing, he was going to make sure that wailing and gnashing of teeth

10

would take place just the same. When Herod began to scratch he thought little of it at first compared with what he regarded as more serious afflictions; but by the time the Greek arrived Herod's itching had become more than he could bear. The Greek had a body slave undress the king. Herod was gross, but his ravaged frame was still muscular; he scratched and scratched, groaning and scarcely coherent as the doctor examined him.

There were swellings under the skin, red and angry from the scratching, and one or two of them had begun to move in gentle pulsation. The doctor watched with lips compressed: he had seen this condition before. In Parthia. Now it was in Syria Palæstina and on King Herod's person.

The Greek administered a potion of nepenthe. When the king was unconscious, his chamberlain, his cousin Achiab and hangers-on hovering, the doctor dismissed everyone but the chamberlain.

The Greek said, 'Have his clothes and everything on his bed burned. Prepare another room for him, with a single leather floor covering. And have that slave killed and cremated at once. But it's probably too late.'

'What is his sickness?' asked the chamberlain.

'Varro holds that there may be animals in existence which are too small for us to see. I follow him. Now kindly do as I say.'

He sent a messenger on a fast horse to Sebaste: the first move in arrangements for turning all he owned into cash. When he returned from his quarters that evening to look at his patient he did so from a distance.

'He tried to kill himself with a fruit knife when he came round,' said the chamberlain. 'His cousin stopped him, but was that wise? Just look at the king!'

Herod was rolling about the bed in intolerable agony. Boils the size of a baby's fist had erupted all over his body. Some were bursting and ejecting streams of foul liquid. The left eye was a melted puddle. Herod was semiconscious, groaning hoarsely. The doctor and the chamberlain withdrew to the anteroom out of hearing of the guards at the royal threshold.

Varro and the Greek doctor were right. The Itch Mite,

Acarus siro, is invisible to the naked eye. It is itself host to the *Harpyrhyncus* mite, which was multiplying in its millions under Herod's skin, every boil as it burst throwing out thousands of larvae.

The patient's environment was totally infected, and the Greek knew this; but the chamberlain had no idea.

He said, 'I had six tentmakers at work. But a leather floor covering . . . ?'

The doctor said, 'Time to think of your own skin, man. The struggle for succession will be very dangerous for you. It's too late to worry over Herod's skin. As soon as he dies get your tentmakers to work again. Sew Herod and everything in the room into the leather, handling only the edges. Let it be double-sewn. Small stitches and waxed thread.'

The chamberlain had turned pale.

He said, 'King Herod was cruel and ruthless, and the people curse his name for the taxes he laid on them, when he was not even a Jew. But he had the energy of an army of men in one body. He rebuilt the Temple even if he did not keep the Law himself; he built lovely cities, aqueducts, pleasure gardens, theatres, ports and harbours. He kept good relations with Rome. And now to see him laid so low! Please tell me the name of this terrible sickness.'

The Greek thought for a moment and then said, 'Oh, Herod's Evil is as good a name as any.'

When the Greek left his instructions were ignored, for Archelaus, Herod's successor, was determined to give the dead monster a royal send-off to the underworld.

The struggle for succession which the Greek had foreseen lay in the future. For the moment all went well. Herod's body was carried to Herodeion on a bier of bejewelled gold, the corpse with crown and sceptre and wearing crimson robes. It went along to its burial in fine state, accompanied by Herod's family (that is, all those he had not murdered) and the entire Judæan Army.

It was twenty-four miles from Jericho to Herodeion, and the itch mite went along for the ride. It soon became endemic in Judæa.

II

In the early part of the year when Herod the Great died* a man named Butin received his honourable discharge from the Roman Imperial Army after twenty-five years' service. He was a captain of auxiliaries, Illyrian cavalry attached to the Roman maniples. He had served with the crack Jerusalem unit, and needed to get back there for a while. Butin was forty-two years old, a laughing man with long fair hair and beard, keen blue eyes and a whipcord body even in his middle years; his nickname was Centaur; he was a horseman beyond compare. No Roman gravity for him: he would laugh with pure delight as he took off your head with his small curved sword, or put an arrow through you from two hundred paces, with an almost flat trajectory from the compound bow he used. It was a Parthian bow, looted from a dead enemy on some long gone battlefield. Butin had picked it up and liked the feel of it. Parthian arrows had never been in short supply. But now Butin was at the Roman military depôt at Cæsarea, and had seen his last Parthian.

War apart, Butin was likeable and popular. The release of the time-expired soldiers was marked by a religious parade to honour the gods, including the Divine Augustus and the Eagle of the Legion from which they were detached. As ordered, Butin reported afterwards to the office of the Camp Prefect at the main administrative block. To his surprise his Tribune and senior officers were present.

The tribune said, 'My faithful captain, we are truly sorry to see you go. Your service has been full of honour and you

*4 BCE

13

are the best officer of auxiliaries I have ever known. You have five awards for bravery, and two of them were earned while you were with these maniples. All of us wish you well.'

He motioned to the Camp Prefect, who handed Butin a parchment scroll.

The tribune went on, 'Your diploma will be sent on to you from Rome. But receive now your citizenship and your grant of lands. The citizenship is extended not only to your male heir, but exceptionally to your wife.'

Butin took the document, his head slightly inclined, restrained into the Roman discipline: but he felt like jumping up and down and shouting with joy.

'There are two other things,' the tribune said. 'Firstly, to your discharge grant all the officers and centurions have added contributions of their own. Secondly, it is the pleasure of the Emperor himself to award you a Roman name. Gaius Julius Cæsar Octavianus, Augustus the Divine, names you Publius Drusus Scipio. Thus your honour is made public.'

Butin fell to his knees and had to be helped up. When he left the office to applause, he was staggering under the weight of a chest of gold pieces to add to his hoard, for he was already a rich man.

Butin reached Jerusalem in a day and a half's hard riding. He transferred his own six horses to livery stables close to his concubine's small house and weaving shed; he had set her up in this business and bought her the slaves who did the work under the supervision of a free-born foreman. The concubine, Maroula, was in her early thirties, dark, plump and comfortable, a soft anvil both for his lusts and for the swift strikes and sparks of his personality. They had seen plenty of each other over the past four years, while he had seen nothing of his wife eighteen hundred miles away; but Maroula has little place in this story. He moved in with her for those few days, and took with him his slave, Targui.

The man was in fact *a* Targui. His family belonged to a people named Tuareg, of which Targui is the masculine singular. All over the world there are geographical features with names culled from obscure languages, and meaning 'No idea', 'Mad foreigner,' and so on. Targui had been the victim

14

of a similar linguistic misunderstanding to begin with. Snatched from a country far south of the known Roman world, far, far south of the North African cornfields, he had been sold aged fifteen on the Libyan coast, disposed of at eighteen to a slave market in Alexandria, and bought there by Butin.

It came about this way. East of the city itself, near the Alexandrian Legion headquarters, was a pleasant little suburb, and part of this had been adapted as a military rest centre for officers. Outwardly it was a typical Roman camp, but contained a complex of buildings and gardens facing the coast. There were officers' quarters and mess-rooms, a theatre, a beer hall and wine bars, good facilities for sports and games, and a luxurious brothel and bath house. The sandy paths were brightened with potplants and flowers under shady trees, and the air was scented with jasmine and hibiscus.

Butin was spending a furlough there, and after two days' rest he was prowling like a leopard. Wide awake on the third night, he stood on the beach. The surf hushed at him, the sand was warm between his bare toes, and westward along the coast the great lighthouse flared its warning, or welcome home. The glare of light dimmed the stars, but the Illyrian captain stared out beneath them, out to sea northwestward, his mind journeying home past Crete, Akhaia, Epiros. . . . He wanted his wife, a fight, a horse to break, a boar to spear.

Next morning he was up in lamplight, washed and dressed. He ate a few dates and a wheaten cake smeared with honey, drank a small pot of beer, and went out into the sudden Egyptian dawn.

Trumpets sounded for the first hour and for the change of guard; as he had planned, Butin arrived at the guardhouse at the same time as the relieving duty officer, to hear at once the password for that night. He was in the Army and the rule was inflexible: he needed to know that password as certainly as if he were in some beleaguered fort on the Elbe rather than in the safety of Alexandria. The password was *Prometheus*.

Butin said in Vulgar Latin, 'Ha! That old eagle: "Liver *again* today?"'

15

The two officers looked blank, and Butin, the barbarian who was multilingual and knew his Æschylus – he had seen *Prometheus Bound* and many other Greek plays – shrugged and walked out with his fast light step. He was wearing mufti, a silk shirt and a leather kilt, bare legs and sandals. He wore no head covering. There was money in an inside pocket of the kilt, and Butin carried a knife almost as long as a Roman shortsword to ensure that the money stayed where it was until he wanted to spend it. The dagger was sheathed at his left side in contrast to Roman regular troops, who wore their swords on the right. He displayed no jewellery, easily snatched in a crowd, but the silver rings on his arms proclaimed him a soldier on leave; these were for good conduct – an effective deterrent to criminals.

At the city outskirts he spoke to a guide.

The man said in Greek, 'You want a girl? A boy? You want my sister? Very clean? Very cheap?'

'What I want in that way I can get without paying money,' Butin told the man with some contempt. 'Show me the city.'

'Yes,' the guide said eagerly. 'I show you exhibitions: girl with donkey; dirty old man and little boy and hot camel sweetbreads; nasty billy goat and –'

Butin was laughing at him and he stopped talking then, because Butin had his thumbs on the fellow's carotids and he went out like a flame under the snuffer. Butin left him unconscious; he would come round quickly. Butin walked on until he found an elderly and scholarly-minded guide who would show him the public buildings, beginning with the great complex of the library. Butin's race had no great tradition of building, but unlike many barbarians, who took the magnificence of Egyptian and Greek architecture for granted, with Roman roads and baths and aqueducts; metered water supply; international postal and health services – all the material trappings of Roman civilization, in fact – Butin was fascinated by it all. He and his guide walked all the way around the main library, the Brucheum, while Butin wondered about the contents.

'There are nearly half a million scrolls housed inside,' he was told.

Even from outside they could hear the din of hundreds of

men reading. They walked along to the annexe, which held almost fifty thousand scrolls, and formed part of a sub-complex known as the Serapeum.

The intelligent Roman citizen passed his days in fear: the fear that there might be an afterlife along the standard Greek or Egyptian pattern. The gods of Rome were immortal, and those of Olympus were humanized, honoured with dozens of festivals and games. But any idea of personal immortality came from the Greeks and the Egyptians. The solid Romans shied away in horror from the prospect of drifting insubstantially through Elysian fields of asphodel. Similarly, having one's deeds weighed after death in the Egyptian style held no appeal at all for a Roman, especially if Osiris' feather balance tilted favourably: the reward was an eternity of work in the fields of Earu. But at some unknown time, to the jackal-faced Anubis was added the jackal-faced Serapis, brother to Horus. The Serapeum was dedicated to this god with his shrine and statue; together with the cult of Isis, of death and rebirth, a kinder immortality was promised.

Butin listened absently to the guide's disquisition on this subject as they walked to visit other buildings. Then they paused for refreshment, and Butin bought his guide a meal, for the man was wilting visibly.

They began the afternoon by visiting the bustling sea front, which Butin had seen only briefly before, on his arrival and at night. They stood on the upright of a T-shape, with the eastern and western harbours on either side of them; the crossbar of the T gave seaward protection, and from its centre the enormous lighthouse towered more than five hundred feet into the sky.

It was a scene of furious activity. There were no large vessels, military or mercantile, arriving or departing at the time of Butin's visit, although many were moored at the quays, including several triremes. But a great number of smaller vessels were plying in all directions among the larger ships, taking passengers to ship or shore, loading water or provisions; touting for trade in goods or women. The Jews of this Greek city controlled the whole maritime trade of Alexandria.

People thronged the quays. There were other sightseers

like Butin, but most were engaged in purposeful behaviour: lines of porters bent under loads, or messengers and officials bearing papyri; passengers with their baggage-slaves; off-duty sailors heading for food stall or inn or brothel, and many just going home; merchants with their retinues of hangers-on; and always the military presence of Rome. A tribune and a centurion stood by one of the triremes while a boarding party under a junior centurion inspected its cargo; small detachments of troops went about their business; and security patrols made their way through the throng. It was hot, noisy and smelly.

The guide said, 'There are about three hundred thousand citizens in Alexandria.'

Three hundred thousand citizens, Butin repeated to himself. He saw a slave auction in progress farther along the quay, and wondered what the total would be if slaves were included. A million? Two or three? But of course slaves never were taken into account. He shoved his way closer to the auction, initially attracted by a group of young women. They were fair-haired, nude for exhibition, and they might have been of his own people. Butin weighed them up idly, then his attention was shifted to a pair of fierce eyes behind the women, a Pharos glare.

The slave was a man, also a naked exhibit with his loin-cloth at his feet, yet he had a fold of material over the lower part of his face, an attempt at a veil which he kept in place with one hand. His skin was a coppery yellow, and as Butin walked round him he saw that the slave's back and shoulders were scarred by floggings, including recent weals oozing blood. The man turned to face him and again Butin met that unservile glare.

He turned to the guide and gave him money, saying, 'Thank you for your trouble. You have a fine head for figures. Now I need to employ my own.'

Butin walked over to one of the slavemaster's assistants, a fat man in a grubby robe.

'That one,' Butin said, and pointed to the slave. 'What is he?'

'Who knows?' the slaver said, noting the silver arm rings and giving an obsequious duck of his head. He led the way

18

over to the man and said, 'He's called Targui. He's difficult, but very strong. It's a problem.'

'Yes,' Butin agreed. 'If you geld him you soften his nature, but you lose his strength. I'll buy him if the price is right.'

They haggled, while the slavemaster watched them and the auction of the women, which was proceeding under another assistant. But eventually hands were struck at eighty-three denarii, with a six-foot length of rope thrown in.

Butin lashed one end of the rope to the collar of his new acquisition, and led him away. The improvized veil was back in position, Butin noted.

He asked, 'Do you speak Latin, Targui?'

'A bit. Not much.'

'Who are you?'

Targui pointed to the south-west and said, 'T'majagh. Imajeghan,' trying to tell Butin that he was a nobleman of his tribe.

Butin said, 'A long way from home? Who isn't, these days?'

They walked, Targui a pace in front; he made no attempt to escape. His cruelly damaged back needed attention, which it would receive at the medical centre in the camp. Then another thought came to Butin.

He said. 'Targui? Is that your usual way of dressing?'

The slave turned his head and sullenly said. 'No.'

Butin stopped him on the rope.

He said, 'Listen now. I will tell you this just once. My name is Butin, and I am a captain of Roman cavalry. You may call me "Captain" or "Master." I want you to dress as near as possible to the customs of your people. Is that understood?'

Again the dark eyes flared, but then softened as the man yielded to Butin's good sense.

'Yes, Captain.'

And so 'Captain' it was to be, Butin thought wryly: this Targui would never call any man 'Master.' But two hours later the slave was dressed in a black tunic, white trousers and sandals, with a dark blue turban, one end of which he used as a veil. As they emerged from the clothier's Targui

19

silently proffered the rope, which had been removed during the tailoring.

'Do I need it?' Butin asked.

'May I ask a thing, Captain? Cavalry is horses?'

'Yes.'

Targui said, 'Then I think you not need the rope again, Captain.'

He had been right, serving Butin well and faithfully during the last three years of his twenty-five in the army of Rome. Targui was an excellent horseman. After a few months Butin had armed him with a long sword similar to that which Targui said his people used, and a leather shield. He was officially a body slave, but unofficially his job had included guarding Butin's back in the field. And because of that Butin was alive, retired and named Drusus.

On the second day of his retirement Drusus called Targui to him and handed him a thin scroll of parchment.

'Where shall I take it, Captain?' the slave asked, assuming that the document was a message.

Drusus told him, 'Take it wherever you wish. That is your certificate of manumission. You are a free man.'

'Truly?' Targui was doubtful, even forgetting to call Drusus 'Captain.'

'Truly. Not just a freedman, pledged to follow me. You are free to return to your own people if that is your wish.'

Targui's eyes lit up, and Drusus clapped his arm, grinning.

'It will take some getting used to,' Drusus said. 'I am a citizen now. We both enjoy a change of status. You can go home if you know the way. Oh – and my name is now Drusus.'

Targui grasped both of Drusus' hands and touched them briefly to his forehead.

He said, 'I thank you, Drusus. I can find my way once I get to the Libyan coast . . .'

His voice tailed off and he stood silent, his brow puckered in thought. Drusus waited until the man had worked out what he wanted to say.

At last Targui said, 'From that first day you have fed me and clothed me, looked after me well.'

To this preamble Drusus said sharply, 'And you have served me well. There is no debt.'

'Perhaps, perhaps not. But let me say this. To the south of Mauretania there are horses. Special horses. They are black with a white star. There are no horses in the Roman world to compare with them. And I know where they are. Shall we go there, you and I, now that I am a free man and you have lands where horses might be bred?'

Slowly Drusus said, 'Horses. Beyond the Peace. . . . My granted lands are in Galilee. Too far and too dangerous to bring bloodstock there from beyond Mauretania. The same applies to my home in Illyria, and anyway I have to give that up. Across the Pillars of Hercules, now . . . that would be feasible. Then to Gaul. I need lands in southern Gaul, and that's feasible too if I grease a few palms to ease the transfer. Everyone wants lands in fertile Galilee.' His face brightened and he shouted, 'By all the gods, yes! Now fetch me some wine!'

Targui turned obediently; Drusus recollected himself and yelled, 'No, not you! You're free, and I forgot, and *you* forgot! We will drink wine together, my friend Targui!'

III

In the twenty-fourth year of Julius Cæsar Augustus, on the fourth day before the Nones of March, Publius Drusus Scipio to his dear wife Teutia, Greetings!

My dear, I write to you from Antioch on my way home, the gods willing for the last time, and then we must journey together.

All three of us have our citizenship. I have my Roman name, and you must decide on your own; and we shall both decide on a name for Klitos. For my service in both Gaul and Germany I have been honoured with the name of Drusus, and for that in Africa with that of Scipio. But have no fear that I shall try to make you into a submissive Roman wife instead of a proud and equal (and often superior!) Illyrian.

Here in Antioch I met an old comrade, now an official, with a permit to use Imperial courier stages on his way to Rome. In Barium he will send this letter to you in a fast ship to Antibarum, and the tidings will reach you two or three weeks before I do. I am eleven days on the way, and another forty should see me home and in your arms.

My father was right when he chose Rome. But we of the Dokleati are in a shaky position. Therefore I am taking lands in Narbonnese Gaul. Go to Birziminium and arrange with utmost speed for the sale of our entire property, horses and all. I mean that: horses and all! We must decide whether to travel to Gaul by land or sea, but if by land we shall take draught horses and mules. Sell the stock at valuation by the factor Patroklus – and tell him I am on my way home. He will not cheat you then! The estate, stud and standing crops

22

would be better at auction: put that in hand, and I should be home to see it through.

My greetings also to my son. To him I say this.

Klitos, the world is changing, and your grandfather realized that we must change with it. You will put on your manhood gown as a Roman, not lack it as an Illyrian. Praise the gods who give this gift!

To you, Teutia, I return as speedily as those gods allow me. I have freed my slave Targui and permitted him to keep his own name. He comes as my companion.

My arrival. When you hear the trumpet my people will stay awhile as I ride on ahead. Then you and I will ride on together up the steps to the portico, so everybody inside but yourself and a good fat cushion!

Farewell.

IV

It was the day after Drusus' letter arrived. Klitos sat in the almost dark kitchen drinking buttermilk and munching bread and honey. The first hour of the day was at hand. A couple of slaves were at the other end of the room, a cook cleaning utensils and a girl tidying round the hearth, but they kept their voices low.

From outside a sepulchral croak announced in Latin, 'Fourth hour of the night and raining tridents.'

Klitos disregarded this blatantly false information: he saw Pylades come into the kitchen and stood up out of respect. The man was old now and white-haired, a Greek freedman who had been tutor to Klitos since the age of seven. He had instilled into his pupil good Latin and perfect Akhaian Greek, written and spoken: had taught him arithmetic and geometry, some logic and music, and a little rhetoric. Pylades had travelled much in the west, and had even visited Britain, so his travels had prevented the scholar's narrow-mindedness and given him a hoard of interesting stories, which he seldom told more than twice despite his advancing years.

He nodded to Klitos, who sat down in silence while Pylades ate a couple of pieces of bread and a dried fig. No other members of the household ate this early meal: it was a children's pre-school breakfast, and Klitos and Pylades had simply kept the custom going, pupil and schoolmaster. Pylades sipped a bowl of milk. Neither of them felt like conversation until they had finished breakfast, Pylades because he was built that way, and Klitos because Pylades had built him that way in turn.

24

The hollow voice outside said, 'Fifth hour of the day and the god Augustus is burning yer god-damned eyes out.'

Neither Pylades nor Klitos took any notice. Pylades put down his empty bowl and they spoke together in Greek.

Pylades asked, 'What are your plans for the day?'

Klitos shrugged and said. 'I'm told that I must catch fish. I'll go this afternoon to the river, where the cold water still runs down from the mountains. But first I have to practise with Kenin. Placidus will be waiting for me soon.'

Pylades nodded and stood up stretching and wincing a little, needing warmth for his old bones.

'Come. We'll see the sunrise.'

They went out into the atrium which Klitos' father had built onto the Illyrian farmhouse. The tops of the pillars glowed with the dawn. The talking bird was on its perch near the pool, and Klitos paused on his way past to tickle its hackle feathers. It was a crow brought home many years before by Drusus. The bird had belonged to slaves whose job it had been to shout out the hours from a sundial by day, and from a water clock at night. Klitos' father had found it while helping to loot a sacked city; the black crow perched full of carrion on the butt of a lance in someone's corpse and calling out the wrong time. It did so still, but no one in the household really heard it any more.

Pylades was quoting Homer on the sunrise, and Klitos didn't really hear that either. He waited and then asked, 'Will you come with us, Pylades? To Gaul?'

Pylades frowned at the sudden question.

He said, 'I am not your father's freedman, merely in his service. He is a citizen now, and so are you and the Lady Teutia. Provincial governors have no power over you any longer; you can't be fettered in prison, or scourged, or put to death unless a court in Rome itself decides that. When I was in Gaul, Klitos, I was a slave.'

The sun blazed suddenly through a niche in the wall of the atrium.

'I must go to my practice,' Klitos said. 'But remember that my father will certainly have need of you in Gaul. And so shall I, by all the gods! You were a slave, but now you are a freedman. I was a free Illyrian, but as a Roman I am now

25

under the terrible power of a Roman father. The sun comes up and the world turns upside-down. As a citizen my father could sell me or kill me without penalty. I can't own land or property unless he emancipates me. Stay and help me, Pylades!'

'You don't need to worry. Your father is a good man. But I will come to Gaul if I'm asked.'

Klitos grinned.

The talking bird said, 'Let this cup pass. Long gone closing time.'

But they didn't hear the talking bird: each man had cast aside problems and doubts for the time being, and in the insouciant way of the Greeks was kissing a hand to the sun.

There were several freedmen on the estate: the majordomo, the farrier smith, the bailiff and Pylades. He was a bachelor and in his day had preferred young men. But he had never laid a finger on Klitos, whom he loved as a son.

At sixteen Klitos had already received more training in the arts of combat than many a recruit to the Army at pass-out. His trainer was a former gladiator named Placidus. Many gladiators gave themselves names that connoted ferocity, like Leopard or Pugnax. Placidus belonged to another school of thought, which held that a pacific-sounding name would lull their opponents into unpreparedness for the speed and venom of their attack. Sentenced long ago for a crime he never revealed to anyone, 'condemned to the Games,' he had survived his three years' fighting and had been given his liberty.

Placidus was in his thirties, hugely tall and strong. He came originally from somewhere to the far south of Nubia. He had been one of the heavily armed gladiators, and it had given him some satisfaction to have been brought by Klitos' father to the shores of Lake Scutari, for the *scutum* was the big shield of the heavy fighter. He spoke camp Latin and broken Greek. He was woolly-haired and amber-black, but the whites of his eyes were clear. His face and body were without one scar from his fighting, though there was a mass of cicatrices round the muscles of his left shoulder where he had been savaged by a draught camel in Seleucia. Like many very big men he had a fundamentally genial disposition.

He was waiting outside the atrium for Klitos. They walked to a little croft. Klitos was already bigger than his father, thickset and heavily muscled; he had a squarish face and dark hair. In repose he had a somewhat stolid expression, steadfast rather than stupid, but as he walked keyed up for action he was every inch his father's son, moving with a light swift grace.

About half of the croft's area had been stripped of turf and sanded like an arena. The bailiff's son was there before them with a pile of javelins and a brace of wooden swords on the sand beside him.

'I hope you're late because you think I'm going to beat you, Klitos.' said Kenin.

Klitos snorted, and raised his eyes to the sky.

Kenin was ten months older than Klitos, but he still wore the soft leather collar which stamped him a freedman's child.

Placidus said, 'Come on. Warm up.'

He ran a dozen circuits of the croft with them, Placidus with a deceptive loping gait. He stopped them when they were breathing hard, then picked up the identical swords and handed them over.

'On guard!' he snapped.

The wooden swords were rather long and decidedly heavy. For defensive practice they used lighter swords and wore leather shields, but these weapons were designed to develop strength in the wrist: the kind of strength that enabled a man like Placidus to wield his sword all day.

'Fight!'

Klitos and Kenin began to circle and probe, sword tips touching and snaking apart. By now each knew the other's defences so well that the contest should always have been even, but this was not so. Kenin had to use his longer reach, for he was tall and gawky, while Klitos had to come to close quarters and nullify Kenin's advantage.

Klitos launched a sudden attack, circling to his right as the swords clattered. Kenin beat him off, then thrust and thrust again, trying to penetrate Klitos' guard. Klitos gave ground, feinted left, leaped right and struck backhanded, forcing Kenin's sword arm to one side; the upstroke ended with Klitos' point touching the amulet on Kenin's collar.

'Enough,' Placidus grunted, with no word of praise or blame. 'Hold out your swords now.'

Kenin gave Klitos a flickering glance of despair at having been so easily beaten, then both held out their swords at arm's length for another strengthening exercise which they both hated.

The ache began in the elbow, then once established it transmitted itself along the muscles of the forearm to the wrist. Placidus watched impassively.

After ten minutes both of the young men were sweating, wrists trembling and arms in agony. Klitos saw that Kenin was on the verge of giving up, since the length of his arm was a disadvantage here. Klitos himself could have lasted one more minute: he always beat Kenin at this exercise. On this occasion he was driven by a sudden impulse to drop his arm a couple of seconds before Kenin.

Now why had he done that? he asked himself as he clapped Kenin on the back.

They took the javelins and threw for an hour, practising distance and accuracy with and without the throwing thongs, but even by the time Placidus let them go for their baths, Klitos had found no satisfactory answer to his unspoken question.

Klitos was fishing in the clear channel where the Moracha river entered Lake Scutari; in toward the banks and along the lake shore stretched a vast green and white carpet of water lilies. To his left and to the south one stark rock lifted from the plain, while to the north the country rose to a massif of black-fanged peaks.

He sat on the thwart of the small boat. One more fish and he could go. The bait was running out. What was more, though he usually enjoyed fishing, his heart was not in it that day. He had caught sixteen good trout on the worm. His tackle consisted of a handline on a wooden frame and a selection of iron hooks. Klitos needed plenty of worms because many were nibbled away by smaller fish such as the bleak which infested the water.

Klitos jigged the handline absently, looking down at it for no reason connected with his fishing: the line was of grey horsehair spun by his mother with combings from the mane and tail of his own horse, Smoke.

The line twitched and Klitos felt the pull. Absently he played the fish for a while, then pulled it to the side of the boat and flipped it inboard with two fingers in a gill: another trout. Now he could stop. He unhooked the trout and killed it with a crack of its head on the thwart, then tossed it with the others. He wound the line back on its frame. Then he picked up his paddle and turned to the bow, heading downstream and turning to starboard along the margin of the lake.

At last he was in the little channel through the water lilies, which was cleared every season by two larger boats with chains stretched between them. He drove the boat into the landing stage. He was panting and sweating with exertion, and rested for a couple of minutes, immobile. As his breathing calmed he became aware of the small sounds of peace: the distant lowing of cows restless for milking; the high whinny of one of the horses; the twitter of sandmartins. A brown snake undulated through the water beside the boat and landed rustling through the dry reeds.

Klitos wiped the sweat from his brow, tied up the boat and walked along the path through the reeds. He left their fusty smell behind as he came into a field in the late afternoon sun, to see two girls heading away from him diagonally, going to fetch the cows in for milking. He called, and they waited until he came up to them. They were daughters of free peasants, members of the tribe, and they did odd jobs about the farm for pin money. One was about eleven, dark and thin, and the other a strapping sixteen-year-old. Two dogs with them lay down, noses on paws.

'It doesn't need two of you to fetch the beasts,' Klitos said. 'One of you bring the fish from my boat. You do that, Nika.'

The big girl grinned and asked, 'You coming with me?'

Klitos clicked his tongue with annoyance. The smaller girl trotted away, the dogs at her heels, and she looked over her shoulder at Klitos as she went: a mischievous smirk.

Nika said, 'Well, Klitos? Shall we rock the boat a bit?'

29

Klitos was strongly heterosexual in a bisexual society. He and Nika had begun to make love since their thirteenth year, if love is the word, since each had only a biological appreciation of the other. For the first month they had rutted like stoats, at every opportunity; then two or three times a day for the rest of the year. It had been the subject of much amused comment by the grown-ups; the consensus had been that Pylades would soon have to introduce the doctrine of the Golden Mean into Klitos' syllabus. In fact it had been Placidus.

A successful gladiator, though socially unacceptable, was a popular hero, a star, and something of this still clung to Placidus, who also loved women exclusively. He had begun to treat Klitos with icy contempt until Klitos had begged him for an explanation.

Placidus had said, 'You fuck too much, but that girl has no baby. Why? You fuck so much your balls turned to water. No good. You can't fight with water in your balls.'

Klitos had been horrified at the thought of his testicles full of water.

'Just a eunuch in disguise,' Placidus had gone on inexorably.

Klitos had quavered, 'What shall I do, Placidus?'

Placidus had held up two great fingers and pronounced sentence.

'Two times a month.'

And so it had been, Placidus as well as Pylades directing him to discipline and dedication, strength of mind towards himself, strength of body towards adversaries: the survival values needful in his world. But it was hard, and his desire grew as he looked at Nika. She was aroused, her lips fuller and her features engorged, nipples tipping her shift.

Klitos said, 'I'd like to, Nika, but I have to see my horse, then the bath will be waiting, then dinner. There just isn't time. Go and get the fish.'

How could he tell the girl that a rule had been laid on him? Whatever he did he would sound like a prig. Sulkily she turned away, but then he stopped her with a hand on one shoulder.

'Nika?'

'Well?'

'Why haven't you had a baby?'

She turned back and stared him in the face with grey eyes, tossed a tress of fair hair and said, 'Either my grandmother taught me what to do, or your balls are full of water.'

The old jibe had no power to strike him any longer and he said quietly, 'The fish. Go now. And our thanks to your grandmother.'

He walked away over slightly rising ground. It was spring in a region which never experienced the cold of winter. The barrier of the Black Mountains bounced the north winds high over the plain and left it unscathed, while farther south the Macedonians shivered in the blast.

Klitos looked round the estate as he walked, and once again felt appalled by his father's decision to leave it all. They were self-sufficient in everything except for olives and sheep. But the Dokleati had good relations with the Avares, who dominated the coast from Butua to Antibarum, and whose olive groves held thousands of trees along the littoral. The Avares supported themselves by merchant shipping and trading, sea fishing . . . and their great abundance of olives. But here, only twelve miles or so inland, it was a different world, and an earthly paradise.

Everything was produced in surplus, and this surplus went to market at Birziminium, except for once a year, when it was held back for a month. At the end of the month a nomad tribe came in, savage non-Illyrians with hooked noses and fierce moustaches, and great flocks of hook-nosed sheep and goats. The species were almost indistinguishable; both had long, silky pelts and only the horns of billy and ram picked out the grown males. There was a week of carousal, barter and slaughter. Then the nomads went their way with the means to a varied diet, and the residents had wool for spinning, lamb and kid to eat, fleeces for saddle and bed, amber and silk and spices which the nomads brought along for trade.

Why on earth disrupt this excellent life? Klitos wondered as he went through into the farmyard. To his right was one of the atrium walls of this bastard Græco-Illyrian structure.

31

Hidden behind the wall a group of the estate's younger children were chanting their money tables:

'Four asses, one sesterce;
Four sesterces, one denarius;
Twenty-five denarii, one aureus make. . . .'

Klitos left them to it and their voices died away as he walked through squawking chickens and swatted welcoming dogs; to his left lay the granaries and barns. Klitos paused to watch a young boar trying to mount one of the sows, thrusting inexpertly at flank and face and ear. The sow stood patiently until an old boar came round the corner of a barn. He shoved the young animal aside with a casual heave, then mounted the sow at once.

Klitos walked on, thinking that his old boar of a father had behaved similarly, only much worse, shouldering everyone away from home. Klitos knew his roots were here, and was sure that his mother felt the same way.

V

The Greek physician left at once after the death of Herod the Great. Herod had been a monster of gigantic stature, yet even the lesser surviving monsters of his family could have sent the Greek on a swift trip to Hades after the loss of his patient. But a couple of days later the Greek was safely in the autonomous Decapolis and in its most important city, Scythopolis. He felt immediately safer there behind the great walls. He went at once up to the Acropolis from where he could overlook the walls and the sweep of the Vale of Esdraelon down to the Jordan.

This was a very ancient city. It had been in existence fifteen hundred years before these events as Beth-Shan, when the Egyptian Thutmose III numbered it among his conquests. It had been held by the Egyptians for over a century, and then by successive conquerors: Canaanites, Israelites, Philistines, Egyptians again; Assyrians and Scythians. But now it was firmly Greek, a bigger city than Jerusalem. When the ten easternmost cities of Syria Palæstina joined in a federation against marauders from the east, Scythopolis was the only one in the league which stood on the west bank of the Jordan. It had an amphitheatre and a hippodrome, baths and aqueducts, and it was an important centre of communications. The road from Jericho to the cities of Galilee passed through it, thus allowing itinerant Jews a north-south route which skirted hostile Samaria.

The Greek doctor visited a shrine of Apollo and underwent a ceremony of ritual purification there, to make a fresh start.

Scythopolis was merely a way station for him. He would

feel fully secure only under the Roman Peace, and moved as soon as he could to Cæsarea, where he settled down, married and raised a family. One of his sons, Luke, became a doctor too, since the practice of medicine tends to run in families; and he was to turn his hand to writing also when the time came at Antioch.

In Scythopolis there was a minority of perhaps ten thousand Jews, most of whom never observed the Law in any way. That is not to say that all were without religion. There were plenty of faiths to choose from: faiths that had seeped in from all quarters. In Judæa itself these waves of belief mostly washed impotently on the abrasive rocks of Judaism and the equally abrasive inhabitants. But freedom of religion was the rule in the Greek cities, as indeed it was in the Roman world, though the Romans in due course were to make two exceptions. In Scythopolis, to give a general sample, there were cults associated with Attis and Isis; Eleusinian offshoots; the Orphic worship of Dionysos; Gnostics and Manichæans. Most of these very different religions shared one thing in common, and that was a ritual meal symbolic of unity, both among the members of the cult and with the Divine through its priest.

For example: there was a religious service in progress in a secret chapel. The house in which it was cunningly concealed belonged to a rich Jewish merchant who kept an abstemious lifestyle in spite of his wealth. This cult had originated from a form of Judaism, so that it was not strictly one of the foreign imports.

The chapel was furnished simply but well, with cushioned marble benches for the congregation, all Jews. There were about thirty of them kneeling before the benches, the men separate from the women. Behind the altar stood their Teacher, with his server at his side. The service had begun with prayers and psalms from the Bible, followed by a sermon. It had then continued with a liturgy originated by the Great Teacher of the cult, who had been slain and hung on a tree at Gilgal by the orthodox a couple of generations earlier.

The present Teacher was tall and thin, with lustrous auburn hair and beard, straight nose and a commanding

34

manner. The server was a youth of sixteen or so. By this time in the service the congregation was in a state bordering on religious ecstasy at the end of a psalm exalting the Teacher in his struggle against the powers of Darkness.

He lifted his robe to reveal a massive erection, then moved round and stood at one end of the altar. Upon it lay a young girl, a virgin. She was menstruating profusely, legs open and knees raised ready for coupling. Beneath her buttocks an open bag containing broken bread had been placed. It was soaked with blood in some places and dabbled in others, for the girl had lain there for hours and often shifted position. She had dark hair and large eyes of an unusual blue, so deep that it was almost purple. Her parents were honoured by her selection and were among the worshippers. The girl's name was Meriem.

'Receive now this sacrifice,' the Teacher intoned, and then penetrated the girl, who yelped involuntarily at his entry. She turned her face sideways with a grimace of pain, dark hair spread over the curve of her cheek and the white marble; tears splashed over the stone.

The Teacher copulated swiftly and methodically, his face showing little emotion even as he approached his orgasm. The object was not pleasure, but to bring down the Divine into him for his own enlightenment and that of the congregation, many of whom were now sexually excited.

At the moment of ejaculation the Teacher withdrew; and his semen spouted among the bread and blood to the moans and gasps of the worshippers. He slid down off the girl and dropped his robe, while she rolled off the altar and slipped on her dress after a ritual ablution; then she limped to join the women. As the Teacher offered up another prayer for mercy and guidance, absolution from sin, and invoked the presence of the Deity, the server mixed bread, blood and semen into a silver bowl with a spatula, then offered it on his knees to the Teacher, who elevated it high over the altar in silent prayer.

At length the Teacher turned and took the bowl to the partakers, feeding each one of them from the spatula, and saying to each one of them:

'Take and eat. This is my Body, and this is my Blood. . . .'

35

VI

They were on the second day out from Rhegium when the talking bird was killed. A short passage had taken them across the ocean to Brundisium, where Klitos had officially become Marcus Drusus Scipio. They had voyaged then in a small coaster to Rhegium, and after a week's wait had boarded a larger vessel bound for Massilia from Alexandria. It was a trading ship of eleven hundred tons, with a big squaresail and a mast of Lebanon cedar; forward a small foresail was rigged on a boom projecting above and afore the bowsprit. It was early June and the wind was fair; but the cargo was dangerous.

The Romans killed half a million wild animals in the Games every year, and the ship was stuffed with them: lions, tigers, leopards, buffaloes, snakes, crocodiles – even a hippopotamus and a rhinoceros. There were no wild elephants, since these usually travelled apart from other animals. The hold could not contain all these creatures, and some were in cages on deck together with the domestic animals that fed them and the human beings on board. There was a constant background noise of snarls, growls and roars. But just as a man living on the bank of a rushing stream will cease to hear it except when he comes home after an absence, so the people aboard the ship came to accept the animal noises – much as Drusus and his entourage never really heard the talking bird.

But they heard its last squawk. Marcus was standing at the starboard side of the ship, watching a school of dolphins at play, diving in and out of the bow-wave and presumably enjoying the rush and tickle of the aerated water. Meanwhile the talking bird had given its version of the time: 'Sixth hour of the night; go home before her husband comes back,' and flown on one of its periodic visits of exploration. The bird was certainly unhinged, and probably bereft of the usual corvine intelligence, for it had perched on a leopard's cage. Marcus heard the squawk and turned just as it was cut off. He was in time to see a few black hackle feathers floating briefly upward from the draught of the leopard's paw-stroke. The leopard licked its chops. There was a burst of laughter from Drusus.

He came across to Marcus, still laughing.

'Poor old bird,' Marcus said.

'Teach you not to go too near a leopard's cage.'

Targui was sitting against the rail to port, gazing out to sea with his mind far away. Drusus had ruthlessly pared down the size of the household before leaving his estate to the new owner from Birziminium. The stud manager had gone; so had the bailiff, the farrier and the head groom, and all the slaves except three. Two were women, to cook and attend to Teutia, who had decided not to change her name to a Roman one. Both of these slaves were capable and unlovely, since Drusus held that pretty women, and particularly pretty slaves, could cause endless trouble on a long journey. The third slave was male, young and strong, Ulpius by name, and he had been brought along as a factotum for Drusus and Marcus. He had spirit and could fight, with a bronze cestus on one fist and a long knife in the other. So there were five fighting men to guard Teutia and the valuables: two chests, one of gold and the other of jewels. The greater part of Drusus' wealth now lay in letters of credit redeemable at Narbo.

Doratus, the majordomo, and his family had been sent on ahead a month in advance, and he was sorely missed. Everybody had grumbled about this arrangement, including Doratus, but Drusus as usual had been decisive.

'We shall all be inconvenienced,' he had said, 'but I'll hear no more of it. You will go to my lands and have some kind of shelter erected, Doratus. Four walls and a roof to begin with: I ask no more than that, and that you see to buying suitable slaves. Now that I am a Roman citizen I have to learn to think in the longer term.'

Munching an apple, Marcus went back to the guardrail and watched the dolphins. He flung the apple core down among them, but the morsel was ignored; it bobbed away from the bow-wave into the stern-wave and the wake, and was lost from view. It eventually missed by no more than a couple of hundred yards the pirate galley which had been shadowing them over the horizon.

They had passed the Lipari Islands, with the smoking volcano on the southernmost, the previous evening. The pirate ship was out of Salina, where it had been hiding in a sheltered cove; but the crew were all Numidians, hard, cruel and vicious. They were not after the animals, but the supercargo and the treasures they would have with them. The other three families travelling in Captain Keramikos' ship were all well-to-do. One was a merchant's and the second a banker's; the third a rich widow with three young children dragooned into iron discipline.

The pirates attacked that night, after the eighth hour and when the moon had set. It was bright starlight. The galley was long and lean, with a beaked prow and one bank of oars. The lookouts sighted it from afar, and Marcus woke to their outcry where he lay beside the shelter, feet thumping past him amid a growing tumult.

The two women slaves had got up at the other side of the shelter, crying as Drusus came out. He herded the women inside with Teutia to calm them, then looked out over the guardrail to assess things with icy calculation among the shouts and cries.

The galley was racing at them, and soon it would overtake the ship; the oar-blades were making swirls of phosphorescence, and it had its own accompanying dolphins.

'Forty-three men,' Drusus said crisply to Marcus. 'Fetch me my bow and a full quiver, quickly!'

Targui and Placidus stood with a batch of throwing spears, Drusus' slave, Ulpius, behind them with his cestus and long dagger.

'What shall I do?' Marcus asked his father.

'Guard my back when the time comes.'

The other families mustered twelve fighting men, and there were eighteen in the crew including the captain. The widow was attended by two eunuchs, and Marcus was surprised to see one of them pick up a spear.

Drusus shouted, 'Those of you who can shoot, pick off as many as you can!'

It was difficult. The laminated bow sang again and again, but Drusus hit only two men. Half a dozen others were shooting arrows at the pirates, with as little effect. The movements of the two vessels made it impossible to strike with accuracy. Drusus drove one arrow through the head of a man rowing three places away from the one he had aimed at, and another lucky shot passed straight through the thigh of a second man, pinning him to the thwart. The galley came on, the rowers still keeping their rhythm, white teeth bared in the starlight.

Targui hurled a spear, which struck thrumming in the beak of the prow. Marcus saw the eunuch throw his own spear high in the air, in contrast to Targui's low trajectory missile. The eunuch's spear fell down and transfixed one of the oarsmen's backs, the point protruding from his chest: Marcus stood amazed while the eunuch capered squeaking with glee. More spears fell, but the galley was level with them, oars high as the vessels came together, oars dragged inboard just before the moment of contact, a glancing grating jar. Targui's spear snapped off between the two ships. The pirates in the galley milled about with purposeful activity, grabbing ropes and grapnels for boarding.

The ship's cook rushed past Marcus carrying a brazier full of glowing charcoal and emptied it into the vessel alongside and below; yells and curses arose. Somebody else emptied in a basket of venomous snakes. A grapnel thudded over the guardrail near the widow's group, and as it was dragged back for a purchase it caught the brave eunuch's ankle; he was hauled off his feet with one leg taking the strain as he screamed and screamed.

Placidus was pulling the leopard's cage across the deck with a rope. He swung it round near the rail, then slashed the door fastenings with his sword, ran round behind and prodded the animal in the backside. The leopard exploded out of the cage and fell into the galley in a blur of rage: it hugged one of the pirates tight with its forepaws and as he yelled in agony it struck repeatedly with its hindpaws, disembowelling the man and shredding his lower body. A cobra struck the leopard in turn, twice in the side as it bit into the man's neck.

Now pirates were coming aboard in twos and threes, wearing only loincloths and carrying an assortment of weapons. Drusus, Targui and Placidus ranged themselves round the shelter, with Marcus in the rear. He saw smoke curling up from the pirate ship. It was on fire, thanks to the cook and his brazier of charcoal. The eunuch was still screaming, but the noise now was such that his mouth opened and shut without apparent sound. Men were leaping aboard without seeing him, and from that moment Marcus lost any general view of the conflict. He picked up the boar spear.

Suddenly Drusus, Placidus and Targui were all fighting. Placidus used his heavy sword and his long reach with such skill and coolness that he was invulnerable to a frontal attack, and Marcus found himself cool and without fear. Placidus had once taught him, 'Never lose your temper when you fight. There is such a thing as battle madness, but a man who allows it to take him is under the protection of the gods – and who knows what he may have done to offend them? Better to keep a cool head and rely on yourself.' The first pirate to attack Placidus swung a sword two-handed, was staring down at his sword and his two hands on the deck before Placidus killed him with the backstroke of the heavy sword, recovering instantly to drive it into the belly of the next man.

Targui was fighting a good swordsman with a curved weapon similar to Targui's own, blades clanging, whispering and ringing. Marcus saw nothing more of this because he was flung into action. Drusus slipped in a patch of blood and landed heavily on one knee. The man attacking him lifted his sword in triumph. Marcus thrust over Drusus with his boar spear into the man's ribs as far as the crosspiece of the spear, straight through the heart. As he died the pirate

40

fell down on Drusus. Marcus tugged, but the spear would not come free although it had transfixed his enemy. Another pirate lunged at Marcus, and at the same moment the slave Ulpius leaped between the pair with his dagger. It was a moment of dreadful confusion. Drusus was on the deck, pinned by the dead man on Marcus' spear, Marcus foolishly hanging onto the boar spear. The lunging blow aimed at Marcus took Ulpius in the chest, and then he was sagging down on the corpse. Placidus grabbed Marcus and pulled him away in the same instant as Targui – who had killed his man – leaped in front of Drusus. Drusus extricated himself swiftly and was using his sword while still on one knee. He got to his feet with a quick glance to see that Marcus was still alive. Placidus threw Marcus another spear, making him shorten his grip.

They had killed their immediate attackers, and now the three men moved forward with Marcus still in the rear. Before they had been fighting individually, but now they moved forward in a miniature phalanx with Placidus at the head and the other two slightly behind on each flank. They passed the eunuch with the shattered lower leg, and the corpse of one of the widow's children, a little girl in the scuppers, and then they began to clear the ship of pirates.

Thirty-four men had managed to get aboard. Drusus and his two comrades killed nineteen of them. Eleven were accounted for by the other fighting men. By dawn there were four pirates left. Three of them leaped into the sea, and the fourth made his hasty exit into the burning and sinking galley with its burden of dead snakes, a dead leopard and a few dead men. Someone cut the cables that had kept the galley swinging perilously close, and it drifted away. The dolphins accompanying the vessels had merged into a single group and stayed well clear, playing and getting acquainted while men killed one another; but now that the fighting had finished, the augmented numbers came back in company as the sails were set and the ship got under way again.

Ulpius was dying. The casualties among crew and fighting men had been high, with ten dead and almost everyone wounded superficially or more seriously; and of the superficial wounds some would in the nature of things become serious. Targui and Placidus were without a scratch. Drusus had skinned a kneecap and bruised his left elbow in his fall to the deck, and Marcus had several bruises, but no recollection of how he had come by them. He was desperately ashamed that his presence of mind had deserted him when he had kept hold of the boar spear, and even more ashamed of the fact that he had given no thought to the man who had saved him from the consequence of his folly. Drusus and Marcus bent over the slave where he lay on a bed of skins just outside the shelter and in its shade. The groans of the wounded could be heard throughout the ship, together with the quarrelsome growls of carnivores being fed on pirate corpses. Keramikos had been slashed across the face with a dagger and kicked in the testicles, and he had been in a foul mood. He meant to make sure that no shades would return to haunt anyone on board; the pirates would suffer such dismemberment as to rule out any hope of an afterlife as well.

Ulpius had a puncture wound in the chest, two bluish lips gaping between the ribs on the right-hand side of his body. A bright froth bubbled at his mouth; his own blood was drowning him. Teutia herself wiped his mouth, for she knew the slave had saved her son's life. For some hours he had lain still, and they had thought that perhaps the wound was not as bad as it had looked. But then Ulpius had suffered some kind of seizure, making convulsive movements like a man poisoned by strychnine, and this had started the bleeding. Placidus came in with Pylades and looked down at the slave. Placidus shook his head.

'He's all but gone.'

Drusus said, 'And I would have given him his freedom today.'

And Marcus said, 'I was a fool.'

Nobody contradicted him. Ulpius had closed his eyes, but they suddenly stared wide, there was a great rush of blood, and the life in the eyes was gone. Teutia laid down the man's head and went to fetch coins for eyes and mouth. Ulpius would be buried at sea, and the coins themselves would fall away, but their ghostly essence would remain as currency for the Ferryman.

Some while later the ship hove-to while Keramikos and Drusus with his household committed the body to the deep. Three sailors lowered it into the water gently, and as they hauled in the ropes it turned on its side for a moment. As the ship gathered way again one of the dolphins nudged the carcase tentatively, but lost interest at the absence of life; then Ulpius was gone.

The rich widow was showering gifts on her eunuch, who bade fair to lose his foot, if indeed the limb did not turn gangrenous. But the eunuch was a freedman, and alive. Ulpius was just a dead slave.

'He gave his life for me.' Marcus said to Pylades. 'Why? A slave can be put to death if his master is executed, but Ulpius put himself between me and another man's sword. Why?'

Pylades was silent for a few moments, then said, 'You never knew? . . . No, of course not. But it's very simple, Marcus. Ulpius loved you. He worshipped your very footsteps. And he died for you, so that you might live.'

Pylades put his hand briefly on Marcus' shoulder, then left him staring at the wake, eyes blinded by sudden tears.

VII

Three days after the religious ceremony in the merchant's house at Scythopolis, the girl Meriem was wandering along the road which followed the west shore of the sea of Galilee. She was still in some discomfort, her vagina still sore from the priest's rupture of her hymen and subsequent copulation, but menstruation had ceased.

She was wearing sandals of flat leather fringed with loops, thongs threaded through them and tied round her ankles. Her underskirt was of white cotton, with a long-sleeved cotton tunic over it, rose-coloured and embroidered with everyday purple, its dye made from lichens steeped in urine. Her hair was tied simply with a knot at the nape of the neck, and it was covered by a small maroon headdress secured by a bronze pin. Beneath it her eyes were of a deeper purple than the embroidery on her garment – eyes in which a man might lose himself for ever. She had no intention of ever giving a man the chance.

There was a grove of pines where tree lizards with fat banded tails flicked among the branches on the warm May day, and Meriem rested in the shade of the trees. She was a few miles south of the village of Hammeth, and the road was busy. Meriem munched a few olives, spitting out the slippery stones while she watched the traffic passing by, her eyes narrowed against the glare from the lake of the late morning sun beyond, where fishing boats plied.

She was no longer a virgin, and hence unmarriageable. The priest had explained to her the proper course of action. She must tear her garments and sit outside her parents' house in the dust, abasing herself ritually. But after a couple of days she would be collected by some members of the sect, and would be looked after. Her father would be given a bride price for her, she would want for nothing all the rest of her life; but she would be in constant demand at services similar to the one she had experienced: a bride of the Deity.

Meriem had other views. She had been deceived into believing that her experience would be one of transcendental beauty. Instead, she had been hurt and humiliated, poked in public by a thrusting, jerking brute. She had felt nothing beyond pain and outrage. And the future laid out before her was a life of being publicly poked by a succession of thrusting, jerking brutes! They could keep it.

She had pretended to go through the ritual abasement, but in the small hours of the night she had sneaked back inside and taken what she needed for a journey. She had been unable to get at her father's money because it lay beneath the mattress under his body, but she had taken her mother's housekeeping allowance.

She had got together a bundle of her own small possessions and a change of good clothes, then added bread and olives, and rolled into a tiny ball between her breasts – her mother's most prized object. The woman had connived at the loss of Meriem's maidenhead, and so she deserved to lose this. It was a scarf of finest silk, a gossamer square of azure blue from China; the price of a good horse had she known how to ride.

Meriem knew that she could find employment as a servant, or even sell herself into slavery, but she was also a self-aware young person, and knew that her nature was unservile, and that a life of punishments awaited her if she took either course. She had no skill with pottery and hated weaving with its endlessly repetitive movements of shuttle through warp and woof. Some women obtained satisfaction from the slow growth of the cloth, but not Meriem. The dyeworks north of Cæsarea would probably be her destination, and her heart sank.

By late afternoon Meriem was still on the road along the lake coast. To get to Cæsarea she ought to have turned left some miles back, along the road which led westward north of Sepphoris and south of Cana. But whatever happened Meriem had decided she was not going to present herself at the dyeworks. It was situated on the coast because a good part of its production was the Tyrian purple. Two species of mollusc had in their heads a little cyst of stuff that looked like pus, and this was spread on material in the sun; it dried into a wonderful purple, lustrous and with a crimson glow. To make the dye involved the gutting of endless sea-snails, and the smell of their decomposition was dreadful. It clung to the workers so that they smelt horribly despite anything that they might do. Meriem had already become a pariah in one sense, and she was not going to encourage her separation from mankind in that way.

But nobody cared. Peasants went by on foot or on donkeys; a small detachment of Roman troops clanked past in the opposite direction under a decurion.

Fishing boats still plied out on the lake beyond a scatter of dazzling white buildings among the cypresses. A camel caravan overtook her, and she drew to one side until it had passed: forty of the beasts and their camelteers, the camels groaning and wheezing and belching their foul cud, taking God knew what cargo north-west to the coast, up through Tyre and Sidon to Antioch – and beyond, for all Meriem knew or cared.

In another hour she was enclosed by hills, and in front of her lay a canyon. The Arabs called it the Wadi el Hammam, the Valley of the Bath, since there was an Arab bathing place there; otherwise it was known as the Valley of the Doves. Its rock walls were a thousand feet high and honeycombed with caves, the habitat of innumerable wild pigeons. Youths and agile young men made a steady living catching them for sale as temple sacrifices, but the risks were great: one slip on the tiny paths by the caves meant death. It was also a haunt of outlaws, robbers and rapists. Meriem gulped and stayed where she was. When a goatherd came by she walked a little way with him until they came to a clump of prickly pear by the roadside, and she asked him to cut a fruit for her. She sat down by the fruit on the ground as the man went trudging off with his bleating flock. Meriem inserted a finger between the spines and rubbed the fruit on the sand until all the spines were abraded away, then she ate it, wiping away the juice as it ran down her chin and spitting out the round white stones. She was putting off her entry into the valley, feeling lonelier than ever. Also she was tired, dusty and hungry, and she needed a bath. Gradually her head drooped to her knees, and she dozed.

Meriem was awakened by the jingle of bells. She opened her eyes and looked up. A small cavalcade was approaching along the broad track that led into the valley. There were four armed men on good horses, and their tack was bedizened with the small bells which gave out a cheerful sound in contrast to the tough bearing of the riders. They wore long, curved swords in decorated scabbards, Parthian bows and quivers of arrows, and spears carried upright. Then came half a dozen women riding donkeys and dressed in different styles: Greek, Jewish, Cretan, Egyptian, Roman, Arabian. They were flanked by four big Nubian eunuchs. Next came a curtained litter carried by eight men clad only in loincloths.

The rearguard was made up of six more armed riders similar to the men in front. There was a sharp word of command from within the litter, and the procession came to a halt opposite Meriem.

'Well, child, and what are you doing here?'

The voice that came from the litter was deep and musical.

Meriem stood up, and gave a bob of deference. Plainly this was some person of consequence, observing her from the spyholes in the curtain.

She said, 'Great one, I have to go through this valley, and I am afraid.'

Another command, and the litter was set down. The bearers all experienced the familiar feeling of rising in the air after having carried a weight, and felt grateful to Meriem for the unexpected break.

The voice said, 'Would you like company, child?'

'Oh yes, please!'

Again a command – what was the language? Meriem did not know, for she had been spoken to and had replied in

47

Greek – and one of the women came forward after slipping off her mount. She spread a cloth for Meriem to sit on, then took off the girl's sandals and washed her feet, drying them with another cloth. She set ewer and cloth aside, twitched the curtains and guided Meriem into the litter. She had scarcely time to sit down on the floor before it was lifted beneath her and the litter set in motion again, her bundle and sandals flipped in after her. Outside the horses' bells were jangling again.

Meriem shifted position slightly and looked up. The interior was filled with a red glow from the light penetrating the material of the curtains. Meriem saw the woman leaning above her, and kissed the hem of her robe. She was a Junoesque figure with heavy breasts and broad hips, large dark eyes, black hair heaped up elaborately on the top of her head and secured with ivory pins. She wore a bejewelled gold necklace and gold rings on her wrists; jewels glinted from the rings on her fingers. She smiled down at Meriem, and asked her name.

When Meriem told her she said, 'Well, Meriem, I am the Lady Tanith. Come up, child and sit by me.'

She patted the tooled leather seat beside her, and Meriem did as she was told. The seat was padded and there were tasselled cushions filled with swansdown. Meriem could hardly believe her luck.

'Thank you, great lady,' she said demurely.

The Lady Tanith said, 'It is my pleasure. Now I have someone to talk to. Tell me, what are you doing, travelling alone?'

'I come from Scythopolis,' she began, and then hesitated. How could she confide her story to a stranger?

'What happened to make you leave home? I take it that you *have* left home?'

Meriem nodded, then made up her mind. This lady was obviously a woman of the world.

She said, 'My mother and father believe that God sent down a Messiah.'

Tanith clicked her tongue and said, 'Messiahs are thick on the ground. What was so special about this one?'

'They believe that he was the prophet Joshua reborn,' said

48

Meriem. 'But his enemies caught him and killed him, and hung him from a tree at Gilgal. That was a long time ago, fifty years or more. But the priests have scrolls which tell of this, and the war between Light and Darkness.'

'The Persians have that war in their belief. So do others. That isn't anything unusual.'

Meriem said, 'It's secret, what they do.' Between tears of shame and anger she made a small, strangled sound, 'I don't care about their secret. Shall I tell you?'

The Lady Tanith put an arm round Meriem's shoulders in a protective gesture and said, 'My dear, I have seen and heard most things. Do not be afraid that you will shock me.'

'I – I have lost my virginity,' Meriem began again.

The arm about her tightened a little, and Tanith said, 'Oh, my dear child, I am sorry for you. Tell me everything, and perhaps I shall be able to help you in some way.'

Meriem told her the whole story, snuggled into the sympathetic embrace, Lady Tanith making equally sympathetic sounds from time to time as the tale proceeded. Meriem began to feel sleepy; deep in the valley now, the light was dimmer out of the sun.

' . . . And so I just left home,' she said at last.

Tanith was silent for what seemed a long time.

Then she said, 'I am a woman of some wealth, with a large household.

'It seems to me that you need time to recover from your ordeal, and I can give you that time. I shall not enslave you or make you a servant. For a few weeks you can be as my daughter – that is, until we decide what you are going to do. Would you like to stay with me, Meriem?'

'Oh, please!' said Meriem.

Tanith hugged her and said, 'Then that is decided. Now rest your head on my shoulder. You are half asleep already.'

When Meriem awoke the litter was at rest and Tanith was pulling her ear to waken her without shock. Still drowsy, she allowed the woman to help her out of the litter; the bearers lifted it at once and trotted away jauntily, a quick bath and a lengthy session of beer-drinking uppermost in their minds; beer and a block of salt to lick. Only after that would they think of food.

Meriem looked round her with wonderment.

'This is a palace!' she exclaimed.

Tanith smiled and said, 'Not quite, though some would think it better.'

They were in an inner courtyard, torches blazing in their cressets, for it was dark now. Meriem turned slowly, taking in her surroundings. Beyond was the outer courtyard, with pools and fountains and pillars. She was standing on a marble floor with a mosaic pattern on it, but she was too close to see what was represented. There were marble pillars, rich hangings, and flights of marble stairs guarded by men at arms. There was furniture, costly and highly polished, but not much of it: half a dozen chairs and a few small wine tables where clean bowls were arranged. As she watched a man came down one of the stairways. He was a rich merchant by the look of him, Meriem thought. Perhaps he was Tanith's husband? But he merely bowed, then went by, leaving behind the scent of sandalwood.

'Come, child,' Tanith said, and led her to the farthest stairway.

They went along a corridor on the first floor up; again marble and expensive hangings. There were rooms opening off the corridor, but Tanith led Meriem to the double doors at the end, where two more men at arms stood on guard holding spears and with sheathed swords. They snapped their spears upright in salute to Tanith, then opened the doors. Meriem followed through the room, which was a large banqueting chamber with a huge cedarwood table and rows of chairs. Beyond that was another dining room in the Roman style, with couches for reclining round a curved table.

'I have seven dining rooms,' Tanith said matter-of-factly. 'This way now.'

Meriem followed her through a bewildering succession of rooms, servants and slaves and guards bowing or saluting. Eventually Tanith stopped by a curtain.

'A good bath is what you need,' she said. 'And so do I. Go in now, and one of the women will bring you to me when we are both refreshed. It's late for dinner, but travellers cannot always choose their mealtimes, and I expect you could manage a bite or two. But first, a bath.'

She patted Meriem's cheek and ushered her through the curtain, then was gone.

A few minutes later Meriem was soaking in a bath of perfumed water with two women to attend her. The bath was of sunken marble, with a surround of grey onyx decorated with gold, and the tiled wall at one side of the bath was embellished with brightly coloured mosaics of sea-creatures: a tunnyfish, a pair of seahorses, crabs and lobsters, prawns and seashells and seaweeds.

She sighed for the sheer luxurious pleasure of the bath, now that her initial embarrassment at being attended by the women had worn off; then she got up reluctantly and stood dripping while the women wrapped her in hot towels and dried her. Then they led her to a side-table with a mirror of electrum, which she had never seen in her life before. She gasped marvelling at her reflection, playing with the mirror like a small girl, while the women scented her and dressed her hair in a cascade of ringlets. Neither of the women had spoken to her, but this was not from surliness, for they were pleasant and gentle with her, smiling and helpful. Meriem spoke only Greek, though she could parrot the Aramaic phrases of the liturgy from which she had escaped. One of the women set the bronze pin in her hair for ornament rather than use with the new hairstyle, then shook her head and went over to a silver box on another small table. She took out a gold pin and brought it over, removing the bronze one and replacing it with the gold, while the other woman held out a diaphanous robe.

'Why, this is silk!' Meriem cried.

The women laughed at her pleasure. Meriem bent down by the side of the bath and picked up the sodden lump that was her mother's prized scarf, and threw it into the bath. One or other of the women would no doubt wash it, but that did not seem of any importance now.

Meriem dined alone with Tanith in a small dining room where a black eunuch presided over the slaves who served the meal. Meriem was ready for much more than 'a bite or

51

two.' She ate a few crayfish, which a slave cracked for her, then a dozen or so pigeons' breasts. She stopped after that, but merely for a break. A slave had filled their bowls, and they drank well-watered wine.

Meriem said, 'Great lady, your kindness knows no bounds. Is it permitted to ask where I am?'

'Of course, child. You are in my house in Migdal.'

Meriem nodded. The name meant nothing to her; and, besides, the black majordomo had beckoned to someone who had been out of sight from the table, but who now came in with a haunch of wild boar on a big olivewood platter; the meat was garnished with lentils and greens, leeks and onions, and the meat had been well roasted over a spit. Tanith spoke of small matters while they ate largely and drank sparingly.

After the meat course they ate fruit and nuts. Meriem had never experienced such a meal before in her life. But one thing began to trouble her. In the Judæo-Grecian household of her parents it had been the custom to say a grace thanking God for her food; but at this meal no grace had been said. Not even a libation had been poured. Then Meriem told herself that the god worshipped by her family's sect was a false god, and so such graces were worthless. Yet something seemed to be missing. That there was a divine Author of all things was something Meriem was never to doubt. So she reached for her wine bowl, and with an assumed clumsiness she spilt a few drops on the floor.

'To you, God, this libation,' she said silently.

Aloud she said, 'How can I thank you, Lady Tanith?'

'No thanks are due. Your company is my recompense, and I am delighted to be reminded that a hungry young girl can eat better than a warrior in the pride of his manhood.'

Meriem grinned and said, 'I feel like a crocodile that's eaten a horse.'

'You don't look like one,' said Tanith.

'All that lovely food, a gold pin in my hair, and a silk robe. There must be some way I can show my gratitude.'

'Well, perhaps, in due course. We'll see. But now it's time for bed.'

She watched as Meriem stood obediently, all the features

52

of her body revealed through the silk. Then she dropped to one knee, and for the second time kissed the hem of Tanith's dress.

Tanith said, 'Goodnight, my child.'

'Goodnight, my lady.'

One of the tiring-women took her to a small bedroom. It had a balcony giving onto the outer courtyard, and as Meriem lay in bed sleepily congratulating herself on her wonderful luck she could hear distant noises of the town.

Migdal? The town had presumably grown up around the site of a temple, *Migdal-Ez* meaning the pulpit of a synagogue. That was most inappropriate to Meriem's present location, and anyhow the place is better known as Magdala. Meriem soon went to sleep. It would be some time before she found out — Antioch excepted — that she was in the best and most exclusive whorehouse in Syria Palæstina.

VIII

'Sometimes I wish your father had stayed in Syria!' Teutia exclaimed, and sneezed loudly.

She was sitting with Marcus on a ruined terrace with three steps leading down to a dilapidated atrium. Beyond was a neglected vineyard, and from it the land sloped down to a green plain with here and there a peak of rock breaking the monotony; abandoned Celtic hill villages with stout stone perimeter walls crowned these peaks. Marcus and Teutia had an extensive view across the distant white buildings of Rhedæ to the river, and beyond the river the ground lifted again into vineyards and timber.

Another cloud of dust drifted over them, and Teutia got to her feet, beckoning to Marcus. Behind them was noise: hammering, sawing, the crunch of breaking masonry. Marcus and his mother walked away, picking their footsteps among littered stonework on the atrium floor.

'All this will take years of work,' she said gloomily.

Marcus was looking back. From this angle he could see Drusus and a few of the gang of men working on the building. They had been at it for two weeks.

He said, 'We're lucky. We didn't know there would be a villa on the estate.'

'A villa!' snorted Teutia.

'Things can only get better,' Marcus smiled. 'We have more land, all the grazing we need. We couldn't stay in Illyria, and who knows what things will be like in Syria Palæstina now that King Herod is dead?'

At Brundisium Drusus had been advised against making

the overland journey to his estate in Narbonnese Gaul because of hostile tribes in the western Alps. They had been fortunate in Rhegium to find passage in a big ship, which had no need to hug the coast, and apart from the early foray with the pirates they had enjoyed a good passage to Massilia. It was a large Greek city, founded five hundred years or more before Marcus set foot in it. In the wars against Carthage – its trading rival – Massilia had sided with Rome, and then invited Roman protection against the Celtic tribes. Rome had jumped at this invitation, and in reward had made Massilia a free city while subjugating the hinterland into a colony: the first part of Gaul to fall under the Roman sway. The city's main trade was in wine, and drinking in a wine-shop with Targui Drusus had heard from a seaman the news of Herod's death. During the passage to Narbo in a trim little coaster Drusus had expatiated on the rightness of his decisions to the point of exasperating Marcus; but during the following days he had come to agree with his father. When they had arrived at the estate, tired and irritable, Doratus had welcomed them into a pavilion of oriental luxury and a splendid feast. He had purchased a retinue of slaves, and on his own initiative had retained the services of a clerk of works and a team of builders responsible for the noise and dust arising behind Marcus and his mother.

In Massilia Pylades had sought out an old friend who now ran one of the city's schools of philosophy and rhetoric, and enjoyed the reunion so much that he had begged permission of Drusus to stay there for a couple of months. Drusus had agreed equably, and Placidus was ordered to look after Pylades and bring him safely onward when the time came. Both men were very happy. Pylades could spend the time bringing himself up to date after all his years in the Illyrian backwater; for him it was the next best thing to a sabbatical in Athens. Placidus was equally content. His size and the glowing quality of his skin would make him stand out like a beacon to all the women of the city, and the discipline of his years at the Games ensured that he would measure out his time of freedom to the best advantage.

'You'll see, Mother,' Marcus said, visualizing all the horses down below. 'There couldn't be a better place than this.'

*

55

Doratus had begun by buying expensive slaves: firstly the Vilicus and his wife. This man was called Lucius, a tall fellow with thin lips and keen eyes, and he was the key person on the agricultural side, in charge of all farming operations. The Vilica was named Julia, and she was housekeeper under Teutia's orders. Doratus had bought a viticulturist who could also look after the olive grove that lay beyond the vineyard; a head shepherd; and a head stockman, as well as menial slaves.

Catch crops were planted, breeding stocks of sheep and cattle acquired, food and fodder and wine bought-in against the time when the estate should become self-sufficient. The vineyard was cleared of weeds, and another gang of men began erecting the farm buildings and stables at the point below the villa which Marcus had pointed out to his mother. Then Targui and Marcus went looking for horses.

They found a few draught animals in Rhedæ, but the general quality was poor, since many of the heavier horses had been ruined by haulage work at the local mines, but they bought six for present use: to travel with, and to use for field work later. Next Targui and Marcus went to Arelate at the head of the Rhône estuary. This was a large town, with a theatre, an amphitheatre and a hippodrome. Targui turned up his nose at the horses he saw, but then had an idea. They had visited the amphitheatre as sightseers; there were no games in progress. Strolling between the baths and the Forum, Targui had suddenly exclaimed and tugged Marcus back the way they had come.

'What is it?' Marcus asked.

'Which faction would you follow in a chariot race?'

Marcus said, 'Why, I don't know . . . If I have to choose, let it be the Leek Greens.'

Targui nodded, then led the way round the amphitheatre to the hippodrome and the stables of the racing factions. Romans were used to differences of dress and skin colour, and though the sight of a veiled man was unusual, Targui attracted no more than a few glances. He bought two colts at the Leek Green stud, both of chariot racing stock.

He said to Marcus, almost making a speech, 'With any

56

luck one of these will turn out to have speed and endurance, and with great luck, both will. Now we look for fillies.'

They were riding the rough horses bought at Rhedæ, changing mounts frequently. Five slaves accompanied them on foot. They had set out with eight, but three had turned for home with the two colts from Arelate. The columns of a great aqueduct towered up to their right, bringing water to the city they had left behind. Marcus was beginning to enjoy himself. The horses were nothing to speak of, but the country was interesting and varied. There was not the intimate interlacing of water and landscape that he had grown up with in Illyria; but there were compensations: the scent of the maquis on the higher ground; the noise of the cicadas in the trees of an afternoon, with the tree-crickets joining in during the evening; and, as they advanced towards Glanum, the enormous backdrop of the Pyrenees to the south-west.

They found a well with a building beyond it fronting a stand of trees, and while the slaves took water and gathered firewood Marcus and Targui strolled towards the building. As they approached a group of men came out in twos and threes, then gathered into a solid group, watchful and hostile. All but one wore trousers and short tunics; the exception was clothed in a white gown and had a gold torc round his neck.

A slave holding a bundle of dry sticks for kindling came up to Marcus and Targui.

Eyes wide, he said quietly, 'Masters, don't go any farther. This is a Celtic holy place.'

He spoke in Vulgar Latin, and Targui did the same.

He said, 'How were we to know?'

And Marcus said, 'It is not in our minds to profane anyone's sacred ground. Have we crossed into it?'

The slave said, 'No, Master: those men stand at the boundary. All is holy beyond, from the shrine to the end of that grove of oak trees. If you permit I will speak to the druid – the priest – and beg him not to strike us dead.'

Marcus and Targui watched as the slave set down his bundle and went forward, dropping to his knees and crawling as he neared the group of men. Behind them Marcus

57

saw that the building was composed of fat fluted columns topped by recesses, and in each recess a human skull was posed. He tried to swallow, but his mouth was dry. The noise of the cicadas in the trees beyond the shrine sounded suddenly alien and malevolent.

The slave reached the priest and bent low. But then he raised his head and was presumably speaking, though Marcus could not see his face. The priest leaned down, the golden torc glinting in the sunlight, and lifted the slave upright, smiling and then placing his hands briefly on the man's head; as the priest spoke Marcus found all at once, magically, that he could no longer hear the insects in the trees any more than the words of the priest.

The slave stood for a moment under benediction, and then turned. As he made his way back to Marcus and Targui the group of men went into the shrine, led by the priest. Targui let out a big breath, and the clamour of the cicadas was back again.

'All's well, Master,' the slave said to Marcus. 'I could make myself understood. We may take water, and dead wood for kindling, but we must not camp within sight of the shrine.'

Marcus and Targui looked at the slave. He was stocky and dark, with brown eyes and a steady gaze, though his hair was dusty and his face sheened with sweat.

'You're a brave man,' Targui told him.

And Marcus asked, 'What's your name?'

'Kradog, Master.'

'Where are you from?'

Kradog said, 'I was born in Narbo, but my mother came from Britain, Master. She was taken in slavery when she was only a girl; she taught me her speech. It isn't the same as that priest's, but near enough for understanding. I don't know who my father was.'

Marcus nodded and said, 'You have done well, Kradog. When we get back home I intend to ask my father for you.' He turned to Targui and said, 'Now let's get away from this place. It makes my flesh crawl.'

Next day they came in sight of the city of Glanum before

58

noon. Ahead of them a range of hills lay, the source of water for the aqueduct to Arelate. The structure descended the hillside in a series of gigantic steps, and on each step a watermill had been constructed: sixteen in all. Neither Marcus nor Targui had ever seen anything to equal this.

Kradog had already attached himself to Marcus and walked by his horse.

Marcus said, 'You, Kradog.'

'Yes, Master?'

'Those people yesterday. Why did they have all those skulls in their shrine?'

Kradog said, 'It was the old religion here. Not many people practise it now they believe the Roman gods to be stronger. But some still hold to the old belief. They were head-hunters, Master. They believe that the head holds the soul and all the strength of spirit, and so it is good to take the heads of enemies.' He shrugged and went on, 'My mother's people's priests were druids also. They would have wicker cages made in the likeness of a horse, and would burn crowds of people alive in the cages to please the gods. But who really knows what pleases them?'

Targui said to Marcus, 'It would please me if he were to shut his mouth. He can sacrifice twice a year to the household gods of Drusus, and that is where the gods finish for a slave. So make an end to this, for I have been a slave myself.'

Marcus thought about this, and rode silently beside Targui for a while.

Then he said, 'Pylades was a slave once in this country, and I wish he were here now. I have learned more from him than I can ever learn from you, Targui. You are my father's man. But as for me, I will question where I wish, and try to learn from the answers I get, whoever gives them. There is more to a man than the prick and the horse between his legs.'

Targui turned on his sheepskin numnah and glared at Marcus as though ready to take the sword to him. The slaves padded along with bated breath, except for Kradog, who was trying to suppress a burst of manic laughter. Marcus set his face and stared straight ahead. He had known for some time that he had to assert himself against Targui, against the sheer weight of the veiled man's presence; and he had been in doubt of the outcome. But he had failed to take account that in Roman law he was now a man, and a citizen, and even in Targui's eyes he was unassailable. And furthermore Targui could not dislike him. Marcus was showing qualities which Targui himself admired beyond personal irritation.

He switched from the Vulgar Latin and said in Greek, 'It is good. Now look: there is the road.'

The road ran south-west through Glanum, a long, narrow town in a deep gorge. At the north-eastern entrance they passed through a triumphal arch showing Gaulish warriors in chains and commemorating the conquest of Narbonnese Gaul. They left the sacred grounds on their right and passed into a district of public buildings, including a temple to the Imperial family, and a great basilica standing opposite a colonnaded Forum; behind the basilica was a grand court-yard. All the public buildings and open spaces were thronged with people.

Narbonnese Gaul was thoroughly romanized, and kept the Roman nine-day week for civilians. Marcus and Targui made their way through the crowds towards the end of the town, where there were houses and inns, past the Temple of Health and the baths. Marcus and Targui secured a room for the night at an inn, together with lodging for the slaves with the horses at livery. Targui performed his ablutions in strict privacy, but Marcus decided to visit the baths, and changed into his toga for the occasion. He took Kradog and another slave with him, leaving them outside with a coin to buy refreshments while they waited.

Kradog's companion could barely communicate. He munched a wheaten cake smeared with curds and drank from the red wine, last year's and tasting of earth, that he shared in a bowl of poor pottery with Kradog. The man was very brown, with an aquiline nose and excellent teeth, but dull eyes.

He said, 'You, Kradog. Where you from?'

'Apple-Land!' said Kradog, and laughed, for he had never seen the place; he merely went by what his mother had told him. 'It is a country where the days are kind, and in that

60

country there is a finger of land sticking up out of an island, where I belong: the Island of Glass it is called, and there every day is like the first bite into a fresh apple. Ynys Witrin in my tongue.'

The man grunted and passed the bowl to Kradog.

Marcus walked through the courtyard into the dressing-rooms and gave his clothes to an attendant. He went into the bellowing, echoing noise of the baths, passing first through the cold room with its plunge bath, men diving and floundering, splashing him with cold water on his way to the warm room, where he waited for ten minutes or so and began to sweat. Then he went through into the hot room and immersed himself in the bath. There were sixty or seventy men present, much better Latin than Marcus had been accustomed to hear resounding round the walls. Men puffed and wallowed in the bath; some in the play area exercised swinging lead weights or doing press-ups; the masseurs worked slapping and pounding flesh, anointing men with unguents and scraping them with strigils, plucking hairs. After the hot bath Marcus had himself shaved, then splashed himself with cold water from the basin in one corner of the room. He went back to the plunge room and dived in, snorting and coming out quickly, then sat next to a plump man who had emerged at the same time.

'Tell me, sir,' he said politely. 'Where would one go in this town to buy horses?'

Marcus and Targui were back at the inn, dinner over. Marcus was in a mood of grim disappointment. They had bought the best fillies they could find, the best that Glanum could offer at its horse fair. The two men sat out of doors in a vine arbour, young grapes overhead, and Targui nibbled chickpeas with his wine. Inside the building someone was playing a lyre, a decorous tune in contrast to a drunken chorus from another room. The sun's last rays slanted through the foliage. Targui seemed oddly content, and Marcus could not understand this.

'We have come a long way and we've precious little to show for it,' Marcus said. 'What will my father say? . . . The

61

best we have bought were those two colts at Arelate. These fillies will never get us a line of bloodstock, Targui. Why aren't the Romans interested in breeding horses?'

'Who knows?' said Targui off-handedly. 'We've done what we can. We'll just have to keep an eye open for news of better stock. But never mind that. I have seen what I came to see.'

And he would not expatiate on this, no matter how Marcus pressed him.

'Let it be for now,' was all he would say. 'You will know when the time is ripe.'

Drusus changed in character as the summer drew on and the villa took shape over the months, belying Teutia's pessimistic forecast. He had not been impressed by the horses, but neither Marcus nor Targui had expected him to be; indeed, Marcus had been pleasantly surprised by the mildness of his reaction.

'They'll do for now,' he had said casually.

And Targui had said, 'Just what I've been telling Marcus. When you finish your building, then we must talk.'

It was fortunate that Doratus had found Lucius, who was a manager of exceptional talent. In addition to the other work he had ensured that the newly-cleaned vineyard would produce a small vintage. He had also used a stream to make a reservoir by having a dam built, diverting some of the builders to this work for a while, and he had stocked the reservoir with trout and carp, perch and bream. The trout died, but the coarse fish were thriving and the water supply was assured.

Drusus' passion was the villa. The atrium was roofed except for a rectangular central space with a pool beneath. On each side of the atrium were three bedrooms, and beyond was the large reception room, which led in turn into the walled garden with its colonnaded walks and a plunge bath at the right hand side; the centrally-heated baths opened beyond the flush lavatory. Crossing the walled garden one came to the dining room on the right, the drawing room in the middle, and a summer room on the left. There was provision for central heating in all the public rooms except the summer room. Slaves' quarters, kitchen and store-rooms and all other outbuildings were ranged along the outside walls, the kitchen sited outside the dining room and the only room of those outside which communicated directly. Although a slave, Lucius did not inhabit the slaves' quarters; he had a comfortable apartment in the farm buildings, and the other specialist slaves were housed there also.

The lot of menial slaves depended entirely on the people set in authority over them. Their lives could be unmitigated hell, or they could be tolerable; much of their condition was regulated by law. Menial slaves received larger rations than people like Lucius himself: during periods of heavy labour they were given 30-odd litres of wheatmeal every month, together with vegetables and olives. For three months after the vintage they were allowed as much wine-must as they could drink, and for the rest of the year the wine ration varied according to the season: less in winter than in summer, but still totalling a little over 200 litres a year; and they could water it or not, as they wished. There were also festivals during which they could forget their condition for a while. At the Saturnalia they were waited on by their masters, and mis-rule was the order of the day; at both the Saturnalia and the Compitalia extra wine was lavishly supplied. Both of these festivals had taken place while Drusus' household had been on the way from Illyria.

When Marcus asked Drusus for Kradog as a personal slave assent was given gladly, but Drusus' brow darkened when Marcus made another request. Drusus composed his face into a mask of Roman *dignitas*.

'Emancipation? No. I shall emancipate you in my own good time. Don't ask again. Why did you want this?'

Marcus said, 'I don't quite know, Father. Now we're citizens, it all seems different somehow.'

An itinerant sculptor arrived together with two assistants, and persuaded Drusus to adorn the walled garden – the peristyle – with busts of himself and Teutia. The sculptor hailed from the great city of Aphrodisias, which was famed not only for its dedication to the Goddess of Love, but also for the abundance of its excellent sculptors. Drusus and Teutia sat for their likenesses for an hour or so every afternoon before bathtime, and after a few days Teutia waylaid Marcus as he went out with Placidus and a bundle of javelins on a golden morning. She tugged Marcus aside so that she could speak privately to him.

'Your father is planning a journey,' she said. 'Now don't ask me what for, or where, and keep it to yourself. When we were sitting for the sculptor yesterday your father had Lucius in, and asked him about pack animals, supplies, travelling conditions and so on. That's all I know.'

It was enough to put Marcus into a state of some excitement. Life had settled into a routine, reclining dinners and all, and boredom began to lurk. Marcus was due to join the Army next year. A trip before he joined up was just what he needed.

IX

One morning before breakfast Marcus and Pylades walked down in semi-darkness towards the farm buildings, and met Lucius and Kradog, who were standing at one side of the path and gabbling in Vulgar Latin so fast that not even Pylades could catch the drift of their conversation. Kradog was holding an uprooted plant in one hand, his fingers grubby with soil. They stopped talking as Marcus and Pylades came up to them.

'What's going on?' Marcus asked.

Lucius said, 'Something of importance, perhaps.' He still spoke in Vulgar Latin, but slowly enough for Marcus now. 'Your body slave attends you well?'

'Yes, of course. But I sent him on ahead of me, and now find you both standing here quacking.'

'Kradog,' said Lucius, 'tell your master what you have been telling me.'

Kradog held out the plant with its light green leaves and said, 'Quickbread.'

'Goosefoot,' Lucius said. 'It is a weed here. But he has more to say.'

'My mother once picked one of these plants,' Kradog said. 'She called it quickbread, and told me that another name for it is fat-hen, because it is one of the best foods for fattening poultry.'

Pylades took the plant from Kradog and examined it.

He said, 'This is a dwarfish thing, but your slave is right. I have seen fields of it in Britain. There it grows taller because it is cultivated as a catch crop. It grows very quickly and

65

makes uncountable seeds, and they can be milled to make flour for bread. When the British Celts take new land they grow this plant to sustain themselves until the wheat harvest.'

Kradog nodded in confirmation. Lucius took the plant in turn and said, 'When we have seeds I'll try a small patch under cultivation to begin with. It grows wild all over the place. Each flower bears only one seed, but the flowers are as Pylades says: innumerable.'

They walked on, and Kradog asked permission to speak with Pylades.

'Have you really been to Britain?' he asked.

'Truly I have,' Pylades said gravely. 'Why do you ask?'

Kradog explained that his mother had been British, and that she came from a region known as Apple-Land.

Pylades smiled and said. 'Why, yes. That is Ynys Witrin, or Avalonia. I have been there. It is an island, with a great and holy sanctuary of the people, and there is a large village there also, built out over the water on strong piles.'

Kradog said, 'The gods are good, to have brought me face to face with one who has seen the birthplace of my mother.'

When the day's tasks had been allotted Drusus dismissed everyone except for Targui, Marcus, Pylades and Placidus. Marcus watched as Drusus composed his face into *dignitas*, and wondered where the laughing man had gone.

Drusus announced, 'Targui has persuaded me that the time has come to speak of horses. Once he told me of a breed beyond compare. and these horses are to be found southward of Mauretania, outside the borders of the Empire. It is my intention now to seek these horses and establish a stud here.'

A prickle of excitement ran through Marcus. He had dreamed of adventure, but to journey outside the Peace surpassed his best expectations.

Targui said, 'When Marcus and I went to Glanum I saw the road. It runs from Italy to the Pillars of Herak. I want to travel that road. I will take Drusus to find his horses, and then seek my own people again: thus I shall end my long exile.'

Marcus could restrain himself no longer.

'When do we leave?'

Drusus said calmly 'You do not leave. You join the Army after the winter festival, and we shall not be back by then.'

Marcus groaned involuntarily. Then Placidus was patting his shoulder, teeth a-dazzle as he smiled.

He said, 'I know how you must feel. So do we all, but there is a compensation for you.'

Marcus swallowed, fighting back the tears which threatened to disgrace him.

And Drusus told him, 'I shall have to emancipate you and set you up with capital of your own, since I am leaving. My record of servce and citizenship certificate have been inscribed on my diploma, but I left Cæsarea for Jerusalem in a hurry, and it must still be following me round the world. Luckily the legion has the custom of awarding an immediate copy on parchment, and before we leave I shall give you this to hold while I am beyond the Roman Peace; you must keep the document safe and with you at all times until I return. Who knows? The journey may take a year. I am going to free Lucius and make him estate manager on a salary. With Doratus in charge of the household there will be two competent people here to look after things while we are away. But you will be your own man, that's the thing. And you'll have your fill of travel in the Army, I can promise you that.'

The process of emancipation was a curious one. In Rhedæ they visited the lawyer who had dealt with the Gaulish end of Drusus' transfer of lands. With the appropriate legal documentation Drusus sold Marcus to the lawyer as a slave for a nominal sum, bought him back, sold him again to the same man, bought him back for a second time, and then freed him. Why the business had to be gone through twice they did not know, but that was the Roman way. On the same day Drusus presented Marcus with his peculium of five hundred aurei, and handed it over smiling; that evening there would be a great celebration. Marcus received the money marvelling at his father's good grace and the contradictions of his character.

X

When Herod the Great died he had left his fifteen thousand hostages penned up in the amphitheatre near Jericho to be killed at his death. No such thing happened because his sister Salome released them and sent them all home. In his will Herod's kingdom was divided among three of his sons. Herod Antipas received Galilee and Peræa; Herod Philip the principality of Ituræa, with Batanæa, Trachonitis and a tract of desert southward of Damascus. The third son, Archelaus, made himself king of Judæa. Of the three sons Philip was the best and Archelaus the worst.

At Pentecost Jerusalem was seething with people, and among them were some relatives of the two scribes and forty other men who had been executed over the matter of Herod the Great's graven image: the eagle on the Golden Gate. These relatives demanded vengeance and compensation, and when Archelaus refused disorder broke out in the city. Archelaus sent in his cavalry and killed three thousand Jews in the Temple precincts, an act of gross and inhuman sacrilege. Honest citizens rose up in revolt all over the country of Syria Palæstina; and so did criminal elements quick to seize advantage from chaos. A small army of robbers captured Sepphoris, looted and burned down the palace, and generally terrorized the countryside. In Peræa Jericho was taken by another league of gangs; again the royal palace was looted and destroyed by fire.

Augustus sent Publius Quintilius Varus in to restore order. He took Sepphoris at once, and crucified two thousand of the rebels on the hill outside the city. Archelaus and other

Herodians fled to Rome, where Augustus heard their case. He deprived Archelaus of his kingship, but allowed him to keep what he had claimed. Herod Antipas was furious because he had disputed the will. Meanwhile the Romans were busy uniting the various factions of Jewry against them, something that the Jews would have been quite unable to do left to themselves. But it is to Varus' credit that he pacified Jerusalem without bloodshed before being recalled to Rome on his way to the frontier of the Elbe.

The mosaic on the ground floor of the Lady Tanith's house represented Leda pierced by Zeus as the swan. All that could be seen of the woman were a shoulder, an arm clasping the god's serpentine feathered neck, and beyond it her head, eyes half-closed and mouth agape in swooning ecstasy. Meriem had seen it on her first morning. Oh well, thought Meriem, Perhaps it's better with a swan, especially if the swan is a god as well. That must be it.

Apart from the occasional fluttering of her own fingers Meriem had not experienced sexual pleasure. Her cold defloration by the priest had left her resentful of men to the point where she could be of use to Tanith only with those of restricted sexual tastes. So she allowed the girl a week of luxury punctuated by casual questioning, and then took action.

After their bath she and Meriem dined together just as on their first evening: silk dress and gold hairpin. But this time the wine was not watered. It was a tincture of wine with oil of hashish.

'A very special wine, my dear,' Tanith said.

After the second glass Meriem was floating, nodding owlishly while Tanith talked to her, sitting next to her and stroking the insides of her thighs through the silk.

'Dear girl,' Tanith was murmuring, 'you mustn't think badly of all men. You have had one bad experience, but it isn't the end of the world, though you thought so at the time.' Meriem's knees were wide apart, and she moistened her lips as Tanith's fingers found her clitoris. 'In a minute I'm going to let you meet a man. His name is Phokion, and

69

you'll like him. By morning you'll like him so much that you won't want to let him go, I promise you that.'

She stood up and beckoned, and Phokion came from where he had been watching unseen by Meriem. He was unclothed, his oiled body built like a discus-throwers, heavily muscled with big shoulders and narrow hips. At a sign from Tanith Phokion picked up Meriem easily, one arm round her waist and the other beneath her knees. He carried her to her bedroom. In the hours that followed Phokion took the girl to orgasm again and again, patiently and skilfully on a journey through the whole gamut of heterosexual experience. In fact it made no difference what sex his partner was. He was Tanith's most prized male prostitute, and his status depended on his prepotency. Tanith knew that by the time morning came Meriem would be enslaved.

They slept until midday, and ate a huge lunch after a bath. At the end of the meal Tanith came in and dismissed Phokion after a muttered exchange which Meriem couldn't hear.

Tanith sat down next to Meriem and said with a grin, 'Well, girl, I don't need to ask whether you enjoyed yourself.' She became serious and went on, 'I wanted to wipe that priest out of your mind, and there was only one way to do that. You'll feel better about it all now.'

Meriem sat and looked down at the remains of her meal.

'No need for false modesty,' said Tanith. 'You'll be doing a lot of bedwork from now on, and with all kinds of men. I keep a brothel, and after a day's rest you begin work.'

Meriem was staring at her, speechless.

'Listen to me,' Tanith said. 'You are unmarriageable, and you have no trade. This establishment is no in-and-out knocking-shop. You will please men, all manner of men, and in your free time you will learn to sing properly and play a musical instrument. A small percentage of your earnings will be set aside for you, and in twenty years' time you will be able to retire and either set up in business for yourself or else do nothing for the rest of your life. Do not enjoy yourself with your customers. And remember. One night a week while you want him, Phokion is yours, and you can enjoy yourself with him as much as you want. Think it all over. You have no choice in the matter, but I'd rather you went willingly to

70

work than have you tormented into submission. I like your spirit, Meriem, and it would grieve me to have to break it.'

She left, and Meriem went out on her little balcony. It faced north and was in cool shadow. She leaned on the parapet and stared unseeing before her, lips compressed, leaning on her elbow with a whiff of jasmine in her nostrils. Somewhere in the street outside children screamed in play, small high voices and laughter. A donkey brayed.

Another kind of girl might at this point have dissolved in tears of self-pity. But Meriem thought carefully about her situation. She had been afraid of the Valley of Doves, but not until recently had she learned how right she had been. Alone, she could have been raped and then killed.

The Lady Tanith had saved her life, and that was a huge debt. Phokion had taught her the pleasures of sex, and she wanted him. So be it, then. If she had to climb through six days of men for a seventh night with him, that was what she would do. She would have had a more or less similar life among the priests of the sect – but unpaid, and on a diet of bread and water, olives, dates and fish. And she would have been used as testimony to a false god until her looks faded. She knew that she had been drugged the night before, but she could not hold this against Tanith: because of it she had been induced to undergo a mental as well as a physical ritual ablution, and she was briefly touched by a sense of the undending paradoxes of the human condition.

So Meriem smiled wryly and said in a small voice over the braying donkey and the screaming children, 'I'll be a harlot, then. Let that be my trade. But I'll be Leda too, and Phokion my swan.'

XI

Pylades and Marcus sat together on a cushioned stone bench in the peristyle of the villa opposite the busts of Marcus' parents, which were bright with fresh paint; the new sundial stood by the pool. Pylades was excited by the fact that he would be travelling again, with Drusus and his party, even though not all the way. Marcus had realized that the old man might not return from this journey, and that in any case Marcus would be away for four years on his first tour of duty. Even if he got back safely from Mauretania, it would be more than likely that Pylades would be dead before Marcus saw Narbonnese Gaul again.

After each tour of duty Marcus would receive a year's leave followed by a new posting, an arrangement which was possible when a soldier joined a legion far from his home. Drusus had left X Fretensis, and this was the legion which Marcus would join at Cæsarea, the port of entry and the site of the Army transit camp. He would officially join the Army and take his oath at the headquarters of the nearest legion, which was XIV Gemina at Lugdunum, and would receive a sum of money for travelling expenses – not nearly enough to cover a journey to Syria; the rest would have to come out of his capital. He would have to travel overland after hugging the coast to Italy, but would be able to stay at Army staging posts on the way. It would be a long and arduous journey, but not exceptionally perilous, since he would have with him neither women nor treasure. But at that moment both Marcus and Pylades were occupied with other matters.

Marcus said to Pylades, 'Are you *sure* you want to travel

with my father and his party? Once you cross the Pillars anything could happen. Why not stay at home?'

'I've been at home for long enough, apart from my stay at Massilia,' said Pylades. 'I should like to see new things, and I've never visited Mauretania. But quite apart from my own selfish reasons, I am part of your father's plans, and must go if for no other reason than that.'

Drusus and Targui were away raising men for the venture, good fighters who would be paid mercenaries' wages and would have no share in the horses. At Tingis in Mauretania they would hire local guides until they reached country which was familiar to Targui; then they would pay off the guides and carry on independently.

Pylades said, 'What about you, Marcus? You are going to be a legionary, a foot soldier. Wouldn't you rather stop at home and breed these horses when your father brings them back?'

Marcus was silent, for Pylades had touched a raw spot.

Then he said gently, 'No, Pylades. My father is still full of vigour, and will be for many years yet, and he is one of the finest horsemasters in the world. Those horses will be his, and woe betide anyone who interferes! My duty is clear. I am to join the Army in place of my father, and he will breed a famous stud, and there is no more to be said about the matter.'

'So be it then,' said Pylades. 'You will need someone to guard your back. Your father had Placidus, and then the veiled one. You should take Kradog with you. As a moneyed legionary you will be able to afford to keep a supernumerary.'

Marcus said, 'I hadn't thought of that. It's an excellent idea. I'll have to teach him to fight.'

'He has British blood. The British can fight, if they can do little else. — Oh, and they can grow wheat. Marcus, you should see the British wheatfields! You'll notice that Julius Cæsar never writes about that. It's the military secret of the age. On a given area of land the British can grow four times as much wheat as anyone else. And they have a machine quite unknown outside Britain: it can reap wheat of varying straw-lengths, so that all the crop can be harvested; there's scarcely any need for gleaners. Believe me, Marcus, the conquest of Britain won't be long delayed, and bread for Rome will be the real reason, whatever others may be advanced officially.'

But Marcus was not listening. He had got to his feet and was shouting at a passing slavegirl.

'You! Find my body-slave and send him to me at once!'

Kradog had trouble with the cestus at first. He was fit and sleek and well fed, but he was not combat-fit, as Marcus and Placidus were. Kradog could walk twenty miles without much fatigue, but Marcus could run twenty and Placidus could run endlessly.

Kradog got there in the end, and enjoyed himself despite the gruelling training. He fought with a kind of bitter ferocity and a deadly perseverance. Marcus thought it strange that a slave should possess these qualities, and said as much to Placidus.

Placidus said, 'You forget where his mother came from. If your service ever takes you to Britain you will see plenty like him. But the British have no idea of tactics or strategy, and they're likely to give up in the middle of a battle and begin to fight among themselves. Ask Pylades. I never got to Britain. But this one sticks to his job, because he is loyal to you, Marcus, just as I was to Drusus when he was Butin.'

Marcus nodded, and the next day he sent Kradog into Rhedæ for two sets of paramilitary kilt and tunic, a belt and baldric for his long knife, and two pairs of heavy walking sandals to break in before their own journey.

Pride of place soon had to be given to the journey of Drusus and his party. Placidus had less and less time to help Marcus with the training of his slave, and then Marcus himself was increasingly drawn into the preparations. There were long lists of supplies to be drawn up, and the supplies themselves to be got; mules and donkeys to be bought and tended; weapons and clothing for Drusus' mercenaries . . . the work seemed endless.

The men whom Drusus had hired were for the most part time-expired soldiers who had settled in the district, had people who could look after their land in their absence, and who had been craving for some adventure when Drusus had advertised for men. They had to swear an oath of loyalty, and they would hold to it. There was a leavening of younger men, but again Drusus had chosen the sons of veterans.

Drusus had embraced Teutia indoors, and she stood with Doratus and Lucius while the cavalcade rode away, Marcus riding with his father for the morning, after which he would make his farewells and return home. Kradog trotted by the side of Marcus' horse. There was a babble of conversation from some of the men who were excited at leaving; others were silent and wrapped in thoughts of the homes they were leaving. Leather and equipment creaked and jingled in the ammoniac reek of the equines.

'Well, we're off,' Drusus said with some banality.

'Yes, Father,' Marcus said, equally flatly; there was a constraint between father and son. Drusus was thinking that by the time he returned home with the horses Marcus might be dead, killed in the service of Rome, while Marcus was sad at thinking how long it would be before he saw his father again. It was perhaps lucky that neither could foresee the true course of events.

'Thirty men,' Marcus said eventually, just for something to say. 'Will that really be enough?'

'More than enough,' said Drusus. 'I shall send ten of them home from Bætica before we make the crossing. I need to travel in some state, but for Mauretania I need the very best men, and I expect to weed out ten of these.'

Marcus hadn't thought of that – something which his father had done so automatically that he had scarcely thought about it either, but from the standpoint of vast experience rather than vast ignorance. Marcus grunted, kicking his horse on. At this stage of the journey Drusus rode to rearward but at one side of the column, to keep out of the dust and to see how the men were shaping. He would maintain this position for several days.

Pylades was riding a quiet gelding, a little gone in the wind but perfectly suited to a scholar's sedate progress.

'Well, Marcus?' he said as the young man drew level with him, Kradog still at the side of Marcus' horse.

75

'I'll be going back at noon,' Marcus said. 'I feel quite sad, though I don't know why.'

Pylades smiled and said, 'Meetings and partings; setting forth and being left behind. The emotions are stirred in face of change. Shall we ever meet again? And if we do, shall we be the same?'

Marcus looked at Pylades accusingly and said, 'Why, you're thinking of going with them, aren't you? The whole journey!'

Pylades said, 'Ahem. Well, Marcus, your father thinks that I shall return from Tingis, but – well, if you must know, it *would* be interesting, but I really don't know yet. Don't tell your father whatever you do.'

They laughed together, and soon it was time for the midday halt, where Marcus took a Roman son's formal farewell of his father, faces set in *gravitas*. Then he went first to Targui.

'Farewell, Targui,' Marcus said. 'I hope you find the horses for my father. I hope, too, that you find your own people again, and that you have a long and happy life with them, health and wealth and whatever you wish for.'

To Marcus' surprise Targui moved forward and embraced him, saying, 'Marcus, I thank you for those words. I swear that the horses will come to Drusus' land whatever may betide. And now, true son of your father, fare you well.'

Then Marcus went to Placidus and said, 'Farewell, Placidus. Come home safely, and in the meantime kill a lot of people, find a lot of women, drink a lot of beer, and look after my father.'

Placidus laughed and said, 'Your father can look after himself, never fear. I look forward to seeing you again, at your first long leave.' And he gave Marcus a bear hug, saying, 'You'll be a tribune when I come back! Farewell, Marcus.'

Marcus was not to see Placidus for twenty-eight years, and Placidus would never again see Marcus; but those events lay far in the future.

To Pylades Marcus said, 'I've been thinking, Pylades. Come straight back home from Tingis. When both my father and I are away my mother will need you as well as Doratus to advise her.'

'Very well,' said Pylades equably. 'I'll do as you ask. I might only become a deadweight travelling in the interior. Will you do something for me in return?'

'Why, certainly. Anything within reason. What do you want?'

Pylades looked at Kradog, Marcus' shadow, and said, 'Whatever else you do, promise you won't sell him. Keep him with you always, and make sure you look after each other.'

Marcus said, 'That's the point of my having made him my bodyguard. If he lasts that long I'll give him his freedom when I've done my service, and a good pension into the bargain. But why do you ask this now, Pylades?'

Pylades said, 'It was a dream I had, a dream in which you and Kradog were at the edge of great events, and I believe that it was a true dream.'

They were speaking Greek, and Kradog understood nothing of this although he stood close.

Marcus glanced round at him and then looked at Pylades again. They embraced and made their farewells, then Marcus fetched his horse and bestrode it, leaning over from the saddle and giving his father a swift Illyrian hug; and then he and Kradog were on their way home.

Marcus led his horse and felt relieved now that the partings had been made, while Kradog walked a pace behind. He wore his ragged old clothes, so proud of his new ones – for all he knew they might be expected to last a lifetime – that he was not going to wear them until directly ordered by his master.

'Kradog,' said Marcus, 'did you understand what Pylades and I were talking about when we said goodbye?'

'No, Master. I speak Latin and my mother's tongue, but I have only a few words of Greek.'

'My mother told me this: when I was eight or nine, Pylades dreamt that my father had become rich; my father was in the dream with a chest of jewels. And he brought one home. And I myself know this; when I was twelve Pylades told me he had dreamed there would be an earthquake, and he made all the household spend next day out of doors. And there *was* an earthquake. It knocked half the farm buildings down, though the house was not much damaged. Now Pylades said that he'd had another dream. In which you and I were on the edge of great events. What do you think of that?'

'We had better look after each other well, Master.'

'Just what Pylades told me,' Marcus said.

INTER SCRIPTUM (i)

When in London Professor Potts stayed at Brown's. There were other hotels which offered faultless service, but not quite the same atmosphere. Potts was a light diner, and he enjoyed small portions of the magnificent cold table, unexcelled anywhere else in London.

He ate a substantial breakfast while glancing through the headlines in *The Times*. It was the morning after his arrival in London. The students had gone back to California from Israel with the lecturer from Potts' department, while Potts had taken a direct El Al flight to Heathrow; he had business in London, and wanted to visit his old tutor at Cambridge.

The headlines in Potts' newspaper were not reassuring. Bomb explosions in Belfast, Paris, Manila; a pitched battle in southern Lebanon; a massacre in Guatemala; the Vietnamese fighting simultaneously on the border with China and in Kampuchea right up to the Thai border.

Potts finished his coffee, took his newspaper to a comfortable chair in a public room, and polished off the crossword.

At ten o'clock he went up to his room. It was six in the evening in Los Angeles, and so he picked up the telephone and placed a call to his wife. Waiting for the call, the words *War, Disease, Famine, Death* beginning to run in his head together with a visualization of the Dürer etching. The phone rang for a long time, but there was no reply.

John Potts was a wealthy man of independent means. In the 1890s his paternal grandfather had bought a couple of streets of houses in Fulham, an insalubrious district of London. In due course Potts had inherited the freeholds from his father. During the 1960s the district had been discovered by the trend-setters of the time; property values and rents had soared, outstripping inflation as the media people moved in together with the dress designers, interior decorators, fashion photographers and dogs' dieticians. Potts had no need to work, but he was driven by a compulsion akin to that of the great Victorian amateur archæologists and explorers.

On Friday evening he would be back home, and Potts was looking forward to it: after three weeks he missed his wife very much. His southern Californian milieu was to blame for the occasional fears of a midlife crisis, but essentially he was a measured and secure person within himself and in the unity of marriage; and so was Helen. It was their only marriage and it had survived the deaths of their twin son and daughter at the age of thirteen.

Chris and Marie had gone out with older friends from the Marina del Rey in a well found motor-sailer on a day near the end of February. The plan had been to sail west of Santa Catalina island and then troll northward, trying for sport fish. A sudden February storm had arisen with a wind of almost hurricane force out of the west and a teeming downpour of rain; the vessel had been driven onto the rocks and broken up in minutes. That had happened two years before this day when John Potts walked among an anonymous London crowd.

He stopped at a pub in Covent Garden for a 'ploughman's lunch' – a poppy roll, two airline-type portions of butter, a piece of mousetrap Cheddar cheese, and a spoonful of Branston pickle. It was a meal which would have sent a ploughman of fifty years before into an apoplectic rage.

Leaving his food half-finished, although the beer had been drinkable, Potts went out into the street, and walked along towards a street juggler, who was performing for a small group of punks with multi-coloured hair.

Potts felt like a stranger in a strange land. As he walked the air about him suddenly rocked, the turbulence followed half a second later by the WHOMP! of an explosion. Potts staggered, masonry raining down. He was unhurt. Then he turned facing the way he had come. The street wall of the pub's lounge bar, where he had been sitting, had been blown out, part of the first floor had collapsed into the lounge, and the wrecked interior was a chaos of broken brickwork, plaster and joists and furniture and bodies. Broken glass was everywhere in the street, together with other debris. And the air that for that half-second had rocked Potts and his companion in silence, was full of cries and screams.

A man heaved himself up out of the wreckage in the lounge bar, his face running with blood, and began to search, weakly calling, 'Jane? Jane?'

Uninjured passers-by were running to the scene, and in the distance Potts heard sirens. Shop windows had been smashed, and their proprietors were hurrying to the pub. Down the street Potts saw an old man pick himself up and calmly walk into a grocer's. He helped himself to a plastic bag and began to fill it with groceries. Potts thought, Good for you, old man.

With a wail of sirens an ambulance followed by two police cars screamed into the street. Police from one of the cars cordoned off the road, while the others and the ambulancemen cleared away sightseers and began to attend the injured and extricate the dead.

'You had a lucky escape,' said Doctor Waldegrave. 'I'm very glad for you. We can't afford to lose you for a while yet, you know.'

The old man at Potts' side was small and stooped. Under a tattered academic gown he wore outmoded jeans and a Fair Isle sweater; his head was bald and he had a straggling white beard.

Potts sat with his former tutor under Milton's mulberry tree in the Fellows' Garden at Christ's College, Cambridge. Roses, an expanse of perfect shaven lawn; weathered ancient stone; seclusion and peace under a tree planted in the seventeenth century by the author of *Paradise Lost*. And the college had been an old foundation when Milton had planted his tree.

Potts said, 'As you know, I've been in Israel. A fairly odd thing happened while I was out there.'

For a while that other, bloodstained world faded as Potts

81

recounted the story of his having found the gold box and its contents. He finished by saying. 'My wife sees a purpose in it all. I don't. After all, what's happened? But then Helen's a native-born Californian, and I suppose that explains it.'

'He'd have had a diploma,' Waldegrave said suddenly.

'Well,' said Potts. 'They found the older parchment was a certificate of service and so on. Perhaps one might call such a document a diploma?'

In the testy voice which Waldegrave had sometimes used to Potts when he was an undergraduate – and made him still feel like one – the old man said, 'You don't know much about the Roman Army, do you, Potts? I'm talking about a diploma in its first meaning. It was a double sheet of copper.'

'I see. The details would have been inscribed on one of those?'

Waldegrave nodded and said, 'Exactly.'

'This parchment was older than the first, and it referred to another man of the same *gens*. Probably my man's father. He couldn't very well carry sheets of copper on him while he was on a military mission. Still, I suppose it might have been a personal copy. I expect that's it. Still, we'll never know.'

'True enough. Now another thing. You were quite right in saying that Sepphoris was near to Nazareth, and a much larger city. But I think you were wrong about Joseph. – How long is it since you read the Gospels in Greek?' Waldegrave added suddenly.

'Never, I'm ashamed to say,' Potts confessed. Only John. Many, many years ago.'

'The Greek is the original text, and in it Joseph is called *tektón*.'

In surprise Potts said, 'A builder! I never knew that.'

Waldegrave said, 'The word meant a workman, but by the first century it usually connoted a builder. Good for you, Potts! Someone else has pointed out that there is no parable of Jesus based on carpentry, but very many on building. Take that word and the parables together, and we may assert with some authority that Joseph was a poor builder rather than a poor carpenter – poor in the sense of lacking this world's goods, naturally. I'm sure he was an excellent craftsman.' He looked at his watch and added, 'If we're to have an aperitif before dinner, we'd better go along and change now.'

They stood up, and Potts touched the bole of the tree in passing. Paradise Lost, he thought: where was Paradise Regained?

XII

Detached elements of Legio X Fretensis at Cæsarea in Syria Palæstina, in the twenty-fifth year of the Divine Augustus, two days before the Ides of April, M. Drusus Scipio to his dear mother this letter and greetings.

– Dear and honoured Mother, I hope that you received my earlier letters. The first was a hasty note which I wrote on shipboard as we trundled along the coast on the first stage of my journey. I wrote the second in the north of Italy when we were snowed in for two weeks, and it was a long letter, for time hung heavy on my hands. Now I have a settled address for you to send letters to me: wherever I am, X Fretensis will find me.

I trust that all is well at home, and that you are in good health. Keep a watchful eye on Lucius and Julia. I was perturbed when Lucius refused his freedom, and repeat the warning which I gave at the time. Do not trust such a slave in a position of importance. He will amass money while abjuring the responsibilities which should go with it.

It was good to see the mares with foals at foot before I left. How are they turning out? I ask Doratus to write to me with a report on this and other matters which I ought to know. The foals will not compare with the ones we shall breed when my father gets home. Have you news of him yet?

For myself I am in the best of health. The journey was uneventful to the point of being dull, especially when the weather held us up. A Roman soldier – even the rawest recruit – and his slave, when both are well-armed, and have overnight shelter at military staging posts, are as safe as in bed at home!

Apart from a few oddities like myself, whose fathers exchanged their lands, the troops here are recruited locally, and the auxiliaries are all Syrian except for one Illyrian cohort. (I must mention that when I passed through Illyria, at one point no more than twenty miles from our old home, I noticed how many Illyrians are joining the Army: I should not be surprised to see many of them reach high rank.) A good few of my comrades are blacker than Placidus, since the Egyptians brought many Nubians here during their occupation of the country; but these are citizens of Rome now.

I have seen little of the outside world apart from route marches. Cæsarea is a recently built city with a wonderful palace built by King Herod, and not far away a stinking factory for the production of the Tyrian purple, and a dyeworks.

My basic training is complete now. I found it very easy, but it almost killed some of the recruits. It was easy for me thanks to my father and Placidus.

Tomorrow I join the relief for Jerusalem, and this day is free, the first since I arrived here. Gods, how the Army works a man! But the food is very plentiful, and the pay so good that I have saved enough money already to defray the small expenses of my journey and the cost of keeping my slave. The capital which I transferred to Antioch is earning interest, and thus growing fatter. Do remember, dear Mother, that Pylades is to write to me at the soonest possible moment after his return.

Julia may be told that my slave Kradog is well: one or two (or ten!) of the girls may be glad of the information.

I have many things to do in readiness for tomorrow's departure, and must now set my hand to them, so take my leave of my honoured Mother.

Farewell.

XIII

When Drusus had left Jerusalem before the death of Herod the Great, Judæa had been more or less at peace, for the Pentecostal uprising had yet to burst into flame. But then that revolt had taken place; and when Marcus set out from Cæsarea the situation was very different, for Rome had used the cestus on its fist. Now the garrison in the city was strengthened, though Cæsarea remained the administrative centre and the Procurator's official residence.

There were five cohorts of X Fretensis stationed in Judæa, each of about five hundred men, plus one cavalry cohort. The First Cohort were the crack troops, always maintained well above strength.

Marcus marched out of Cæsarea with the Ninth Cohort. As he had said in his letter to Teutia, he had found the basic training easy. There were two drill periods a day for the recruits. Weapons training was carried out with heavyweight swords and spears, which Marcus had been using since puberty; he was very strong and accurate. He learnt to use his slingshot and his issue shield, but at swimming and riding he had nothing to learn, and the twenty-five mile route marches left him almost as fresh as when he started out.

The cohort's heavy baggage was carted, but Marcus still had to carry all his own equipment. He was wearing heavy marching sandals, and a mail shirt over his red tunic with strips of mail hanging down over its kilt. Belt and baldric held his shortsword and dagger, sword at right and dagger at the left. His helmet was slung from his shoulder. On his shoulders behind his head he held his leather kitbag tied by a thong to a stick which he held in his left hand. The kitbag had a light wooden frame; from it on the left hung his entrenching tool, and from the right-hand side his water bottle and mess-pan. Then below the kitbag Marcus carried his shield in its leather cover. Tents and encampment stakes were carried in the baggage train.

The troops marched ten miles due east, and then turned south along the good Roman road through the Plain of Sharon. It was a warm spring day, not hot enough to be uncomfortable, and Marcus was at ease despite the weight he was carrying. Whatever the official order of battle, the men thought of themselves as belonging to a particular century, and then the smallest unofficial unit, the eight men who shared a tent or barrack quarters.

Marcus was very much a new recruit, but so were the seven men who lived in proximity with him. They got on well, and marched together. Marcus had his two friends on either side of him. Quintus was short and barrel-chested and genial of disposition, while Claudius was tall and thin, but strong and wiry. His forename was Servius, and his father, who was originally from Britain, owned a farm in Galilee. Claudius never tired of singing the praises of that part of the world.

Claudius said, 'Look behind you at that pair. They've sneaked right up behind us.'

They were marching on a curve, and Marcus could easily see the two men who were tagging along at the end of the troop, instead of staying in the rear with the baggage train, slaves and other travellers taking advantage of Roman protection.

'What are they playing at?' he asked.

Because of his family's residence, Claudius was well versed in the ways of the country.

He said, 'We're plumb in the middle of Samaria, and those two Jews are scared stiff, I bet. They'd march in the middle of the ranks if they could.'

'Why's that?'

'The Samaritans think they're the true Jews, but the Jews think the Samaritans are a bastardly lot of mongrels. Jews were never safe in Samaria if they want to travel up to my part of the world they go round through the Decapolis. And now with the troubles breaking out again, those two could get picked off as easy as kiss your arse.'

The marching troops were escorted by mounted Syrian auxiliaries scouting ahead and to each flank. So far the journey was passing without incident. Whatever the two Jews might fear, the Romans had little to worry about until they reached Judæa.

The troops paused for refreshment and a meal at midday. Marcus eased himself out of his burdens and slipped them to the ground, stretching thankfully.

Kradog loped from his place with the baggage train, weaving his way through the crush until he reached Marcus. Quickly he detached Marcus' mess-pan from his kitbag and took it away.

Quintus was given to teasing Marcus about his slave, but Claudius was envious, and said so.

'It's good that a soldier should have a man to fetch and carry for him,' he said. 'Leaves him with more energy for fighting.'

When Kradog brought Marcus his issue of wheaten biscuit and cheese, Marcus took it and his water bottle so that he could sit as close as possible to the two Jews; Kradog stayed behind to guard the kit: as in armies everywhere, a soldier who had lost an item of equipment would try to 'win' a replacement before the next kit inspection.

The Jews were deep in conversation. Both wore identical head-scarves and dark coat-type robes with long sleeves. They had full beards and ringlets hanging over their ears under the head-scarves. One was older than the other, a grey beard and a black. They spoke Alexandrian Greek. Marcus, with his perfect Akhaian, had no difficulty in understanding the words, but he listened with deepening amazement at the concepts being expressed.

Blackbeard said, 'Finally, Job refutes the friends' indirect allusions to him because, the principles not applying, he cannot be an example.'

'But note these points,' said Greybeard. 'He is horrified at the profound mystery of the wicked man's prosperity. The rich men deliberately decide to ignore God and leave him out of calculation in their scheme of life. Yet – and mark this: *prosperity comes from God.*'

Blackbeard nodded and said, 'So, in the first cycle of speeches the friends have failed in their arguments based on the general nature of God, and in the second cycle they have failed in their arguments based on fact.'

'There now remains only one weapon: to charge Job explicitly with great sins.'

Marcus was staring. What was all this *about?*

Blackbeard said, 'So now we come to the third speech of Eliphaz. He charges Job with great wickedness. He suggests that Job has committed the sins common to rich and powerful rulers in the East: inhumanity, avarice and abuse of power. Eliphaz exhorts Job to make God his treasure and turn away from worldly prosperity.'

'Yes. Incidentally, by "the old way" we are meant to understand the way of the wicked man before the Flood.'

When a pause came in the discussion Marcus leaned over and said, 'Please excuse me, learned ones. I couldn't help overhearing something of your conversation, and it puzzles me. Is it permitted to ask what you are talking about?'

The younger man's mouth curled in contempt, and he was about to make some cutting answer, but Greybeard touched his arm gently and stopped him.

'Wait, Reuben,' he said. 'We are under the Roman helmet while we travel. Besides, remember Isaiah: "The Gentiles shall come to thy Light." Who are we to gainsay Isaiah?' He turned back to Marcus and said, 'Young soldier of Rome with the perfect Greek, we are Jews on a pilgrimage from Alexandria to Jerusalem. We believe that there is one God, one only, and that he chose us as his people. He gave us laws and commandments, and if any one of these is broken, then a sin is committed. We were discussing one of our holy books, which is much concerned with the question of sin and the judgment of God.'

Politely Marcus stood up holding his water bottle and mess-pan, for the warning trumpet was sounding: at the third trumpet they would form up in order of march.

'Thank you,' he said.

'You should find a copy of the Book of Isaiah in Greek,'

Greybeard began, and if he had any more to say Marcus never found out, because a hand gripped his shoulder and he was spun round with great force. It was his centurion, Gaius Naso.

Gaius was a black African citizen, a strapping man with a strong and unyielding face. His greaves, body armour and helmet shone silver, and his crimson crest ran sideways across the helmet from earpiece to earpiece. He wore his sword on the left and dagger on the right, and in his right hand held his vine stick. Marcus stiffened to attention. Away beyond the centurion by Marcus' kit he saw Kradog come alert. Marcus had warned him that if ever he saw his master undergo military punishment he must not interfere: if he fought with a Roman citizen in military authority he could be crucified. The vine stick twitched back in Gaius' hand, but then Claudius had Kradog by the belt, and Quintus had him by one arm. He saw no more for some moments because Gaius slashed him across the cheek. Marcus stayed rigidly at attention in smarting agony.

Softly the centurion said, 'You will not hob-nob with civilians without permission when you are on the march.'

That was all. Gaius turned away, the second trumpet sounded and Marcus ran for his kit, Kradog helping him into it.

Marcus said to Kradog, 'I may have to beat you tonight. Now get back down the line.'

They marched on after the third trumpet.

'Why did you get walloped?' Quintus asked.

Marcus said, 'I was talking with those two Jews, and it seems that was not the thing to do. Nobody told me.'

'Nobody tells you anything,' said Quintus. 'Fucking Army.'

'How does your face feel?' Claudius asked.

'Hurts,' Marcus said succinctly. 'Throbbing.'

'Fucking centurions,' said Claudius.

Marcus said nothing. After they had halted for the night and built camp he did not beat Kradog. Instead he bathed his face in cold water and thought about the strange conversation of those Jews. He would have to find out more about all that.

*

90

Drusus stayed a week in Tingis with his party. He bade farewell to Pylades, then hired a guide called Bogut; he had red hair and beard, and blue eyes. Drusus, Placidus and Targui had eighteen companions apart from Bogut, since Drusus had rejected twelve men in Bætica rather than the ten of his earlier estimate.

They passed into a countryside of steep slopes and rushing rivers, and then into the mountains of the Middle Atlas, where Bogut led them through a pass. Beyond the watershed the rivers flowed southward through forest and maquis and steppe until they lost themselves in evaporation in the desert. And as the party moved south Targui became talkative. Farther south, a long desert journey, lay his home, and when the horses were safe with Drusus he would travel on that journey and find his people again.

On their seventeenth day they were in grassy steppe-land, and Bogut told them that they would pass into the tribal territory of the horse-breeders on the next day. Then he asked for his fee.

'I go no farther,' he said. 'I have brought you where you want to be, and as far as I'm concerned that is my job done.'

Placidus was for turning the man away empty-handed, but Drusus disagreed.

'No,' he said. 'I'll pay him and let him go. It is as he says, and if he wants to travel back alone he's welcome.'

So Drusus paid off Bogut, and they never saw him again. The next day they began to see wonderful white-starred horses, and people; and it was almost midday when they reached the village of the Magnoun, escorted by two horsemen and a rabble of children.

The chief and the village elders assembled. Latin and Greek were unknown here beyond the Roman Peace. With Bogut gone Drusus had to fall back on sign language, but he made his wants known easily, pointing to a stallion and holding up two fingers, then to a mare, ten fingers upheld. Then he showed some gold.

The chief of the Magnoun was a burly man with blue-black whiskers and a predatory air, but his eyes lit up at sight of the gold. Attendants fetched mares' milk and cold mutton, and bargaining began over the meal. By the end of it Drusus and the chief had reached agreement: Drusus would have his horses, and for a mere ten aurei, which Drusus could scarcely believe. An hour and a half later he had made his selection with Targui's help, and they were on their way, unable to credit their good fortune. They made camp early that evening where the steppe fell away in short cliffs to the bed of a stream. Drusus went round the horses with Targui, superfluously singling out their points of excellence.

'Targui,' he sighed. 'Truly I am in your debt for ever. Can I persuade you to come back with me and share the fame that these horses will bring?'

Placidus had joined them while the others in the party saw to their own mounts, collected firewood and prepared food.

Placidus said, 'Targui thinks only of one thing now. Home! Am I right?'

Targui said, 'Yes. I can think of little else. I have been away too long. I have a long, long ride through the desert, but I know where to find the oases, and within a month I shall be with my people once more. Long ago, when you freed me, Drusus, I said that I would take you to find these horses. Now my task is done, and no one will stop me from going home.'

There was no more to be said on the subject. They ate a light supper of dates and olives washed down with cold, clean water from the stream, and then went to bed by firelight.

The Magnoun attacked at dawn. They were skilled in field-craft, and the three men who were taking the last watch were killed in complete silence. A few other men were waking, and had barely time to yell a warning before the Magnoun were among Drusus and his party.

Drusus awoke to a great outcry. There were eighty or a hundred of the Magnoun, and a crowd of their women in the background, encouraging their menfolk with shouts and screams. Drusus grabbed his sword, but had no time to use it as eight men overwhelmed him.

Targui was gone. At the first outcry he had run to a mare of the Magnoun's breed, leaped on its back, and was galloping away southward, clearing a path with his sword; then he was safe and out of sight.

Nobody could hold Placidus. He tore himself free and

killed the two men who had grasped him, lifting one off his feet in either hand and dashing their heads together; their brains spattered on the ground. Then Placidus tried to beat his way to Drusus, but there were thirty men separating them, so Placidus changed direction. He killed six more men before he got to the cliff. He hesitated for a moment, then jumped.

Five of Drusus' party were killed in the attack, and twelve of the Magnoun. The Romans were stripped and pegged down naked, arms and legs wide; then they were given to the women. Three of the Romans were selected to begin with. The women collected kindling and brushwood, piled it on the men's bellies, and lit three fires; that was when the screaming began, and the captives as yet unscathed struggled in vain to free themselves.

The Magnoun women began to practise variations on three new victims, cutting off their eyelids and smearing honey round the wounds to attract flies; slicing off the men's genitals and pinning them to their mouths with long thorns.

Placidus came to himself in agony, but when he heard the sounds coming from above he steeled himself to remain still. It was a hellish commotion: men crying for mercy, screaming, sobbing, yelling, all mingled with guffaws from the Magnoun and the eldritch screeches of amusement from their women. Placidus was eventually able to pick out Drusus' voice; and it was loud in his ears for a long time. But the noises of men in agony gradually began to fade as they died, and by the end of the afternoon of that dreadful day they had all ceased. The last sound Placidus heard from above was a whiffle from one of the horses which Drusus had congratulated himself on getting so cheaply.

Placidus waited until dark, then dragged himself to the water and drank. He took an hour to pull himself up the cliff path to the scene of torture and slaughter, finding Drusus' body burnt and mutilated. There was nothing that Placidus could do except try to save his own life. He did not give much for his chances, but even with two broken legs the man was indomitable. He began to drag himself slowly towards the east.

XIV

The youngster on top of Meriem threshed and spouted into her for the third time; the third time inside Meriem, for he had ejaculated spontaneously at sight of her naked body. Meriem moved and made the obligatory sounds of pleasure as he gasped endearments.

Then the youth sagged, opening his eyes on the boundless purple wells of Meriem's. He was panting, but as his breathing slowed he slid off her body and lay beside her.

'Oh, thank you, thank you!' he sighed.

He was about fifteen, Meriem guessed, and probably from a strict household; Meriem had long since ceased to wonder at the variations of sexual customs which she encountered.

'You are only the second woman I have known,' he said shyly, 'and the first one was . . . not nice. Old. But you: you are more beautiful than anyone I have ever seen. I think I'm in love with you.'

Meriem fetched the bowl of jasmine water and washed his sticky groin and belly while he lay back in a fantasy of life with her. She brought him down to earth with a thump.

'Pay the two eunuchs downstairs,' she said.

'Oh. Yes, I will.'

As soon as he had left Meriem gave herself a thorough douche after removing her pessary, changed it for a fresh one and anointed herself with scented olive oil. She ate a fig, and sipped from a bowl of water with no more than a dash of wine in it, waiting for the next customer.

This one was a middle-aged Jew with a knobbed and corrugated glans, which could have given Meriem some

94

trouble had he been as vigorous as the youth who preceded him. But he was fairly drunk, which he should not have been as a Jew, and in a brothel, where he most certainly should not have been; and during the proceedings he began to lose his erection. Meriem slewed him round and bestrode him, riding him until he came.

Men, she thought when he had gone and she was renewing her ablutions. I've washed this so often it's a wonder I haven't worn it away.

Apart from eager youngsters the Lady Tanith never gave Meriem to customers who had not been vetted by other girls of the establishment: they had to be sexually straight. And well-to-do. Meriem had made her commitment to whoredom, and carried out her job efficiently and without recrimination or guilt, but she was thankful to escape the attentions of the quirky. Tanith had seen at once that Meriem was an asset to be used with care. She was on call five mornings out of seven, and six nights, but the rest of her time was free. She was taking singing lessons and learning to play the zither. She went to the instrument now and plucked the strings, singing in a clear, reedy voice:

'Deathless Aphrodite, throned in flowers,
Daughter of Zeus, O terrible enchantress,
With this sorrow, with this anguish, break my spirit.
Lady, no longer!

'Come to me again! O now! Release me!
End the great pang! And all my heart desireth
Now of fulfilment, fulfil! O Aphrodite,
Fight by my shoulder!'

'Well, well. Sappho?' said a clear and pleasant baritone voice behind her, and as she turned: 'Yes, I'd imagine the Isle of Lesbos has its attractions.'

Meriem had seen this man before, she knew as he came forward and cupped a hand beneath her chin. He had a square and pleasant face, rich robes, and he smelt of sandal-wood. Keen grey eyes looked into hers.

'Did you use up all your voice with the song,' he asked.

'No, sir,' said Meriem, and this time she used the honorific without mockery. 'I think I have seen you somewhere before.'

95

He gave her cheek a light pat and said, 'Now those are words which *I* should use, but in different circumstances. At a party, say.'

'You were here the evening I first got here. I remember now: you came down the staircase. I'd just arrived with the Lady Tanith and some girls.'

'More than likely. My name is Petros. I come to Magdala once a month on business,' he said, disrobing. 'Socrates had a shrewish wife in his Xantippë, and I have my Chloë. Or Hydra or Gorgon; take your pick. A marriage of my father's commercial interests. But you, now: you are something out of the ordinary.'

Petros caressed her thoroughly, bringing her nipples up. He did not enter her for some time, probing her clitoris with his penis, keeping up a steady rhythm; despite herself Meriem became excited by this contact. She had soon tired of Phokion, had obeyed Tanith's order that she was not to enjoy herself with the customers, and had turned to Tanith herself for sexual relief. But this man Petros had entered her now, and she could not prevent herself going into spasm. She almost blacked out, and as she slowly recovered she was aware of him smiling down at her.

Petros said, 'Thank you, my dear. That was most excellent. And how about you? I hope that Lesbos palls in comparison.'

Angrily Meriem said, 'You shouldn't have done that!'

'But, lovely girl, *you* did it. Or to tell the truth, we both did. And that's the point. Chloë never enjoys it, but I cannot get my pleasure unless my partner is fully with me. Now give me a quick wash round. I'm going to see Tanith.'

Meriem was called to lunch with Petros and Tanith; while eating Petros expounded the idea that had occurred to him.

'This girl is exceptional, Tanith.'

'Tell me something I don't know. I've had her as well as you.'

'I guessed as much; but you haven't understood me. Take my own case. In future I shall let you know in advance when I'm visiting Magdala. I want Meriem's exclusive services for one day and a night.'

'Done.' said Tanith. 'I don't need to ask whether you can pay.'

96

Petros merely raised an eyebrow and said. 'I don't want to spend the whole time in mindless copulation. Meriem has an excellent voice, and a bright mind into the bargain.'

Tanith said a little defensively, 'She's learning the zither, and having singing lessons, too.'

'That's good, but it isn't enough, Tanith.'

Meriem sat in silence while Petros took a hand in shaping her future. Here was a man who from the first teasing moments had treated her as a person and not a thing. Against all the rules of the game he had brought her to the most satisfying climax she had ever experienced. Lesbos, in the shape of Tanith, certainly did pall in comparison with Petros. And so did all the mechanical wiles of Phokion in retrospect.

Petros said, 'Meriem should be taught all the domestic arts as well as those of the bed. Besides the zither, she must play the harp and the lyre and the pipes. She should learn to embroider and make lace, to converse intelligently, and to help with your accounts.'

'This is going a bit far, surely?' Tanith protested.

'Not at all. Look at the girl. As she is, Croesus himself would throw himself into the pools of her eyes. If she is made into a rounded personality she would be absolutely beyond price. You would reserve her only for clients of my standing, who want her on similar terms to myself. This girl has not yet been corrupted by whoredom, but the moment the process begins, you have a wasting asset. Think it over.'

Tanith turned to Meriem and said, 'What do you think, child?'

'May I learn to dance?' Meriem asked. 'I've always wanted to.'

'Of course,' said Petros. 'Did I forget to mention that? I expect there'll be other things too, if Tanith agrees with my idea. I'm sorry to say this to your face, Meriem, but it's a question of profit and loss, no more and no less. You understand?'

'Oh yes,' Meriem said, for, with his face turned to her, he had just given a small wink.

Tanith was making calculations. At first she had been hostile to the whole idea, but as Petros unfolded his argument she came round to his point of view. If she trained Meriem as a top-flight hetaira Tanith could set her own enormously increased kudos against the expense of Meriem's education. And in fact Tanith had people, slaves or freedmen, women or girls, who could impart all the skills to Meriem at no cost.

Meriem sat with her hands in her lap and her eyes downcast, hoping. The new way of life which Petros had suggested was better than anything she could have thought of for herself.

Tanith said, 'So if and when Meriem is made, what fee should I charge for her services? I should be grateful for your advice.'

Petros glanced at Meriem, then bent and whispered in Tanith's ear. Tanith's eyebrows shot up, while Meriem's spirits sank.

Tanith composed her face and turned to Meriem: 'From now on your days will be taken up with education; you will have the Sabbath free, and you will work that night and the next two. I have to have some return on my investment. What do you say?'

Tears were running down Meriem's cheeks.

'No need to cry,' Petros observed.

'Men!' said Tanith. 'She's crying for joy. Can't you tell the difference?'

Meriem whispered, 'Lady, I kiss your feet,' and did so, but Tanith raised her up and called for wine. The three of them drank unwatered bowls, and as always, Meriem spilt a few drops on the floor. She said silently, 'This libation in thanks to all the gods.' Petros gave her a glance which said plainly that he knew what she was doing, while – though Tanith must have known also, she never gave a sign – they were all three happy together.

Then Meriem said, 'There *is* one thing. I hate sewing,' and she couldn't understand why the others burst out laughing.

XV

Pylades in the twenty-sixth year of so on and so forth, nine days before the Kalends of May, to his erstwhile pupil the Soldier Marcus Drusus Scipio, a greeting to you and my long-delayed news.

We had an uneventful journey to Bætica, and a smooth crossing to Tingis; the much-roaring sea, I am glad to say, with thanks to Poseidon, kept quiet. Your father sold all the animals in Bætica, and bought new after we had landed, and left after ten days for the interior, leaving me in Tingis. The place is something of a hole, to be frank; what is not barbarian is wholly Roman, and scarcely a Greek in sight, though it has a good wide bay. Seen from the sea, the city looks for all the world like an amphitheatre.

Your father asked me to send his greetings to you when I wrote, and this I now do, months after you would have expected to hear from me. For, like a bear which has slumbered through the winter, living on its fat and growing steadily leaner, until in spring it wakens and goes ravening through the sheep-folds, so the ocean awoke and ravaged the Pillars of Herak. By the time the storms had subsided, the travelling season had ended, and I was marooned in Tingitan boredom for the winter. I pass over that exile in silence; there was some compensation in the fact that when the sea was open again I took a ship directly to Narbo, thus saving myself the uninteresting trip back over ground already traversed.

Your mother is well and sends her love. She asks you to write more often, saying that she intends to learn herself;

but naturally she is only speaking in jest: she knows it is an impossible thing for a woman of her class. She counts herself fortunate in reading as well as she does.

Doratus has already sent you an account of his stewardship and that of Lucius, so you know that all goes well with the estate. You expressed some reservations when Lucius would not take his freedom; but in fact the man is working very well. If it pleases you to do so, perhaps you might tell Kradog that there is an experimental patch of goosefoot under cultivation. I was able to give some advice on this, from my memories of it in Britain.

Learn as many languages as you can. You have a natural linguistic gift. I would not have dreamt of telling you that while we were under the same roof. It is well now that you become aware of this talent: in the military life it is of exceptional value, for it can afford entry into different cultures and different literatures. Prices come down too!

I have never visited Judæa, and I should welcome an account of the inhabitants and the situation at present. Of course I have heard plenty from your father, but things change, and one likes to keep up to date. Your mother has decided that I may spend two months in Massilia every summer, that great lady having seen how I benefited from my sojourn before.

Marcus, do not worry if your father does not return here for some time. From what the veiled creature said, there is a long and arduous journey to be undertaken. On the way your father's party will no doubt find itself in sight of Mount Atlas, where the superstitious believe that the eponymous giant King of Mauretania lies frozen into stone by the Gorgon's glance. Ignorant louts! – But to resume: Just between ourselves, I estimate that the journey could take two years. Remember that the return trip involves a horse-drive. And remember too that it would be unwise to mention my estimate to your lady mother, who sends her love along with my affectionate

Farewell.

XVI

During the great Pentecost revolt of the previous year Varus
had brought two more legions south with him as well as the
whole of X Fretensis, but these two had been withdrawn
when Marcus arrived in Jerusalem. He missed the sea air
and the comfort of the camp next to Cæsar's palace not far
from the great aqueducts which brought water to Cæsarea
from Mount Carmel. Jerusalem was a splendid city built
largely of a tawny granite which could look golden in a
certain angle of the light; and the city centre was massively
impressive. It was dominated by three huge buildings erected
by Herod the Great: the Temple, the Antonia fort, and
Herod's Palace with its three colossal towers. Yet for all the
space and beauty of the centre, Jerusalem was always to feel
claustrophobic to Marcus; and most Romans, save for the
most insensitive, felt the same. They were very certainly not
at home there. The very fabric of the place felt hostile.

The size of the city was limited by the two valleys enclosing
it, with a third valley running down the middle. Herod's
Palace, to the west of this central valley, was joined to the
Temple precincts by a viaduct: the Valley of Kidron to the
east, then, Hinnom to the south-west, and the Tyropæon
running roughly north-south just to the west of the Temple
area.

This was an enormous courtyard surrounded by a spiked
wall with a cloister running all the way round inside it. To
the south were the Royal Porticoes extending the cloister,
and to the east the double portico of Solomon's Porch.

The northern portion of the area contained a great sanctuary composed of the inner and outer courts; the inner court had three sections, one each for priests, laymen and women. Another great porch led to the Altar of Sacrifice, with places beside it for tethering animals and slabs for slaughtering them; the blood ran away down drains. In the inner sanctum there was first a little lobby, and then the holy place where the seven candles burnt perpetually. The Holy of Holies itself was a chamber fronted by double curtains and lit only by the Menora, the Light of Jewry.

Marcus saw none of all that as he went out on his first free afternoon with his friends Claudius, Quintus and another man of their eight named Philo. They got as far as the Court of the Gentiles, and Claudius pointed to a notice on the wall. It was written in Greek, Latin and Hebrew in that order, and it read *No Gentile is allowed to pass these bounds. Anyone doing so does it at his own risk, and the penalty is death.*

'What's it say?' asked Philo, and Claudius read out the interdiction.

Marcus said, 'Gentile. My father told me anyone who's not a Jew is a Gentile, but it didn't make me *feel* like a Gentile. I feel like one now, though. There are places where a Roman soldier can't go. It's a funny feeling.'

Quintus said, 'Yet the architecture's Greek.'

'So are all the public buildings,' Philo said.

'All the best *builders* are Greek,' Claudius said, adding in self-defence, 'Or Roman. The Greeks got here first, that's all.'

Marcus looked at the vast complex of buildings. They had been part of his father's daily life, and had touched some part of him, Marcus now understood. Opposite the Temple stood the huge mass of Herod's Palace, and dominating both structures reared the fortress-palace of Antonia, named by Herod in honour of Mark Antony. The three great buildings were connected above ground by colonnades (to say nothing of subterranean secret passages), and the Roman troops were stationed in the Antonia. Marcus' duties so far had been limited to guarding one approach to the fortress, and he gazed round from his vantage point at the magnificent works: golden stone, fluted shining marble, enormous bronze doors.

102

And from part of all this the Romans themselves were excluded! He shook his head in amazement.

There was a *splat*, and a rotten fruit exploded on the wall by Quintus' head. They looked for the assailant, but in the press of purposeful activity to and from the buildings could see no one who might have hurled the fruit. Teeth gleamed in the face of some soldiers of Archelaus guarding the Temple: they had seen the event, but were too far away to have been guilty.

'Come on,' Claudius said. 'I think we've outstayed our welcome here.'

They went downhill into the bustling, narrow streets, crossing the Tyropæon, where the conditions favoured dairying and cheese-making, hence the name Valley of the Cheese-makers. They skirted the business quarter, and gawped at the opulent bazaars and shops. Each specialized in certain articles: rugs and carpets; footwear of all sorts; jewellery; textiles. Trades were plied in the street: the copper-smith hammering away; the scribe writing and his assistant counting the words on finished work, for scribes were paid by the hundred words; the carpenter busy with saw or hammer or adze. There were luxury shops where the spices of the Orient were sold, and balsam of Jericho, worth its own weight in gold. There were food stalls, sellers of soft drinks, boozing shops, fishmongers and butchers in the side-streets. There was no wheeled traffic because the streets were too narrow and hilly, but there was scarcely room to move because of the press of people and draught animals. Marcus and his comrades squeezed through the crowds, past donkeys and horses, mules and camels, while Marcus remembered the mass of scars on Placidus' shoulder, and gave the camels the widest berth he could. It was hot and busy and smelly, noisy and undisciplined. After an hour they looked for some-where to sit down. They found a Gentile wine bar, sat grate-fully, and Quintus said, 'Well, what do we want? Nuts and wine all right?'

Claudius said, 'Just grape juice for me.'

Philo and Quintus asked for nuts and wine, and Marcus for beer. When the proprietor came up Quintus spoke and was answered in a language strange to Marcus.

'What were you speaking?' he asked Quintus.

'Aramaic.'

'You can speak Aramaic?' Marcus said in surprise.

'You said it. It's my second language after Latin. I put Greek a bad third. My old man's lands are up near a place named Magdala.'

Claudius said, 'I speak Aramaic too. It's easy. Pity I never learned to write it.'

Marcus said, 'I want to learn it. Will you teach me?'

'How much for?'

'What'll you pay?' said Quintus and Claudius simultaneously.

There was some discussion, after which Quintus withdrew his offer on the grounds that it had been an impulse, and he would never make a teacher; it would be boring, and anyhow, Claudius was cut out for the job. Marcus and Claudius settled on a small fee.

'Waste of good money,' Philo said. 'Latin's good enough for me, with enough Greek to get by, and a finger to point with.'

Philo was the son of a time-expired auxiliary, as was Marcus, but his grandfather had been a Parthian, and the family had plunged into the Latin ethos to dodge the slurs. He was swarthy and self-opinionated, quick in his movements but slow in the workings of the brain, a good private soldier who would never be promoted. Quintus might make decurion, or optio, as the rank would be called later. Marcus and Claudius had already been noted in the Prætorium as worth watching: promotable material, possibly.

They finished their refreshment and headed back uphill for the Antonia, shoving their way through the crowds. They had reached an intersection where the traffic of people and beasts of burden jostled in three directions and in more than usual confusion. Trying to make their way uphill, the Romans were pushing against two contrary tides, with constant body contact; Marcus was thrust violently from behind. In the crush there was a welter of impressions: beards and headscarves, lustrous feminine eyes, a wrinkled face and a white beard, a camel's unspeakably foul breath. He stamped in the opposite direction, bringing himself to rest.

Quintus was at his heels and Philo at his right side; of Claudius there was no sign. The babble of chatter and shouts swelled and dropped in volume like surf on a beach.

Philo suddenly cried out, 'Ah! My back!' and slumped against Marcus, who put an arm round him.

'He's hurt, Quintus. Quick, lend a hand!'

With much effort the pair supported Philo into a sidestreet. Philo was wounded in the back towards the right side, but he could walk with help; he had not yet experienced the full pain of the wound, and shock had not begun. Out of the corner of his eye he had seen the glint of a knife, then felt the thud of impact of the blade.

Marcus and Quintus helped Philo along to the other end of the street, where they turned uphill again. This street was rather less crowded, and halfway up they met a foot patrol under a decurion, coming down. At the decurion's command the patrol halted.

'What's happened?'

Marcus said, 'This man's been stabbed in the crowd. We didn't see anything at all, but he saw the knife before it went in.'

'Can you manage as you are?'

'I think so,' Marcus said. 'He can walk with our help.'

The decurion said, 'Right. Report at once to the guard commander when you get up there.'

Laboriously the pair resumed the uphill trudge, while Philo grew steadily heavier between them, groaning now with the pain of his wound. His tunic was soaked with blood, and Marcus was unsure whether to regard this as a good sign. At least it might mean that Philo was not bleeding internally; Marcus remembered that the slave Ulpius had scarcely bled externally at all.

One of the vast courtyards in the Antonia housed the Ninth Cohort, and they had made it into a Roman camp, of exactly the same design as any other camp, whether for an overnight stay or a centuries-long permanent habitation, from one end of the Roman Peace to the other.

Marcus and Quintus sat glumly in an office next to the guardroom. They were doing what forms a good part of Army existence: waiting for a long time without being told anything. They had taken the barely conscious Philo to the guardroom, and a stretcher party had rushed him to hospital. The guard commander had ordered them to wait, and there they were.

'We should have taken that Kradog of yours with us,' said Quintus. 'Better off with him behind us with his eyes peeled, instead of sitting in the billet cleaning your kit.'

'Yes,' Marcus agreed, 'that's a lesson learned the hard way, and I won't – '

The two men had gone from relaxed passivity to quivering attention and total silence as their centurion, Gaius Naso, strode in. He stared at them impassively for what seemed a long time.

Then he said, 'Stand easy. Now tell me in your own words exactly what happened. Don't be afraid of interrupting each other.'

Hesitantly and self-consciously at first, but then gaining confidence Marcus and Quintus gave their version of the afternoon's events. They were frightened by Gaius, who was harsh and sometimes brutal; and they were not yet experienced enough soldiers to realize that they were men of Gaius' century caught up in a matter which had gone beyond the century. Gaius listened, his black face showing no expression. Only his eyes shifted from man to man.

It was not a long report, and when they had finished Gaius said, 'Drusus Scipio, you can write. Let me have this as an internal report; I'll incorporate it in my own. And write in Latin! I'll have tablets and stylus sent in. – Now then, I have to report to the Camp Prefect. You are recruits only recently passed out. Yet you did not panic. You brought your wounded comrade out without damage to yourselves or further damage to him. I shall not recommend punishment. Instead I shall commend you for your swift action. That was a Sicarius at work.'

Gaius saw their puzzlement. These had the makings of good soldiers, so he said, 'There's a faction among the Jews who call themselves Zealots. Most of the Jews hate us Romans, but the Zealots hate us worst. Maniac nationalists. They use assassins that we call Sicarii: daggermen. You're damned lucky he didn't get the lot of you.'

*

106

The men were billeted eight to a hut, with the centurions' quarters at the outer ends of the centuries; each centurion had his own private billet. Marcus took his finished tablets in and handed them to Gaius, who read them and then looked up. Marcus was still at attention.

'That'll do very well,' Gaius said, and then peered at Marcus. 'Have you got something you want to say? If so, you have permission to speak.'

Marcus said, 'The wounded man, sir: Philo. Are we allowed to visit him?'

Offhand Gaius said, 'Oh, he's dead. You'll be seven to a billet until a replacement comes in. Now take this and get out.'

Dusk came to Jerusalem; for the Jews the first star meant the beginning of a new day. For the Romans dusk meant the evening trumpets and the new password for the night. For Marcus it meant the canteen and some beer after he had finished some small duties and inspected the kit which Kradog had cleaned to perfection.

'Good work, Kradog,' said Marcus. 'Take this and get out.'

When he entered the canteen Marcus was astonished to see Claudius sitting with Quintus, both drinking unwatered wine.

Marcus went quickly to them and said, 'What the Hades happened to you, Claudius? I thought you'd got your stupid self killed.'

With a mockingly accented vocative Claudius said, 'O man of action, perhaps I'm not so stupid. I saw a gap open up ahead and ran like a deer up the street.'

Marcus sat down and ordered his beer from one of the serving slaves.

Quintus said, 'Did you hear about old Philo?'

'You know, then?' Marcus asked. He was a little disappointed because he had thought he would have the mixed pleasure of being first with the news.

'This is the Army,' Claudius said. 'Everybody knows. We three are famous. Lost the first casualty in the cohort.'

107

Marcus was annoyed.

'Some fame, having your comrade wounded to death and doing nothing about it.'

Quintus said, 'You're in the Army. Philo's just the first.'

'How did you get on with Gaius Cerberus?' Claudius asked.

Marcus chortled and took a big draught of the beer as soon as the slave set it before him.

'He gave me a denarius, for nothing! – No, hear me out: he just handed it over and said, "Now take this and get out".' I gave the money to my slave. What's a denarius to me? *Kradog* is in the money: to him a denarius is riches. Why, he'll never have held a silver coin in his hand before in his life.'

XVII

From his first months in Jerusalem Marcus had felt the hostility of the place. Philo's death was succeeded by the murder of two other soldiers at the hands of unknown daggermen, and the garrison, Marcus included, was permeated by fear. In set-piece attack and in prepared defence the Roman Army – with one or two exceptions – was invincible, doggedly persistent and unafraid. But Jerusalem was different. The whole city had breathed forth its enmity, and now it had been seen to have very real substance. Life had to go on, but for the soldiers off duty it went on with much looking over the shoulder, icy prickles at the back of the neck; fear of the dagger in the crowd: the Jerusalem Terror became part of the way of life.

Despite this, and with plenty of money in the bank at Antioch together with local drawing facilities, Marcus decided to find himself an apartment to use during his leisure time. After some enquiries and searching, always with Kradog alert at his heels, he found three rooms in a single-storey block, pleasantly shaded by trees: a kitchen, a dining-cum-living room, a bedroom, communal use of the flat roof, and a tiny private courtyard screened by a lattice of vines.

The proprietor was named Orthos, a quiet man with an aquiline nose and black whiskers trimmed short, possibly with Hittite or Hurrian blood. He presented Marcus with a list of rules for the conduct of the apartment, then turned to leave, but turned to face Marcus again.

He said, 'Oh yes, one thing: you'll need to see the Jewish authorities about the water.'

'Eh?'

Orthos pointed to where a section of an aqueduct was visible and said, 'That's what I mean. These buildings take their water from the Temple supply.'

'Thanks for telling me,' said Marcus.

Marcus found the department and sent in his application in Latin, then waited in an unsegregated anteroom while the document was processed. He was finding out that Jewish bureaucracy was the same as bureaucracy everywhere else: like the Army, it involved much waiting. He called Kradog.

'Here's two asses. Fetch me some beer and have one yourself.'

'At once. And thanks, Master.'

Marcus rearranged the rough straw cushion on his marble bench. He was alone in the anteroom. Most of the applicants were Jewish, and they were dealt with in the main offices for the exclusive use of Jews.

A man came into the anteroom from the general office.

Marcus stood up and said courteously, 'Peace be upon you,' then added, 'I'd begun to think no one was ever coming,' speaking in Aramaic. He saw a man perhaps five years older than himself with light brown hair sweeping out from beneath his headscarf. He had eyes the colour of his hair and a golden skin with a straight nose and moulded lips. A walking Praxiteles, Marcus thought. He's *too* beautiful; and then he felt oddly relieved when the man opened his mouth and spoke, revealing two false upper incisors. They had turned yellow as ivory dentures always did, in strong contrast to the rest of his perfect teeth.

'Peace be upon you also,' the man replied. 'We're so busy in there you'd hardly believe it.'

Marcus said, 'Yes, I thought it was something like that.'

'Forgive me – but you're not a native Aramaic speaker?'

'No. I've been taught by two comrades.'

The man said, 'You're very good. There's only a slight accent – apart from the Galilean, of course.'

'That's because they were raised in Galilee. They couldn't help that.'

The moulded lips tightened a little, and there was the hint of a frown, both reactions brought instantly under control.

'Perhaps not,' the man said. 'Well, to business. The application has been approved, as of course it had to be: a formality. We can make the connection two days after the Sabbath. Can you arrange to be on the premises then?'

'I'll try,' said Marcus. 'If I can't be there in person I'll send my body-slave. I'd trust that one with my life, let alone my water supply.'

'Good. Two days after the Sabbath, early in the morning.'

It was, of course, afternoon when the workmen from the water authority arrived, together with the golden-skinned official. 'Would you care to come inside?' Marcus asked him. 'I'm slowly getting the place to rights.'

'No, thanks. I have to watch these men.'

'A drink, then?' Marcus suggested, and called for Kradog, who was in the kitchen. 'I've plenty of good Egyptian beer. Wine too if you prefer it.'

The man hesitated, then said, 'Perhaps a little grape juice.'

'Certainly. – Kradog, go and fetch grape juice for the Adonai. Find a Jewish vendor.'

So the two men companionably watched the plumbers until Kradog came back with a leather skin of grape juice. He handed it to Marcus, then brought a glass bowl and a crock of beer.

'Peace be on this house,' the man said, and drank, his headcloth and his golden face dappled by the shadows of the vine leaves above.

Marcus had his nose in his beer. After a long draught he looked up and across his earthenware crock.

'Thank you,' he said. 'I value the blessing.' He spilt beer on the floor, tactful enough to make no mention of gods which he knew would given offence to a Jew, and added, 'To you, long life and happiness.'

They drank together again, members of separate exclusivities. As the thought occurred to Marcus, another followed it.

'Adonai, could you kindly tell me where I might find a book called Isaiah?'

111

The hazel eyes narrowed into a searching gaze.

'Why do you ask this?'

'A wise old man said that I should seek this book Isaiah, which has things to say about the Gentiles.'

'It has a lot more to say than that,' the man said seriously. 'This is the book of the Prophet Isaiah, one of our holiest books. But your wise man was right, and it seems to me that you are right to ask. I have a copy in Hebrew, and would gladly lend it, but I doubt if you could read it.'

'I couldn't,' Marcus admitted. 'I can read anything in Greek or Latin, but I can't even read Aramaic.'

'Copies in Greek are available. That would be your best plan: look for a Greek copy.'

'Yes,' said Marcus, 'I may do that. And thank you very much for your advice.'

They put down their drinks as the plumbers finished work and tested the supply. Marcus, the official and Kradog stood in the kitchen and watched the water gush from the faucet, a coruscating stream in a shaft of sunlight; then at a sign from Marcus Kradog turned it off.

As Marcus saw the official out and tipped the workers the man said, 'Sometimes there are problems with newly-connected supplies. If you have any difficulty send a message with your slave, in Latin. Personal to me: I'll sort things out at once. My name is Nakdimon. Nakdimon ben Gurion, but in Latin I am called Nicodemus.'

112

XVIII

All the Jews disliked the Romans, for it was unthinkable that the ground of Israel should be trodden by an occupying force; but there was a party which advocated collaboration, temporizing until God should deliver them. This faction took the attitude it did because it hated Herod Archelaus even more than the Romans.

Archelaus was weak and vicious; he vacillated between trying to curry favour with his people and subjecting them to torture and execution. Augustus had given him control over Cæsarea, Sebaste, Jerusalem and Joppa. Salome the younger, his niece, was given the palace at Ashkelon.

What rankled with many of the people was that the Herods were not even Jews, but of Arabian descent, so that whichever way they turned there was a yoke around Jewish necks. One was harsh and implacable, but at least consistent: the Roman; the other yoke was the Herodian reign of terror. Some people acknowledged that at least they knew where they stood with Rome, and when God had punished Israel enough to purge its sins, they would be set free of foreign oppressors.

Marcus neither knew nor cared about any of this as he travelled into Galilee with Claudius, Quintus and Kradog. Marcus had a good bay horse under him, which he had galloped that morning and now walked, Kradog at his side. Claudius rode a quiet hack, and Quintus a desert pony. Apart from his lack of a woman, Marcus had not been so happy since those far-off Illyrian days.

The country had a lot to do with his mood, he decided.

Galilee. It had everything anyone could desire. The vintage had begun in the middle of the summer, and it was still continuing in September, together with the harvest of olives and figs. The people were not hostile here: they were too busy gathering the fruits of the earth and socializing. Everywhere work combined with alfresco partying under the sun. Grape pickers filled great baskets with the vintage; others filled the presses, crushed the grapes and poured the must into the fermenting vats. In the groves of olives and figs the people swarmed, harvesting the fruit, children and youngsters clambering about in the branches of the fig trees. The corn harvests had been gathered in spring and early summer. Galilee was as rich in animals as it was in the fruits of its trees: sheep and goats, cows and pigs, poultry and bees, and there were huge wild flocks of edible birds: quail and pigeon. The paradise-gardens – game preserves – held deer, hares and rabbits, while even the smallest tenant farmer had his rabbit hutches and bee skeps.

'The gods keep the locusts from Galilee,' Marcus said fervently, and the others echoed his prayer.

Marcus was reclining at dinner next to Marcus Claudius' sister, and finding it difficult to enjoy his food, though it was remarkably good. He had eaten seafood with a spoon, and put it aside to eat the next course with fingers: venison with pulses and greens. He had washed his hands when a slave had brought round basin and cloths, and participated in the mid-meal grace, throwing a few left-overs into the glowing charcoal of the hearth. Now he was nibbling sweet cakes, and lying on his erection.

Claudius' father was a tall and scholarly man, most of whose education had been acquired since leaving the Army and gaining his citizenship. A few days before his time expired a war elephant had trodden on his right foot, which gave him a limp for life and the *gens* name that would later be shared with an emperor. His wife was a fat and jolly woman who was born in southern Italy. Marcus Claudius had a younger brother, who helped with the lands, and one sister, the cause of Marcus' acute discomfort.

Cressida was seventeen and an opulent blonde with full

114

lips, hair dressed in ringlets to the shoulders and curls on her brow. She was looking lazily at Marcus, having asked him where he originally came from.

Marcus said, 'Illyria, to the south of the country. But now my home is in Gaul of Narbo. My father was given lands here in Galilee, but he exchanged them.'

'How strange. Think of it: we might have been neighbours!'

'Not really,' Marcus said, gazing at Cressida's soft breasts. 'The lands were north of here, I think, near a village not far from a place named Capernaum.'

Cressida smiled and said, 'But that's only twenty miles. A day's ride. Would you have liked it if we *had* been neighbours?'

'Very much,' Marcus said, adding silently, *Gods, keep me from staining my couch!*

He had been without any sexual outlet for a month now, and was in torment. For the first few days Cressida had been cool and aloof in her attitude to him. But now he was being given an explicitly carnal invitation; if anyone else around the horseshoe table was aware of it, no one gave any sign.

There were nine people at dinner: the four members of the Claudius family, Marcus, and two married couples who had neighbouring lands. The older people had been deep in discussion about the affairs of their estates, but now as slaves brought the wine round, conversation became more general. A girl in one corner of the room began to play a double flute. Kradog got up from where he had been crouching, half hidden, under Marcus' couch, and held out Marcus' bowl for the household slave to fill it. He gave the bowl to Marcus and resumed his place.

Marcus raised his bowl, poured a small libation and then said, 'I drink to you, Cressida.'

'And I to you.'

They drank, then Marcus said, 'When I go to stay with my other comrade Quintus I'll get some riding in. I'm looking forward to that.'

Cressida smiled and asked, 'Would you like to ride with me tomorrow?'

Marcus was amazed and said, 'Ride? You? I'm so sorry, but I don't understand.'

Cressida laughed and said, 'It's nothing. You don't need to apologize. But where my father came from women ride, and drive chariots too.'

'I suppose they fight too and have only one breast, the better to draw their bows. But how could your father come from the country of the Amazons, since their menfolk live in a neighbouring state?'

Cressida shifted position and cheekily revealed two pert nipples. Marcus gaped back at her; she rearranged her dress and went on, 'My father is of eastern Britain.'

Quickly Marcus dropped a hand and found Kradog's collar, holding him down; he was already tensed and about to leap up and say or do something for which Marcus would have been obliged to punish him in public.

Quietly Marcus said to the slave, 'Hold still, Kradog. I'm going riding with the lady Cressida tomorrow, and you'll be coming too.'

One of the neighbours was saying, 'Yes, I have a statue of Myron, almost five hundred years old; the provenance is impeccable. You recall the story about his sculpture of a cow, so lifelike that a bull tried to mount it.'

Claudius' father said, 'That must have dented his pride.'

Marcus wasn't listening; he was busy working out how he and Cressida would create their own opportunity the next day. Their eyes met, and he lifted his bowl to her again.

They lay in sweet grass, limbs tangled, Cressida's oat-gold hair tumbled over Marcus' face, their breathing slackening. Cressida was skilled and experienced, which was another surprise to Marcus, but she said her father had no worries about her virginity or lack of it; in Britain women were as free to choose their partners as men. Her mother, however, held decidedly opposite views, and they had set out for their ride accompanied by two eunuchs and three female chaperones ... and Kradog. By pre-arrangement with Marcus and Cressida, at a given signal from her he had jabbed the end of a brooch pin into the rump of her horse. She had screamed in simulated fear as the animal had bolted;

116

Marcus had shouted that he would catch the runaway, and galloped after her. The escort were on donkeys, and Kradog on foot, happily leading them in the wrong direction.

Marcus brushed the girl's hair from his sweaty face, and moved slightly against her. She moved round and rested her forehead on her arms as he drove into her again effortlessly and with perfect rhythm for twenty minutes, giving her three vociferating orgasms to his final triumphant one.

When they had recovered Cressida looked at the gazing horses and said, 'We ought to go. Oh Marcus, I have never had anyone to compare with you. I can hear myself beginning to babble and shout out when I'm coming.'

She was looking at him with wide eyes, confident in her femininity. Marcus caressed her, running a hand along the smooth contours of her thighs and up to her breasts.

He said, 'I have to leave here and stay with Quintus. I don't want to go.'

'Then stay here for the rest of your leave. I wish you could stay here for ever.'

Marcus said, 'Your mother will never let you out of her sight again while I'm here. And I told Quintus I'd join him for the second half of my leave. I can't let him down. Now let's get dressed and find those idiots my slave is bamboozling.'

They were riding close together; Cressida leaned over and nuzzled Marcus' cheek.

She said, 'When I get to Britain I'll be away from my mother. After our sport today I expect you'll want from time to time to have news of your child.'

That evening Marcus gave Kradog a gold aureus. This was a munificent gift from master to body-slave, and if Kradog employed it carefully it could result in his building up wealth over the years. As he held the coin his eyes shone, and he was about to abase himself before Marcus, but his master held him upright.

'No more of that, Kradog,' he said. 'No more of that from now on. Go and see if there is any beer to be had in this household, and bring it together with two pots.'

They were in Marcus' bedroom, and Marcus had hurried

117

his bath before dinner. Kradog sat at his feet as they drank their beer; he had brought a small amphora with its stand.

Marcus asked, 'Have you been spoken to by Primus Claudius?'

'Never, Master.'

'I had to hold you down when the Lady Cressida said he was from Britain. You could have found a way to make him speak with you.'

'That is not for me, Master. I am your slave.'

'Very well. Suppose she drops me a child, do you know what the custom would be in Britain? Would the child be exposed and left to die, for example?'

'I don't think so, Master. The lady would need money; then the child would be accepted into the tribe if a grandparent were British, and the child born to a lady herself of British extraction. Her husband would be softened by the cash.'

Marcus said, 'Well, then, if you're sure Primus Claudius won't poison my next meal I'd better have a word with him.'

Primus Claudius heard Marcus out in silence, and then he said, 'I see now why my daughter wanted you, and took no precautions. I thank you for coming to me now, not even waiting to see if there is a baby on the way. I have known what it is when the blood runs hot! Now I ask this of you: you will keep in touch, and if Cressida is correct in thinking she is in kindle, then you will have to pay maintenance for the child. This is easily arranged. I know a merchant, an up and coming young man, who has already made three round trips to Britain, and we can do it through him. If the child dies at birth, of course there's no more to be said. The British do not expose unwanted children at birth, and count either sex of equal value. A child may even inherit through the mother.'

'I agree to your conditions,' Marcus said. 'But, Dominus, she is very lovely, and I still want her.'

Primus Claudius regarded him with slate-grey eyes and smiled.

He said, 'And I have to live with my wife. For you the harvest of the figs is over.'

118

XIX

The man had seemed normal enough to begin with, and presumably had behaved normally during Tanith's vetting, but he had not been in need of a hetaira's services. A brief pressure on Meriem's carotids had knocked her out, and after she had regained consciousness she had found herself gagged with her own silk scarf and tied to the bed with arms and legs spread wide. Her client stood naked before her, his penis flaccid and a flagellum in his hand. He began to whip Meriem's breasts and his genitals alternately, slowly achieving an erection. Meriem shouted into her gag, but could not make a noise loud enough to be heard by the guards. She struggled against the bonds that held her, silken articles of her own clothing. The man dropped his flagellum and masturbated slowly, almost to the point of orgasm, then he stopped.

'Time to make a hole for me now,' he said conversationally.

He went over to his clothes and rummaged for a moment, then turned, a knife gleaming in his hand. Meriem knew that she had minutes – perhaps even seconds – to live, and with strength born of despair got her left hand free as the man bent over her to make his foul incision, snatched her gold hairpin and stabbed repeatedly into the man's eyes. He screamed, dropped the knife cold on Meriem's belly, then was staggering blind round the chamber as the guards burst in.

*

119

'This is a fine mess,' Tanith said. 'A tribune to the Governor of Syria!'

Meriem said defiantly, 'I don't care if he was Augustus Cæsar. He was going to kill me. Did you expect me not to defend myself?'

Tanith said, 'That's neither here nor there. Now let me think, and keep quiet.'

They were in one of Tanith's sitting rooms. The guards had made a mess of blood and excreta when they had killed Meriem's blinded client, and her room was being cleaned. Tanith sat in silence, her face set at first, but her expression gradually brightened.

Meriem watched Tanith without speaking, assuming that the woman was working out how to cover up the tribune's death or dispose of his body, and she was disconcerted by Tanith's next words.

'I have to punish you. The question is what form the punishment should take.'

'I don't think I should be punished at all,' Meriem said indignantly. 'It seems to me that you should be thinking about that filthy tribune.'

Tanith said, 'That's no problem. His attendants are already poisoned. Wine on the house! They and the tribune will be victims of terrorists, and evidence planted to prove it when the bodies are found, miles from here. But you have to be punished for the good of the house: an internal matter.'

'He was going to make an internal matter out of me,' said Meriem. 'How could he think he'd have got away with it?'

Tanith said, 'It's natural you should overvalue yourself. I have spent perhaps half a talent on your education,' she lied, 'and you will possibly earn me ten talents before you retire, perhaps a little more. But that filthy tribune would have paid me twenty talents to cover up your death.'

Tanith had seemed to care for Meriem, and the girl felt a great sense of loss at the realization that Tanith cared more about profit. She knew then that sometime, somehow, she was going to escape from this house.

Tanith said, 'You go back on general duties for a week. You will take on all comers. That'll keep all the other girls in line: they'll know that I'm not to be trifled with.'

*

Her first customer held her by the shoulders and looked at Meriem for a long time, then spoke in beautiful Akhaian Greek.

He said, 'The Blue-Eyed Maiden, Minerva, has given you eyes that are lovelier than her own. What is your name?'

'Does it matter?' Meriem said. She was determined to spend her week's punishment in sulky intractability, and this man's approach disconcerted her.

'Yes,' he said. 'It matters very much. Last month I met the loveliest girl I had ever seen. We made love all one afternoon, and then I lost her. She is going to the ends of the earth to be married, taking with her — so she says — my child in her womb.'

Meriem frowned and said, 'Then you are both lucky in a way. Think: there'll be no time for love to go sour.'

'And I shall never see her again, nor my child if there is one. But you are more beautiful than she was: that's what I wanted to say.'

'But I'm only a common harlot.'

'And I'm only a common soldier. My name is Marcus Drusus Scipio. Now tell me yours.'

He sat her down beside him on the bed with an arm around her shoulders.

He said gently, 'I thought this girl was my other half apple, but perhaps it's you.'

'I'm not the half of anyone's apple, and never will be,' exclaimed Meriem.

Marcus was wearing a light orange robe over a civilian tunic. He stood up and took them off, while Meriem stared. She saw a man of above average height with columnar legs and thighs, hard wads of stomach muscle, pectorals like a moulded cuirass, huge deltoids and biceps. This was a man of enormous strength, she knew, and fervently hoped that his tastes were normal as his penis rose.

'Well,' he asked once more, 'what is your name?'

'Meriem,' she whispered.

'Thank you, Meriem. Turn and put your brow on the pillow. I'll see those eyes next time.'

As Meriem obeyed she feared the attack of a bugger, but Marcus stayed in her outer lips at first with a powerful but considerate rhythm, with none of the tricks of Phokion and far more power than Petros. If he had been anything but the first customer of the day she would have been able to resist him now that she was under training; but after five minutes her juices were flowing. Marcus retained his climax until the end of hers, and afterwards he lifted her round to face him and laughed at her with joy.

'A good beginning, little one! I booked a girl for three hours. But don't worry: we'll spend the second hour with food and drink and talk; maybe some music and a song or two. And don't undervalue yourself. Common harlots don't do what you just did with me!'

Marcus treated Meriem like the hetaira she was training to be. He was much less urbane than Petros, but both men had consideration in common. Meriem felt valued again as a person in her own right, and as the afternoon progressed her spirits lifted.

During their second hour they ate curds and wheaten bread followed by olives, nuts and figs. Meriem drank watered wine and Marcus beer. After the meal he sipped more beer as Meriem played the zither and sang to him, a song about Ino's transformation into the sea-nymph Leucothea.

When she had ended Marcus said, 'Thank you for the song.'

'I am the one who should thank you,' said Meriem. 'You have given me a sea-change; just a small one, but it has been good for me. Lately I've been told that I have overvalued myself, but you are the one who is right. I will never let myself be cowed.'

'Thank the gods,' Marcus said. 'Or perhaps you have done so already? I saw you pour your little libation before we began drinking.'

'I don't know who the gods are,' Meriem said seriously. 'And I got into this place because of a false god. But there is great evil here, and I think it follows that somewhere else there must be great good. I pour my libations to that good, in the hope that the gods will understand.'

'Plato and Polybius write of God rather than the gods; but Polybius also writes of the gods. Who knows? I met a man

122

who believed in a god named Lugh. I think it may be that people get the god or gods they deserve. I don't bother my head with all that. I perform the observances demanded of a soldier. But this is my last day here. I'm well rested, bless the friend who sent me here, and I think I hear somebody calling out our last hour together.'

XX

In the four thousand nine hundred and ninety-ninth year of our Order, the sun in the house of the Ibis, I the White Magus set down this.

My Colleagues concur. The Magus of Light and the Magus of Treasure are speeding to me here at Philadelphia of Peræa, and then we travel together after completing our computations. The astro-conjunction roughly predicted will take place, and it remains for the three of us to become one in collaboration to define the precise time and location. One thing is certain: our Order's fifth millennium will see the birth of a King for the Israelites; and more than a King if we have read the skies aright. There is an added advantage, which may or may not be an anti-climax. Following upon the symbolism the parents will be able to convert our valuable gifts into cash should the need arise – for example, to leave their country in haste for any reason.

Gold, then, for royalty; for Godhead, frankincense. And myrrh, for the destiny that we perceive.

These are the words of the White Magus, which being interpreted is Caspar.

XXI

The people who collected taxes for the Romans in Imperial provinces or possessions were recruited locally, and were invariably corrupt and despised by everyone. The official level of taxation was not in itself high, though comprehensive: it varied from one to one and a half per cent. It was levied on assessed income as a poll-tax, on food, and on sales and transfers of real estate. There was a general purchase tax, customs duties on exports, and a general profit tax.

The collectors, or publicans, held office for five years and would be expected to bribe the Roman Censor in the Procurator's department to renew their term. In turn they would squeeze more tax than was due from the common people, while taking bribes from the rich to lower their assessments. The Procurator, who was appointed usually for four or five years, would raise a special levy once in his term of office, and on these occasions people had to report to the head of the family's place of birth.

For the Procurator's levy garrisons were stationed all over Judæa, and Marcus' century found itself encamped outside a small village for the winter festival. There were eighty combat troops in a century, but in the garrison there were over a hundred and fifty men when supernumeraries and slaves were counted. The murdered Philo had been replaced by a Syrian named Dysmos, a small, wiry man with keen black eyes and a chin sooty with stubble.

The weather was cold, and a light snow had even fallen in Jerusalem; the days were dark until a strange phenomenon appeared in the eastern sky. The augur attached to the century said that it was caused by two wandering stars coming together, but if it portended anything it was for the Jews; the Romans would get on much better by looking at the entrails of poultry.

Dysmos said, 'That one's just a tenth-class augur. Everyone knows that the stars body forth portents.'

Claudius agreed and so did Marcus, while Quintus was less certain.

'I don't know,' he said. 'The man must know his job, or he wouldn't be allowed to keep it.'

Dysmos said, 'But he's *limited*, don't you see? A gutsgazer, that's all he is and all he'll ever be.'

And Marcus said, 'It looks like just one star to me, and you could swear the thing's hanging over the far end of the village.'

The place was crowded. Claudius said that long ago it had been a city founded by a king of the Jews named David, but it had long since declined in importance. There was a detachment of Jewish troops in control, together with a tax collector, and the Romans were under orders not to intervene except if civil disorder arose and threatened to get out of hand. But although the village was crammed full it was peaceful enough, and the Romans unbuttoned for their winter festival. Their centurion, Gaius Naso, and the decurions served the men with food and drink; a Lord of Misrule poked fun at the officers, and after a few short religious ceremonies saw to it that everyone got drunk.

Marcus sat with the other men of his eight. Ladon and Eusebius were hard-bitten soldiers; but Ladon could play the lyre and Eusebius had a pleasant baritone voice; they sang together until they were too intoxicated to continue. Pyrokles was small and thickset, a Macedonian Greek who used the Macedonian calendar whenever he could, which was not often, since there was a difference of two weeks from the Roman. Pindaros was the last member of the eight, a Greek from Antioch with red hair and green eyes.

The men all spoke camp Latin, and during the early part of their carousal began a discussion about the benefits which barbarians enjoyed in return for their taxes.

'My old man pays taxes in Galilee,' said Quintus, jerking a thumb at Claudius, 'and so does his. The barbarians are lucky we came. They get all the benefits of Roman civilization.'

'Roman peace and *Greek* civilization,' Pindaros said, his green eyes narrowed truculently.

Marcus interposed quickly, 'No quarrels today. We can argue for weeks about that and get nowhere.' To stage a diversion he beckoned to the centurion. 'Hey you, Gaius!'

The others watched in astonishment, waiting to see Marcus beaten unconscious. Instead the centurion came over and stood meekly by their table.

'What is your pleasure?' Gaius Naso asked.

'More beer,' said Marcus. 'A big crock of the best Egyptian.'

'Why, certainly,' the centurion said, and hurried away while the others laughed and clapped Marcus.

Marcus said, 'That's all right. He'll stand for that, but you can't go too far or he'll have it in for you when the festival's over.'

The centurion brought a large crock of beer and set it in front of Marcus.

He said, 'Thank you, Gaius Naso. Will you do us the honour of drinking with us?' thus wiping out any offence he might have given.

Gaius Naso said, 'Yes, I'll take a drink with you,' and sat down. 'Who has red wine?'

Quintus and Eusebius were drinking red wine from an amphora. Eusebius lifted it from its stand while Quintus held out a bowl, and when it was full gave it to the centurion. Gaius poured out a few drops and muttered some words, among them one which sounded like *mithrus* or something similar.

'May I ask to what god you pray?' Marcus asked politely.

'Never you mind,' the centurion said. 'Instead let me drink to your father: to Publius Drusus Scipio, whom I knew for many years as Butin.'

Marcus was surprised, not that Gaius had known his father, but that he had never mentioned it. Then he realized the centurion's good sense. An inexperienced soldier might have been tempted to curry favour with a former comrade of his father, and incur disfavour.

He lifted his pot of beer and drank with the centurion, who asked for news of Drusus. Marcus briefly told him that Drusus had gone beyond the Peace in North Africa in search of a fabled breed of horses.

'It's almost two and a half years now,' he finished, 'and last time I heard from home he still hadn't got back.'

Gaius Naso said, 'Don't worry. On a trip like that he could be away for five years.'

He thanked them for the wine and then resumed his duties.

'Five years!' said Marcus. 'That could mean he still might not be back when I have my long leave. . . . Oh, well, it's in the lap of the gods, and there seem to be enough of them about for one of them to look after him. Let's have a singsong and then get drunk.'

Pindaros said, 'Here, Marcus, drink this and you'll feel better. It's only a drop of posca with some white wine.'

Posca was the common drink; wine vinegar diluted with water, tart and refreshing. Marcus grabbed the bowl from Pindaros and drank, then clutched his head.

Claudius said, 'Suffering Silenus, you were pissed out of your mind last night. You wandered off and we lost you.'

Marcus groaned and drank more posca.

He said weakly, 'I can't remember anything. Not a thing.'

'You just staggered off into the village,' Quintus told him. 'You could have been robbed or killed. Claudius and I found you.'

'I don't remember,' Marcus said helplessly. 'Oh, my head!'

'You were standing staring into some house when we caught up with you,' Claudius said. 'Under the light in the sky. I had a peep inside. Just the usual thing: men and women at one end and stock at the other. And a few people over with the beasts. But you could have got into dead trouble. Three of the men looked very important.'

'Rich robes and head-dresses,' said Quintus. 'The three of them turned and saw us. And they weren't Jews, that's the strange thing. One was as black as Gaius Naso, another had that eastern eyefold – '

128

Claudius said, 'The third one could have come from anywhere. But we didn't wait to find out; we were fairly well gone ourselves. We dragged you back here and put you to bed. You went out like a candle.'

'I think I need some beer,' Marcus said.

Eusebius gave him a small pot, telling him to drink one only. 'And then eat something, if it's only a wheat cake and a bit of cheese.'

The men ate together. Marcus was so fit and strong that the ill effects of his drinking bout soon wore off, but the memory of his night out still eluded him. When the evening came it was dull and starless, with rain or snow threatening, and the soldiers looked at one another in puzzlement, for the light in the sky was gone.

Marcus was dreaming, wandering disembodied in a field of reeking asphodel, shades about him: he could see the stems of the plants, paler than straw, through them, and hear their tinny voices, but the words made no sense. Then he was in lush grass with Cressida, and yet it could not be Cressida, for the eyes were deep purple: Meriem's eyes. This dream-composite was stroking him and moving against him, and at the edge of his vision – though sharply clear – he could see a baby watching with unblinking eyes in the face turned towards him. Somewhere a cow was lowing; chickens clucked, and then Marcus was staring down into the coils of a hen's entrails. He woke in the early morning feeling depressed and unrested.

Dreams were always the subject of much discussion, and in the first place Marcus recounted what he could remember to his slave Kradog.

Then Marcus added, 'The eyes belonged to a girl you never saw, from Magdala. But you know the other one: it was the sister of my comrade Claudius. What do you think, Kradog?'

Kradog said, 'The Lady Cressida left with her father for Britain last autumn, and she said she was carrying your child. Would that be the baby in your dream? I don't know about the hen, but you Romans are always staring at chickens' guts.'

'I'm not at all sure about the baby,' Marcus said. 'But I

129

remember talking with the others about our augur. It's a pity you got drunk with the slaves the other night. It seems that I needed you.'

'I had your permission, Master,' said Kradog. 'I got drunk, but not too drunk to come and have a look at you when you were all asleep. You were talking. Drunken talk. But you seemed to think you'd seen something of enormous importance. Then you said things I couldn't understand in Greek.'

Marcus said with self-disgust, 'I'll never get as drunk again. It's a pity your Greek isn't better. What could it have been? Probably nothing at all.'

All the same Marcus brought up the subject of his dream at the morning meal with Claudius and Quintus.

Marcus said, 'Remember when you fetched me from the village? Bits are coming back to me: I know where the house is. But you talked of important people there. I don't remember them, but they were in the dream along with Cressida, so I must have seen them. Then again, we'd been talking about the augur, so that accounts for the chicken guts. What I want to know is this: was there a baby in the place?'

'I didn't notice,' said Claudius.

But Quintus frowned and said, 'Yes, I remember. There *was*. Lying in one of the mangers.'

To the east of the large village or little town the background was the towering hills of the Judæan wilderness, but to the north there were olive groves together with open fields where sheep grazed on poor winter keep.

Gaius Naso was in no hurry to return to the fear and claustrophobia of Jerusalem, or the boring training sessions of Caesarea, as the case might be. He waited for orders, and meantime gave his men one drill a day, and plenty of free time, though he still mounted a guard. Marcus took to spending his afternoons at javelin practice in the fields, a form of exercise he had always enjoyed since the early days with Placidus. Marcus was deadly accurate with the javelin. Unfortunately a ram took it into its head to make a sudden charge at one of the ewes, and ran straight onto the point of the javelin as it curved down to earth.

The animal was transfixed, and Marcus ran forward, finishing it off with a stroke of his sword. A herdboy of about ten years ran up, shouting and waving his arms. Marcus cleaned sword and javelin by thrusting them into the grass and earth, then turned to the boy and explained what had happened.

'Tell me where to find the owner,' he finished. 'I'll pay compensation for the ram.'

He listened carefully to the boy's directions, picked up the rest of the javelins, and made his way to the village.

All was far from well there. As Marcus approached he could hear screaming and wailing. An insanely braying voice: 'They're killing babies!'

Marcus turned into the street, and saw nothing but one soldier of the Herodian Army. There was bloody murder taking place, outcry upon outcry, but it was happening indoors. The only visible soldier was about to enter the house where Marcus had leaned in his drunkenness at the winter festival.

Marcus dropped his javelins and picked up a jagged piece of rock, the ram forgotten as he selected instinctively the ubiquitous weapon of Judæa rather than a Roman spear.

Marcus hurled the rock with all his strength just as the man, touched perhaps by some filament of foreknowledge, turned his head to Marcus. The soldier was carrying a drawn sword in his right hand and a spear in the left. The rock hit him in the face. He died at once, nose and frontal ridge driven immediately into the brain, teeth spraying from the ruptured jaw. The man dropped his sword and sagged against the wall; the spear lodged under one armpit and its haft wedged on the ground, so that he remained upright.

Marcus rushed past him into the house. There were men and women cowering against the far wall, one woman holding a baby.

'Get out!'

Marcus began to manhandle them to the rear exit of the house.

'Get out! A dream. . . . There's no time to explain. Quick, go south!'

The party were clutching bundles of possessions. No one spoke, but they took the opportunity that had arisen in the form of a Roman soldier out of nowhere. Marcus watched them hurry away, then followed by the same exit. When he reached the main street he bellowed to turn out the Roman guard.

There was, in the event, nothing to be done. A Jewish matter entirely. Gaius Naso was sympathetic. Marcus had been right to turn out the guard before the centurion's own inquiry proved that the Roman troops would have been powerless to intervene between the Tetrarch's troops and people. So, by the time their orders came in, the matter had blown over for the Romans, if not for the families mourning their slaughtered infants. As for Marcus, he made no report about his own intervention. That was a personal matter, he decided; it made up a little for his earlier disgraceful drunkenness. But he quite forgot to pay the owner of the ram.

INTER SCRIPTUM (ii)

Professor Potts came out of one of the computer rooms, where he had been checking the work of one of his post-graduate students, and walked along to his office. He sat down at his desk and began to tidy it. As he sat he felt the seat of his chair leave him briefly and then strike him in the buttocks a couple of times. He was used to these common-place earth tremors, and was scarcely disturbed. He finished tidying, and locked the office behind him; his secretary had left half an hour earlier.

He drove north up Sepulveda Canyon into the Santa Monicas. climbing steadily along the upstroke of a T; he and Helen lived on the crossbar formed by Mulholland Drive, and the latter admittedly a wavery one drawn by a drunk or a very small child. He ascended into the clean air aromatic with the vapour from the eucalypts, sand drifted across the road in places after he had turned west. The houses were built on sand, he thought wryly, but their architects had driven the piles down to bedrock. Architects: practitioners of *tekhtoniké*, he thought idly. What did that remind him of?

Helen was at home and as usual had left her car outside. Potts parked his own in the garage and then Helen's, equably. He went through into the house, where he could hear the hiss of the shower.

'Helen,' he called. 'I'm home.'

'About time. How about a drink?'

He made her a vodka martini with a twist, iced it and poured himself a finger of Glenmorangie with neither ice nor

133

water, then took the drinks to the patio, which was open to west and south. He sat by the pool and took a sip of the delicate twelve-year old malt. To the south and below the smog blanket extended: La Cienega Boulevard swooped down into it like a ski-jumping ramp from West Hollywood.

'Down, down, through the Cities of the Plain,' Potts said to himself aloud.

'What was that?'

Potts hadn't heard Helen approach on bare feet, but he felt the slight disturbance of the still air, then her perfume through the eucalyptus aroma as she kissed the top of his head.

He handed her the martini as she sat down.

'Nothing, really,' he said. 'Talking to myself.'

'Finish your drink. You'll feel better then.'

Inside, the phone rang. Potts went to answer it.

The operator said, 'I have a collect call for you from Cambridge, England, sir. Will you accept the call?'

'Certainly,' said Potts.

The thin high voice of Doctor Waldegrave might have been coming from next door.

He said, 'That you, Potts?'

'Speaking.'

'Some aspects of our conversation intrigued me when you came to dinner.'

There was no hope of hurrying Waldegrave, so Potts said patiently, 'I remember the occasion with great pleasure.'

'Jesus began his ministry in the synagogues: in other words, he was a rabbi. He is addressed as "Rabbi" in the Gospels. Now the Mishnaic Law states explicitly that "A bachelor may not be a rabbi." '

Potts said, 'Good heavens. In other words, you're saying – '

'I'm saying that Jesus had to have been married, Potts. It doesn't matter whom he married. *All* rabbis were married. For all I know they still are. It would not have been thought worthy of remark at the time. Now don't think I'm the first to pick this up. Several authors have suggested the same thing, and even advanced candidates. Some of them are fairly wild: Mary Magdalene, for example! But I don't think that

134

is of importance. The main point is that marriage was compulsory. I hope that gives you something to chew on, Potts.'

'I think one might safely say that it does,' Potts said. 'I'd better do some reading and revision. If I come across anything, may I get in touch? I should welcome the benefit of an exchange of ideas with you.'

'By all means, dear fellow. Just one thing, though.'

'Yes?'

'Don't reverse the charges to my end.'

Although Potts had decided to look further into the matters which he had discussed with Doctor Waldegrave, in the event he had to postpone his studies. There was just too much to to do in his professorial field. He would take his own vacation when Helen had her own, from the middle of August to mid-September. Though the university itself was on vacation, there were still plenty of students on campus, and Potts set aside one morning a week for undergraduates who wanted to see him. Three afternoons were taken up with postgraduate and postdoctoral students and fellows, and the rest of Potts' time was swallowed up by conferences, committees and other administrative and academic meetings. He was also fighting for funds to enable the renewal of his department's computer system. He and Helen could count themselves lucky to take a month away in Europe.

Potts thought of the immemorial peace of the Fellows' Garden at Christ's, allowing himself a wistful moment while locked in the morning traffic on Sepulveda in smog, throat irritated and eyes smarting. He had a busy and frustrating day, the funds for the new computer system as far away as ever, and Helen absent, her work having taken her to San Francisco for three days. That evening Potts thought about visiting friends, but knew that his mood was not compatible with company. He drank three glasses of Glenmorangie, barbecued a T-bone steak and ate it with a side-salad. With the meal he drank a bottle of Châteauneuf du Pape, two glasses of port with his cheese, and two glasses of Rémy Martin with his coffee. Later he was to blame his dream on his dinner and its drinks.

135

That night Potts dreamt of kings. He knew in his dream that they were kings, though they were not conventionally attired. One was dressed in white robes. He wore silver slippers turned up at the points, an enlaced silver belt, and a silver circlet confining his headdress. He had a pale, sensitive face with a fairly aquiline nose, a short moustache and beard. The second man was black and clean-shaven, a big man with a dark reddish-purple robe. He had a short and padded cylindrical headpiece, and this and his robes blazed with jewels. The third man wore robes of golden-shot silk, a gold necklet, and a round golden cap; his black eyes had the epicanthic fold and he wore a long, thin moustache.

These were the Three Kings, Potts knew in his dream. He was unable to observe them together: each as it were presented himself individually to the dreamer's gaze. There was no sound in his dream, only bright colour. Then there came fire, and one by one the men passed into leaping flames but were not consumed. During this episode in his dream Potts saw a baby inset on the edge of his vision, looking at him and the kings who passed into the fire. Then within the fire he saw his wife in agony, her clothes blazing, hair burning, her face convulsed and mouth opening and shutting in soundless screaming. And still the baby was watching. Potts had felt no emotion during the first parts of his dream, but now Helen had appeared in it he was filled with a hopeless terror and foreboding.

Potts awoke sweating and in fear. When he had calmed down he made a cup of hot malted milk and sipped it slowly, but it did not help him get back to sleep.

XXII

In the thirtieth year of the Divine Augustus, Servius Claudius Baratanicus writes on leave from Antioch six days before the Kalends of October to his friend Marcus Drusus Scipio, at the Villa Belinuncia in Gallia Narbonensis. A good slap on the back!

O Marcus, I write only twenty days after you went on long leave. You will forgive the pun when I say that I could wish this letter had a vexillium or two to waft it on wings to you!

My esteemed father arrived home the day after I got there, and only a few days after you departed. He sent a rider at once to Cæsarea. Ordinary people can expect to wait three weeks for a ship, but being Marcus, you had found one almost at once, and were gone.

I think my father did not want to leave Britain, for he spent almost three years there: plenty of time to see your son Aeron grow into a lusty infant. It is amazing to think he is now almost three years old.

Could you use your next leave in a visit to your son? My father says that you would have to be very careful, and scarcely even look at Cressida. But the boy is yours and you are providing for him. As his father and provider you would be tolerated.

Everything jogs along here. I am dividing my leave between home, Quintus' place and Antioch. While staying with Quintus I tried for a session with your purple-eyed beauty of whom you used to rave; but she is beyond my price. Quintus and Eusebius are here with me; the others on leave elsewhere. After regrouping we shall be stationed here at Antioch, but this is a wonderful place, a soft billet, great either to serve in or spend a leave. Riches and magnificence abound here. Judæa seems just like a bad dream: I can't imagine anything good ever coming out of there! Quintus and Eusebius join me in telling you (not that you will need telling) to drink some beer and wet your son's head. And think of us from time to time. Now I say farewell.

XXIII

It took Marcus some time to settle down when he and Kradog returned home. When he had left for Judæa the place was new and some parts were still not quite finished; but now it was in its sixth year: signs of wear were perceptible in some places. Horses had had time to make smooth spots on the bark of trees. Paths had been worn on fields which Marcus remembered as grass-covered. And indoors furniture which had been brand new had a scratch here and a dent there; ceramic items had been broken and replaced.

Pylades and Doratus seemed to have exchanged their avoirdupois, for Doratus was now thin and Pylades fat. The vilica Julia had a son and daughter, and Julia was fat and sullen; motherhood did not seem to suit her. Lucius the vilicus was unchanged. But Marcus' mother Teutia's dark hair had a white streak in it, and her former mettlesome spirit was quenched.

'You've been missing my father,' Marcus said to her as they sat in the peristyle opposite the sundial, its copper gnomon tinged with green.

Teutia's eyes, once so lustrous, had lost their light as they turned to him and then to the bust of Drusus.

She said, 'It's been too long without a word. Not a single word all this time. When your father was serving he would always write, and if he had been killed I would have been informed. Why, why did he conceive this crazy notion of going outside the Roman Peace? And all to look for wretched horses!'

Her voice was high-pitched and querulous. Marcus took her hand and stroked it sympathetically.

He said, 'My centurion in Judæa was a man named Gaius Naso. He knew my father, and when I told him about the expedition Gaius said it would take at least five years. I wasn't going to mention it, but – '

Teutia brightened a little.

'Did he really say that?'

'And he knows what he's talking about, Mother. You know my father. He can look after himself, and with Placidus and Targui there's an invincible trio. You saw that yourself on the voyage here when the pirates attacked the ship.'

Teutia hugged him and said, 'Bless you, Marcus. I shan't be myself again until your father comes home, but at least you make me feel better. It's so good to have you here again. I'll have to find a girl for you.'

A couple of days later Marcus felt rested after his travels. He had been lying in bed until the sun was up, but now he rose while it was still dark. Kradog got up from his pallet across the threshold of Marcus' bedroom and attended him as he washed and dressed. As they left, Marcus saw Lucius on the way into his mother's room.

'What are you up to, Lucius?' Marcus asked.

The slave said, 'Your Lady mother has called me to her to give me her orders.'

Marcus had difficulty in seeing the expression on Lucius' face in the gloom, but thought he detected the suspicion of a sneer. But he let it pass, nodded curtly and went out with Kradog.

Pylades was alone in the farm kitchen, his once austere face plump and rosy. He smiled with delight as Marcus came into the room.

Pylades said, 'I've been coming here for the last few days in the hope that you would turn up, Marcus. It's good to see you now you've recovered from the rigours of your journey.'

'I had a feeling you might be here,' Marcus said, gratified. 'Quite like old times.'

They breakfasted together and drank buttermilk, then

went out as the sun rose and kissed their hands to it, keeping the Greek way.

With Kradog in attendance they walked past the stables and the corral through the vineyard, working slaves bobbing or smiling at Marcus, then through the pastures where the horses grazed. The wheat had been harvested before the vintage, but Pylades pointed to a field which was a sea of greenish flowers almost hiding the plants.

'There's your fat-hen, Kradog,' said Pylades. 'That's the third crop this year, and Lucius says we could get much more. In the first year we made flour and bread that was just about edible, while the wheat got established, but now we use it for poultry feed and sell the surplus.'

'So that's how the fields look in Britain,' Marcus mused.

His memory of Cressida had faded. Paradoxically he was haunted from time to time by the eyes of the whore Meriem, and by the memory of her personality, but he shrugged away the thought of her: by now probably she would be raddled and her character rotted by her trade.

'Only some of the fields,' Pylades explained, 'where new ground has been cleared. But it's been very useful, and our thanks are due to your slave.'

Their conversation was in Greek as usual, but Kradog knew the words for *thanks* and *slave*. He coughed behind Marcus' back.

Marcus turned and said, 'Yes, the words were about you, Kradog. The whole estate is grateful to you for your fat-hen. I'm going to ask Doratus to go through the farm accounts and pay you ten per cent of the profits, back-dated to the first harvest of this crop and continuing until such time as we cease to grow it. I don't think that will ever happen, but anyway Doratus will invest the money for you where it will earn interest.'

Marcus had spoken in Latin to Kradog, and the man stammered his thanks. Except by an extraordinary stroke of good fortune it was impossible for a low-status slave to acquire capital, let alone an unearned income; yet now Kradog had both.

Marcus added, 'And we'll go to a magistrate and have a document drawn up. It will state that if I'm killed or die in service you are to be given safe-conduct home, and I'll make provision for that in my will. Now find Doratus and ask him to see me this evening after my bath.'

Kradog capered away, leaping for joy and never for a moment realizing that he had earned his luck.

Marcus experienced the happily self-righteous emotion of one who has given a splendid present to an inferior, but Pylades' next words quickly shattered this feeling.

He said, 'Marcus, I am going to tell you something now which I have decided you should hear from me rather than learn by accident. I beg you to keep your hand from your dagger.'

Marcus stared at him, suddenly silent and alert.

Pylades went on, gravely and formally, 'The Lady Teutia, your mother, misses your father greatly. He has been away a very long time, and she is still a woman.'

'What of it?' Marcus demanded. 'I suppose she finds a man from time to time. She's human. But that makes no difference in the long run. It's none of our business.'

'The slave Lucius *is* your business, Marcus.'

White-lipped, Marcus said, 'I saw him this morning going into her room. He said he was going to get her orders.'

'The Lady Teutia knows nothing about running a farm, so consider the nature of those orders.'

Marcus swallowed and took a deep breath, keeping his clenched fists at his sides. Any other person than Pylades would have been dead by then.

Gently Pylades said, 'Think, Marcus: the man is a slave, and is bound to obey. Think again: in the great cities like Rome or Alexandria the situation may be said to be a common one, because it has the advantage that a permanent embroilment is impossible. I think that if you can assess the affair dispassionately you might conclude that it is a good arrangement so long as the man does not get above himself.'

The days went by, and with their passage Marcus became resigned to his mother's affair. He grew distant and offhand with her, and watched keenly for an excuse to beat Lucius; but the man never put a foot wrong.

He began to spend more and more time with the horses.

The head groom was a likeable Arab named Akbar, who spoke Alexandrian Greek and got on well with Marcus. This was exceptional. All of the people on the estate accorded Marcus the respect and deference due to his position, but the fact remained that he was an interloper to be seen every lustrum: Marcus could never form part of the continuity of their lives, and he sensed this; it forced him into a certain aloofness in his dealings with them. He had even shied away from Pylades. Though they met as often as before, Marcus had put up a mental fence after Pylades had revealed his mother's affair. He had allowed Pylades to lead him by the nose as though he were still under the man's tutelage; and even if it had been for the best of reasons Marcus would not let it happen again. But with horses he was knowledgeable and happy, on common ground with Akbar. The man was no more than twenty, three years younger than Marcus, but horsemanship takes no account of youth: he had been in the saddle since he could walk, and managing horses since he was five or six.

Three weeks after his conversation with Pylades Marcus and Akbar were schooling two horses, bringing a young one up to the standard of the older horse, which Marcus was riding while Akbar trained the pupil in a united canter, balance and collection, and finally a half-circle of small jumps, three of them over water. It was all easy, uneventful routine, and Marcus was enjoying himself immensely. They finished the short course, gave the horses a honey cake each and then handed them over to the waiting lads.

Marcus said, 'I enjoyed that, Akbar. You've done very well here without my father, but you weren't head groom when he left and I joined the Army.'

'I got the job when he died, Dominus. The majordomo promoted me.'

Marcus grinned and said, 'Doratus always knows what he's doing. I think you've improved the stock.'

They were walking back towards the stables, still talking horses, when Kradog came into view. He trotted over and said to Marcus, 'Master, it is the majordomo. Can you come and see him in his office?'

Marcus lifted a hand to Akbar and went with Kradog to

the office at the villa, a large room with marble tables; the walls were lined with scroll-holders filled with accounts and documents. When Marcus came in Doratus shooed away the accountant, the steward and clerks, telling them to come back when Marcus' slave came for them; then he placed a second chair by his big marble table. The two men sat down side by side, Doratus with a grim face.

He said, 'When you asked me to check on sales of the goosefoot crops to allot ten per cent to your slave I did the work at once. Then, since I had the accounts out from the first year of your service, I decided to do a complete audit with the accountant and the steward. It was the steward who pointed out a discrepancy in the given yield of wheat in that first year. I was able to corroborate it because everyone was waiting to see how the first year would turn out.

'Naturally, I ran some further checks, and these led me to make a full investigation. There were discrepancies every-where. So then I went to the Market Inspector and got copies of the receipts for our sales. Briefly, the figures given in to the accountant here were ten to twelve per cent less than was sold at market.'

'Who compiles the figures?' Marcus asked.

'Lucius, of course.'

'My congratulations, Doratus. I get more out of you and my slave Kradog than a man has the right to deserve.'

Marcus went to find Lucius. He was in the olive grove with two menial slaves inspecting the trees, and turned when Marcus called his name.

Marcus said, 'When my father offered you your freedom you refused. It would have been well for you to have accepted, for you would at least have received a trial for the crimes you have committed.'

With that he struck Lucius in the chest directly over the heart, a Heraklean blow that sent the slave staggering back a few steps; then he voided his bowels and fell dead.

Marcus went to the house and found his mother, who was watching some girls carding wool. There were six girls working, and Marcus had been to bed with four of them. On the estate he had no lack of partners for his sexual activities, though he would never force a slave girl, but

144

waited for a feminine signal of invitation from a girl who was already amorously inclined.

Marcus took his mother aside.

He said, 'Mother, I'm sorry to have to tell you this, but I've killed Lucius.'

Teutia paled and would have fallen, but Marcus caught her and supported her to a seat. Then he turned and snapped, 'One of you girls fetch wine! The rest of you get on with your work!'

Turning back to his mother he said quietly, 'This was nothing to do with you. Nothing at all: understand that. Lucius had been embezzling since he was first taken on here. No wonder he was so good at his job! The better the profits the bigger his cut, the thieving bastard.'

When the girl came with wine Marcus gave it to his mother and said, 'Drink now, and then I'll drink as well, to better times.'

Trembling, Teutia drank while he steadied the bowl for her; then they drank together, while Marcus consoled his mother. He finished by saying, 'I think this is for the best. Father may come home any day now. How would you have felt if he'd come home this morning?'

There was a long pause then Teutia said, 'I would have felt like killing myself.'

The steward, Milo, was twenty-five, cheerful, willing and a hard worker, but hopeless at calculation. Marcus refused to consider it at first when Doratus suggested promoting Milo to vilicus.

'How could you think of it? He doesn't know the difference between the signs for one thousand and ten thousand! He can't add five and four and get nine!'

Patiently Doratus explained, 'It's easy. We put Casca to oversee that side of it, and pay him something out of the percentage Lucius was stealing, so as to compensate him for the extra work.'

Casca, the accountant, was small and pasty-faced, with a bald head and pale blue eyes; he never made a mistake in arithmetical computations.

Doratus added, 'Divide and rule. Casca would never

145

embezzle a denarius, and Milo wouldn't know how. I think you will find my suggestion a good one.'

Marcus gave up. Doratus always thought things through to the last detail, and Marcus resolved that he would try to do the same. He would not succeed entirely, because although he could learn subtlety, the kind of deviousness which includes far-sightedness cannot be learned, and would always elude him.

He said, 'What about Julia?'

Doratus considered, then said, 'I think she should go.'

'Very well.'

Marcus called for Kradog, and ordered him to fetch the vilica. Julia was clearly apprehensive at facing the man who had killed her mate, and she stood at some distance from Marcus and Doratus in the peristyle.

Marcus said, 'Julia, after what has happened I think you would be happier in some other situation. Be ready to leave at the end of the month.'

The woman nodded without speaking, then turned and hurried away, bursting into tears as she went. Doratus and Marcus took no notice of this. Marcus stirred the pool with a foot, sending fish darting.

'Well, that's that,' he said.

'I thought you were going to send her packing at once,' Doratus said.

Marcus took his foot out of the water, looking at the busts of his father and mother, painted in lifelike colours and placed forever together.

He said, 'Julia has committed no crime. And she has two children. I couldn't sell her immediately: that would be an injustice. We can try to prearrange a sale in Rhedæ or Glanum to some suitable buyer.'

They were at dinner on the same evening: Teutia, Marcus, Pylades, with their neighbour and his family. Doratus and Julia supervised the attendants. The furnishings in this dining room were the same as those in Illyria: the oil lamps were alight, the gold and silver ornaments, polished olivewood and crockery glinted with highlights, and the crimson hangings were the same ones.

146

Their neighbours were viticulturists and olive growers, rich in both vines and olives; they also possessed huge flocks of sheep on the green uplands which had been cleared of maquis a century ago. Caius Lessius belonged to an old-established family of equestrian rank. He was as bald as Marcus' accountant Casca, but with a fine head and an eagle nose. His wife was a faded beauty turned shrewish; she had given him five daughters and then gone barren. Her name was Donata.

Three of the daughters had survived, and they were present at dinner: for Marcus' inspection, he realized with some amusement. Teutia had said she would find a girl for him, and here were three. He had been looking them over throughout the meal. It was unnecessary to marry a woman whom he loved — indeed, that would be a disadvantage for serving soldiers, absent for such long periods. They were not supposed to marry at all, strictly speaking; but by Marcus' day this rule had been unofficially relaxed. A moneyed and landed soldier needed a wife at home, and she had to possess certain special qualities.

The three girls had been making shy conversation with Marcus during the meal, Kradog as usual down by Marcus' couch. Daphne, Aspasia and Cynara: fourteen, fifteen and seventeen years of age respectively. Daphne was pretty and smart as a sandpiper, with small breasts and a mischievous smile which said, 'You don't know how much I know about men. Would you like to find out?'

Aspasia had her younger sister's dark hair, worn in ringlets, while Daphne's was uncut and hanging down her back. Aspasia was serious and intelligent, with a figure as luscious as Cressida's had been, and Marcus would have delighted in a day in bed with her, to find out into what other areas her intelligence extended.

Cynara's face had the classical beauty of bone structure which her mother possessed, but a serene temperament and a similar amusement to Marcus' at this dinner of inspection. Her hair was a little lighter than her sister's, and piled up on her head. She wore a dress which revealed little of her figure, and her smile said, 'You'd like to find out what's under this robe, but you won't until I decide to let you!'

Teutia was saying, 'An odd name, Villa Belinuncia, but my husband liked it and so we kept it.'

'It's Gaulish,' said Caius Lessius. 'A poisonous herb: arrow poison. The villa would seem to be under the protection of the god Belis.'

Julia came over with the jug which contained the perfumed water for Teutia's wine, and was about to pour when Doratus stepped forward and said, 'I'll take that.'

He poured some of the water into a clean bowl and offered it to Julia, saying, 'Now you drink this.'

Julia started back and was about to turn when Cynara leaped from her couch behind Julia, grabbing her by the hair with both hands and grinding a knee into the small of the woman's back. Julia yelped and whimpered, then screamed as Doratus forced her mouth open, the scream turning to a gurgle and then cut off as the majordomo held her nose and made her drink. Cynara held the woman immobile.

'Doratus, I know you will have your reason for this,' said Teutia, 'but will you explain to the company?'

Doratus said, 'It was the mention of the name Belinuncia and poison that started me thinking. The vilica has no cause to love you, Lady, and Milo reported this afternoon that she was gathering belladonna in quantity. Now all we can do is wait.'

Marcus was looking at Cynara while everyone else watched Julia. Cynara's speed, decisiveness and capability were admirable. If their personalities proved compatible, then here was his châtelaine and the mother of his heirs: heirs to a rich estate indeed.

Julia was mouthing curses. Doratus leaned forward and peered at her closely.

'Yes, belladonna,' he said. 'The pupils are dilating. So it begins.'

And Marcus said, 'Kradog, take the woman away and lock her in her quarters with one of the slave girls to attend her until she dies. And Mother, you would do well to drink unwatered wine this evening, or else drink beer with me.'

148

XXIV

Marcus sat on the corral fence with Akbar, reading the letter from Claudius which Kradog had just brought to him. It did not occur to him to seek privacy while he read, so the other two men heard every word.

'Congratulations!' Akbar said when Marcus finished reading. 'A fine son!'

'A son in *Britain*,' Kradog muttered.

Marcus said, 'The mother promised to write to me, but if she did the letter went astray. More likely she was prevented. As long as the payments for the child's upkeep go through he'll be all right, and I'll get reports about him every so often. It's all in the hands of a good man I was introduced to in Judæa. He comes from Ramathaim, or Arimathea as we say. A bright young man, well-travelled and businesslike; he should go far.'

He was rambling, and knew it; but he was thinking wildly of Claudius' suggestion that he travel to Britain to see his son. Akbar left to get on with his work, and Marcus looked down at Kradog. A horse whinnied in one of the pastures, and another replied. In the distance a bulling cow kept up a muted but perpetual background series of strangled roars.

'Well, Kradog?' said Marcus.

'I think you should talk with the Lord Pylades, Master.'

Pylades was standing at his lectern in the room which he used as a study, slowly unrolling the scroll in its holder as he read Pindar: dull verse in an inflated style, Marcus always thought. Pylades' sight was worsening in his old age, and he

149

was reading with a lens. He was beginning to lose weight, and rapidly losing strength also; he leaned heavily on the lectern as he read, craned over the scroll. Engrossed as he was, he did not hear Marcus come in, so Marcus touched him on the shoulder.

Marcus said, 'Forgive the interruption, but Kradog is of the opinion that I should speak with you.'

'Is Kradog here?' asked Pylades.

'Of course. Waiting outside.'

'Can he come in and join us? I like Kradog.'

Marcus shrugged and called his slave. It was quite true that Pylades and Kradog had always got on well together; there was a tie between the two men, as sometimes happens irrespective of age, race or social class: an indefinable affinity, sexless and mysterious. Marcus himself had felt it with the whore Meriem.

'Now then, Kradog,' Pylades said. 'Tell us what is in your mind.'

Kradog said, 'My master has fathered a child, now in Britain. It is in my mind that it would be a good thing for my master to visit his son.'

Pylades said gravely, 'And for a certain body-slave to visit his motherland, no doubt?'

'Well,' Kradog said, and coughed. 'There is that too, of course.'

Pylades sat down and sighed with relief at getting his weight off his feet. He stared at them, considering, and then he spoke.

'You might have done this in Julius Cæsar's time before he destroyed the Veneti, but I don't think you can do it in the time that remains of your leave; not now. The Veneti were a great and powerful tribe in north-western Gaul, in Armorica. They were civilized, though non-Roman; they even had a senatorial type of government, and they controlled all sea traffic with Britain. Voyagers from the south who paid their dues were given swift passage to the island, for the boats of the Veneti were stronger and better-found even than Roman boats. But they were unskilled in naval warfare, and Julius overwhelmed them. Now you could

150

waste weeks in trying to get a passage. No, Marcus, you will have to wait.'

Marcus said, 'I was hoping you would find a reason for me not to go. Kradog would have nagged me until I killed him, and you know that I should not do that because of the dream which you yourself had years ago. Now that he has heard your words I expect I shall be left in peace.'

'Is that so, Kradog?' Pylades asked the slave.

'The Lord Pylades has spoken,' Kradog said, then added, 'It was worth trying, though.'

Marcus clapped his slave hard between the shoulder blades and said, 'Fetch beer and some fruit. You'll never see Britain unless the Divine Augustus decides to conquer the country, and then only if I'm with the legions which attack. So make the best of it.'

And when Kradog had gone Marcus turned to Pylades and said, 'I wouldn't mind seeing my son: in fact it seemed a wonderful idea at first. But I can't be absent without leave for *any* reason. I'm a serving soldier. And there's too much to do here for the rest of my leave. I'm going to get married, Pylades.'

Julia the vilica had died in agony and delirium on the afternoon following the dinner party at which she had tried to poison Teutia. There had been some excited discussion among the party after Kradog had taken the woman away, but Marcus had gone straight to Cynara.

'I thought you handled that very well.'

Coolly she had said, 'I think I can handle most things.'

'Can we meet, Cynara?'

'We can *meet*, but not to handle things,' she had said, gazing at him with frank amusement. 'You've a long way to go yet, Marcus, before you and I'll be handling anything belonging to each other, if that's what you're thinking of, my rich legionary!'

Marcus had grinned and said, 'I'm not rich. My father's fairly well off.'

'Your father's *dead*.'

They sat outside a shepherd's hut on the high sheep pasture

151

just within the boundary of Caius Lessius' land. Cynara had brought a slave girl with her, who sat out of earshot. Kradog sat not too far away from the girl, and was moving gradually closer.

Marcus asked Cynara, 'Why did you say my father is dead? Your father called for his slippers, and so I couldn't ask you before.'

'How long has he been gone?'

'Almost six years now.'

'Then it stands to reason, doesn't it?'

Marcus absently watched Kradog, who had an arm round the girl's waist. His free hand stroked her cheek, then moved down. Marcus had instructed Kradog to seduce any female companion whom Cynara should bring with her as chaperone, leaving the field free for Marcus with Cynara. But now thoughts of sex were far from his mind. This girl whom he scarcely knew had brought him abruptly face to face with the truth which up until then he had tried to hide from himself: the death of his father. And at once she echoed what was in his mind.

'Poor Marcus, don't you want to believe it?'

Marcus breathed out deeply, looking into Cynara's clear hazel eyes.

He said, 'I *didn't* want to believe it, Cynara, but I do now. Thanks to you.'

'Do you blame me?'

Marcus said, 'For making me see the truth? I'll never blame you for that. My father has probably been dead for years. I think other people have tried to soften the blow, but that isn't the way to go about things. Your way is by far the best.' He took her hand in friendship and added, 'I thought we might proceed to . . . But it isn't the right time now. Come, I'll take you back to your father. I'm going to ask for his permission to court you, Cynara. You are all I could ever wish for in a wife here.'

'We'll see about that,' she said, but then put both hands on his shoulders and swiftly rubbed his nose with hers, leaving him with little doubt about her feelings.

He got to his feet, tugging her up by one hand. They walked downhill through bleating sheep on the way back:

to his marriage; to the eventual merging of the estates; and to the duty which ruled his life, leaving the slaves to their random pleasure.

XXV

Legio IV Gallica, year thirty-one of Divine Cæsar Augustus, three days before the Nones of March.

Marcus Drusus Scipio to his beloved wife Cynara, greetings!

First of all I must give you a warning. In case you do not know or have forgotten, remember that my Lady Mother reads as well as you, although she cannot write. Do not let her see all of this letter. Towards the end I will put in some stuff which will give you an excuse for keeping it to yourself. You can tear up the letter, drop that bit and fail to retrieve it. My mother will read it and turn all sly with you!

As things stand I am merely an emancipated son, and without clear evidence of my father's death I shall so remain: to the end of my life, perhaps.

The time will come when your honoured Father is no more, and our estates will become one. To prepare for that day it is necessary for my majordomo Doratus and my Vilicus Milo to become familiar with the running of your father's estate. Could you persuade him to give informal permission? Doratus will cause not a ripple, and he will see to Milo.

I was delighted by the news that you are pregnant. Needless to say I hope for a son, but I was Illyrian before I became a Roman, and a daughter who takes after you will do very well to be going on with!

This legion is in a backwater. Drill, parades, weapons training, route marches — I might as well be a recruit once more. There are three legions stationed to the north-east of us: XVII, XVIII and XIX, and it's possible that they may see some action. They're commanded by Quintilius Varus, who did a good job in Judæa; he left there just before I arrived.

The weather is damnably cold here, though they say it warms up towards the middle of April.

My dear one, I miss you greatly, and long to be in your arms (and between your legs) again. I count myself the most fortunate of men to have found a wife such as yourself. Next summer I get a month's annual local leave. Ostensibly local, for I have decided to come home to you every year. It is a stunning idea of Kradog's, though he wanted me to travel north! And it is a great comfort to have money enough for my plan: to have a relay of fast horses set up so that I can cover over a hundred miles a day. It's how my father used to travel. We shall have only a week or a little more together, but to me it will be worth it.

Thank the gods that I am a horseman as well as a foot-slogging legionary! I can't wait for the summer and to be with you again, and in bed with you, my love.

And now farewell.

XXVI

During his first year with IV Gallica Marcus managed to spend a week at home with Cynara after a gruelling journey which taxed even his superb fitness. Both sorrow and joy awaited him on his arrival at the Villa Belinuncia.

Pylades was dead. During the spring he had shown Cynara a black mole on the third toe of his left foot.

'See this,' he had said. 'The melanoma. I shall be dead within two months.'

And so it had proved. Pylades had taken to his bed and died six weeks later, his body cruelly wasted. Whether he had felt pain no one knew, for he had taken the Stoic line during his last days, lapsed into silence and refused food though he had taken liquid refreshment.

When Cynara told him of Pylades' death Marcus turned away from her, unable to quell the sudden rush of tears down his cheeks.

Cynara put an arm round him and said, 'There is better news, Marcus. Come now.'

There in the matrimonial bedroom Teutia sat, rocking two wicker cribs, the proud grandmother of twin sons. Marcus forgot all about Pylades for the moment, looking down with amazement at the babies, lifting them gingerly one by one as if they were made of delicate ceramic ware; then he hugged Cynara and his mother, cackling with joy.

Marcus had been in some doubt about how his wife and mother would get along. Although of different temperament, both were strong characters, and Marcus had feared a family struggle perhaps leading to a feud between the two women.

The arrival of the twins scotched that at once: Teutia loved Cynara from that moment, and this opening of Teutia's heart had a side-effect.

That evening during dinner, while Marcus was bringing himself up to date with the matters of the estate, Teutia suddenly interrupted.

She said loudly and clearly, 'My husband Drusus is dead.'

Marcus and Cynara stared at her, at a loss how to reply; a few moments went by, and then Cynara nodded.

'Yes, Mother-in-Law. I think you're right. It's just been too long, hasn't it?'

She rose and went to Teutia, kissing her cheek with an arm round her shoulders.

'You're very brave.'

She resumed her place, and Marcus felt a great sense of relief that his mother had finally accepted the fact of Drusus' death. The difficulty for Marcus was that there was no proof. But his leave was too short to worry about that. He spent his few days in the pleasures of love and playing with his children, Marcellus and Appius; and then it was time for the punishing ride back the way he had come. He arrived back at his legion two hours before sunset on the day his 'local' leave expired.

The legion IV Gallica was stationed a few miles west of the Rhine, while far to the north-east Varus was pushing the bounds of empire onward. In the late autumn of the year when his twins were born Marcus was promoted decurion, and immediately experienced the gap which opens up between a non-commissioned officer and the rank and file. The next two years passed without incident, the only disturbance being that he was unable to repeat his interim visit home.

Marcus had taken to spending much of his free time in the legion's horse lines, and he did not take Kradog with him. In the time before Marcus had made his unofficial journey home Kradog had nagged Marcus constantly, trying to persuade him to travel instead to Britain and visit his son Aeron. And when Marcus went home there had been no question of taking his slave with him: the man simply was

157

not up to the feat of horsemanship involved. Kradog must have been nursing his resentment during Marcus' absence, for on his return the slave restricted himself to the letter of his duties, which he carried out perfectly as before; but he had ceased to offer those extra touches which had made their relationship a companionable one. During the time when he had thought often of Pylades Marcus had recalled the old scholar's portentous dream concerning himself and Kradog. So he let Kradog be, hoping that time would bring him out of his sulks; and being the man he was, Marcus turned to horses.

He met Uddo on his first visit to the lines, where auxiliaries, grooms and farriers were looking after the horses. Marcus was wandering idly along when he felt a touch on his shoulder. He turned to see a middle-aged man with long fair hair bound with a brow-band, and a full set of whiskers. He had grey eyes, and his teeth were still good. He was as tall as Marcus, but slim and lithe despite his years.

The man said, 'I was on parade at Cæsarea of Judæa when a captain named Butin got turned into Publius Drusus Scipio; but I always knew him as Centaur.'

'You knew my father?'

'Say rather that I was in awe of him,' the man said with a broad smile, and clapped Marcus on the shoulder, something which a barbarian auxiliary should not have done to a citizen and a decurion; but Marcus found himself unable to take offence. 'My name is Uddo. You don't look like Butin, but the way you carry yourself reminded me of someone I knew, so I made inquiries. Welcome to the horse lines. Now would you like to see my horses?'

So Marcus took to riding in his free time. Uddo was a Germanic Celt who had given his allegiance to Rome, as had most of his fellow tribesmen. He regarded the Teutonic tribes as interlopers who had stolen his original lands. In three years' time his service would be complete, and then he would have his citizenship and new lands in north-western Gaul. Meanwhile he served Rome, and killed Teutons when he could. He was trilingual, in camp Latin, Celtic and Teutish. He owned twelve horses, but his favourite was a superb chestnut mare named Triutinne.

158

Inspecting Uddo's stable, Marcus' eye was held by a black stallion.

'I like the look of that black,' he said.

Uddo chuckled and said, 'He's yours any time you want to ride. Shall we go to the tack room?'

Marcus took a couple of paces towards the stallion, then stopped. The horse was tossing his head with the whites of his eyes flashing, ears laid back.

'Go on,' said Uddo. 'What are you waiting for?'

Marcus said, 'I won't ride him for a week. If I go near him today he may never let me get to know him. Tomorrow's soon enough to start.'

Uddo gave him a long look and then a nod. He had passed a test.

Marcus gave a cackle and added, 'There's another small thing, Uddo. If I'd gone near him just then I'd have been on my way to the moon!'

So their friendship began. When he was free next day Marcus found Uddo and then went to see the stallion, who was named Liutpold. Uddo stood back and watched as Marcus went up to the horse towards the left quarter, talking quietly. As he did so a moment came to him from a sunlit field in Illyria long ago, of himself as a youth talking to his grey stallion, Smoke; and the memory made him catch his breath. He had not thought of Smoke for years. Illyria was devastated now in Augustus' Balkan War, half the population killed, disease and famine rampant. Then Marcus shrugged, thinking, The past is gone. Only in the last moments of his life would he learn that the past is never gone.

'Good old Liutpold, there's a clever fellow,' Marcus was saying. 'Not as if you're an unbroken horse, is it now?' He produced a wheat cake smeared with honey from behind his back. 'What have I got here? Never knew a horse that didn't like a honey cake.' He proffered the cake, and Liutpold took it and began to munch, relaxed while Marcus slid the hand that had held the cake round to stroke Liutpold's nose, and his other hand patted the neck and scratched behind an ear, while he talked and talked. Soon Uddo joined him and they talked across the horse.

Uddo said, 'You took a month's local leave and went home to Gaul of Narbo on horseback, didn't you, Marcus?'

Marcus found it difficult to restrain himself from making the kind of sudden noise that would undo all his good work.

He gulped and asked, 'How in the name of all the gods did you know that? Only my slave knows.'

'Only the whole legion knows,' Uddo corrected him. 'You had to use Army staging posts, didn't you?'

That was quite true. It was also true that no one had asked to see a movement order: Marcus looked so obviously a fast courier that he had passed everywhere unquestioned.

He said with relief, 'So that's how. I had to sign my name and give my destination. I couldn't give false information. But no one's said anything at all, let alone punish me.'

'Why d'you think you're a decurion, Marcus? A slave from my tribe was serving drinks when the Legate held a meeting after you'd got back. You didn't overstay your leave, and it was decided that in this case an exception would be made in defining the term *local*. And your initiative was to be recognized by promotion to decurion. How else could you have got promotion?'

'I never thought about that,' Marcus said, feeling chastened rather than elated.

'This is the place where nothing has happened for years. Nothing ever happens. When someone does what you did it causes a stir, I can tell you!'

Marcus nodded and changed the subject, but he felt uncomfortable. No one in his century – in his eight, even – had so much as hinted that they knew about his journey. It was true that until his meeting with Uddo he had formed no really close friendships; and with the exception of two men from Spain all the men of his century were Gaulish or Germanic Celts, with a sprinkling of disaffected Teutons.

'It's very simple,' Uddo said. 'As soon as you came back to the legion you set yourself apart, half way to a god. And now you *are* apart as a decurion. The Army does sometimes know what it's doing, Marcus, though I grant you it isn't very often.'

Next day Marcus talked with Liutpold as before, and on the

third day walked him with a headrope, while Uddo walked the mare Triutinne by Liutpold's side. On the fourth day the performance was repeated, but beforehand Marcus got the horse to accept bit and bridle; and on the fifth day the military saddle with its four pommels.

Uddo said, 'Aren't you going a bit too gently, Marcus? Liutpold's been ridden for two years, though he can be the hell of a handful.'

'That's why I'm going gently,' Marcus told him. 'I don't want to show off bringing a hell of a handful under control, and having to fight him. I want him quiet for me, and his full power at my disposal. This is one of the best horses I have ever seen, Uddo. I wish I had him down on my estate at stud for a season.'

Uddo's eyes gleamed with pride.

He said, 'I leave the Army and you take your year off at the same time. Would you like me to come home with you and bring Liutpold for a few months? I'd charge very reasonable stud fees.'

Marcus said, 'I'd like nothing better. I have a very good head groom at home, and he's doing his best to improve the stock, but Liutpold would do wonders.'

So they agreed on that course of action, though in the event things were not to turn out quite that way. For the present he went riding with Uddo after two more days. On the sixth day the stallion was walked as before, and lunged on the seventh. On the eighth day Marcus lunged Liutpold very vigorously to take some of the steam out of him, and then mounted him. The horse stood quietly, charged with vibrant power at Marcus' command, while Uddo clapped his hands twice in congratulation.

Marcus thought carefully before deciding to take Kradog with him when riding with Uddo. A slave was needed to attend to the riders' creature comforts, and Kradog would do that, even if he kept up his meticulous but distant attitude. For another thing, Marcus wanted Kradog to be able to ride properly. He could keep a donkey going with much kicking and cajoling, and could even sit a horse after a fashion. But he had no notion of a horseman's aids to riding, for the

161

simple reason that no one had ever taught him. This was a deficiency which Marcus intended to make up. Sooner or later some emergency would arise which meant that Marcus would have to be somewhere else very speedily, and it would make sense to have Kradog with him. His only doubt was whether Uddo would fight with Kradog: Marcus didn't want his slave killed by his friend. Both were Celts, and Celts were notorious for fighting among themselves.

As it happened Marcus had no need to worry. The two men could converse well enough, as Marcus found as they went out together, Kradog on a quiet gelding. Uddo was interrogating Kradog as they rode out from the Prætorian Gate on a cloudy day with a hint of rain, Liutpold still behaving himself perfectly, and Uddo on Triutinne. Kradog began by answering Uddo with a slight frown, his voice low and without much expression; but after a couple of minutes Uddo made a short speech. When he had finished Kradog looked at him for a moment and then barked with laughter.

'What was all that about?' Marcus asked.

Uddo chuckled and said, 'Kradog tells me that you have a son in Britain, Marcus. When you took your famous local leave Kradog wanted you to visit your son there.'

'Yes: and take Kradog with me. He is mad on the idea of seeing his motherland. It was out of the question. But why did he laugh?'

'Oh, I just told him that if I wanted to visit the children I've fathered I'd have to leave the Army and spend *all* my time in the saddle!'

Grinning, Marcus said, 'Fine. Kradog needs to learn some horsemanship. Will you teach him, for the first hour as we ride out together, Uddo?'

So Kradog got his riding lessons, and Marcus a contented slave. In the IV Gallica backwater there was plenty of free time, so Kradog's horsemanship improved rapidly. They developed a routine. Kradog would have his hour's lesson; then the two soldiers would pick a suitable spot for lunch, and they would leave the slave there to hobble his horse and prepare an alfresco meal from the pannier which the horse carried. It was a pleasant time for Marcus. Once on a windy

162

day a fragment of torn clothing fluttered out of the trees at
the edge of Liutpold's vision. He shied, snorting and ready
to bolt; but Marcus held him firmly and without harshness,
stroking his neck and talking to him, gentling him. He
calmed down very quickly. Uddo nodded his approval.

He said, 'No one else waited eight days before getting on
Liutpold's back. I've a mind to give him to you!'

This was a Celtic impulse which a Roman had to stifle. If
Uddo acted on it, sooner or later he would as swiftly regret
it, and Marcus would have lost a friend.

He said, 'Thank you, Uddo my friend, but we agreed he
will come home. At stud he will give me more Liutpolds,
and who could ask fairer than that? Now let's get a good
gallop in before lunch!'

So they galloped through the broad rides which the
Romans had cut in the forests when this part of the country
was pacified. Marcus had never penetrated among the coni-
fers, nor did he want to. To a Roman mind these almost
impenetrable, green-black fastnesses were alien and hostile,
the dwelling-place of who knew what dreadful gods. He
stayed in the middle of the rides until it was time to walk
their horses back and have lunch.

They found Kradog standing trying to mop the streaming
blood of a scalp wound, and with two dead men at his feet.
Near one edge of the cloth which Kradog had been spreading
on the grass lay his cestus with bloody flesh adhering to it;
his long knife was back in its scabbard. The face of one
man was unrecognizable; the other was unmarked, but there
spread out a patch of blood through his jerkin over his heart.

Kradog said, 'You wouldn't think it to look at them now,
but they were twins, like as two peas.'

'What happened?' Marcus asked.

'I was just spreading that cloth when I saw something in
the trees, so I fitted on the cestus and pretended I'd noticed
nothing while they crept up to close quarters. I got inside
their swords.' He reached behind him and picked up two
identical long swords with slightly curved blades, then added
with relish, 'Some robbers! It didn't last long.'

Marcus turned as Uddo broke out into helpless, almost
hysterical laughter. The two others smiled, but looked at

163

each other in puzzlement. The would-be bandits had got their deserts, but what was so funny? They had to wait until Uddo recovered sufficiently to tell them.

'You'll . . . you'll be . . . more famous than ever, Marcus,' he choked at last. 'Only action for years . . . *your slave* kills two men *single-handed!*'

XXVII

For the next two years Marcus took his local leaves locally. The centurion of Marcus' century, Quintus Cornelius Piso, saw to that.

The Roman centurionate held many gradations, and there were usually fifty-nine of them to a legion. The senior centurion, the First Spear, had the powers of a lieutenant-colonel in a modern army. Each cohort had six centurions, and the most junior, the Rear Spears, were roughly equivalent to warrant officers. The centurionate held many gradations of ambition, too.

Quintus Cornelius Piso was a nobleman and a Roman of the City. He could think both politically and strategically. In his early manhood he had perceived the great change which had taken place: the Roman Emperor since the day of Julius Cæsar was chosen not by the civil administration, and still less by the people. The Army picked the Emperor. It was as simple as that.

It followed that a person who desired high advancement should have an intimate knowledge of the Army, and so Piso had enlisted as a legionary. This rank again held all manner of men, from aristocrats like Piso, through rich and landed soldiers like Marcus, down to barely literate citizens who had joined because their circumstances were desperate.

Piso was taller than Marcus, and with a Grecian rather than a Roman profile. He held his rank through ability and not through nepotism, and he was on his way up from it as fast as he could go. When the time had come for Marcus' furlough, Piso had sent for him.

165

'I see you're off on local leave tomorrow, Decurion,' he had said. 'There's a coincidence: so am I. We'll go together, to Remi.'

The leave passed pleasantly, for Marcus, and also for Piso, but in a different manner. He saw in Marcus a soldier of exceptional potential, but completely raw. Marcus had little idea of advanced tactics, and none at all of strategy. So Piso took him in hand, giving him a grounding in military science.

He said, 'You may think you'll never need all this, but your time will come.'

In fact when Marcus' time came it did so in a manner which could not have been foreseen. He was at the horse lines, cleaning the military two-piece snaffle which went with Liutpold's tack, when an orderly appeared.

'The centurion Piso wants you, Decurion. He said right away.'

What now? Marcus wondered idly as he followed the orderly. A new method of witholding the centre while charging with the legions' flanks?

The orderly led Marcus to an office in the Prætorium. Quintus Calpurnius Piso was seated at a marble table, and at the other end was a Teuton. Marcus knew that he was a chieftain because he was wearing a helmet, which was permitted to no one else among the Teutons. He had on a mail shirt over a blue tunic, and long brown trousers. The man's fair hair and beard showed from under the helmet, but had been trimmed.

As Marcus waited at attention there was a movement behind him, and then Uddo was standing rigidly at his side.

Piso said, 'Stand easy and sit down there.'

Marcus and Uddo found two stools at the other end of the table to the Teuton, and kept silent.

'This man,' Piso continued, 'is an ally of ours. His name is of no importance, and indeed might put his life in danger. Let us call him . . . Chief Coluber.'

Marcus suppressed a grin. To call a man 'Chief Snake' told him something of what Piso thought about people who changed sides, even if the majority of the Prætorian Guard in Rome were Teutons.

Piso said, 'You know that the Seventeenth, Eighteenth and

166

Nineteenth Augustan legions are pushing north-east under General Varus, escorted by huge numbers of allied Teutons; their commanders are named Arminius and Sigimerus. Chief Coluber comes to me with information that Arminius at least – and maybe Sigimerus too – schemes to attack the legions. I myself, and the two of you, together with your slave, Decurion, have been detailed as a fast detachment with the mission to alert General Varus. We leave in two hours.'

XXVIII

When it became apparent to Rome that the rule of Archelaus offended all standards of good government, Judæa and his other fiefs were declared an Imperial province, and in the following year Coponius was appointed Procurator of Judæa. He was a man of equestrian rank, as was usual with procurators; they could thus never aim to supplant the governors of provinces, who were senatorials.

The Governor of Syria Palæstina at that time was Publius Sulpicius Quirinius. His name was one of the oldest in Rome: the cult of the god Quirinus centred on the Quirinal, and this god was related to Mars himself; Quirinius was one of the names taken by Romulus, joint Founding Father of the City. It was scarcely surprising that this man was appointed to a second term as Governor.

None of this cut any ice at all with the Jews. They were aware that the Roman governors enriched themselves by a levy of taxes during their term of office: this levy took the form of a census on property. They were enraged when Quirinius did this a second time, and Judæa erupted in an uprising, which was put down with normal Roman severity and mass crucifixions.

Galilee and Samaria were fairly quiet. All over the province there had been a property boom since Herod the Great's time, and a builder in the prime of his life, one Joseph the son of Jacob, saw the upturn in his fortunes begin. He had started off in a small way. But the Greeks were always building, and the Romans; and for all his faults, so was Archelaus, following the Herodian tradition. Again, a popular rebellion by definition entailed destruction of real estate, the interruption of water supplies and similar damage. It was a good time for builders if they were in with the right people. Nakdimon ben Gurion had now been appointed to the Sanhedrin, and had political influence; he had recently taken over charge of the water supplies to Jerusalem, an immensely important post. And he was a friend of Joseph's. So too was another Joseph, who had venture capital at his disposal. He was the man from Ramathaim, not yet thirty years old, and a plutocrat. He had pioneered a fast route to Britain with a staging post on the island of Tresco, and had done it at the age of seventeen, maintaining a stranglehold on it ever since. He had the obsessive eye for detail of a genius, and neglected no opportunity to amass cash, even to the ten per cent he took for looking after the upkeep of a Roman soldier's son in Britain.

So Coponius sat in the Antonia in Jerusalem looking out over the mass of crucifixes on the Mount of Olives. Quirinius sat in Antioch counting his money. Nakdimon sat in the Sanhedrin helping to direct public and religious matters. The two Josephs were too busy to sit anywhere at all. The man from Ramathaim, whom his friends called Joram, was making his fifth trip to Britain with a shipload of oriental goods which he would exchange for commodities, and Joseph son of Jacob was building, building.

XXIX

The tiny flying column of four men rode out from IV Gallica in the early afternoon. The day had begun with bright sunshine, but now there was patchy cloud scudding across the sun. In the forest ride a bear at the edge of the trees rose on its hind legs and sniffed the air, then dropped to all fours again as it trundled into the forest, the good stiff breeze having given the bear the scent of men and horses long before their passage was audible.

They crossed the Rhine in late afternoon by ferry. Twenty-odd miles to the south, Julius Cæsar had built a magnificent bridge over the river in ten days, then, after duly impressing the tribes, he had destroyed it.

Piso paid the ferryman, and the four men turned their backs on the wide and swift-flowing river, and remounted.

Piso said, 'We've anything between ninety and a hundred and twenty miles to go before we make contact with General Varus' rear elements. Three legions and a baggage train! They'll be spread out over a great distance.'

Marcus nodded and said, 'I've never seen one legion in action, let alone three. What do you think the general will do when he hears the intelligence?'

'Get out as best he can,' said Piso.

Uddo said, 'He may be a good general; I don't know about that. But it's common gossip that he treats the Teutons badly. He's high-handed and insulting, and they won't stand for it. They're proud and they're touchy.'

'Well,' said Piso. 'What we have to do is push on as fast as we can. What Varus does is up to him.'

*

170

By noon of the next day Piso and his men began to reach country which Varus and his legions had pacified by putting the inhabitants to the sword, burning their dwellings, and making off with crops and livestock. Varus' engineers had cut great swathes through the forest, and the land was wholly devastated and almost deserted, though here and there the riders saw a few survivors. These people cowered in fear if they were close to the Romans, but if they were far enough away they laid dreadful curses on the soldiers' backs. Marcus and Piso wore sword and dagger, Uddo was armed with a long sword and a spear, while Kradog as usual had cestus and long knife. They bore the curses with fortitude; they were under orders to get to Varus as quickly as possible, and that was their intention. They had already reached the litter left by armies on the march: fruit peel and stones, dead camp fires, worn-out sandals and marching boots, a cast horseshoe whose crosspiece betrayed its Roman origin, and all the rubbish that marching armies leave behind.

In the evening they made a roaring fire and ate their meal by it, listening to a distant howling of wolves. Much closer they could hear a boar snuffling, honking and grunting.

'Should have brought a boar spear,' said Uddo.

Shortly Piso said, 'We're not on holiday.'

And Marcus said, 'The only time I used a boar spear was years ago. And it was on board a ship!'

Piso expressed curiosity, so Marcus told the story of the pirates' attack, making much of his father, Placidus and Targui, and not trying to minimize his own foolish behaviour in the fight. Piso listened with interest and so did Kradog, for the story was new to him also, and he kept an ear cocked as he tended the fire.

Piso said to Marcus, 'You're too hard on yourself. You did well enough for a first encounter. Pirates always fight like tigers. I never met your father, but I'd like to have done, together with those two other men.'

Of course that led to the story of Drusus' expedition. When it was ended Piso looked thoughtful.

'I have been to Tingis,' he said. 'Not much of a place: Roman merchants and so on; no troops. But it has strategic value, because it commands the other shore of the Pillars.

We'll get around to developing it in due course.' He yawned. 'And now bed. We take watch and watch, with your slave first, Decurion. He's worked while we've talked, and he'll be first up, so he gets the easiest watch.'

And then, as they bedded down for the night and Kradog sat by the fire with his long knife drawn, Piso yawned and said, 'Decurion?'

'Yes, sir?'

'Pity about your father. You're quite right to have given up hope. Ah, well. We should catch up with the legions in a couple of days.'

Piso's estimate of time assumed that the XVII, XVIII and XIX Augusta legions were still marching, but in fact he and his party began to catch them up on the following afternoon. They were no longer marching because they were dead.

Although he had put down the Pentecost revolt in Judæa quickly and efficiently, Varus was not a campaign general. He was also not very bright, and what he lacked in mental power he made up for in high-handedness. Uddo had been quite right.

Historically it has always taken three nations to beat the Germans in war. The Teutons of Marcus' day formed a vast moving kaleidoscope of tribes. A tribe would be reported down south in Rhætia one month, and in a couple of months it would be on the Baltic. But the Teutons had that basic Germanic capacity for extreme hardness in battle. Varus had led three Roman legions through the Forest of Teutoberg in column of route. Fifteen thousand men had marched along *six abreast* and with a huge baggage train in the middle which effectively cut the long serpent in half. He had not even sent scouting cavalry out on the wings, because he had so many allies with him! And this was the man whom Augustus had appointed as 'Governor of Germany' and Commander-in-Chief.

There were a few survivors, and Marcus learnt later what had happened. Arminius and Sigimerus, whose Teutonic names were Herrmann and Siegemyrgth, had become completely disaffected by Varus' treatment of them and his

172

allied troops. After escorting the legions for some days they had asked permission to withdraw and bring even more reinforcements. They had then joined these previously alerted troops, who were already lying in wait.

It was pouring with rain and the ground was slippery when the Teutons attacked, and because they were in column of route the Romans were broken up. In four days the slaughter was over, and Varus had fallen on his own sword. A hundred and twenty men escaped, but Piso's party did not meet the survivors because they took a different route. Forty of these survivors were lost, picked off as they made their way through the forest.

The first inkling that something had gone dreadfully wrong came not by sight but by the cawing of thousands of carrion-eating birds, mainly crows and ravens, which grew to almost unbearable intensity as Piso and his men approached what had been the rearward elements of the legions.

There were buzzards, red kites and black kites among the corvines scavenging the carrion, wolves and dogs quarrelling as they tore into the dead flesh. As Marcus picked his way forward with the others the birds rose in furious clouds, settling again as the men passed. A wolf raised its mask to Marcus, a gobbet of flesh in its jaws. He took the wolf's head off with one sword-stroke, then he and the others began an orgy of slaughter which lasted only a minute or so because it began to seem pointless.

Marcus knew he was witnessing something unprecedented in the history of Rome. Death had visited here on such a scale as to mute the party's physical reactions after that first instinctive outburst, and they began to walk through the long trail of butchered men in a state of detachment, objectively. There were dead Teutons in plenty, but the majority of course were Roman: heaped corpses for mile after mile through that ghastly forest, until at last they came to Varus and his tribunes. The last had been stripped of their finery, but Arminius had commanded that Varus should be left as he was, resplendent in his tunic edged with golden tassels, his silver muscled cuirass with its belt of Tyrian purple, and his gold-fringed red cloak. His soft leather boots were clogged with clay, and the finery smudged and dirtied; his own sword protruded from under the cuirass.

Piso said, 'That was Varus, and we were too late.'

No one else said anything. Moved by a common impulse they led their horses away. They passed through groves where rough altars of logs had been erected and Roman unit commanders sacrificed on them, disembowelled and decapitated, their heads hanging from the trees. But eventually Piso and his men found a clearing which seemed at peace, away from the noise of the carrion-eaters.

Kradog passed into a state of shock, eyes blank. He walked like an automaton, and when they eventually found a clearing with no traces of human presence, he was unable to perform the menial tasks he should have carried out.

Marcus said, 'I'll gather firewood and so on. My slave will be better by tomorrow.'

He loosed Kradog's grip from his horse's bridle, sat the man down, then hobbled his horse as well as Liutpold. The three men gave the horses their nosebags filled with hay from a pannier, for there was no grass in the forest; then Marcus moved into the trees and began to gather dead wood, his mind filled with the terrible images of dead men.

Those images vanished at a sudden outcry behind him from the clearing. Marcus dropped the firewood and ran, sword leaping to hand. As well as hearing shouts he could now glimpse a confusion of movement. He burst into the clearing, in time to see Uddo stagger backwards transfixed by a spear through the chest. He fell heavily, thrashing feebly like a speared fish. Kradog still sat in catatonia. Piso was standing with his back to a thick tree trying to fight off three Teutons armed with stabbing spears and shields, deflecting their thrusts with sword and dagger.

Marcus rushed at the Teutons from their right, away from their shields and taking them by surprise. Then he was upon them. He yelled and cut down hard at the first man's spear arm, leaving it dangling at the elbow, the spear on the ground. He slashed at the second man's neck; the blow had little effect because it landed on a leather scarf. But the diversion enabled Piso to step in with his own sword and run the man through the belly; he coughed curses in his

174

native language and fell to his knees. Marcus finished off his first opponent with a slash to the throat, and as the man gargled in death throes Marcus turned to see that Piso had decapitated the third man: spouting great gouts of blood the corpse collapsed onto Uddo's lower body; but Uddo was no longer moving.

Marcus killed off the man with the stomach wound with a swift thrust into the heart, then he and Piso stood panting together. When their breathing had calmed they both bent over Uddo, but he was dead as they had feared.

Marcus said, 'That was a good man. He was coming home on long leave with me, and bringing his stallion at stud. Now I'll keep the stallion and the mare too.'

Piso shrugged, with the urban Roman's complete lack of interest in horses, and looked over to where Kradog remained unmoving.

'Look at your slave,' he said wryly. 'I don't think he even knows what's been going on. Can you get him moving? We can't stay in this accursed forest now.'

Marcus went over and examined Kradog, who was without a scratch.

'Kradog?' he said. *Kradog!*'

The slave slowly turned his head and then looked at his master. Then Kradog frowned and looked all around him. He put his hands on the ground and painstakingly pushed himself to his feet.

'Master?' he said.

They pushed south-westward through the forest, and continued in fear through the night, making extremely slow progress. They were helped for a few hours by a low moon, but as it rose they had to move with the few flickers of light through the dense trees. There is no undergrowth in thick coniferous woodland, merely the endless blanket of dead needles; but there are fallen trees in plenty, and dawn found the three men scratched and bruised. To some extent the horses had found the way for them, but a military horse which is led sees to its own safety.

Kradog had recovered during the night, but he was very subdued as he prepared a makeshift cold breakfast. Marcus

175

wondered whether the slave's thoughts were running parallel to his own, but he kept those thoughts to himself, and sat down to eat with Piso, who stopped calling Marcus 'Decurion'.

'Well, Marcus,' he said as they ate, 'I never in my life thought I'd see what we saw yesterday. Plenty of promotions going now!'

In fact Piso was wrong in his assessment. When the terrible news reached Rome, Augustus deleted the three lost legions from the Army List; but neither Piso nor Marcus was to learn this for a long time.

Marcus nodded and said, 'I suppose so.'

'I am going to become a tribune and then leave for Rome. I shall recommend you for a medallion and promotion to centurion. You saved my life.'

After the meal they rode the horses back towards the safety of IV Gallica. Marcus dared not confide his thoughts to Piso. The promotion would go through, as would his decoration for bravery, and Marcus would be happy to receive both. But the slaughter in the forest had a profound impact on Marcus as well as Kradog.

From infancy in Illyria Marcus had been conditioned to believe in the invincibility of Roman arms. There was no force in the world that could stand up to them; and this had been drilled almost daily into Marcus when he came of understanding. His father, Placidus, and later Targui, had been living and breathing examples.

No doubt there would be excuses in plenty, but the defeat and massacre of three legions would send Rome into a national trauma second only to the guilt which crept into the Roman soul after the extirpation of Carthage. But the rout had a different effect on Marcus. He had not been part of those legions, and had acquitted himself well in action. The fact remained that the Roman Army could be beaten, and it followed that Drusus and Placidus had not been telling him the truth. This shaped his future course of action. As always he would do his duty, but he would seek no further promotion beyond centurion, doing his job as steadily and efficiently as he could for the years that remained of his time. But unlike Piso who saw opportunities for advancement in

176

the defeat, a great void had opened in the world of Marcus, and he wondered whether there was anything which could possibly fill it.

XXX

On his long leave Marcus took the stallion Liutpold and the mare Triutinne home with him, taking his time. He and Kradog had four other horses with them, so their mounts were never over-extended. They arrived at the Villa Belinuncia in the middle of September. For every year of long leave which Marcus was permitted the Army added a year to the eventual date of his release.

As soon as he rode in Marcus delivered the horses to a delighted Akbar, and then went to his family, which included twins who were five years old and had no idea who he was. They screamed with fear at the sight of this fierce centurion with his silvered body armour and transverse helmet crest. Over the coming days they would gradually accept him, but for the moment Appius rushed to Teutia and Marcellus to Cynara. Marcus put his arms round both women.

'Gods, but it's good to be home!' he said, hugging them both.

Cynara said, 'You look magnificent in your uniform.'

'I can't wait to get out of it and into something comfortable.'

'Then I'll come with you and lend a hand,' said Cynara.

So they went to their bedroom, took off all their clothes and made love; and it was as good as it always was with Cynara and Marcus. By tacit agreement neither inquired into the activities of the other during Marcus' long absences; but Marcus knew that whatever arrangements Cynara made they would be most discreet, and for physical relief only. What had begun as a businesslike alliance had turned into a love match that withstood the test of time.

In contrast to his previous leave, Marcus found that little had changed outwardly on the estate, which was thriving under the joint administration of Milo and Casca, supervised by Doratus, who asked leave for his son to come to the estate for a vacation.

Marcus thought, Doratus will never change, and laughed.

He said, 'I don't suppose for a moment it has entered your head that your son might some day – in the far distant future, of course – replace his father!'

Gravely Doratus said, 'He has been working in Rome for years, but it might be interesting to see how he shapes up in the country. He'd have a lot to learn. Nothing need be decided in a hurry. So may I invite him for a holiday? I'll say no more than that for the time being.'

'Certainly, Doratus. Send off at once and he'll be here well before the winter festival.'

Away from the Army, that emptiness Marcus had felt at Rome's vulnerability receded, and he was entering one of the happiest periods of his life, enhanced by his deepening relationship with Cynara and delight in his children. He sent a letter to the man in Massilia who had been Pylades' friend, asking him if he would be kind enough to find a young tutor who could carry on Pylades' work with Marcus' own children.

Doratus' son arrived early in December. He was plump and podgy like his father, but with bright blue eyes and a shock of unruly black hair. Festus was thirty-three. He had his wife, Livia, and a son, Primus, with him. Marcus decided that they should all be accommodated in the villa and take meals with him, even though Doratus would still function as majordomo. He consulted Doratus beforehand, and the man nodded.

'A good idea,' he said. 'You will be able to observe closely, and so shall I, even though it's odd that a man should be heading the slaves who serve his son.'

Festus was a wizard with figures, and he had a direct character, in strong contrast to his father's deviousness. A thoroughly urbanized type, he was at first completely bemused by the life of the estate, and confessed as much to Marcus.

'But it's interesting,' he said. 'Very interesting. I could get to like it very much because it's all so varied.'

Marcus was getting to like this man, and he said, 'Let's go and have a word with your father.'

The upshot was that Festus and his family would stay on for a trial period, and if that proved satisfactory to both sides, then the family would settle down on the estate. There was plenty for Livia to do, and the lad Primus would fit in with the other children.

The young man whom Pylades' friend had chosen as tutor to the twins arrived in the middle of December, ten days or so after Festus and his family. Phalaris was his name, and he spoke the same excellent Akhaian Greek which had been one of Pylades' gifts to Marcus. He was in fact a Massilian Greek, thin and poor, but he carried himself proudly.

Marcus said, 'We'll see how you get on. I shall have a subject for you to engage yourself upon. It's the Phalaral-imentum: getting food into Phalaris.'

He told Kradog to fetch the twins to their tutor. They were not quite six, and hence it was a little early for them to begin their education, but Marcus wanted to see to this himself and not at whatever distance the Army thought to remove him on his next tour of duty.

Marcus went for his bath in a quietly satisfied frame of mind. As he emerged from the plunge he heard a loud commotion arise in the distance. He sent Kradog for his clothes, dried himself and dressed hurriedly, for the row was still going on. Then he ran outside.

There was a group of men in the corral, strangers with horses. Akbar stood in front of them with a spear, facing Casca, Milo and a group of slaves and servants, and a shouted slanging match was in progress. Marcus ran down towards the corral.

As Marcus approached he could see the strangers more clearly, and a more villainous-looking bunch he had never

180

seen before in his life. But then he saw the horses that were with them, and a great sob burst from him.

He pushed through, flinging people aside until he reached Akbar.

Akbar said, 'They killed two slaves who took them for bandits, but I had to make the others wait for you. They're just savages, *but look what they've got with them!*'

Marcus sent his own people away except for Casca and Milo — and Doratus, who had just put in an appearance.

Then he said to Akbar, 'Can you speak with these men?'

'We can just about understand one another.'

'Then in the name of all the gods tell them they are a thousand times welcome here. They will rest and drink, and tomorrow there will be a feast in their honour.'

The new arrivals were filthy, with rat-tailed hair hanging over their shoulders, tattered robes — and very serviceable curved swords, some of which were drawn. Fierce faces were turned threateningly to Marcus, but as Akbar spoke the men relaxed, began to smile, then they were laughing and cheering.

Marcus was looking at the horses, a stallion and six mares with foals at foot. They were horses of the breed that his father had gone beyond the Roman Peace to fetch, wonderful black horses, each with a white star.

He said to Akbar, 'These horses have been on the way for thirteen years. It isn't possible; I don't understand it, but I'll feast these men until they burst, so long as I find the answer.'

XXXI

On the day following the arrival of the horse-drovers, the whole estate gave itself over to celebration, an occasion in which the slaves were permitted to join, in the instinctive gesture which Marcus had made to pacify them after the deaths on the strangers' arrival. There was music, dancing and a lot of drinking. Early in the afternoon Marcus took Akbar aside together with the leader of the newcomers. He was as filthy as his men, but his clothes were not torn, and he had a gold chain round his neck.

Akbar said, 'This man's name is Moulay. He belongs to a tribe known as the Muskeen, and as far back as anyone can remember they have always been sworn enemies of a tribe to the south, the Magnoun. It was the Magnoun who were the horse-breeders.'

With some impatience Marcus said, 'Ask him if he knew my father.'

Again an exchange, then Akbar said, 'He has a message for you, but he will come to that in his own time.'

Then Moulay spoke at some length, Akbar listening with his brow furrowed and his lips moving.

Finally he said, 'Thirteen years ago an army of veiled men – warriors from the far south – came up on horseback and massacred the Magnoun, leaving not a man, woman or child alive.'

'Targui!' Marcus exclaimed. 'Go on.'

'They took most of the Magnouns' horses south with them, but gave the Muskeen some breeding stock. On their most solemn oath and under penalty of suffering the

Magnouns' fate if they broke their word, the Muskeen were made to swear that they would deliver similar breeding stock to Marcus Drusus Scipio at the Villa Belinuncia in Gaul of Narbo. He would defray the travel expenses, and perhaps even reward them. These are not the first horses, but their children and their children's children. Now the Muskeen have done this, they may even live in peace and change the name of their tribe, which being interpreted is the Poor.'

'I think I got most of it,' Akbar said as he finished. 'May we talk about the horses, you and I?'

'Very soon,' Marcus said. 'But what about the message?'

Another colloquy, then Akbar said, 'This is the message: "The Roman, Drusus, is dead, killed by treachery which Targui has avenged. Farewell, Marcus, you who live under the curse of Rome." '

Moulay grinned and nodded, then reached behind him and picked up a parcel wrapped in folds of unsavoury, coarse cloth. He handed it to Marcus, who unwrapped it. Then he saw what he held, breath catching and eyes stinging.

It was his father's bow.

There was a long pause, and at last Marcus looked up at Moulay, and spoke to Akbar.

He said, 'Say that Moulay and his men shall go from here laden with gold. What is their word for *happy*?'

'*Mabsout.*'

'Then from this time forth let them be called the Mabsout, for they shall never be poor again. Let Moulay continue the feast, telling his men my words, for now at last I have proof of my father's death.'

That night Marcus got merry with the other revellers, but on the next evening after dinner he led Teutia and Cynara to the room which had been Pylades' study, and now was used by Marcus. In one corner of the room he had placed an iron chest fitted with lugs at the bottom outside, and set in concrete. He kept his treasures in there, including Drusus' copper diploma (the parchments he still kept in his tortoise-shell box, always on his person), and now he lifted out the compound bow.

Teutia burst into tears when she set eyes on the weapon,

but Cynara was soon able to calm her, for she had long been convinced of Drusus' death.

'So now we have the proof we needed,' Marcus said. 'You can remarry if you want to, Mother, and I can inherit. After all these years I am my own man.'

He stood with the bow in one hand, and ran the fingers of the other over the laminations.

'It brings my father back to me,' he said. 'I remember the first time he showed me the bow. He placed the bow in my hands. And he said to me, "Marcus, look closely at my bow. The middle is a wooden frame. On the side nearest the archer there are layers of water buffalo horn glued down, and on the side nearest the arrowhead there are layers of sinew, beaten into strips. When I draw my bow the horn on the inside doesn't want to be bent, and the sinew on the outer face of the bow doesn't want to be stretched. So when I let an arrow go, each side wants to get back where it was before as fast as it can. And that will send the arrow through armour." '

'Very interesting,' said Cynara, and stifled a yawn.

'I'm coming to the point. He had more to say. "Marcus," he said, "the wood on the inside is Rome, and the layers of horn and sinew are the nations under the Peace. Rome always brings them back to stability." But after those legions were destroyed, I've often wondered if he was right.'

Cynara said, 'Oh, put the thing away again, Marcus,' but Teutia asked to be allowed to hold it. Marcus gave it to her, and she grasped it tight for a minute or so.

Then she handed it back and said, 'I wondered whether I should feel anything, but I didn't. Nothing at all.'

INTER SCRIPTUM (iii)

'Don't pick it!'

John Potts brushed Helen's hand away from the delicate pink flower. They were in Cheddar Gorge, at the head of a grassy slope from which the limestone walls towered up another four hundred feet, vegetation clinging to every cranny.

Potts said, 'It may not be the Grand Canyon, this place, but those flowers grow nowhere else in the world: the Cheddar Pink confined to the Cheddar Gorge.'

Helen was fitting a close-up lens to her camera.

As she busied herself she said, 'At least Cheddar's got something to itself, John. Not like the poor old cheese. Irish Cheddar, New Zealand Cheddar; for all I know we make American Cheddar.'

Helen took three exposures of the flowers, and then said, 'Climb, John.'

Obediently Potts found an easy pitch and went up it like a fly. He waited for Helen to take her photograph, and then came down.

'Enjoying yourself?' he asked.

'You bet. And I loved your old Doc Waldegrave.'

They had spent two days in Cambridge. Potts had shown Helen some of the sights, including Milton's mulberry, and they had taken Doctor Waldegrave out to lunch on the first day and dinner on the second.

Over coffee after lunch he had said, 'By the way, I ran a computer check, and I turned up your Publius Drusus Scipio.

At least, I turned up *a* Publius Drusus Scipio. No telling if it's your centurion's father, but it's at least likely.'

This had rekindled Potts' interest. Putting down his coffee cup he had said, 'Good heavens, I'd no idea. Why didn't you telephone me?'

'I'll tell you why, Potts,' his old tutor had said. 'After we spoke last time – you recall I reversed the charges – a woman rang back and said, "Your collect call to Los Angeles cost forty-eight dollars." Bit steep, I thought at the time. And if P. Drusus Scipio's waited almost a couple of thousand years, a couple of months couldn't do any harm.

'There are two items in the Musée Gaulois at Arles – that's the ancient Arelate of course. Much of it's unreadable, I'm told, but the names tally, and the bits of the record of Army service which can be deciphered tally also.'

Potts suppressed an impulse to scream, and said politely, 'What are the items in question?'

'Oh, sorry, Potts. The first is an Augustan military diploma: the double copper sheet we once mentioned seems to have turned up. But the grant of lands doesn't tally with that on the parchment you found near Qumran. The lands granted on the parchment were in Galilee, as I recall, whereas on the diploma they're in *Gallia Narbonensis*, which makes sense given the provenance of the diploma.'

'Can you think of any explanation for that?'

The old man had sipped his coffee delicately and then said, 'You remember I advanced the possibility that the parchment was a temporary document? If that had been so, and an exchange of lands had taken place subsequently, that would account for the discrepancy.'

'The diploma relates to a Publius Drusus Scipio?'

'Of course,' Waldegrave said a little testily. 'Didn't I say so?'

NO!! Potts yelled within himself, and said aloud, 'Just running through the facts. I don't see how we can prove it's the same man. But what was the other item? You spoke of two.'

'Oh yes, but it can't be of help. Along with the diploma and one or two odds and ends there were the remains of a laminated bow.'

Potts sat up straight and said excitedly, 'But that's wonderful! The people who used the compound bow in the first century lived to the north and east of Syria. Our man – the father, I mean – could have picked it up in Parthia, for example. There's a feasible geographic line from there through Judæa to the South of France.'

They left the Cheddar Gorge and drove to Wookey Hole, where Potts had professorial business. Two days before leaving for Europe he had the long-awaited permission to update his departmental computer system. As a caver he was tickled that he would get the world's best storage and retrieval system at Wookey Hole – at the Thorn EMI unit there. He left Helen at the cave entrance, and in twenty-five minutes he found her in the cave. Potts was grinning as he rejoined his wife.

'You found what you wanted?'

Potts nodded and said, 'Absolutely. I'll put the requisition through from London. Now let's have a look round: from computer systems to cave systems. There are only three caves with public access, but there are sixteen or seventeen more.'

Potts took Helen away from the conducted party, and after they had toured the caves they had tea, then drove to Wells. He was giving Helen a sightseeing trip; she was enjoying it, and both were happy, Potts particularly so because of the serendipity of his visit to Wookey Hole.

That evening Potts read *The Holy Blood and The Holy Grail* by Baigent, Leigh and Lincoln, leafing through the text, for he had read the book before, a blockbuster of historical mystery. Potts was profoundly impressed by the authors' hypothesis that the Magdalene was the wife of Jesus, and that the marriage had taken place at Cana. And he noted the apparent contradiction between two legends: that Mary Magdalene had taken the 'Holy Blood' to southern France, while Joseph of Arimathea was said to have taken it to Glastonbury.

Next morning they drove through gently rising country with many orchards, and Potts said to his wife, 'This is Avalonia,

187

the Land of Apples. A.F.A.L. with the *f* pronounced *v*, is Welsh for apple.'

'The Little Apple, not the Big Apple?'

'That depends,' Potts said, 'on size, significance, antiquity – a number of things. The place is stuffed with legend, from King Arthur to Joseph of Arimathea. And there's one thing I've learned.'

'What's that?'

'To take legends seriously. Time and time again, what seem to be outrageous fabrications turn out to have a basis of fact.'

They walked round the ruins of the Abbey and paused by a small arch in the Lady Chapel; within the arch was a small well, unadorned and with a rough stone rim.

'Saint Joseph's Well,' Potts said. 'The Lady Chapel's twelfth century, but the well was dedicated in the fifteenth – and to Joseph of Arimathea. You've seen thorns that flower at Christmas. Joseph of Arimathea again: green thorns from the Crown of Thorns, so legend asserts. Now come this way through the Galilee. This is fourteenth century.'

'The Galilee?'

'It's the term for the porch at the west end of an abbey, from the opening of the festival hymn "When Christ went before them into Galilee".'

They came out of the porch onto the greensward, looking across to the Tor.

Pott said, 'Glastonbury is Ynys Witrin in Welsh: Glass Island. In ancient times it really was an island surrounded by swamp and water. The Tor was the highest point of land for miles around; there was a great earthwork, and beyond it what seems to have been a kind of three-dimensional maze with a pagan religious function. Let's walk over.'

They walked as far as the well-house of the Chalice Well and looked down at the ornate hinged cover.

'This well has been here from time immemorial,' Potts said. 'So has Saint Joseph's Well. Legend says that Joseph of Arimathea brought the Holy Grail here, or the Holy Blood, if we go on from that book I was reading last night.'

After tea they drove out of Glastonbury, heading back to London through the Somerset flatlands in the hire car. Potts was a fast and efficient driver, but his speed began to slow and his mind was evidently elsewhere. Helen looked at him curiously.

'What's bugging you?'

Potts said, 'The whole bloody enigma. A compound bow in the south of France. Four hundred years after my centurion, the horse archer with his compound bow helped put an end to the Roman Empire. Then there's Joseph of Arimathea. Mary Magdalene. Joseph of Arimathea's supposed to have built a wattled chantry at Glastonbury and dedicated it to Mary Magdalene. That chapel we saw, the Beckery, *is* dedicated to Mary Magdalene.' His voice sharpened almost into annoyance. 'Jo Rim. Mary Mag. Holy Grail, Royal Blood. Helen, there's some gigantic mystery afoot. Those authors haven't put their fingers on it, and what's more, I'm damned if I can either. I'll book a flight to Marseille at the weekend.'

XXXII

Joseph of Arimathea was known to his intimates and close business associates as Joram, which name Nicodemus used in his correspondence with Marcus. It was a half punning reference to the second book of the Jewish prophet Samuel: to the man who brought vessels of silver, gold and brass to King David, usually transcribed as Jorum, with a neutral second vowel.

When Marcus still had a month's leave to run Joram sent him an emissary. Marcus was busy with Akbar and the horses, as he usually was in those days. He and Akbar had weeded out all the stock descended from the Narbonnese horses, even those mixed with the marshland stallions, and started two distinct bloodlines. The first was out of the north-east Gaulish mare Triutinne by Liutpold, and the second from the extra-Mauretanian stock brought by the Muskeen, who had departed rich and happy as the Mabsout.

Marcus said, 'Akbar, if you agree I am going to free you. As my freedman you will have authority over all dealings with the horses in my absence. I'll get Doratus to advise me on a suitable emolument, and from the way things appear to be shaping up it will be a big one.'

'Thank you, Dominus,' Akbar said. Then he added with a smile, 'I am glad for the horses' sake. It's not fitting for a slave to be set over such as these.'

Triutinne was in foal, Akbar examining her and Marcus standing by in the loose box, the smell of straw and ammonia and dung in his nostrils while he ran a hand over the mare's flank; then he heard Kradog calling him.

190

'Master. . . . Master?'

Marcus came out of the loose box and beckoned to Kradog, who seemed excited.

'What is it, Kradog?'

'There's a man waiting in the peristyle. He's from Britain, Master.'

Marcus went past the busts of his parents, noting in passing that they needed repainting, and went to the man standing by the plunge bath.

'Peace,' the man said in Aramaic. 'I am Shimmon bar Abbas.'

'And to you peace,' Marcus said, then called the Kradog for cloth and towel. He bent and took off Shimmon's sandals, then washed and dried his feet, the custom coming naturally to him from his time in Syria; but he was none the less gratified when he felt the man's hand briefly on his head in token of approval.

Marcus said, 'You are most welcome here, Adonai. You must be in need of rest and refreshment. Would it defile you to take them under my roof?'

Shimmon was short and stocky, with light-brown hair and a full beard and moustache. His eyes too were light brown, and he wore the capacious robes and headcloth of a prosperous Jewish merchant. He smiled warmly at Marcus.

'Indeed it would not,' he said. 'I am under permanent dispensation, for I spend most of my time abroad on the affairs of my associate, whom we know as Joram.'

Marcus led Shimmon to the dining room next to the kitchen, calling for cold lamb, bread and wine, then seated his guest.

'I trust Joram is well?' he asked.

'The last time I saw him was ten months ago. He was well at that time,' Shimmon said.

'I'm glad,' said Marcus. 'By the way, have you a following with you?'

'Three men only. There were four, but one stayed in Britain. In the earth.'

Marcus called Kradog and told him to send a pair of slave girls to attend the three men. Food and wine arrived, and Marcus served Shimmon, who ate with a will. Kradog

191

squatted up against Marcus' legs, and Marcus could feel him quivering.

Eventually Marcus said, 'Was your man murdered there?'

'No,' said Shimmon. 'A boar killed him. We have long had peaceful and mutually enriching connections in the island. We come and go as we please. We bring out commodities mainly, and import art objects.'

'Such as vessels of silver, gold and brass?'

Shimmon asked in surprise, 'Have you read Samuel?'

'Never. Nakdimon ben Gurion told me when he arranged for Joram to receive the payments for my son.'

Shimmon said, 'Usually we make our journeys entirely by sea, but on this occasion I made a slight diversion to bring a gift.'

He reached into his robes and brought out a square wrapped in washleather. Marcus unwrapped it and found himself looking at the painted likeness of a child on an ivory base. The hair was yellow-gold and the eyes bright blue, but the bone structure under the puppy fat was that of Marcus.

'Thank you a thousand times, Adonai,' he said. 'This is my son.'

'Keep the likeness well wrapped up and in a dark place,' Shimmon said. 'Joram commissioned it last year from a Greek artist living at Londinium. Your son Aeron's tribe occupy territory to the north-east of the town, but there are many Trinovantes in Londinium itself. The boy was ten when that portrait was painted.'

Marcus looked again at the painting and then rewrapped it with care.

'Adonai Shimmon,' he said, 'I owe a great deal to Nakdimon ben Gurion, and of course to Joram. With him it's a business arrangement, but he goes beyond the letter of it. I've been thinking. I am starting a stud of two breeds of very special horses, and one of them will be suitable for Syrian conditions. Now I have a friend in Galilee. He is a Roman soldier, but like me he speaks Aramaic – in fact, he taught me – and since his father died he owns a farm. He is uncle to my British son. Next year I shall be able to spare two mares with foals at foot. Could you or someone else in Joram's organization transport the stock to Galilee for

Nakdimon and Joram? My friend would be able to look after the horses and perhaps also begin a stud: it's not my place to work out a division of the profits. Perhaps you yourself might also benefit in some way, and I would hope so, since you brought me the likeness of my son.'

Shimmon smiled and said, 'They told me you were a Roman soldier with a difference, and they spoke truly. Do as you suggest, Dominus; when the time comes I'm sure Joram and Nakdimon will accept your gifts with pleasure.'

Shimmon left on the following day with a purseful of jewels, and Marcus sent Kradog with the party to escort them as far as Narbo.

He said, 'Kradog, know this: I shall make you my freedman, as I have done with Akbar. And then I shall send you with Joram's men to bring my son Aeron to me from Britain. It is not fitting that a slave should carry out this mission.'

When the party had gone Marcus poured himself a beaker of beer and went into his study. He put the portrait of Aeron in his iron chest and locked it. For the present he intended to say nothing to Cynara about his intentions over Aeron. When the time came he would present her with the accomplished fact of Aeron's presence.

He drank some beer, then put down the beaker and went over to the inside wall of the room, still stacked with the scrolls which had belonged to Pylades, and were now a valuable library belonging to Marcus. The scrolls were arranged in their holders alphabetically. Marcus was looking for Plato's *Republic*. Rummaging through the scrolls, he found the ones he wanted and carried them over to the lectern, where he fitted in the first scroll and began to read. After half an hour or so he stopped, went back to his beer and sat down to think.

In deciding what kind of vision of the world his philosophic rulers should have, Plato makes Socrates say that he is unable to present this directly: he can only use metaphors. There is a supreme Principle, a Sun giving life and light to natural objects. But in that world men are prisoners in a cave with a fire behind them, perceiving the shadows on the cave wall as reality. The Philosopher king must release himself from the cave, go out into the sun and experience the transcendental reality of things, including the Supreme Good.

Marcus finished his beer and leaned forward, frowning. For Plato, most people were prisoners in the cave, and Marcus found the idea unattractive. He couldn't see anything wrong with his own perceptions of reality. A memory of something Pylades had once said had sent him to Plato, and Marcus felt vaguely disappointed. He sat on a little longer, until other perceptions sent him outside to the shrill voices of his quarrelling children.

Appius and Marcellus, though identical twins who behaved as one in many things, were going through a stage when violent disagreements blew up over trifles with dramatic suddenness. Phalaris came into view and ran towards the twins, but Marcus was there before him. He leaned down and pulled the children apart, then held up one at the end of each outstretched arm, and looked at each by turn until Phalaris arrived.

He said to Appius, 'Marcellus, did you start this?'

The twins were quiet, suspended effortlessly in the air by Marcus.

Phalaris said to Marcellus, 'Or was it you, Appius?'

Marcus looked on with amusement. The twins wore silver chains with pendants in the forms of Greek capital letters: Alpha for Appius and Mu for Marcellus. But they were always exchanging these, and only Marcus, Cynara and Teutia could tell one from the other. He set them down on the floor, took the chains from their necks and then fitted them correctly. Phalaris looked rueful.

He said, 'They're always doing it. I feel a failure.'

'Well, don't,' Marcus told him, giving each twin a light smack on the bottom and sending them away. 'Short of tattooing them there's nothing to be done.'

Phalaris said, 'I like them both.'

Marcus said, 'I think I'll look for a military and physical training instructor for them.'

'Do you intend them to follow your career in the Army, Dominus?'

'No,' Marcus said succinctly, and left Phalaris to catch up with the twins.

Their destiny would be different from his. Caius Lessius was a sick man, and could not be long for this world. The twins would be tied to the estates as tightly as if they were slaves.

XXXIII

Six weeks after the death of Caius Lessius, Cynara gave birth to a healthy daughter, Octavia, and when the excitement had died down Marcus gave thought to the further education of his sons. He employed a time-expired centurion of the Prætorian Guard, and he was a Teuton, Siegfrith by name, a man of potent presence who exacted instant discipline from the twins. And he loved children, all children. Once a week in the evening he would hold court under an old chestnut tree, and tell stories which kept them enthralled.

Marcus inherited Caius Lessius' estate, and trebled his wealth. He appointed Festus' wife, Livia, as vilica, and had a shrine built to the goddess Fortuna, and he worshipped regularly there. He was not sure whether that had any effect on his next posting, which was to Judæa.

Marcus stood in one of the pastures with his sons, his father's bow in his left hand. The bow had been newly strung. With his right hand he reached to the quiver behind his right shoulder for an arrow, nocked it and then drew the bow, muscles corded and mouth tight with effort, aiming at a straw mannikin a hundred yards away.

Marcus said, 'Romans draw a bow to the chest, but the Parthians draw it to the ear like this.'

He released the bowstring, and the boys whooped as the bow sang and the arrow hissed away. Marcus was out of practice at archery. He missed the target, and the arrow embedded itself in a tree. The twins ran as fast as they could over the sward, while Marcus followed at leisure.

The tree was a fine old oak seven or eight hundred years old; now it had an arrow in it seven or eight inches deep.

Appius asked. 'Will you give me the bow when I put on my manhood gown? I'll try and try until I can draw it.'

'Well now, if I give you the bow, what shall I give Marcellus?'

Marcellus said, 'Give me the vineyards, Father.'

Nakdimon sent Marcus a letter written on the fourteenth day of the month Tébéth, together with a copy of the Book of Isaiah in Greek. Since the gift of horses Nakdimon had unbent, and this was his way of showing gratitude. Marcus put the scrolls away carefully, meaning to begin reading the next day, but he did no such thing, for next day Kradog came home.

An excited shepherd boy came running in with the news that a party of men was heading in on the road from the coast with Kradog among them, and Marcus was delighted. He put on his finest toga and waited in the atrium in a state of high expectancy, which melted into complete anti-climax when Kradog arrived with the four men of the Joram Line who had set out with him for Britain. And there was something wrong with Kradog: he looked much older and very tired, and there were blue marks on his forehead.

'Kradog!' said Marcus. 'Where is my son?'

Kradog said, 'Greetings. Your son would not come. I talked as you instructed me, of the fine life here, and of the horses.'

One of the escort said, 'This man was a fool to go alone among the Trinovantes.'

'What happened?'

Marcus strode forward and saw that letters had been tattooed on Kradog's forehead.

Marcus read aloud: '*Te remitto canterium Marci*. "I send thee back Marcus' gelding." What in the name of all – ?'

Kradog said, 'Eight of them held me down, and then your son castrated me with a white-hot knife.'

Marcus gave a great groan and said brokenly, 'Kradog, Kradog, what can I say? You, and my own son. . . . How can I ever make this up to you?'

'For a start,' said Kradog, 'you can stop thinking of Aeron as your son. I well remember the day when I fooled those servants while you went riding, in more ways than one, with the Lady Cressida. One afternoon. You had your pleasure and I had my fun; and now the wheel comes full circle for us both.'

Marcus sat in his study pondering Kradog's words. *Had* they done anything on that long-gone golden afternoon in Galilee which deserved retribution? Marcus believed they had not.

Marcus put away the portrait sadly and he went to find Kradog, who was in one of the tack rooms with Akbar with a large amphora of wine in its stand on the floor between them. They were getting drunk. Marcus was about to reprimand Akbar, but then restrained himself. Kradog was bereft of his greatest pleasure, the bedding of young women, and should be allowed to take solace where he could.

'I'll join you,' Marcus said, and sat down on a saddle while Akbar poured him a beaker of four-year-old wine from the estate. Gloomily Marcus shared the bottle with Kradog and Akbar, drinking most of the wine himself in puzzled silence.

Marcus watched as Kradog poured a libation and said, 'May Epona stamp every one of the Trinovantes into the dust!'

'Epona? That's a new name to me,' said Marcus, and took a draught of the red wine.

Kradog laughed without humour and said, 'Epona is the horse goddess of my people.'

Marcus said gently, 'Kradog, I am going to forget my son Aeron. Why don't you forget Britain, too? When all's said and done you were born and raised in Gaul of Narbo. Britain has not been kind to you.'

Kradog drained his glass and refilled it.

Akbar said, 'I'll drink to a horse goddess any day. Kradog. To Epona, and may she carry out your every wish!'

Marcus scrutinized Kradog, taking in the lines of pain, the indelible blue message on the brow.

'Who knows what the gods have in store for us?' Marcus said, and finished his wine. He had been minded to stay for a drinking bout, but felt no inclination now; instead he went to his study and rummaged until he found Nakdimon's letter enclosed with his gift of Isaiah.

Nakdimon had written:

'Much of this work you will not understand, but no matter. More than one author writes here "Isaianically," but there is a single authentic voice, and it will speak to you, whether in the vibrant energy of a man in his prime, or from the wisdom and serenity of old age.'

Marcus picked up a scroll at random, fixed it in its holder on the lectern, and began to twiddle his way idly through, picking passages for haphazard reading. But then he was soon reading in continuity. Much of what he read might have been written by someone from beyond the stars. Prophecy was not new to Marcus, but it had taken the form of oracles, which almost always could be taken more than one way.

'I the Lord have called thee in righteousness, and will hold thine hand, and will keep thee for a covenant of the people, for a light of the Gentiles; to open the blind eyes, to bring out the prisoners from the prison, and them that sit in darkness out of the prison house.'

Marcus went to his chair and sat down heavily, leaving the scroll where it was. For the first time he realized that his perception of reality might have been wildly at fault, and that he himself might have been to blame for the way Aeron had treated him, and not only him, but Kradog also. He stood up and went back to the harness room, where Kradog and Akbar were taking a recess from drinking, munching bread and olives. They were drunk, but not yet incoherent.

'Kradog?' he said.

'Marcus Drusus. Back again. Hassome wine.'

'Wait. Tell me something, Kradog, even if it means speaking of things I said I would never mention again. Who tattooed the words on your forehead?'

'The one who cut off my balls, o' course.'

Kradog ate an olive and spat out the stone on the floor.

'Did Aeron copy the words?'

'No. Jus' picked up the needle an' went to work. Said

199

he'da done it on my eyeballs but you would'n be able to read it. Have a drink, Marcus Druse.'

'Yes. Yes, I will.'

Marcus took his glass and filled it, then moved to the door and stared out over the corral, the vineyard, the rising turf with a stand or two of cypresses, the azure sky dotted with blobs of white cloud. He took a deep draught of his wine, and turned.

'Kradog,' he said, 'what you have just told me means that my son Aeron can read and write in Latin. I could have written to him, Kradog! If I had, over the years, who knows what might have come of it?'

'Too late to worry now,' said Kradog. 'You owe me my balls.'

Marcus said, 'I'd do anything to set the time back. I'm going to make you my steward, and take you back to Judæa with me. I should never have sent you to Britain.'

Kradog stood up, swaying, and said, 'Both to blame. I kept on at you for years. But I tell you one thing: you try and get in touch with *him* again, you'll never get an answer.'

Marcus flung his glass shattering on the floor, then spun on his heel and strode away. He wandered round the estate, ignoring greetings as he went. He passed the old oak tree, then turned and went back to it. Someone had broken off the arrow flush with the bark of the tree, but the head and the buried part of the shaft would remain until first the wood and then the iron became a part of the oak, assimilated by it if it took a century, a short time in the life of the tree. But Marcus knew that for his part he could never come to terms with the shaft that had lanced out as he had been reading, for the guilt had pierced his heart.

XXXIV

Since Kradog was promoted, Marcus told him to keep an eye out for a man who could act as replacement.

After a few days Kradog came to Marcus and said, 'There's a slave in Rhedæ who belongs to the innkeeper and hates his job. He's a warrior.'

Next day Marcus took Kradog to the inn, saying nothing of their purpose to the innkeeper. Kradog pointed out the slave, who had pale skin and close-cropped black whiskers. He looked surly, but worked efficiently enough at his menial tasks, washing up and sweeping the floor, while pretty girls waited on the customers.

As soon as the innkeeper left the room Marcus called the slave over. He stood straight before Marcus and Kradog, staring from one to the other with eyes that held no hint of servitude. They reminded Marcus of someone.

'What's your name?' Marcus asked.

'Khosro, Dom'nus.'

'What are you?'

'Kardokhos,' the man replied.

'A Kurd, eh?'

Marcus threw a sudden punch at Khosro, very fast but not with his full strength. The Kurd deflected the blow with his forearm and was inside Marcus' guard like an eel, a thumb on Marcus' left eyelid. Then he stood away, the back of his hand touching Marcus' wrist ready for any signal of intent.

'What's going on?' the innkeeper shouted, having come back into the room. 'What's my slave up to, Dominus? I'll have him beaten to death if he's annoying you two gentlemen.'

Marcus grunted and said, 'Your slave could have had my eye under his foot on the floor. I'll buy him from you, innkeeper. Many years ago I came to Rhedæ looking for horses, and found a few poor ones. We may or may not have had a drink here; I don't remember. But I remember the man who was with me at that time.'

'Targui,' said Kradog suddenly. 'I never liked him.'

'Liking didn't come into it with me,' Marcus said, looking at the slave. 'He was my father's man entirely. That's why I'm buying this one. You made a good choice, Kradog.'

During the three weeks that remained of his leave Marcus was busy with affairs of the estate, but the day after their visit to Rhedæ Marcus called Kradog to him. The words on Kradog's forehead were no longer legible. He had visited a tattooist, who had inscribed a square with a diagonal cross over each letter; it would be taken by those who gave it a second glance for some tribal decoration.

Marcus said, 'Kradog, take Khosro to Siegfrith. I want a slave who is combat-fit. And you must learn the ropes of stewardship. Doratus will retire, with a house and a pension. Milo and Casca will take over. We'll all have our hands full, be sure of that.'

XXXV

In the first year of Tiberius Cæsar, three days before the Ides of October, M. Drusus Scipio from X Fretensis to his dear wife, greetings.

It seems to me most strange to begin my letter as I have done. The Divine Augustus ruled for more than fifty-seven years, and the news of his death will have shocked the Empire as much as it shocked me. But Tiberius was a very fine general, and I am sure he will be as good an emperor.

I am on garrison duty at a little place called Marisa in the lowlands of the country. Apparently there were rumours of a possible uprising here, but they have come to nothing. I have a local leave due in three weeks. I long for you and slippered ease, but will content myself with travelling north to seek out old friends.

Tell Milo and Casca to prepare and send me full reports. If any problems of estate management arise, they should consult Doratus. His wisdom is to be relied on even though he is officially retired.

Our children thrive, I hope, as I hope do you also, and my lady mother.

Farewell.

XXXVI

Meriem was lying on her back in the brothel at Magdala, and enjoying herself immensely in orgasm with Petros.

Their association had been a long and happy one. Petros had remained the only person – one Roman soldier excepted – who could satisfy her sexually. Afterwards she and Petros sat and took refreshments, and she smiled happily at him. He had streaks of grey in his hair now, and crows' feet at the outer corners of his eyes, but he was still tender and considerate with Meriem. But what he had to say took the smile off her face at once.

'My dear, my father is dead. I had the news by courier from Alexandria. This means that I must delegate all affairs here and take over the head office in Egypt. I leave the day after tomorrow.'

Meriem burst into tears, and he took her into his arms with her head cradled on his chest.

Petros said, 'I'm sorry, Meriem. I shall miss you. I still remember coming downstairs one night and seeing a young girl standing shy and ill at ease in the hallway. But now we part.'

Meriem sniffed, detached herself from the man's grasp, and blew her nose.

Shakily she said, 'I don't want you to go, Petros. You *made* me. I am a hetaira, and it's only because of you.'

Petros smiled and said, 'Perhaps I may still do something.'

He called out, and a slave came in with a box, putting it on the table at Petros' side and then leaving with a bob of his head.

'There are two hundred gold pieces in this box,' Petros told her. 'In three days go to the chariot races. Then back the Whites in the last race. You should get a hundred to one, because the Whites almost never win. But they'll win for you, my dear, because I've fixed the race.'

Meriem caught her breath. A small percentage of her earnings was put away for her by Tanith, but Meriem never had any worthwhile amount of cash in hand, merely pin money.

She said, 'Petros, this could be my freedom!'

'Exactly,' he said, and chucked her under the chin like a brother. 'You've always been too good for this existence. It pleases me to do this one last thing now my father is dead. And I'm divorcing my wife, thank all the gods.'

Meriem said, 'But what shall I do, Petros? I've always wanted to get out of here, but I'm frightened now it's possible. . . . Are you sure the race is fixed?'

'Absolutely.' Petros thought for a moment and then went on, 'Use your accomplishments, but don't hurry. What you should look out for is an appointment as châtelaine to a great family. You'll be happy in a household, and your character fits you for a position of importance. You can entertain the great, and you can keep accounts. The best is yet to come, my dear.'

Marcus shoved the attendant eunuch away, and slammed the door with his heel. Meriem turned swiftly, not knowing what to expect, then Marcus was grinning, striding across to her, enfolding her in his arms.

Meriem pounded his chest with her fists, and Marcus realized she had no idea who he was, a disconcerting thought at first.

He held her away from him and said, 'Meriem, I should have known you would have forgotten me. We met here only once, and at first you didn't even want to tell me your name.'

Meriem stared at him wide-eyed, then her gaze softened.

'The Roman soldier?' she asked.

Marcus said, 'Yes. It's been a long time, but I've always held you in my mind. Your eyes have haunted me, and now I see them again.'

Slowly Meriem said, 'Yes. Yes, I *do* remember you . . . Marcus?'

He led her to the bed, and they disrobed. Marcus was pleasantly surprised. He had been expecting her to show signs of the life she led. She was more mature of figure, but her face was unlined, and the bloom was still on her skin. Over on a marble table there was an array of musical instruments: lyre, zither and flute, and her room was opulently furnished. Meriem had gone up in her world. They coupled, more like lovers than prostitute and client, came together, then lay side by side until their breathing slowed. The memory of their first encounter came back forcibly to Meriem then. Marcus, and Petros.

She said, 'I've been dying to tell somebody, and I can tell you. You're a Roman, and I can trust you. Marcus, I've come into some money. I've been told to wager it on a chariot race tomorrow. The race has been fixed.'

Marcus said, 'Damned chariot racing. How much are you putting on?'

'Two hundred aurei.'

Marcus whistled and said, 'Then I'd better come with you just the same. Get dressed now. We have to think up a story for your madam. . . . No. All she needs to know is that I want you for a whole day.'

To most of the hellenized spectators at the races Magdala was known by its Greek-Roman name, Tarikheæ. Marcus sat among them with Meriem, watching the races. He was stone-faced as race after race was run. Each race was of seven circuits around a turning point of four marble columns, and it was at the turning point that most damage to the horses took place. By the fifth of the ten races twelve horses had been badly injured and put down. The sixth race was simply a gory shambles of broken shafts, displaced wheels, and injured men: the first two chariots collided and brought down the rest of the field. Marcus took Meriem away to a refreshment stall while seven more horses were killed off, and they ate and drank in silence.

Then Meriem said, 'I've never been to the races before,

and I don't ever want to again. I didn't know it would be like this, really.'

'You hear them all shouting and screaming, that crowd?' said Marcus. 'As long as they can see blood they're happy. Now we're here we'll go through with it, however. Let's go and place your bet.'

'On the Whites?' said the bookmaker. 'Two hundred? Why, certainly, certainly. Ninety to one, the last race. Oh yes, indeed.'

He rubbed his hands as they went and stood apart from him. The last race. The Leek Green driver swerved in front of the Blue, and as it overtook, the horse-yoke broke free of the pole. The two Leek Green horses dashed away, loose; the pole hit the ground, and the Leek Green driver was catapulted forward to a bone-shattering impact, while the Blue crashed into the wreckage. White and Red surged one after the other through the narrow gap at the turning point. White was going to win easily, and Marcus moved behind the bookmaker with a dagger at the man's back.

Pale and sweating, the hapless bookmaker looked round at the touch of the dagger, his eyes pools of disaster,

Marcus said pleasantly, 'We'll go with the lady as far as your bank, I think,' and prodded him forward.

At the bank Meriem opened an account, and the bookmaker transferred into it the sum of eighteen thousand gold pieces, moaning of ruin and suicide.

Marcus said, 'Don't be a fool. You're a known millionaire.'

Marcus and Meriem left the bank, and Meriem said, 'I can't believe it, Marcus. I'm rich!'

'What are you going to do?'

'Buy my freedom, of course.'

'I'll come back with you,' Marcus said.

They had reached the mosaic of Leda and swan-Zeus when Marcus halted Meriem and turned her to face him.

'Meriem,' he said. 'Would you come to bed with me? Set the seal on the day?'

Meriem studied him seriously.

At length she said, 'If you hadn't come with me to the races I'd never have got away with that money. Yes, Marcus, but I'll tell you one thing: you'll be the last man I shall take to bed for a long time. If ever.'

Marcus sat on the bed with a crock of beer watching Meriem. She was singing to her own accompaniment. Her singing voice had been pleasant to begin with, but now it was trained. Both she and Marcus had dressed. Marcus was enjoying himself, when he became aware of another sound: a high-pitched scream, suddenly cut off.

Marcus leaped off the bed, the beer-crock flying into a corner and shattering. He rushed out of the room and down the corridor, flung open a door as guards came running from the opposite direction and Meriem came from her room. Tanith lay on the floor with her throat cut, her head in a pool from the blood which was still pulsing from the wound, while on top of her a thin, hairy man was copulating energetically. Marcus dragged the man off Tanith's body by his hair and hurled him to the guards babbling and jerking, his eyes rolling: the man was plainly deranged. More people began to arrive, the place in uproar. Marcus grabbed Meriem's hand and slipped with her back to her own room.

'Now's your chance,' he said. 'Get your things together!'

When he and Meriem came out into the corridor with Meriem's possessions the confusion had grown worse. Roman and Jewish troops had arrived, and were getting in one another's way. No one took any notice of Meriem, nor of Marcus in his civilian clothes. He took her to an inn and made it clear to the innkeeper that she was under the protection of a Roman centurion.

They sat in the courtyard of the inn under a lattice where sprays of jasmine twined golden.

'What are you going to do, Meriem?' Marcus asked.

Meriem looked down at her hands, folded and perfectly still on the table.

She said, 'I'm going to think about it, Marcus, and then I'll tell you. For today, it's enough that I have my freedom at last. Tanith took hashish more and more, and in the end she hardly knew what she was doing. So I'm free.'

The cloying scent of the jasmine in his nostrils, Marcus

208

said, 'I'll help you if I can. We've met only twice, but . . . there's something special.'

'Yes,' she said. 'Yes, Marcus. Come and see me tomorrow.'

The next day they had lunch together at the inn. As ever, Meriem had thought carefully through her situation.

'I know what to do now,' she told Marcus. 'I have all the money I need. I shall go to Sepphoris and turn myself into a Jewish widow. I'll dye my hair, buy jewels and rich clothes. Then I'll buy two slave girls: a body slave and a tiring woman. I'll be kind to them, and tell them my husband was killed by a leopard near Jericho; he had no surviving brother to marry me, so I was left alone. I'll eat kosher food and go to the women's section of the synagogue. My slaves will go everywhere with me, and they will cement my new identity. Then, after a month or so I'll look for a high-class house-keeper's job.'

Marcus chuckled and patted her hand, saying. 'You don't need any help from me, that's for certain.'

He called at the inn the following day to see her out of friendship, but Meriem was gone.

XXXVII

From M. Drusus Scipio at the Villa Belinuncia in the sixth year of Tiberius Cæsar, four days before the Nones of December, to S. Claudius Baratanicus at X Fretensis, greetings.

I am posted to Judæa again, my friend, so look forward to seeing you in the New Year. My long leave has passed uneventfully, apart from the death of my dear lady mother, but you never knew her.

I shall be with Headquarters this time, and not on piddling garrison duty. That is something to be thankful for.

Farewell.

INTER SCRIPTUM (iv)

John Potts and Helen took picnic gear out of their hired
Citroën and walked slightly uphill to the place they had
spotted from the car: a likely place for an alfresco lunch.
Potts put down the hamper and opened it. The couple sat
with their backs against the stump of an ancient oak tree
and took their meal: a brace of partridge with salad and a
bottle of claret. Potts munched and looked sourly up at the
hilltop village of Rennes-le-Château, the houses, the church,
the château itself. Ancient Rhedæ once lay in the valley
below.

He said, 'All that stuff in Baigent and Co. about the Zion
Priory and so on is very interesting, but it's become irrelevant
to my concerns. What's getting at me is the same as at
Glastonbury: all this emphasis on the Magdalene. They say
that tradition maintains that she and Joseph of Arimathea
were in a party which got to the south of France, Lazarus
among them. We've just seen the Magdalene Tower here. I
feel we're on the edge of great events, but I can't see my way
in. I may try handing it all over.'

'What's that supposed to mean?'

Potts said, 'Oh, I mean handing it over to my guardian
angel.'

His wife raised her eyebrows and opened her eyes wide in
puzzled amusement.

'John, you've got to be joking!'

'Far from it,' he said seriously. 'Let me try to explain. I'll
have to do it by analogy. Think of your personal computer.
You want to hook it up to a printer, and for that you need

211

an interface. If the interface isn't immediately compatible you have to key in the appropriate code.'

'Right. So what?'

'The key is that magic spell which gets the result you want. Different interface, different code: another spell. Now it's a common way of sucking people into Black Magic to suggest they can be brought to know and converse with their guardian angel. Whatever they may see in the end, it isn't that. The guardian angel is an interface, and you can't communicate with an interface, only through it.'

Helen said, 'You're not only not joking, you're beginning to grab my interest. Through it to what?'

'To God. Forget any idea of God as a person, male or female. God is unknowable. That's why people need intermediaries. But an infinitesimal fraction of what we call God can be likened to a computer of endless capacity, quite able to take account of the fall of a sparrow, thank you very much. Baptism and confirmation power you up. Then, when you really need it, you can key in the code.'

'John, you amaze me. You've actually done this?'

'Three times, when I felt on the edge of the pit.'

Potts stood up and leaned with his back against the ruined tree, while his wife gazed at him, her mind elsewhere.

Eventually she said, 'You've never pressured me, John, and I'm grateful for that. But I'm going to take religious instruction. I want to get ahold of those codes.'

On the flight back home Potts reflected on what he had so far. It was unsatisfactory. There appeared to be some connection between the part of ancient Gaul which they had visited and Glastonbury, Mary Magdalene and Joseph of Arimathea. They had seen a chapel with a Shield of David as a window decoration, and a Magdalen Tower. At the museum they had seen some fragments of what they had been told was a compound bow, and a battered copper diploma, which the French would not permit Potts to inspect with any rigour, since he had no standing in that field: he would have to enlist Dr Waldegrave. It was confirmed that the diploma did refer to one Publius Drusus Scipio. But tracing any interconnections was beyond Potts, and he felt frustrated.

Back at his office Potts looked at his backlog of mail. Included in the pile was a note from the Department of Antiquities in Jerusalem, enclosing photocopies of the documents which Potts had found in the gold box near Khirbet Qumran. He put it to one side and buzzed for his secretary, dealt with the more urgent correspondence then picked up the documents and studied them while he drank coffee.

Both documents were in Latin majuscule. The square capitals of the older document were cramped and full of lacunæ. A scholar in the Department could venture only a partial and tentative reconstruction, identifying Publius Drusus Scipio as captain. He must have been an auxiliary before being granted citizenship, and his lands were *APUD CAP* 'near? Capernaum.' His record of service could not be reconstructed beyond a reference to *AEG* '*Aegyptns* (Egypt).'

This was of no immediate interest to Potts. He put down the father's document and picked up the son's. The square capitals of the Latin script were neat and well-spaced, but without vitality: a typical product of military bureaucracy. Potts himself could read enough to understand that he was looking at a combined operational and movement order. The centurion M. Drusus Scipio was ordered to proceed to Secacah with two decurions and sixteen men, make an arrest, and stay overnight at a nearby garrison.

Preceding the order Potts could make out a very faint X. And at the very end there was an equally faint P. He puzzled over these two letters, because their characteristics differed from what had been restored in the remaining text. He decided that he was looking at an amendment in another hand. The first letter could refer to X Fretensis, but he could not even hazard a guess about the letter P.

213

BOOK TWO

THE CROSS

After this he (Pilate) stirred up further trouble by expending the sacred treasure known as Corban on an aqueduct fifty miles long. This roused the populace to fury, and when Pilate visited Jerusalem . . . they shouted him down. But he had foreseen this disturbance, and had made the soldiers mix with the mob, wearing civilian clothing. . . . He now gave the signal . . . and the Jews were cudgelled so that many died from the blows, and many were trampled to death by their friends as they fled.

— Flavius Josephus (Joseph bet Matanhias), *The Jewish War*, trans. G. A. Williamson, ed. E. Mary Smallwood, Penguin Classics 1981, p. 139.
The Jewish War first appeared c. 75 C.E.

XXXVIII

Marcus was now Fore Spear of the Third Cohort of X Fretensis, on parade with the legion outside Antioch. There were seven cohorts present out of ten, one at Cæsarea, one at Jerusalem, and one split up into garrisons in Judæa.

Marcus stood at the right of the front rank of his cohort. At the head of it were the guard sergeant, the standard bearer and the trumpeter. Away and in front to Marcus' left the auxiliary cavalry were formed up together with scouts and despatch riders. To his right the First Cohort's ranks protruded from the general body of men because of its greater numbers, and at the head of that cohort were the senior officers. The Legate bestrode a caparisoned horse; a few paces to the rear stood the Adjutant Tribune and the Camp Prefect; to their rear in turn stood the Eagle Bearer with the five junior tribunes lined up on him. Standing out on the far right of the legion stood the First Spear. Guard sergeant, standard bearer and trumpeter headed the ranks of all the cohorts. Trumpets blared out, and the legion began to unwind itself slowly. Eventually Marcus' trumpeter sounded the signal, Marcus barked the order, and the Third Cohort moved forward in column of route, six abreast, the air thick with dust and the sun over the men's heads as each three eights merged into four sixes for the march, with the cavalry deployed on the wings and the scouts ahead. The troops were out for the day on one of the regular twenty mile route marches, and it was Marcus' first few days of this tour of duty with the legion.

Marcus had never been as far north as this: the countryside

was different, somehow soft and effete, like the local inhabitants. But Marcus slogged along, and gradually the legion began to engulf his personality as he marched in unison with the others.

What little free time he had snatched Marcus had spent looking for old comrades, but had met none. As the legion formed up into column of route Marcus thought he had caught a glimpse of a face he recognized, but could not be certain: the Rear Spear of the Second Cohort. But the face had been lost in the movement of so many troops. The centurion was now marching in front of Marcus. At the first rest period he would find out if the years had given a friend back to him.

When the trumpets called a halt Marcus went quickly round the legionaries under his command, drank some posca and then went swiftly forward to the centurion. It was Claudius, jumping to his feet with his eyes alight.

'Marcus, old friend!' he exclaimed.

Marcus said. 'It does my heart good to see you again. How are things with you?'

'Passable,' said Claudius. 'More than passable, if the gods permit.'

Marcus said, 'We'll meet this evening in the canteen. I must get back to those men now.'

Marcus and Claudius sat together in the centurions' canteen, their slaves at their feet. Khosro had been well schooled by Kradog, whom Marcus had sent at once to the neighbourhood in Galilee where Drusus had exchanged his lands for the estate and villa of Belinuncia; Kradog was looking for a suitable building site there for Marcus to purchase and put work in hand on a small villa. The work would have to wait until Marcus' first local leave.

Claudius said, 'Cressida's well, and writes once a year. Her first husband died. She had five children by him, and two survive. Then she married a man of the Durotriges; the children, a son and a daughter, remain under the care of Aeron and his wife with the Trinovantes. Cressida's living now at some place in the west called Ynys Witrin.'

'Kradog will be interested in that,' said Marcus. 'That's

218

where his mother came from. He's away looking for a building plot for me. Now tell me about the horses.'

'They're doing excellently,' Claudius told him. 'You shall see them on our first short pass: Villa Batanya is yours whenever you want to use it. I've met Joram and Nicodemus, as well as Shimmon. They wish to be remembered to you, and want to arrange a meeting as soon as it's convenient to all parties.'

Khosro was in Marcus' bad books. That morning he had dropped and broken the tortoiseshell box in which Marcus kept the parchment copy of Drusus' diploma. Khosro trailed glumly along with Claudius' Nubian slave, Gesmas, who was cracking jokes in camp Latin, and getting no response from Khosro.

Marcus was admiring Antioch. The plan of the city was copied from Alexandria, in four quarters intersected by two great colonnaded streets at right angles: its geographical position in the Orontes valley ensured that east-west trade ran through it; the Lebanese mountains lay to the south and the Taurus to the north and east, squeezing trade into the flat and fertile valley. The city had all the features of a great Roman capital. There were magnificent temples, baths, theatres and amphithreatre, a hippodrome, together with a reputation for Oriental vice.

Claudius said, 'Have you seen enough for now, Marcus? If so we'll go to a street of goldsmiths. I fancy we can find the very thing you need.'

They did, in the first shop they entered, leaving the slaves outside. Marcus chose a gold box, and said casually, 'I'll take this,' his eye already caught by a jewel which would make a gift for Cynara: a finely-chased golden lion's paw with extended ivory claws clutching a perfectly spherical ruby. The box would replace the tortoiseshell, and that was that; but here was something worth bargaining over. The goldsmith seated them and gave them sherbet, and the haggling began.

On his first local leave Marcus went with Claudius to the Villa Batanya, delighted to be back once more in lovely

Galilee. Claudius' mother was still alive, but senile and incontinent, attended by slaves. After a bath and a light lunch Marcus and Claudius went to inspect the stud, and Marcus made the rounds of the horses with satisfaction.

They left the stables, Marcus giving an aureus to the head groom and a handful of denarii to the lads. Claudius took his friend round a stand of cypresses to where a group of slaves was busy erecting a pavilion which would be hidden from the villa, and the man supervising the workers was Shimmon bar Abbas, who had brought ten-year old Aeron's portrait to Marcus at the Villa Belinuncia. His face lighted at sight of Marcus, and he came forward with outstretched hands, smiling.

'Peace! Well met, Dominus!' Shimmon said. His eyes twinkled as he added, 'The Lord God works among the Gentiles to good purpose!'

'Greetings, Shimmon bar Abbas, and peace,' Marcus said, answering in the Aramaic which Shimmon had used. 'I don't know about the Lord God. I think Galilee suits my breed of horse as well as it suits me. My man Kradog, who once saw you off on a journey, is looking for a place where I may build a dwelling. It doesn't seem easy.'

'There's a lot of money about these days.' Shimmon said, 'and a building boom that's been going on for years. You're rich enough, but you'll still need the help of influence. I think you'll get it. See what I'm building!'

Claudius said to Marcus, 'Joram and Nakdimon are coming. I expect them in two or three days. This pavilion will house them and enable them to observe their Law with Shimmon. As for you, Marcus, I'd gladly give you a building plot if I could spare the land. But it was farmed to capacity even before the horses came, and now we have to rent extra grazing. I can't spare a footprint's worth of ground.' And to Shimmon: 'You're going to put in a word in high places?'

Shimmon nodded and said, 'Yes. It's no more than is due.'

Marcus went to bed that night in a happier frame of mind than he had enjoyed for some time. He was dozing off when he felt a tug at his toes: it was Khosro.

The slave said, 'Master, there's a girl outside. Do you want to see her?'

Marcus grunted, then sat up and rinsed his mouth with posca.

'Yes. First fetch a torch.'

The girl was no more than sixteen or seventeen, with flaxen hair and a slight figure; she stood modestly with eyes downcast, the torchlight flickering over her features. Khosro was grinning, eyes darting from the girl to his master and back.

'Who sent you?' Marcus asked her in Latin. 'My host, the Dominus Claudius, I suppose.'

'No. It was the Adonai Shimmon. I am one of his slaves, and I have not known a man. He bought me when I was ten, and later this year I shall be free, for the Jews enslave only for seven years.'

'Where do you come from, and what is your name?'

The girl had a reedy but pleasant voice, and she said, 'My mother came from somewhere in Seleucia, and my name is Kollura.'

' "Little Cake"?' Marcus chuckled. Then he said, 'Go away, Khosro, and take the torch with you. And you, Cakelet, come to bed with me, and have no fear. Just a small nibble tonight, and then we'll see how things go.'

When Kollura slipped off her clothes and moved into bed close to Marcus he found himself in a fever of sexual excitement; but even so he did not take the girl's virginity. He kissed her: neck, eyes, mouth and nipples, feeling her mouth go slack and her nipples harden. Then he hugged the girl and called for Khosro.

'Khosro, fetch me some beer, and some fruit for Kollura.'

'Yes, Master. Do you want anything to eat?'

Marcus laughed and put an arm round the girl, saying, 'For a long time to come I'll be eating little cake, I hope.'

Marcus sought out Shimmon the next morning as soon as breakfast was finished at the villa. The pavilion was almost completed, the workers hanging tasselled rugs on the walls and laying rich carpets on the floor.

'Peace, Dominus,' Shimmon said. 'Did you have a good night?'

'Peace. Thanks to you, the best night for a long time, in a way, for the girl is still a virgin. You do me too much honour, Shimmon, but I want her.'

So Marcus sent Khosro for Kollura, and Shimmon said to her, 'Kollura, the Dominus wants you permanently, as his concubine. If I free you will you go with him on that basis?'

'Make up your own mind, Cakelet,' Marcus said gently.

Kollura said, 'Yes, I will. I have made up my mind, and I'll go with you wherever you want, Marcus Drusus Scipio.'

'How did you learn my name?'

Kollura leaned up and drew down Marcus' head to her mouth, then said softly into his ear, 'I got it from your slave. It didn't seem right to be doing what we did last night and not know your name. I'm looking forward to another lesson!'

Marcus released himself and grinned at Shimmon.

'Now I'll have to find an apartment near the fort by Antioch,' he said.

Joram and Nakdimon sat outside their pavilion with Marcus, Claudius and Shimmon. Nakdimon's skin was still golden, but there were wrinkles at the corners of his eyes, Marcus scarcely recalled his one formal meeting with Joseph of Arimathea. As they drank grape-juice and ate fruit Marcus studied Joram carefully.

He saw a man of immense vigour, still only just turned fifty, with a hooked nose and red lips, flashing black eyes and a full beard, black and wiry. He was bulky and muscular, and of massive intelligence.

Shimmon said to Joram, 'Adonai, the freedman Kradog is searching for a building plot, and can't find one anywhere.'

The Jews ate in the pavilion and the Romans at the villa, where they talked of old times.

'Where's Quintus these days?' Marcus asked Claudius.

'He died six months ago. Killed. He was on guard duty. Fell off a tower. It was a silly way to go, really.'

Marcus clicked his tongue with brief regret, and they talked of other things. Marcus drank little, and after a decent space of time he went in search of Nakdimon, finding him

222

outside the pavilion again under a bright full moon; Joram could be seen in the pavilion by torchlight, still at his food.

'May I join you?' Marcus asked politely, and sat down at a nod from Nakdimon.

Marcus said, 'I want to thank you with the words of my mouth for your gift of the words of your prophet Isaiah. I have never read it straight through, but have often dipped into it. There's so much I don't understand.'

'The best thing is to find an old Jew who is bilingual, and take up your studies in Greek. He needn't be a priest – in fact, you would do better not to approach a rabbi at all, but some old man who will have heard Isaiah discussed for years.'

Marcus thanked Nakdimon and stood up as Joram came out of the pavilion.

He said, 'I've been thinking about you. I know a builder who will get you land, and build you a house on it into the bargain.'

XXXIX

Ten days before the Kalends of June in the Fourth Year of Tiberius Cæsar, Servius Claudius Baratanicus to his friend Marcus Drusus Scipio at X Fretensis, Greetings.

The stud continues to thrive. Joram and Nicodemus paid another visit last week, and they are highly satisfied. Joram had news for you, which I won't spoil by telling it, for that is his prerogative.

They took me to a Jewish wedding last week: imagine! It's a pity that you wouldn't take this local leave with me, for they would certainly have taken you as well. However, now you have your apartment and its delightful resident I can understand your wanting to stay at Antioch.

This wedding. Local bigwigs and bigwigs from Magdala. I had to stay outside and take a back seat, but so did a lot of people; there must have been a couple of hundred guests. A nineteen-year old bridegroom, son of a building tycoon named Joseph son of someone or other, and a fourteen-year old girl from Magdala. Cana was awash with wine: it ran like water!

But that's not important. Marcus, there was a woman who, so they told me, was housekeeper to the Magdalene family. She was a widow, but had thrown back her veil for the occasion — and she had eyes of the most astonishing deep purple, the like of which I've never seen in my life before. I've always remembered the tale you told of the girl in that high-class brothel — and, of course that was at Magdala too. Is it possible that a whore could get a position like that? I suppose she would have to have been reformed a good long

224

time ago. Or perhaps it's just a coincidence, and there are two women with eyes of that astonishing colour. I couldn't find out her name, being on the fringes of the crowd as I said.

I don't need to ask whether you're having a good time with your charming Kollura. I think it's high time I got married if I'm to raise a family; but my father always expected me to marry a British woman. I may write to Cressida and see what she suggests; I'm getting on now. And so farewell.

XL

On the third day of Tammúz in the World Year 3777, Joseph of Ramathaim to the Centurion M. Drusus Scipio at Headquarters, Legio Ten Fretensis, greetings. The news is what you would wish to hear. Through the good offices of a friend I have obtained a plot of land for you with permission to build a villa; the small estate includes an olive grove and a vineyard, both mature but overgrown. The property is situated in a hamlet on the outskirts of Capernaum. The original building on the site was destroyed years ago in war. My friend, also Joseph, will send a clerk of works to you with draft plans and will have the man discuss them with you. A deposit will be required together with further payments as the work proceeds. A temporary dwelling can be swiftly erected should you wish your freedman Kradog to supervise construction in your absence.

Nakdimon tells me that you have been reading the Book of the Prophet Isaiah. Praise to the God of Israel!

Farewell.

Post scriptum: The land as distinct from the building is a gift to you from Nakdimon and myself.

XLI

Headquarters duty with X Fretensis consisted in the main of training. Antioch had long been pacified in the military sense; but the Antiochenes were a turbulent people. They behaved as they did out of no nationalistic or religious belief as did the Jews. The Antiochenes were sloppy, depraved, corrupt and quarrelsome, and when Marcus was not training he was engaged in petty military police work, sorting out drunken brawls, separating fighting gamblers, jealous lovers, quarrelling families, thumping the heads of young bloods out on the town and terrorizing the common people.

He had found a small apartment half a mile from the fort and installed Kollura there, spending most of his free time with her. His patience had ensured sexual compatibility. Kradog stayed at the apartment when he was not on Marcus' business, and Marcus bought her a tiring-woman. She was thirty, and ill-favoured, an Antiochene named Melissa. She had made advances to Khosro, who had repulsed them with contempt, so there was bad blood between those two.

On the evening after Marcus received Joram's letter he went along to the apartment with Khosro. It was a fairly poky little place in a tenement building.

Kradog had been in residence for a couple of weeks when Marcus arrived that evening. He was plump and rosy-cheeked. Kradog was very comfortably off now, thanks to the investments which Doratus, and later Festus, made on his behalf from the percentage of profits on the fat-hen crops at the villa Belinuncia.

227

He got up smiling when Marcus came into the apartment, pleased to see him as always.

'Greetings, Marcus Drusus,' he said, having always addressed Marcus in this way since freedom. 'Is there any news?'

Marcus told Khosro to fetch him some beer and then said to Kradog, 'Yes. News at last. Where's my concubine?'

Kradog pointed to the bedroom and said, 'Where else? Making herself lovely for you.'

Marcus was wearing a civilian toga, which was hot and uncomfortable, but compulsory dress for a centurion leaving the fort in mufti. He took it off now and tossed it on a marble table, then sat down in one of the tooled leather chairs, red with gold trimmings, and took his beer from Khosro.

'We'll wait for Kollura,' he said. 'The news will concern her also.'

He sipped his beer and ate some fruit, and a thought occurred to him.

'Kradog,' he said, 'there is an item of news unconnected with what I shall have to say in a moment, but this is of interest only to you. My comrade Claudius had gone to visit his sister and to look for a wife. Perhaps I never mentioned it, but the Lady Cressida lives in Avalonia now.'

Kradog bit his lip, and asked Khosro to bring him a glass of wine.

He said, 'Ynys Witrin? He will see Avalon with his own eyes, and taste the summer apples, the orchard grass beneath his feet! If I had known of this, I would have asked you for permission to accompany him.'

'I know,' said Marcus. 'That's why I said nothing until now. Lachesis weaves very strange threads, but a man can take a hand now and then.'

At that moment Kollura came out from the bedroom, radiant in a filmy light-blue robe. She wore a circlet of emeralds set in silver round her head, and her flaxen hair cascaded down her back. She hurried to Marcus and embraced him. He loved her. Their relationship had yet to ripen, but already it was quite different from that with Cynara. Marcus had married her for business reasons, and

228

love between them had grown as a vintage matures with the years. With Kollura Marcus had felt an instant magnetic attraction from the moment that she had stood before him in the torchlight with her head demurely cast down. And now he held her away from him, laughing.

He said, 'It does me good to look at you. But go and sit down, for I have news.'

Marcus gave the sullen Melissa money and told her to go out and enjoy herself – an unlikely happening – and then took from his tunic the parchment from Joram.

He read the letter and then said, 'Well now: what do you think of that?'

Kollura said, 'I don't want to go to any villa. I'd rather stay near you.'

'You'll stay close to me wherever I am, here or at the villa, never fear. Now go for a walk, Kradog, and you go with him, Khosro. We have to be back before Lights Out, for I'm on early duty tomorrow, so come back in an hour.'

Marcus and Khosro were walking back to the fort in a pleasant sidestreet lined with cypresses, aromatic in the evening air, when the footpads attacked. Marcus looked like a prosperous civilian out for an evening stroll with a slightly-built man, slave or servant, attending him. Two big louts came surging from the shadow of the trees, shouting. 'Stay where you are!' and 'Your money, now!' One held a long knife, and the other a club.

'Take the one with the club,' Marcus said to Khosro.

Marcus disarmed the knife-man, then broke his right arm. The man was making a lot of noise, so Marcus hit him hard in the throat. After that he turned to see what all the other noise was about. The club was lying on the floor. Khosro had stepped inside the blow from the club and used his thumbs; both the man's eyes lay on his cheeks, and he was staggering in circles and screaming. Marcus went behind him, squeezed his carotids, and laid him down on his back, replacing his eyes in their sockets.

'You didn't use your dagger?'

'No time,' said Khosro. 'When a man's eyes are sitting on

229

his face it gives me time to think what to do next: draw my knife and finish the job, or do what you just did.'

The hamlet was called Elon. There were six houses there, but no sign of building activity. The houses in sight were fairly small, built of mud bricks with straw sticking out, and flat roofs which were also used for outdoor living. An old Jew with a long white beard was nodding on a stool in the shade by his doorway, and Marcus leaned down from his horse Abraxos, for the sound of the horses had wakened the old man.

'Peace,' said Marcus.

The old man mumbled, 'Peace.'

Marcus went on in Aramaic, 'Forgive the disturbance, Adonai. I am looking for a building site: work should be in progress, but I can see nothing.'

'Not surprising,' the old man said. 'See the olive grove at the end of the street? The building is going on behind it, and that's why you cannot see anything.'

'Thank you,' said Marcus, and kicked Abraxos up into a canter.

Once past the olive grove Marcus saw that more demolition than building had taken place. A group of labourers in loincloths toiled stacking old stones into a cart drawn by four horses, the men's and the horses' bodies streaked with sweat and dust. But that was the last cart of detritus, and already two men in light tunics were marking out the foundations; Kradog and the clerk of works were watching, accompanied by a stranger clad in magnificent robes. In the background, halfway to a neglected vineyard, a pavilion stood away from the dust, presumably Kradog's living and sleeping quarters.

Marcus and Khosro dismounted, and Marcus gave his reins to Khosro. Greetings were exchanged, but not introductions, because the stranger broke in before they could take place.

'Those are fine horses you have.'

Marcus patted Kyllaros and said equably, 'This is Kyllaros, named after one of the horses owned by the founders of Rome.' He stroked Abraxos. 'And my horse is Abraxos. In

230

Greek numerology the letters add up to our year's length: three hundred and sixty-five. And in Greek mythology Abraxos was a horse belonging to rosy-fingered Aurora, to whom some still kiss their hands.'

The stranger snorted and said, 'Never mind all that Gentile rubbish. What I want to know is where you . . . got them.'

Marcus stared, then said, 'I got them from beyond Mauretania to my estate in Gaul of Narbo, at the price of my father's life. I sent a breeding nucleus to the Villa Batanya by Cana of Galilee, as a gift to my friends and associates, who are Nakdimon ben Gurion and Joseph of Ramathaim. I trust that provenance will suffice? I am Marcus Drusus Scipio, centurion.'

'My apologies,' the stranger said. 'I should have known. This is your villa-to-be, and I'm your builder, Joseph bar Jacob.'

Marcus smiled and said, 'Well met indeed. I'm honoured to meet you, Adonai. I was going to ask Nakdimon for a letter of introduction, but now there's no need. I'm surprised to find you here.'

'In a couple of hours you wouldn't have done,' Joseph said. 'But I check the foundations of every structure built in my name, house or palace, paradise or fortress.'

Khosro brought Marcus beer, and Joseph asked for goat's milk, which had to be brought from the hamlet. Kradog set chairs outside his pavilion, which was a plain thing after the ornate pavilion at Claudius' villa, and Joseph sat with Marcus, who drank his beer and called for more.

He said, 'I heard about the marriage of one of your sons: it seems to have been greatly to your credit, if I am permitted to say so.'

Joseph looked keenly at Marcus as though detecting some insinuation.

He said, 'Perhaps,' and then abruptly changed the subject. He went on, 'The foundations of your villa will be of concrete, which the Romans taught us to make. We are always happy to avail ourselves of new technology if it does not conflict with our Law.'

Marcus wondered if he had offended against some point of etiquette of which he knew nothing.

231

'I must be going,' Joseph said. 'I have many houses. One is the other side of Capernaum, and I stay there tonight.'

'Shall we meet again?' Marcus asked.

'I'll be here for the topping out.' He reached into his robes and brought out a piece of tawny stone. 'This is what we shall be using, similar to the Jerusalem stone, though a little lighter in colour. Keep it.'

Joseph made his farewells, then the clerk of works went into the first trees of the olive grove and called out; in minutes Joseph was riding away with a retinue of spearmen who had been resting in the shade. Marcus looked down at the small peice of stone in his hand.

'I'll call this villa after a horse,' he said. 'One of Hektor's horses: Galathë.'

' "Cream Colour"?' said Kradog, whose Greek was greatly improved by this time.

'Exactly. We'll see what our Joseph has to say about *that* particular bit of Gentile rubbish.'

XLII

SECRET

FROM   Military Intelligence Directorate
                    Prætorium, Rome
TO   Intelligence Office Sen. Trib.
                    Prætorium, Jerusalem
DATE   iv before Ides Sept., 775 After
                    City Foundation; vi Tib. C.
SUBJECT   M. DRUSUS SCIPIO, Cent. Fore Spear
                    II Cohort, X Fretensis

Short-term: None.

Long-term: After present tour of service and long leave, Subject to be posted to fighting service elsewhere in the Empire for one lustrum. Following this period, Subject to be detached to Intelligence duties based on Prætorium, Jerusalem.

Release from military service is withheld indefinitely. When Subject's Intelligence work ceases to have value, Subject will become expendable.

P. ÆMILIUS PAULLUS, D.M.I.

XLIII

Meriem was leading a settled and orderly life in the household of Judith of Magdala. Barnabas died six months after Mary's marriage at Cana, but Judith was extremely wealthy, and sought no union with a brother for protection.

Mary had been living with her in-laws at Cana, but came home for the first anniversary of her father's death, for the stone-setting ceremony. She announced that she would be staying for some time. Her husband had gone away for what might be an extended period of study as one of the Jerusalem academies, and Mary felt happier in her old home.

The young Magdalene herself had settled down after marriage. When Meriem had first known the girl she had been wilful and selfish, cruel to slaves, evil-tempered and lazy. Her marriage had changed all that; in fact she seemed transformed.

'My husband said he'd cast seven devils out of me,' she confided to Meriem. 'He meant the Seven Deadly Sins.'

'Well, marriage certainly seems to suit you,' said Meriem. 'Your mother and I thought it would, and we were right, weren't we?'

But despite the outward calm of Meriem's existence, she was in an inner ferment over Mary's husband Jeshua. Before the couple had sat enthroned under their canopy – before the ceremony proper had begun – Jeshua had turned his eyes on Meriem and plumbed the depths of her soul. Meriem had known in that moment that he was aware of everything she had ever said or done, and that she would be free of it, even

234

though the time was not yet. He had nodded to her and smiled, then gone to join his bride.

Meriem's well-developed sense of curiosity had led her earlier to make an inspection of the arrangements for the wedding guests – and she had also rationalized the inspection as being possibly useful in the future, should Judith ever decide to stage some splendid celebration. Meriem was intrigued to find a very considerable number of big jars brimful of cool fresh water: she tasted a drop from each jar like a conscientious housekeeper on her own premises.

It was during the wedding feast that the miraculous happened. Jeshua's mother, also Mary, came to him in agitation, telling him that the wine would be insufficient for the great crowd of guests. Meriem knew of course that among the Jews it was a deep disgrace to run out of food or drink at a wedding feast. Jeshua had seemed angry at first, but then had nodded to his mother and continued the feast. The wine went on flowing in abundance – and it was being taken from the jars which had been full of water when Meriem had tasted them. She had been present throughout the feast, and no substitution had taken place. Water had turned into wine.

XLIV

There were five Jews in the hamlet of Elon, and the old man of whom Marcus had asked the way to the building site was their patriarch; his name was Asa ben Amon. He was bilingual in Aramaic and Greek, his Greek rather better than his Aramaic. At that time there were very many Jews who spoke nothing but Greek.

While the Villa Galathë was building Marcus cultivated the acquaintance of Asa and his family. The hamlet lacked men of working age whatever their creed: the young men had been murdered casually by soldiers of Herod the Great on the way north in the last year of the monster's reign, and by this time they would have been in the prime of life. So Marcus helped his neighbours, sharing food and drink with them in return for undemanding work in the olive grove and the vineyard. For heavy work he hired day labour. Much of this was organized through Kradog, who was permanently in residence. Marcus visited whenever he could.

The Villa Belinuncia and Cynara, away in Gaul of Narbo, were one world, and Marcus knew that he would have to go back to it in due course; but here was a new world, and a new set of interests and responsibilities. He neglected neither of the two worlds. For some years Cynara had been pressing Marcus to purchase equestrian rank, and a month before the Villa Galathë was finished Marcus did so, beginning the process at Antioch: it would be completed in Rome. He decided that when his knighthood came through he would apply to be transferred as knight in charge of an auxiliary cavalry unit, not knowing that the Army had different plans for him. He himself was not a seeker after rank, but it would keep Cynara happy, and had the added advantage of putting him on equal – or more equal – terms with Nakdimon and Joram.

During his local leaves Marcus began the study of Isaiah with Asa in Greek, the Judaic prophecy informed by the Greek spirit of inquiry, and as their studies progressed Marcus gradually made sense of the work, since Asa was able to separate the various sections, point out the threads of continuity, and show Marcus which passages were prose and which poetry. Marcus came to believe that the God of the Jews was the right one for him.

'What's His name?' Marcus asked Asa.

'*Théos* or *Eloi*,' said Asa. 'Either will do.'

Marcus protested, 'But that just means "God." He must have His own proper name.'

'Indeed He has,' said Asa, his beard waggling and his eyes a-twinkle.

'What is it, then?'

'It is not permitted to reveal the names of God to a Gentile.'

Marcus said with exasperation, 'Here is this God, for whom I am perfectly willing to throw away the twelve major and twelve minor gods of the whole Græco-Roman pantheon. I can't see Him, I'm not allowed to make an image of Him, and now you tell me I'm not even allowed to know His name!'

Marcus kept his new-found belief to himself, and continued to do his duty at Antioch. Though Marcus never sought promotion, it was inexorable while serving at legion head-quarters, and Marcus had for some time been Fore Spear of the Second Cohort. The days of military police work were over, and Marcus found himself dividing his time between supervising training and drill, and administration.

'Bullshit and bumf,' he said to Kollura. 'Never mind. A month's leave coming up, and we're off to Elon. We'll have a feast. You and Kradog can look after the Gentiles: Claudius is home from Britain with a wife. Asa ben Amon's women-folk will attend to the Jews and see that they have kosher

237

food with crockery and so on from Asa's household. Lots of wine and beer – and afterwards, a Cakelet.'

There was a babble of conversation from the feast, which had three sections, for Jews, for Gentiles and for the building workers. In fact they were all eating exactly the same food; the difference lay in the preparation and utensils.

All the women were having their own feast in a fourth section in one of the Villa Galathë's dining rooms. Claudius and his party had arrived when everyone had just begun eating, and no introductions had taken place. Joram and Nakdimon were over at the Jews' section with Joseph bar Jacob and Shimmon, Joram holding forth about something and at the same time tearing into a leg of lamb.

Claudius said, 'My wife has heard much about you, Marcus. What's more, she has a gift for you.'

Marcus expressed polite interest, but his mind was else-where, on the clean lines of the cream-coloured stone in front of him. The focus of the villa was its large peristyle with its intricate mosaic floor and large pool. Marcus felt very happy. Khosro belched from where he squatted beside Marcus. Like Joram, he was eating a whole leg of lamb, and when he had finished it he would go and drink with the other slaves.

After they had eaten, Marcus and Claudius went inside the villa to the atrium. Marcus called for Kollura, and she came from the dining room with Claudius' wife. She was a tall woman, twenty or so, with fine breasts and raven-black hair; but her eyes were blue. Claudius and she were plainly in love. He introduced her as Geneura.

Geneura smiled at Marcus and said, 'I have this for you,' handing him a tiny packet wrapped in silk.

Marcus took the packet and thanked Geneura.

Claudius said, 'It's from my sister Cressida.'

Marcus had intended to open the packet later, but now wanted to open it at once. He unwrapped the silk carefully, finding a silver box studded with garnets inside. Marcus opened the box, and took out a little silver whistle, finely engraved. Putting the whistle to his lips he blew . . . and there was no sound. He thought, It should be a Jewish

238

whistle: a whistle you can't hear would go well with a God you can't see.

Geneura said, 'It's a silent dog whistle. Dogs can hear it, but people can't.'

Marcus was saying, 'I don't keep dogs, but it's a pretty little thing, so I'll – '

He stopped speaking. Khosro had rushed into the room looking wildly about him; then he slowed and dropped to one knee before Marcus.

'Please forgive me, Dom'nus,' he panted. 'I thought there might be trouble. I was on the way to the drinking when I heard this high whistle. Didn't know what it was.'

The others looked at one another in some amusement while Marcus blew the whistle again. Khosro winced.

'Aiee! That's it: the whistle!'

Kollura was fanning herself with a large ivory fan.

She said. 'If Khosro can hear his master call when no one else can, it could be most useful. Things aren't always what they seem.'

'Quite right,' said Marcus, and after some more talk with the women, went out with Claudius to find his own drinks. He took a crock of beer and went over to Joseph bar Jacob and his companions, who were drinking wine sparingly. They complimented him on the feast. Marcus made a short speech in praise of Joseph's building, and the conversation became general.

Joseph said to Marcus, 'Have you any children?'

'Three. Twin sons and a daughter.'

He felt the box containing the whistle in his tunic; despite the gift from his mother, Aeron no longer counted as a son; but even at this festive time Marcus felt the twinge of guilt and inner emptiness.

Joseph said, 'I have three sons. The one of whom you spoke is a trouble to me. He's always been wayward and precocious.'

'The one of whom I spoke?'

'Who married at Cana,' Joseph said with a touch of impatience.

Marcus said, 'Yes. I remember now.'

Joseph said, 'There was a man named Judas of Galilee.

239

He formed a party known as the Kenaïm. They are known in Latin as the Sicarii, though I don't suppose you've ever heard of them.'

'I certainly have,' said Marcus. 'At close quarters,' and he recounted the story of how Marcus' comrade Philo had met his death.

Joseph nodded, his face grim.

'There were only a few of them then, but they're getting stronger.' he told Marcus. 'My son has a friend named Simon Zelotes, and I'm afraid of the man's influence. The people of the Kenaïm are sworn to kill everyone who breaks the Law of Moses.'

'Oh,' said Marcus. 'You surprise me. I thought they were just anti-Roman.'

'That too, but they may cause general disturbance. That is why I'm so worried.'

'I expect it'll all come right in the end,' said Marcus.

Privately he decided to send in a written report on the Kenaïm, and was to be surprised later on when called to the intelligence office at Cæsarea: a general air of jocular conspiracy prevailed there concerning Marcus, and it would be seven years before he found out the reason.

Joseph had turned away and was calling for his servants, making ready to leave. Marcus felt a tug at his sleeve, and turned to see Asa, his face full of concern.

'Why, what's the matter, Asa?'

Asa said, 'There are five more Jews coming to live at Elon! Whatever shall we do?'

'I don't understand,' Marcus said. 'I'd have thought you would have been very pleased.'

'Oh,' said Asa. 'I forgot. Our Law says that when ten male Jews dwell in one place, a synagogue must be built. What can we do? We can hardly find the money to put one brick on another!'

Marcus thought for a moment.

He said, 'Never fear: I'll cut your Gordian knot. Wait here, friend.'

Marcus went to Joseph bar Jacob, who turned and said, 'Dominus, I was about to come and say that I must be going, and to tell you that I have greatly enjoyed your feast.'

'Thank you,' said Marcus. 'I wonder whether you can spare a moment before you leave. My old friend and teacher, Asa ben Amon, tells me that if there are ten Jews living in one place there has to be a synagogue.'

'Quite correct,' said Joseph.

Marcus had originally intended to tease Joseph about the name of the villa and its 'Gentile rubbish'; but now he was glad that he had refrained, because it might have soured their relationship. Perhaps he had felt intuitively that there was a way in which they might work together.

'Will you come and speak with the man?' he asked Joseph.

They went over to Asa, and Marcus said, 'This is the great builder, Joseph bar Jacob. What we have to do now is ask him to build a synagogue at Elon, and if he agrees, then I will pay for it.'

INTER SCRIPTUM (v)

Professor John Potts' class had been comparing two documents. One was a facsimile of the complete Isaiah scroll found at Qumran and published by the American Schools of Oriental Research, designated 1QISa, and the other was a facsimile of what had been the earliest known Isaianic text before the Qumran discovery. Fully unrolled, the Qumran scroll was eight yards long by one yard wide, and complete except for a few small lacunæ and tiny holes, easily restored. Potts was concluding his lecture.

'... And so we have made an admittedly superficial comparison of these documents separated by approximately one thousand years. At the beginning of this lecture I said that we should be looking at scribal accuracy. Well, we have seen so few variations between these two texts that I think it fair to say that not until the advent of the word processor have such standards of accuracy been achieved. That's all for now. Next week we'll take a look at the very fragmentary 1QSAb, and go on to the Commentary on Habbakuk.'

Potts stood up and watched his students leave. No one asked a single question. The class had been awed by the scrupulosity of ancient scribal memory: seeing with their own eyes almost identical texts a millennium apart had floored them. Potts grinned as the lecture theatre emptied. Time for coffee.

Potts drove home, thinking of his next week's lecture to that class on the Habbakuk Commentary, 1QPHab. '*For behold, I am arousing the Chaldeans*. . . . This interpretation refers

242

to the Kittim, who are swift and formidable in battle, bent on the destruction of peoples.'

Potts inclined to the view that the Essenes were here using a code. The *pishro* or interpretation of Kittim for Chaldeans led him to agree with the view that the Kittim were the Romans.

He switched on the radio, listening to the latest horror's recounting – a skyjack – among the commercials, and then switched off in disgust.

Bent on the destruction of peoples. To the Essenes, perhaps the Romans had seemed that way, but the Essenes were never allied with Jesus. Potts believed that Jesus must have studied Essene doctrines, but his way was of peace, while the Essenes were ready to allow violence against 'the wicked.' And there the whole basis of their teaching foundered, since 'the wicked' would inevitably be those who disagreed with the sect. Jesus had gone into the desert and returned bearing the message of love prefigured in Isaiah, a message intolerable even then, when the world lived by its own sets of standards and values.

Solzhenitsyn had been right, Potts thought: the West had forgotten God. That the communist world had abandoned God needed saying too. And yet these were only partial truths. For 'the West' read 'western commercial society'; for 'the communist world' read 'the communist hierarchy' and that would perhaps be closer to the truth. Helen was baptized and confirmed, and everywhere small people were swimming against the tide.

Helen was not yet home. Potts poured his finger of malt whisky and took it to his study, where he sat down with the air letter from Doctor Waldegrave, which had arrived two days before.

Waldegrave had written:

'Publius Drusus Scipio was given a grant of lands *mutatæ*. That is the only reference, but it is quite enough for us. He exchanged his lands in Galilee for lands *apud Rhedæ* in Narbonnese Gaul. You might have walked the very ground yourself!'

Potts shook his head. He recalled leaning against an oak

243

tree, long ruined by repeated lightning strikes. The tree might have flourished for centuries, until, for example, someone diverted a watercourse in such a way as to provide a path for lightning through the tree. Potts might have touched a tree which had been green and growing in the days of the centurion, whose father had possessed land near Rhedæ. It might even have been inherited by M. Drusus Scipio; but Potts would never know one way or the other.

XLV

Marcus was forty years old. He had completed nineteen years of active service, and was on his fifth long leave, twenty-four years after joining the Army.

Now Marcus was back at the Villa Belinuncia, and he was extremely busy. The estate was running smoothly, and would have continued in this way even if Marcus had not returned; but he felt the natural compulsion to bring himself up to date: he spent the first month touring the estate, and two more weeks closeted with accounts and other documents.

His children engrossed him, too. The twins were sixteen, and his first sight of them had astonished Marcus. A parent seeing his children daily finds himself amazed at the pubertal change. To Marcus, who had not seen them since they were eleven, they were at first unrecognizable young men. And his daughter Octavia was on the verge of womanhood at eleven.

Cynara had changed little if at all in outward appearance, and after their usual passionate first weeks she and Marcus lived in amicable domesticity. But he sensed a certain reserve in her from time to time, and it puzzled him.

Marcus stroked Liutpold's nose, while at the same time Triutinne lipped his tunic sleeve and pulled; he clouted her affectionately and then resumed his inspection of the two studs with the others.

Akbar said, 'We need more water down here. Men are always carrying water down from the reservoir when they could be better employed doing something else.'

Marcus took out his silver whistle and blew silently.

Khosro appeared and Marcus said, 'Fetch me my major-domo, Khosro.'

Appius said, 'I still don't understand. How does Khosro know he's to come when you just breathe into that thing?'

'Syrian magic,' said Siegfrith darkly.

Marcus ignored this. He waited until Festus joined the group and then led the way uphill. He had told no one the secret of the silent whistle. They walked up to the reservoir and looked down from it to the corral and the stable buildings.

'What do you think, Festus?' Marcus asked. 'Could we run a feeder down from here to some dip in the ground? There's a hollow in front of that tree.'

Festus pursed his lips. There were streaks of grey now in the bush of black hair. His father Doratus had died the month before Marcus' return, but Marcus had mourned him only briefly: the man had died in his sleep after a full and happy life of devious twists and turns; but always Doratus had been in control of himself and others, and he would have wished no hypocritical expressions of grief.

'I don't see any problem,' Festus said.

Marcellus had been looking over the reservoir. By this time it had grown rich in animalculæ and algal growths; a bloom of algæ tinted the surface where fish rose dimpling it.

Marcellus said, 'You could have a cascade down to a pond, Father. I know just how to do it.'

'Very well, then. You're in charge,' said Marcus. And to Festus: 'Give him what he wants, within reason. We'll see how he shapes up.'

They walked the ground again, and Appius said, 'I think you'll find Marcellus shapes up very well. He's always with the vilicus and he's learned a lot.'

Marcus asked, 'What about yourself?'

Siegfrith and Akbar both spoke at once, and Marcus held up a hand for silence.

Then he said, 'Akbar?'

Akbar said, 'He's become a wizard with horses. Primus too but more of him later. You recall, Dominus, that you left the key to your chest with the Lady Cynara?'

'Of course.'

Akbar whispered in Appius' ear, and the youth ran swiftly away. Marcus raised his eyebrows, but said nothing: if he could have his secrets, so could other people. He continued his tour of inspection, and they found Primus in a large shed beside a small corral.

Akbar said. 'You gave Primus two horses, stallion and mare. See the ponies he has bred?'

There were eight ponies in the corral together with their parents.

'Primus is breeding them for chariot racing,' Akbar went on. 'He'll be in the shed.'

Primus had learned how to build chariots, and was putting the finishing touches to a *biga*, a two-horse racing chariot. After the Celtic and Gaulish fashion he had used metal tubing for the axle and pole; the pole was cunningly inlaid with enamel. The chariot-builder looked up at Marcus with a grin, then jumped to his feet.

'Greetings, Dominus,' he said. 'I hope you will think I've used your gifts well. The second generation of stock is outside. I sold the first for capital to buy materials to build my chariots. Fifty per cent of net profits I give to my father for the estate.'

Marcus clapped Primus on the shoulder and said, 'Well done, Primus! Fifty per cent is too much. Tell your father we take twenty, and ask him to make the adjustment retrospective.'

Primus beamed and blurted out words of gratitude, but Marcus had turned away, hearing Appius call for him. He went outside, and his mouth tightened. His son was mounted, and in his hand he held Drusus' compound bow.

Marcus said angrily, 'What play-acting is this?'

Appius said nothing. He took an arrow from the quiver at his shoulder, nocked it . . . and drew the bow. Marcus caught his breath with amazement. Very gently Appius released the tension until the bowstring was slack, then replaced the arrow in its quiver.

'That is impossible,' said Marcus. 'Yet I've just seen it myself!'

Siegfrith said, 'Your son Appius can put out his full strength.'

Marcus knew what the instructor meant. Like absolute pitch, the ability to put out full strength is a rare gift. Under extreme stress – particularly when a loved one's life is threatened – human beings are capable of feats of strength quite impossible under normal conditions. But some few people can do this at will, and Appius was one of them.

Marcus breathed out heavily and said, 'I was going to scold you, Appius, but I've changed my mind. The bow is yours.'

'Thank you, Father!'

Marcellus took four slaves, and under his direction they made a watercourse with a cascade leading to the hollow ground by the oak tree; he himself made a sluice outside a retaining wall.

When the time came everyone on the estate who was free assembled. Festus wanted Marcus to sacrifice a sheep to the Genius of the Place, but Marcus curtly refused, telling Festus to do it himself if he felt so inclined.

Festus said, 'But I cannot. It's *your* duty as head of the household.'

'No more,' said Marcus. 'I follow a different God now.'

So there was no sacrifice, but Marcus said, 'Don't worry: if all goes to plan we'll have a feast.'

Phalaris had been standing with Siegfrith, but now he came to Marcus and said, 'I don't think my charges have much need of me any more. Do you wish me to leave?'

The tutor had filled out with the passage of the years, and had taught the boys well in their subjects. Also, Phalaris had an extremely long span of attention, and he knew many aids to learning: he had passed on these abilities to Marcellus and Appius.

Marcus said, 'No, Phalaris, I don't want you to leave. You have a home and stipend here for as long as you want. It's the only way I can make certain of conversing in good Greek when I come back.'

Phalaris flushed with pleasure, and stood by while Marcellus dug away the retaining wall and lifted open the sluicegate. The watercourse which had been excavated was lined with concrete; water gushed and chuckled along, people making the excited noises which such an occasion provokes. The water tumbled splashing down the cascade, and the pond began to fill. Marcus applauded with the rest. Marcellus had carried out his father's suggestion perfectly. Marcus told off the four slaves to spell one another and close the sluice when the pond was full, then went off happily to the feast with his sons. The horses would get their water. But Marcus had once alluded to one of the Fates, Lachesis, who spins the thread of a man's life while Klotho holds the distaff. They were two of the Cruel Fates in the pantheon which Marcus had abandoned – called cruel because of their total indifference to human desires; and the third was Atropos, who cuts the thread and ends life.

Marcus made no friends among the other estate owners in and around Rhedæ, but Cynara kept up a social life among their womenfolk, and had made a particular friend of a woman named Lavinia, the wife of a landowner who lived a few miles away towards Carcaso. Lavinia was blonde, Junonically built, with cornflower blue eyes; she visited Cynara two or three times a month.

One afternoon Marcus announced his intention of riding to Arelate with Akbar, but after twenty minutes his horse cast a shoe and he turned back, telling Akbar that he should go on; Marcus would walk back and take a fresh horse. He would meet Akbar later on.

When Marcus led the horse in he was sweaty. He gave it to a groom and ordered a fresh mount, but the walk had made him thirsty, and he went to his quarters in search of beer. Passing the bedroom which he and Cynara shared he heard strange sounds, and peered in. Cynara and Lavinia were lying naked on the bed, heads between each other's thighs, gobbling, slurping and moaning, each oblivious of everything but pleasure.

Marcus burst out into a huge peal of laughter. The lurching bodies on the bed were suddenly still; then two smeared faces detached themselves and looked up at Marcus in shock and embarrassment.

Marcus said, 'Well, a sapphic afternoon. I'm sorry I interrupted: just passing by for some beer.'

The women had sat up, and Cynara said accusingly, 'You said you were riding to Arelate.'

'We started, but I had to come back. Get yourselves cleaned up and dressed. I'll see you in the peristyle.'

Marcus sat with his beer by the pool. He had never had the remotest suspicion that Cynara found her own sex attractive, and when she joined him – telling him that Lavinia had found a pressing reason for going home – he looked at his wife with some interest.

He said, 'I never knew you liked the pleasures of Lesbos. When did that start?'

Cynara said, 'Well, Marcus, I was a virgin when we married, as you well know. But I've been going with girls since I was about fourteen. I never do when you're here, that is in the usual way of things. When you're away I never do anything else. This afternoon . . . well, it just happened.'

'Did you finish things off?'

'No. Lavinia was so ashamed she just ran away as soon as she could.'

Marcus stood up, took Cynara's hand and pulled her to her feet.

He said, 'I don't know why it is, but the thought of you two sends me into a fury of desire. Come now, and we'll finish what was begun.'

They made love, and afterwards Marcus lay alone thinking; Cynara went to bathe. A few lines of a song were going through Marcus' head:

'What is here the longing more than other,
Here in this mad heart? And who the lovely
One beloved thou wouldst lure to loving?
Sappho, who wrongs thee?'

Marcus was frowning as his memory took him back to Meriem. He began to doze, then fell fast asleep, and never got to Arelate that day.

It was a dull and muggy afternoon, very hot and humid. In such conditions running water is irresistibly attractive to children. The water in the pond had fallen in level, and Octavia was easily able to persuade a slave to open the sluice gate. She and some twenty other children played in the stream, ignoring the rumbling sky as thunderheads built up along the coast to the south-west. Wet and muddy, shouting and screaming as they splashed one another, the children were having a splendid time.

Cynara came along carrying a towel in search of her daughter; it was time for Octavia's lesson with Phalaris. At first Cynara could not identify the girl in the welter of playing children among the jewelled water-drops; but at length she leaned over and took Octavia by her arm, pulling her out and getting wet too.

'Come along, my girl,' she said. 'Lesson time.'

Gasping, Octavia said, 'I'd forgotten, Lady Mother. We were having such fun!'

Marcus was in the estate office going through some accounts with Casca and Milo. The pair amused Marcus, for they were forever shifting position, sweating, dabbing necks and brows. This kind of heat affected Marcus not at all while he was in a loose civilian tunic; in armoured military uniform he would have sweated gently.

The storm broke overhead quite without warning. The interior of the office lit up with the dazzle of the lightning flash, and the simultaneous thunderclap deafened the three men for a moment; then they were aware of babbling and screams, this time not of play but of shock and agony. They hurried outside.

Cynara had taken her daughter over to the oak tree and begun to dry her when the lightning had struck. And now Marcus beheld the smoking riven tree, children stumbling out of the water, two or three badly burned, the body of his wife lying still at the foot of the tree with her clothes on fire, and Octavia writhing feebly beside her. Marcus rushed uphill, splashed water at the burning clothes, but saw at the same moment that Cynara was dead, riven and burnt like the tree, as was Octavia. As Marcus went to her, his daughter stopped moving. A great cry burst from him at the loss of all the love and promise. When Milo and Casca reached him he was kneeling in the pouring rain, with his hands on the corpses of his loved ones.

After the obsequies Marcus shut himself away for two

251

days in bed without food or water, then on the third day he came out again and went to his study.

His copy of Isaiah consisted of eight scrolls, each about three feet square. Marcus was carrying them all under his arm when he met Festus.

Marcus said, 'Festus, some months ago I remember telling you that I worshipped a different God. That was the God of the Jews. I have paid for it dearly. It seems to me that the Jewish God may reign in Syria Palæstina, but not in Gaul of Narbo. Call him Zeus Pater or Jupiter, *He* was the one who sent the bolt from heaven, and Atropos the Cruel Fate that cut off the lives of my wife and daughter. Now I hold here a book of one of the prophets of this Jewish God, and I am going to burn it. After that I shall make appropriate sacrifices to the twelve great gods which Greece and Rome hold in common.'

'May I see?' asked Festus, and Marcus handed him the Book of Isaiah.

Festus examined the scrolls and counted them, feeling their texture. Then he looked up at Marcus.

He said, 'I think it would be a pity to burn all this. It's good soft leather. All that squiggly foreign writing spoils it for other purposes, but we've got sixteen breechclouts for slaves here.'

Marcus thought for a moment, then his lips twisted in an ironic grin.

'Keep them, Festus,' he said. 'Sixteen slaves will sit in comfort, their arses wrapped in Isaiah.'

XLVI

On the fifth day before the Ides of July, eleventh year of Tiberius Cæsar, Servius Claudius Baratanicus at X Fretensis to his friend M. Drusus Scipio at III Ægypta, greetings.

I write to say that I returned to Antioch from local leave three days ago, and on both my outward and return journeys called at the Villa Galathë, where all is well. Your steward keeps all in good order: there is a fine vintage and the olive crop looks as though there will be a bumper harvest.

I believe you were wise not to bring over the nucleus of a stud to your villa. Joram and Nakdimon would be in competition with you. As it is you have their friendship. Your villagers at Elon think enormously well of you, not only for the synagogue you built for the Jews there, but also for your connections with such important people. The donation by Joram of the ritual bath, and the furniture of candlestick, ram's horn and whatnot impressively and stylishly handed over by Nakdimon, simply add to your kudos.

Kradog visits my villa every two months or so on the pretext of asking advice from my own steward, but in fact to talk with Geneura in their common tongue. They get on so well it's a good thing I can never have grounds for jealousy!

Things are very quiet here – though I don't know about Judæa. There cannot be much going on, or we'd have heard about it; as far as I know our detached maniples are still shuttling between Cæsarea and Jerusalem. One small item of news. There is a new Procurator down there, an equestrian. L. Pontius Pilatus, 'Speared' because his old man won the Spear of Honour on some battlefield. Valerius Gratus has bogged off with a shipload of loot, and this one'll be just like the rest of them, out for Number One. Still, it'll all be the same in a thousand years. . . . So from the fleshpots of Antioch to the fleshpots of Alex, with my remembrances to Kollura, farewell.

XLVII

The wind blew strongly and was as hot as though it blew straight out of an oven, giving Marcus, his century and supernumeraries dry, cracked lips, parched mouths and throats and incessant, insatiable thirst. Behind them and far below the Red Sea stretched like a purple pool shimmering in the heat. They marched along a rocky path past a Roman quarry where slaves toiled and some of them died in their chains and under the foreman's lash. The soldiers spared hardly a glance for the slaves; the detached maniple of III Ægypta was on the march in Africa into the blistering southerly wind. These soldiers would not falter or faint. If they had been able, they would have grumbled, but until they could find water they had no voices to grumble with. But they would march on until their centurion called a halt; and if they had to, they would fight for the rest of the day without quenching their thirst. It was this simple quality of sheer, plodding endurance and steadiness which had helped to make the Roman Empire.

The deaths of Cynara and Octavia had sent Marcus into an inward desolation of guilt. The concept of an Act of God absolving mankind from blame was wholly alien to his thinking. The lightning bolt had been sent by the Most High Zeus to punish Marcus, and for no other reason. He had sought a priest of Apollo and undergone a ritual cleansing, then sacrificed to all the gods, afterwards scarcely daring to speak to anyone except Khosro, beyond giving necessary instructions to household staff. When his orders for Egypt had arrived Marcus had abased himself at the altar to

255

Fortuna, but said no prayer. He had secretly hoped that the gods were beginning to look favourably upon him again, for he had desperately wanted to avoid a return to Syria Palæstina. It had never occurred to him that he was simply fitting in with the Army's long-term plans. Marcus had left Festus and Livia in charge at home, and gone to Alexandria determined to do his duty and appease the gods.

So here he was, marching with his century in the burning wind. The service had almost killed Marcus to begin with, for he had grown plump and unfit for combat during his long leave; his bereavement and mental agony compounded his lack of training. Only his iron constitution saved him, but now he was fit and spare.

The country was infested with snakes, and the supernumeraries went on ahead, carrying sticks or swords and clearing the line of march. Two hours before dark they found themselves in among barren brown and yellow rocks which closed in around them. They came to a wellspring: a shallow rock basin fringed by ferns. The slaves and others ran to the water croaking with delight like a flock of crows. The Romans built their camp. They could not dig a ditch round it because of the terrain, so they lugged together a rampart of stones at a distance from the wooden walls; and only after that work was complete did they drink, Marcus last, his mouth streaming with sweet, cool water. They devoured their rations of hard bread, dates and olives washed down with more water: they felt that they could never get enough of it. Some of them wondered at this. Although body armour had been unbearable to the touch, they had not been aware of sweating. The fact was that their sweat had evaporated at once throughout the march, and they were all dehydrated.

After everyone had washed, Marcus held a foot inspection and then attended to himself. At last he sat down, taking out the silver whistle and blowing for Khosro. Then he smiled at his absence of mind: not even Khosro could hear him in Alexandria.

He looked idly at the whistle. Soon after he had acquired Cressida's gift by way of Geneura, Marcus had noticed Latin letters among the delicate chasing. They read MUCRAMDA. Marcus was as used to reading from right to left as from left to right, and sometimes alternately; and he was also accustomed to finding out for himself the spaces between words. *Ad Marcum* – 'To Marcus' – leaped out at him.

And now, the sun going down quickly over Africa, he thought of Cressida and some lines of poetry from long ago came into his mind:

> Of little threads our life is spun,
> And he spins ill, who misses one.
> But is thy fair Eugenia cold?
> Yet Helen had an equal grace,
> And Juliet's was as fair a face,
> And now their years are told.

P. Horatius Flaccus, he thought, instilled into him in Illyria by Pylades. And there was something else by the same poet:

> I am not such as in the reign
> Of the good Cynara I was; refrain,
> Sour mother of sweet loves, forbear
> To bend a man, now at his fiftieth year. . . .

Mortal things touching the mind, Marcus drowsed; too much sadness in life. . . . He jerked awake, made his rounds and checked the sentries, then went to bed by torchlight.

Marcus was up in the dark next morning, and as the sky began to pale he pulled in the sentries and made every soldier assume the tortoise formation, locking his own shield in above his head as well; the supernumeraries cowered inside the formation. The dawn attack came, and the Romans stood stolidly almost in boredom as the first flight of flimsy little arrows pattered on their shields, arrows tipped with deadly venom which would kill a man in minutes. The tribesmen never varied their tactics when they made contact with Roman troops: perhaps they were not very bright, or had religious reasons for their behaviour. The dawn flight of arrows was always poisoned, but none afterwards. Perhaps they simply ran out of poison, Marcus thought as he yelled orders.

They spent the day hunting and killing these puny opponents of Rome, little sun-dried men, wiry and full of stamina, but powerless. They would not stand to battle, and

257

the soldiers could throw the heavier of their two spears as far as the tribesmen could shoot with the bow. In twos and threes they were flushed from cover and transfixed, with no Roman casualties.

They made camp again by the well that night, and at the dawn stand-to no arrows clattered onto the tortoise. So they struck camp and refilled water bottles, then resumed their line of march. Until late morning they saw no sign of life beyond the snakes and a few spiny grey rats; then at midday the unit reached a small oasis with the miserable huts of the tribe huddled in the shade of palms. There were no menfolk there, only the women and children, and there was nothing worth looting. But there *were* the women, so Marcus gave a nod to his decurion, and turned away.

Half an hour later the huts were burning, and there was no person of the tribe still living. Marcus and his people moved away. In two days the rocks gave way to sand, and in two more days they could see the band of deep green on the horizon where Nile-fed crops and vegetation grew. Soon they would be back in Thebes and Marcus would make his report: another small patch of territory made safe for Rome.

XLVII

After a year based on Thebes Marcus was given two months' leave. His movement order in his gold box, where he carried such things along with its permanent contents, he sailed down the Nile in an Army ship: north past Ptolemais, Hermopolis, Oxyrhyncus and Memphis, and past monuments of ancient Egypt. Huge, ponderous and mysterious, the sun-baked pillars and temples reared into the sky, gigantic pharaohs and animal-headed gods staring into the morning sun. Marcus poured furtive libations to them. Better safe than sorry.

At the delta the ship took a north-westerly arm of the river to Rosetta on the coast. Marcus got a horse from the Army staging post and rode along the beach with the dazzle of the salt lake on his left. It was an easy ride; the horse he had signed for was hard-mouthed but docile, and Marcus delighted in the sea breeze on his face, cool and refreshing after his time in the interior in the steamy heat of Thebes and the oven-blasts of the Red Sea uplands. By the time he reached the headquarters of III Ægypta Marcus was revivified.

He handed over the horse to an ostler and received his chit for it, then handed in his movement order at the Camp Prefect's office in the Prætorium. Then he was free, though he would have written reports to complete while on furlough.

Marcus went to the baths and changed into civilian clothes. On his way out of the camp he called at the office of the First Spear.

'Can you do something for me?' Marcus asked. 'It's over

two years since I applied for a posting to cavalry. Could you look in Records and see what's happened to it?'

The First Spear was ten years older than Marcus, grizzled and with one eye. He peered up at Marcus with it and grinned, showing surprisingly good teeth.

'I don't need to look,' he said. 'I know. Part of my job, isn't it? Your application's shelved. Don't ask me why, because I can't tell you. All I can say is that you'll never get into the cavalry.'

Marcus stared at him, then shrugged.

He said, 'Oh, well. Eighteen months and my time's served. I've got all the horses I need at home.'

The First Spear smiled pleasantly, but in the one eye there was a hint of something which Marcus was unable to fathom.

'Enjoy the thought,' said the First Spear. 'And have a good leave.'

Marcus had remained celibate throughout his service in Upper Egypt from choice, and so had Kollura: Khosro had seen to that, whatever her private inclinations might have been. She and Marcus spent two days in bed, attended by the three giggling girls supervised by Khosro. At forty-three Marcus was still extremely fit; his service in the uplands of the Red Sea had brought him to a physical peak. He and Kollura made love repeatedly; and Marcus thought often of Cynara. He remembered the afternoon, shortly before her death, when he had surprised Cynara with the woman Lavinia. He could not understand the reason, but this had startled him into a sexual rejuvenation which, for a few brief days, had revitalized their marriage. Then Cynara had been blasted from him, and his daughter also.

Marcus presented Kollura with gifts: an ivory comb studded with jewels, a necklace of crocodile teeth tipped with gold, and a tiny amethyst statuette of Isis suckling Horus.

He took this back from her and studied it.

'What gods reign in this city?'

Kollura pouted and said, 'How should I know? That slave of yours has kept me so close I might as well have been in prison. Who cares about the gods?'

'I do, for one,' said Marcus. 'I mean to take Khosro and

find out. A man neglects ruling deities at his peril, as I have reason to know.' He handed back the statuette and added, 'Khosro has done his duty and done it well, but there is something in what you say. I will find out about the gods, but first you shall enjoy yourself.'

They saw the sights as Drusus had done many years earlier; but their tastes were more far-ranging than Drusus' had been. They went to the theatre and the amphitheatre; the hippodrome. They saw *The Boastful Soldier* of Plautus, preceded by an obscene farce, both in Latin; then they went to see Aristophanes' *Lysistrata*, in Greek.

'Men and women, both put in their places,' said Marcus as he bought Kollura sweetmeats at a stall. 'Are you enjoying yourself?'

Kollura nodded, eyes wide and mouth full, her ivory fan busy in one hand.

They watched the street shows: conjurors and acrobats, fire-eaters and strong men, dancing bears and jugglers. They were watching a juggler when the attack came, their eyes held by the sucession of dazzling crystal balls which the showman was manipulating.

They heard a thud and a grunt behind them. Marcus swung round to see Khosro falling to the ground unconscious, felled by a blow from the haft of a dagger. Marcus saw a big man, eyes flashing in a mass of black hair and beard under a phrygian cap, the dagger reversed in an upstroke at Marcus and the gold in his purse. He had no time to reach for his own knife, yet he would be able to disarm the man without difficulty. But Kollura stepped in front of him inside the man's dagger arm and stroked her fan across his eyes. He screamed and dropped the dagger while Marcus watched in amazement.

A Roman foot patrol was on the scene quickly. Marcus held the sobbing thief until they arrived. Establishing his identity he said, 'This man has been blinded. I hand him over to you.'

Khosro was getting to his feet, rubbing his head bemusedly.

'What happened?' he asked.

Marcus said, 'You were watching that juggler too closely.

261

You will never watch a juggler again.' Then he turned to Kollura. 'What did you do?'

A small crowd had gathered, but it was beginning to disperse now that the excitement was over. Kollura had her fan open again, but she closed it as she had done when the thief attacked, and a small blade snapped out of the head; then she showed Marcus the small catch on the handle of the fan which activated the spring below the blade. Retracting it into concealment she said, 'Remember, Marcus? I told you once things are not always what they seem.'

A few days later Marcus met another centurion on leave from Thebes. His name was Lucius Pompilius Massilus, and he was as black as Marcus' first centurion, Gaius Naso. They had a few drinks together, and Marcus mentioned that he was trying to find which gods held sway in Alexandria.

Fireball, for that was the man's nickname because of his bustling manner, laughed and said, 'All the gods there are. But I worship only one.'

'Like the Jews, you mean?'

'No,' said Fireball. 'Not at all like the Jews. This is a military god. And it's secret.'

'Can I get to know the secret?' Marcus asked.

'Certainly,' Fireball said. 'We're looking for people like you. You'd better show me where you live. I'll call for you in the morning while it's still dark. There will be an initiation into the lowest grade, and so you can see what you'd be in for.'

He was as good as his word. The main streets of Alexandria – like Rome and Antioch – were lighted at night, but soon Fireball hired a linkman and said something to him. The man preceded them into the dark sidestreets with his flaming torch held aloft; Khosro brought up the rear, alert as a hunting lynx.

Fireball said, 'My nickname got me into this, in a way. You see, the god I spoke of is the god of light, in perpetual struggle with darkness and evil. He is known as Mithra, or Mithras in Greek. He was born out of a rock, and he pursued a sacred bull, which he sacrificed, as we do in memory of him; he ascended into heaven in the Chariot of the Sun. We

262

have to live according to strict rules, and then after death on earth we shall live for ever. What other god should a man with my nickname follow?'

'I see the sense of that,' said Marcus.

They reached an opulent house on the outskirts of the city. Pompilius Massilus paid off the linkman, told Marcus to send Khosro to the kitchens, where he would find food and drink, then led Marcus down a flight of steps, pushing aside a hanging.

There were a dozen men standing in a cellar or crypt. At the far end of the room there was a deep recess with a grille, and in front of it a bull was tethered. Below the bull's head and neck Marcus could see the head and naked shoulders of a man who was standing in a cavity in the marble floor. Four men held the bull with ropes at the rear legs, but one man held its head easily by the nose-ring. Another man, presumably the chief priest, stood by with a short sword, chanting sonorously.

'What language is that?' Marcus asked quietly.

Fireball said, 'It's Persian. I don't understand it any more than you do, but it's all going to be translated into Latin and Greek. . . . Watch now.'

The light was growing in the room. The priest's chanting redoubled in volume, the congregation calling out responses. Then all were silent.

The bull bellowed as though forewarned of what would happen to it. The sun's dawn rays blazed in an aureole around the animal's head and the priest struck, a massive blow into the jugular, twisting and rending. The man below raised his arms and bathed in the torrent of blood, then climbed out quickly before the animal collapsed on top of him. He stood to one side and the dying bull's head was laid where the man had stood, so that the blood could drain away. There was a short benediction, and the service was over.

Marcus collected Khosro from the kitchens; he said he was full of the best bread he had ever tasted.

Shortly Marcus said, 'Well, we haven't had any breakfast. Come on, Fireball.'

They found a street stall and ate bread and cheese washed

down with goat's milk. Fireball's proselytizing mood had been heightened by the ceremony, and he talked enthusiastically about Mithraism. Marcus was doubtful. Kissing his hand to the sun was one thing; sacrificing bulls to it seemed a little too much.

'It all brings *purity!*' exclaimed Fireball hotly. 'To follow the example of Mithras, and to have eternal life. Doesn't that appeal to you?'

Marcus said, 'I bought my concubine a statuette of Isis and Horus. The priests of Isis promise eternal life.'

'Charlatans!' Fireball snorted. 'Come with me and I'll show you.'

They went to a temple of Isis, where there was a large congregation, confined to two-thirds the length of the building; the remaining area was roped off, and within it were larger-than-life statues of Osiris and Isis, horned head symbolizing the cow of fertility; she held Horus in her arms. Osiris the Many-Eyed was also horned, as the Ox. The priests were going through a rigmarole as Marcus and Fireball entered, Khosro behind them . . . and the statues began to move, Osiris backwards until the statue disappeared from view through some hangings, the Setting Sun, while Isis moved forward as the Dawn and Rebirth: the congregation went '*Ooh*' and '*Aah*' at this apparent miracle.

Khosro said. 'Devils' foreign magic!'

And the Dawn stood with the promise of eternal life in her arms. When the service had finished and the congregation dispersed Fireball said to Marcus, 'Come on!' and ran forward, leaping the barrier with Marcus behind him. Scattering clucking priests the two men shoved through the hangings behind which the statue of Osiris had vanished. It stood there immobile on a track, next to a cylinder with a fire beneath it. Fireball yanked at a connecting pipe, and there was a jet of steam.

A priest shouted, 'You defame the holy temple of Isis!'

Fireball ignored him and said to Marcus, 'See what I mean? They work miracles – with steam.'

Khosro had his dagger out, and circled protectively as the two Romans left the temple.

Marcus said, 'I don't understand how they do it.'

'Simple,' said Fireball. 'You've seen a pot boiling with a lid on top. The lid bobs up and down. Steam can push things. It pushes those charlatans' statues: as simple as that!'

They were passing through a market, dozens of stalls set up with produce from the countryside.

Fireball said, 'I have to leave you now.' His voice rose in intensity: 'Come to Mithras, man!'

Marcus said loudly, 'Don't push me, Fireball: I'll make up my own mind. If I decide anything I'll come to the leave camp; otherwise I'll see you again at Thebes. Have a good time.'

Fireball paused, then nodded and pushed his way through the throng of people shopping and chaffering round the stalls. Marcus felt a sudden grip on his tunic and turned swiftly to see an old woman; Khosro had already intercepted her, but Marcus waved him aside.

'What is it, Grandmother?'

'He said, "That is Klitos",' the old woman quavered. 'Will you come, great lord?'

He stared at her, the thin white hair under a headscarf, the brown face a map of wrinkles, faded dark eyes slitted as she looked up at him in the almost vertical noonday sun. He smelt fruit and human bodies, hearing the chatter and babble of voices in his ears. *Klitos?*

They had no more than a couple of yards to go, to a stall piled high with fruit and vegetables, and standing at the side of it a man who had once been tall, but was now stooped and white-haired with age. The old woman called, 'Husband?' and the old man took a couple of steps forward holding onto the side of the stall. He was crippled, Marcus saw, legs deformed, and as he looked at the questing directionless head he could see that the man was blind also, the eyes in the amber-black old face frosted with cataract.

'Have you brought him?' asked the old man. 'Where is Klitos?'

Marcus stepped close and said, 'Old one, who are you to talk of Klitos?'

'It *is* you!' the old man said triumphantly. 'I knew your voice at once. Klitos, Klitos, they gave you a Roman name,

265

but I've forgotten what it was. Don't you remember . . . Placidus?'

Then the two men were holding each other and weeping, while the old crone and the slave looked on in mystified amazement.

XLIX

Marcus sat in the small courtyard of the house where Placidus lived with his wife and three sons, who worked the smallholding which Placidus owned while the old couple sold the produce at market. One of the sons had come to pack up the stall on a donkey-cart, and Marcus had gone home with them. Now he and Placidus sat drinking beer together; Marcus thought with sorrow of the cruel sport which the years make of humankind.

They talked of old times, and then Marcus asked, 'How long have you been blind, Placidus?'

Placidus said, 'I'm not quite sure. About three years, I think. Totally blind, I mean: my sight started to dim some years before that. It's not so bad. We're not rich, but we make a living, and we're never short of food or beer. I reckon I've seen everything in my time, and I never was a reading man, so who cares? It would have been different without those lads. They're all married, but we get looked after a treat.'

Marcus said, 'Have some more beer,' and refilled Placidus' pot.

'Thanks,' said Placidus. 'Talking of reading, what happened to old Pylades?'

'Dead long ago,' said Marcus. 'My mother too. And I'm a widower. I've got a girl here, though I found her first in Galilee.'

That started another round of questions and answers, but when Marcus had brought Placidus further up to date he broke off.

'Tell me what happened to my father,' he said.

Placidus sighed, and then recounted what had happened to the ill-fated party, Targui's escape, and his own.

'I got to the next tribe, dragging myself eastward. Then I paid for care and shelter until I could walk. I kept heading east, doing odd jobs along the way to Leptis Magna. There I joined a camel caravan and came here. I married the daughter of the man who owned this little place, and when he died it came to me.'

Marcus touched him briefly on the shoulder and said, 'You could come to my estate, in Gaul or Galilee, all of you. You'd never lack for anything. What do you say?'

'I'm grateful,' said Placidus. 'But I'm too old and set in my ways. And I'm not a citizen, but I'm under the Peace here. Yet to the south the regiments of *my* people run with spears through the grass. I'm in Africa, and that's where I belong.'

Marcus blew for Khosro, who came in and stood by; Marcus turned back to Placidus.

Marcus said, 'You've got it both ways, Placidus, and you have found wisdom. Now tell me: was Targui right when he spoke of the curse of Rome?'

Placidus considered Marcus' words, turning his beer pot in his hands and staring down with his sightless eyes, but employing his inner illumination.

Then he said, 'It depends who you are, and it follows from what I've just been saying. No matter what tag they put on you, Klitos or Marcus or Drusus Scipio, you are the same: your own man. And you are in and of the Roman Peace. I'm inside and outside, as I said. But when I got back inside I was never so glad in my life. For Targui it was just the opposite: he was a caged hawk, and his freedom was somewhere else. Who can make rules, in the end, for what a man is or does?'

'I wonder,' said Marcus. 'I must go. But I'll come and visit when I can. It's so good to have met you again, Placidus. And now at last I know what really happened to my poor father.'

L

Marcus said irritably, 'I need to be three people!'

He was lying in bed with Kollura, hands behind his head and one knee bent; Kollura was tracing the network of scars on his arms and legs, tickling him, but Marcus took no notice.

'I want to be with you when my long leave comes up,' he went on. 'I want to be in Galilee. It's too long since I saw Kradog and the Villa Galathë. And I *have* to be in Gaul. It's a puzzle.'

Marcus was on his second local leave, splendidly fit. Soon after returning to Thebes he had gone down with fever, but that was a year ago, and he had long since recovered. But his service based on Thebes had become a hardship to him. And the Army was not letting Marcus go. The date of his time-expiry had come and gone, and when he had asked a military tribune about this, the officer had shrugged his shoulders and said, 'Rome still has need of you.'

'It's a puzzle,' Marcus repeated.

Kollura stopped trying to tickle him. She slid up onto his chest and said, 'Solve a bit of it, anyway. Take me with you.'

Marcus sat upright, making Kollura grunt as she was slewed round with the force of his movement.

'Yes!' he exclaimed. 'That's it! We go to Galilee together, spend a month there, and then together we sail for Gaul of Narbo. Why didn't I think of that before?'

Marcus went to visit Placidus, and took gifts: a fine oil lamp for the old woman, and a *mancala* board for his old instructor. Both were delighted with their presents, Placidus' wife because her blind husband had not been able to notice that the lighting had deteriorated, and Placidus because a blind man can play *mancala*, a game in which pellets are taken or transferred from little pigeon-holes in the board by certain rules.

He said, 'Bless you, Marcus. I can have my cronies in, and we can play for money instead of just drinking and talking.'

After a good midday meal of fish and vegetables Marcus left Placidus and found a street of scribes near the great library. Marcus had often thought of his precipitate action when he had destroyed his Book of Isaiah at the Villa Belinuncia. He had done so in blind grief, but now by and large he had come to regret what he had done. And it struck him forcibly that to return to lands under the sway of the Jewish God without making some kind of amends would be rank folly.

After some inquiries Marcus found a Jewish scribe with excellent Greek, and commissioned him to take a copy of the best Greek version of Isaiah in the library. They settled on a fee, half to be paid on commencement and half on delivery to Marcus' apartment, plus the library's copying fee, paid in advance.

Marcus said, 'Use only the best quality skins.'

The scribe was in his early thirties, heavy-faced and full-bearded.

'Of course only the best quality,' he said. 'Now to details. Do you want a continuous or a sectional scroll . . . ?'

They had an easy passage from Alexandria to Cæsarea, and after spending a night there rode to the Villa Galathë at Elon, Marcus carrying his new Isaiah scroll in his personal baggage and looking up at the sky from time to time. They had an uneventful journey, however, and in the little hamlet of Elon they were greeted with much enthusiasm. Marcus saw his old mentor, Asa, and dismounted, throwing his reins to Khosro.

Marcus went forward to Asa and then knelt before the old man, who raised him up as a father raises his son. Asa called for cloths and a ewer, and washed the traveller's feet after exchanging greetings.

Marcus called to his slave, 'Khosro, ride on with my lady.'

There were thirty or more houses in the hamlet now. Asa brought out bread, olives and wine, and the two men ate together while Asa gave him the news.

'All is well here,' said Asa. 'Herod Antipas has built a new town on the shore of Gennesareth, and called it Tiberias after your Emperor. There have been small outbreaks of fighting in Judæa, but nothing much after the first big outburst, in the first days of the new Procurator.'

'What was that?' asked Marcus.

'I don't understand the ins and outs of it, but he sent standards with images on them into Jerusalem: images of Cæsar. The Jews in crowds besieged Cæsarea, where Pilatus was in residence, and when Pilatus' soldiers threatened them with death they bowed their necks to the swords. He removed the offending standards.'

'What else has been happening?'

'Pilatus stole some holy treasure to build an aqueduct, and he forestalled a revolt by having disguised soldiers mix with the crowd. The soldiers had clubs under their mufti, and when disturbances began they beat many Jews to death; many were trampled to death in the crush.'

Marcus rode away, thinking that L. Pontius Pilatus was a cruel and cunning man. But then the Villa Galathë came into view, and at sight of the light tawny walls he spurred his horse towards the figures of the people running out to meet him.

Kradog had turned in middle age into the stereotype of the eunuch. He had become fat and hairless, though his voice had changed little, perhaps two tones higher in pitch. Denied the pleasures of sex for so long, he had turned increasingly to the pleasures of the table, and had grown indolent and scant of breath in consequence. But like Doratus in his later years, Kradog had delegated his work with skill, and kept overall control as firmly as Doratus. Going through the various accounts with him, Marcus was able to offer his congratulations.

271

'I'm very happy with it all,' said Marcus. 'I shall leave this estate and villa to the Lady Kollura in my will, so that if anything happens to me, she will be settled here.'

Kradog said, 'She'll do very well out of it all. That seems to happen to people who get on the right side of you. I remember sitting on the ground eating with another slave, and drinking bad wine. I've come a long way since then, balls or no balls. And I've grown reconciled to *that*.'

'And in yourself?' Marcus asked. 'Do you feel homesick for Gaul of Narbo?'

'No,' said Kradog.

Marcus grinned and said, 'We all change as the years go by, Kradog, but there are some things in which a man is changeless. You still feel homesick for Britain, don't you?'

'For a *part* of Britain,' Kradog corrected him. 'I want to see the sun rise and set over the place where I belong.'

Marcus looked at him for a while, until Kradog began to fidget. His elbow knocked some scrolls from the table to the floor, and he fussed with them picking them up. It had been a long time since the two men had met, and Kradog had forgotten the strength of presence which Marcus exuded when he was concentrating on another person.

But at last Marcus said, 'You want to go back to Britain, and so you shall, by all the – I mean, by the invisible God who reigns here,' he amended hastily.

Kradog was staring at Marcus with mouth agape, a smile beginning to dawn.

Marcus continued, 'Those two you've trained can manage the estate for a year and a half. That should give you a whole year in Britain. I'll arrange it all with Joram, but you must pay the expenses yourself.'

Marcus rode with Khosro to the Villa Batanya, starting their journey on a fresh morning that promised heat later. There was plenty of time. They walked their horses south along the lake shore away from Capernaum, the Village of Nahum, a town built of black basalt which most of the inhabitants whitewashed into a dazzle. On the lush coastal strip they crossed the Waters of Meron, shrunk to a summer trickle, and carried on until they reached Magdala. They struck inland to Arbela, and left the road there, riding across country with forested hills to north and south, crossed a wadi, and disturbed a she-bear with cubs. She gave a rasping roar and rose on her hind paws before dropping down to the attack; but Marcus and Khosro were in full retreat, trying to control their fleeing horses. The rest of the journey was without incident. The day was hot but dry, and the tree-lizards were busy in the pines, the air full of their clean aroma.

Not only was Claudius at home, but he was time-expired long ago. He had joined the Army at the same time as Marcus, and had been released from service at the due date. They had been out of touch.

After his bath Marcus sat down to dinner with Claudius and Geneura. Claudius was no longer thin, but had put on some weight, and looked every inch a worthy Roman of a type to be seen from Iberia to Nabbatæa, from northern Gaul to Upper Egypt.

'A Roman dinner in Galilee,' Marcus said. 'Who will be dining here in a thousand years? Two thousand?'

Geneura was matronly now, but still attractive. Marcus and Claudius each wore a light summer tunic, while Geneura had on a single flimsy silken robe in bright blue. Her breasts were still good, though now she had two sons and a daughter.

'A Roman dinner,' she said. 'Claudius is half-British, I'm pure British, and you're what, Marcus with the mixed up names?'

A little stiffly Marcus said, 'Illyrian, to begin with.'

In a corner a girl was playing a flute, while another touched a zither and sang quietly in Seleucian Greek; horses whickered in the corral.

'Rome can accommodate it all, absorb it all and make it Roman,' Claudius said.

And Marcus said, 'I agree. For some years after the Augustan legions under Varus were lost I felt somehow that I'd been lied to, that Rome could be beaten. But then I studied the campaign. Varus was a rotten general. Claudius, this wine is making me thirsty. May I have some beer?'

Beer was brought, and Marcus drank deeply, then asked Claudius, 'Have you heard from your sister Cressida?'

'Not for a long time,' said Claudius, 'nor has Geneura.'

Marcus and Khosro came back to the villa at a thundering gallop the next morning, Claudius far behind, the first two riders panting as they dismounted and walked their horses into the yard, watching while grooms rubbed them down and Claudius finally trotted home puffing. Marcus thought, Mustn't let myself grow fat. It looks bad for one thing, and for another I'm sure it can lead to trouble.

But he said to Claudius, 'Thank you, old friend, for giving me and even my slave the best horses.'

'Think nothing of it,' Claudius said; easy-going now, he was appeased before he could even become annoyed.

They went together for their bath, finishing with the cold plunge, where Khosro and Claudius' slave, Gesmas, waited with towels and clean clothes. The Nubian was older and fatter than when Marcus had last seen him, but still cracked bad jokes which were funny only to himself. Khosro waited until the Romans had moved away, then shoved Gesmas in with a huge splash. The man heaved himself out of the water like a bull seal, gasping and shivering with the shock of the cold water.

'What do you mean by it, t-taking me by s-surprise like that?' he chattered, water pouring from him.

Khosro said, 'A sudden thought: that there was something *I'd* laugh at, and *you* wouldn't.'

From a cool marble seat in the shade of cypresses on the next day Marcus and Claudius looked at the property. The olives were being gathered in and the figs were ripening. The stud horses had been exercised in the cool of the early morning.

Marcus said, 'By the way, I was disappointed not to meet any of my Jewish friends. I thought Shimmon might be here looking over the stud, or even Joram and Nakdimon.'

'Not this week,' said Claudius. 'Some big Jewish festival going on at Jerusalem. Better luck next time.'

INTER SCRIPTUM (vi)

John Potts stood among the crowd in the Master's Garden at Christ's with a glass of pale fino sherry in his hand. He had paid his respects to the Master, and was looking for his old tutor, but he could not see Waldegrave anywhere. The babble of conversation was increasing, the sherry doing its job. Potts emptied his glass. He took another from a tray carried by a passing college servant and replaced the empty one, scarcely interrupting the man in his progress.

Potts had been in Washington D.C. for an Oriental Schools conference, and had taken Concorde on to Heathrow. Now he was in Cambridge for the annual Christ's College Club dinner. It had been a splendid summer day in London, but here the air was hot and humid, the sky gunmetal, purple and black. Thunder rumbled in the distance. Then, quite without warning, it began to pour with rain, hissing and spattering. Potts shielded his glass as he joined the rush for the Fellows' Parlour.

When the rain stopped fifteen minutes later Potts came out with the other people going back to the lawns, a leisurely tidal flow. Then Potts saw Waldegrave, moving against the tide. He was wearing full academic finery topped by its floppy Renaissance beret. Above that he held a large golfing umbrella in red, white and blue. Even though it had stopped raining, the umbrella's spikes deterred the people going in the opposite direction from moving too close. Potts went to meet him.

After greetings Potts said, 'I'd like to talk.'

'Let me get a glass of sherry,' said Waldegrave. 'We'll find a corner in the Senior Common Room.'

'Are you here for long, Potts?' Waldegrave asked when the two men were ensconced in comfortable armchairs.

'No. Going back tomorrow. Listen: I was waiting for you when that shower drove me into the Fellows' Parlour. I was squashed between two women – physicists, I think – and they were talking about quarks. Matter being created, wiped out and recreated, endlessly. At least that's what it seemed like to me. Matter created from nothing and then back again *ad infinitum*.'

Waldegrave said, 'The Hunting of the Quark. I've heard of them, but nothing specific.'

'It reminded me of something else,' Potts said. 'It was about the Turin Shroud. Someone wrote that the marks on it could be consistent with a body's having undergone a thermo-nuclear implosion: a big bang *inwards*. If that had taken place, combined with a dissolution and recreation of living tissue. . . . It could explain the Resurrection.'

Waldegrave sipped his sherry, then sighed and said, 'It's all very well, you know, Potts, but I don't think there'll ever be a scientific proof. We strain at quarks and nuclear gnats. What's the point if it all ends up in some scientific Potts-hole? We believe or we don't: it comes down in the end to a question of faith.'

Potts said slowly, 'I haven't told anyone, not even Helen, but I've started having these peculiar dreams about that bloody centurion. I dream in Latin or Greek, and sometimes I even dream in Galilean Aramaic, almost a semitic equi-valent of Mummerzet.'

'Reincarnation dreams?' asked Waldegrave sharply.

'No. In that event I'd have gone straight to a psychiatrist. No: I seem to be there as an observer, just watching the action with no power to interfere with it. The dreams don't make any sense.'

'Examples?'

Potts said, 'Well, for instance I was at some villa in the Middle East. I'm pretty sure it was in Israel, part of the ancient Syria Palæstina, because I could see pine trees, and there were arboreal lizards of a kind I've often seen myself.

As I say, I was outside this villa. There was a man and a girl close by, and she called the man Marcus. He wore a civilian tunic: on leave, I suppose. There were all sorts of other people milling around, but I couldn't see them properly. It was a kind of selective vision I always get when I'm dreaming.

'They were setting out on a journey, and there was a man near Marcus whom I could see clearly: a nasty-looking little piece of work. Marcus said to the girl in Greek – beautiful Greek it was, too – "so Kollura, farewell now to the Villa Galathë." Then a fat man who looked like a eunuch came up and they all moved off on horseback.'

Waldegrave said meditatively, 'That's most interesting. Those names, I mean.'

'Just the sort of silly thing you'd get in a dream, surely?'

' "Small cake. Cream-coloured." Why silly? "Mavis" is a thrush. And you don't need me to tell you that lots of house-names in Britain sound silly.'

' "Cream-coloured",' Potts said. 'I could see part of the villa walls. They *were* a light tawny colour, lighter than Jerusalem limestone. . . . And I've seen Marcus and his Small Cake in other places. Riding; on board a ship several times. What's happening, Doctor Waldegrave?'

Waldegrave said, 'I think you're subconsciously involved with this centurion far more than you're consciously aware of. You're doing some sort of dream reconstruction. You've always worked too hard, and you're working on this in your dream life. Do you feel any sense of nightmare and menace in these . . . centurion dreams?'

'No, nothing at all,' said Potts. 'I'm just a selective observer with no say over what's selected.'

'Then I shouldn't worry,' Waldegrave told him, and there the matter rested.

Potts brought out the photocopy of Marcus' military order and handed it to Waldegrave, saying, 'Have a look at that. The two faint marks at the beginning and end are odd. X and P. What do you think?'

'You're a palæographer. I'm not,' said Waldegrave, but he studied the document closely just the same. Then he said, 'Your two marks. They might have been incised, not written.

277

On a photostat they would look faint.' Then his face changed from a studious interest to the expression of a man who has made a discovery.

'What is it?' asked Potts.

Waldegrave looked up, composing his features.

He said, 'The wildest of guesses.' He put up a hand to forestall objection and went on, 'I'm not going to tell you what it was. If it were wrong it would be cruel to you. I'm coming to San Francisco in November on a lecture tour, so I'll pop down on the shuttle and inflict myself on you for a weekend. Can you get to Jerusalem before then?'

'Doubt it,' said Potts. 'In the Christmas vacation, perhaps. Why?'

'I strongly advise you go and look at the original document, that's why, Potts.'

LI

Six days before the Kalends of September in the fourteenth year of Tiberius Cæsar, M. Drusus Scipio at the Villa Belinuncia in Gaul of Narbo to his son Aeron, among the Trinovantes in Britain.

My son: events of many years ago lie so heavily on me that I am compelled to write this letter. I very much doubt whether you will reply, if indeed you still live (for I have no news from your part of Britain), but the words must be written.

When you were born I considered that I had done my duty as a father by ensuring your maintenance in money. So great was my ignorance of your country that it did not occur to me for one moment that you could read or write in Latin – or, indeed, in any other language. I realized it only when you sent back my freedman gelded and branded at your hands.

At that time there was no reply that I could make. The insult was too great then. But as time has passed I have come to see that I insulted you greatly also by my presumption. I have made very many mistakes during my life, but the greatest was to assume that you would be an unlettered savage.

My son Aeron, I cannot again insult you by offering you money, though there is a great patrimony in gold and jewels which is yours by right, not by my condescension. It is very many years since your mother and I met, but I still think of her with great affection, and I have reason to believe that this is returned.

I desire peace between the two of us, and as earnest of the strength of my wish I send this letter to Britain by the hand of the man whom you ill-used. He will not come to you in person, but he bears the letter willingly to your shores since he too desires peace between us. More than that I cannot ask.

Farewell.

LII

When Marcus arrived at the Villa Belinuncia he found that much had changed. Everything was prospering, the vintage in full swing and the stud thriving, although Appius and Akbar no longer bred the Gaulish horses. They had kept on Liutpold and Triutinne out of respect for their father. But first the mare and then the stallion had died while Marcus had been in Upper Egypt, and that was the end of the Gaulish breed which they had begun.

The twins were twenty-two years old. They were polite and respectful to Marcus, and to Kollura; but treated their father with a coolness and a distance which wounded him. Their attitude persisted, and it was a minor factor prompting Marcus to carry out finally his plan of writing to Aeron, even though the idea had first been conceived at the Villa Galathë.

So the days passed. Festus was showing more grey streaks in his bush of hair, and Livia's face had lines of pain as well as those of advancing age; she began to suffer from arthritis. Their son Primus was now much less interested in the horses than in the business of producing more and more elaborate chariots for the Gaulish nobility. He had turned away from Roman dress and customs, wore his hair long and had a full set of whiskers, wore trousers in loud patterns and nothing above the waist save for a cloak in the cold weather. But he was growing rich and employed six free workmen.

A party from Joram arrived, and Kradog set off for Britain

with them, accompanied by Siegfrith and half a dozen fighting men whom he had recruited.

'Keep the peace,' Marcus warned Siegfrith. 'You are a defensive force, and you fight only if pushed to it. When you return I shall be where the Army has sent me. Your task is to take Kradog safely to Britain and bring him back safely here; then he goes to my Villa Galathë.'

The party left and Phalaris wept. Marcus had him to dinner with Kollura and some neighbours the next evening, when he and Marcus aired their beautiful Greek and Phalaris acquired the kudos which consoled him.

So all went superficially well, but only superficially.

One late afternoon Marcus drew rein with his companions on a high point of land from where he could see the fangs of the Pyrenees, and could look back over all his own property: all of the ground, the crops, the livestock, the buildings.

And he said bitterly, 'What am I doing here? I have become superfluous! Akbar, in my father's time it was the custom to eat an early breakfast, slave and free together to allot the day's tasks. We knew where we *were*. But now I, who own all this, do not know where I am at all!'

His mount tossed his head, showing the whites of his eyes, disturbed by the vehemence of Marcus' voice; Akbar leaned over and gentled the horse, talking softly and stroking his neck.

Akbar straightened up, his own horse standing like an equestrian statue. Khosro had dismounted and was urinating noisily in some bushes. Cicadas chattered and dragonflies shimmered in the quivering air of the afternoon, a moment to incise itself on Marcus' memory to be set against another one long ago. Kradog and the druid. The cicadas had stopped then; now their sound carried on after Khosro had ceased pissing.

And Akbar said, 'Your father, whose exploits have been handed down by the great lord of blessed memory, Doratus, gave freedom to his son. You freed me and Kradog. What of Appius and Marcellus?'

Marcus took a quick gasp of breath, and looked again over the landscape of his property, green and brown and purple, a white wall of the villa sending a bright message into his mind from the westering sun.

'Thank you, Akbar,' he said.

Next day Marcus called his sons into the study.

He said, 'I'm an absentee landlord, and an absentee father. Before my own father absented himself he emancipated me. Can you ever forgive me for not having done the same?'

Appius said flatly, a bearing rein on his emotion, 'Yes. But when you came back here again and brought your concubine with you, we didn't know what to think.'

Marcus said, 'Know these things. My sons, I will emancipate you this week. In most things you are as one, but you, Marcellus, have taken over the agricultural side of the estate, and you, Appius, the livestock. This is good in itself, but as you grow older also your interests may diverge, and I wish at all costs to avoid the possibility of conflict between you. Therefore all receipts will be merged into one, with Festus in financial control, and you will share half and half from the net profits in future. This shall be your *peculium*. I will take nothing further for myself.'

'But how will you manage, father?' asked Marcellus.

'I have enough,' Marcus said. 'Enough and to spare. My only regret is that I did not take this decision earlier. On the ninth day we'll put all this in hand, and then have a feast in celebration.'

By the time Marcus' orders came in the estate was a happy place. He was posted once again to X Fretensis in Syria Palæstina, and the orders filled him with both joy and foreboding, for he had come to feel that his destiny lay in that land. As for the Villa Belinuncia, it was in excellent hands and Marcus was content, for he did not intend to visit it again.

283

LIII

In the year after Marcus met Placidus, and Pontius Pilatus became Procurator of Judæa, Tiberius retired to Capri, where he devoted himself in a lack-lustre fashion to sexual deviations. All of the Imperial family and much of the Roman aristocracy had taken to eating pills of lead. For more than ten years Ælius Sejanus had played an increasingly important part in affairs, and Tiberius had given him plenary power. But before leaving for Capri Tiberius persuaded the Senate to appoint a Foreign Affairs Committee, and then embarked on slaughter, executing Sejanus among the victims.* Sejanus had done what Tiberius wanted by having all his grandsons except Caligula murdered.

Meriem joined the household of Mary at Cana in the same year, after the death of Judith the Magdalene; the dear old lady had caught a fever after visiting relatives near Jericho, and Meriem was greatly distressed by her death.

The Magdalena and Meriem had been to the women's ritual bath adjoining the synagogue, and they returned to the house at Cana, where some workmen of the Magdalena's father-in-law were laying a mosaic in a stylized floral pattern round the fountain in the courtyard.

Mary of Magdala said to Meriem, 'We shall soon have enough of water. My husband has a cousin some months older than himself, a man named John the Baptizer. He looks scruffy: hair in elf-locks, beard in rat-tails, ribs sticking out; all wild eyes and gleaming teeth. He has a power, though, and he dips people in water, in the Jordan.'

*31 C.E.

'Why?' asked Meriem. 'It seems a very odd thing to do.'

'See it this way. We've just come from the bath, and we're ritually clean as well as clean in body. John baptizes people so that they are reborn to be claimed by the Messiah. Now John has baptized Jeshua . . . he *knows*. He is the Messiah, Son of God, King of the Jews.'

Meriem said, 'I think that is true. And if he could turn water into wine beforehand, who knows what he is capable of now?'

They digested this in silence for a minute, but then the Magdalena said, 'I'm frightened. Not for me: for him.'

'But your father-in-law is rich and powerful, and he has influential friends. Surely they'll be able to protect him?'

'They are not Romans, are they?' asked the Magdalena; and to this Meriem could find no answer. The workmen finished, and the fountain was turned on. At first the water gurgled and dribbled from the spout, but then suddenly it gathered force and burst upwards in a fan of spray coruscating in the sunlight.

LIV

When Marcus arrived at Cæsarea with Kollura and Khosro they were put into close confinement as soon as they left the ship, Marcus apart from the others.

Herod the Great had found an almost ruined town with an equally corrupt name. Tower of Strato: originally probably Tower of Astartë. Herod demolished everything and built a new town, including a great harbour and breakwater against the Mediterranean surf, with huge towers and statues, the latter highly offensive to the Jews; the buildings of the town were constructed of limestone, dazzling in the sun.

As Marcus disembarked with his two followers and other passengers onto one of the arched landing-stages a tribune stepped forward.

'The centurion Marcus Drusus Scipio?'

'Yes,' Marcus said, and showed his identification and orders. 'The two with me are my concubine and my slave.'

The tribune nodded and gestured to the soldiers behind him. A decurion and eight men surrounded Marcus and his companions, then marched them quickly away to the Roman fort and transit camp. Marcus found himself alone and mystified. He took in his environment. He was in a tribune's apartment in the transit camp. The furniture was good; fruit and a small amphora of wine, together with a jug of fresh water, stood on a side table with plates and glasses. Marcus took some comfort from this, for it was not the reception which would be accorded to anyone suspected of wrong-doing. Experimentally Marcus clapped his hands, and an orderly appeared.

'Yes, sir? Is everything to your liking?'

'I badly need some beer and a bath,' Marcus said. 'I expect the bath will have to wait, but the beer . . . ?'

'Surely,' the orderly said, and brought a crock. As he put it down he said, 'Knock some back quick, Centurion: the Camp Prefect's on his way, and he's got company.'

Marcus took a good swig, washing the sea-salt from his lips, and then sat down; his surroundings rocked and swayed, and would do so for some time before he regained his landlegs. He did not have long to wait, jumping to attention as three men came in: a hawk-nosed and swarthy civilian of rank, wearing a formal toga trimmed with purple; the dour old martinet who was Camp Prefect; and the tribune who had met him at the harbour. Marcus saluted, fist over breast.

The Prefect said, 'All right, stand at ease.'

'No, no,' said the civilian. 'Things will go more easily if we all sit down. I see you have some beer, Drusus Scipio; I'll take wine, and no water.'

Marcus served wine to the civilian and the tribune; the Camp Prefect took nothing, probably offended by the informality. Marcus had noticed that the civilian had given him his correct formal address. Who was he, and what was afoot? The question was answered for him.

'I am Pontius Pilatus, Procurator of Judæa. Now then: the people with you. Do they know that you speak Aramaic?'

'Yes, sir.'

'Who else knows?'

'Everyone in the hamlet where I have a villa just outside Capernaum in Galilee. In Judæa, only a handful of people.'

Pilatus nodded, putting down his glass and steepling his fingers.

He said, 'Now listen to me. You are as of now detached for service in Intelligence. I can find all the Aramaic speakers I need: it's the native language of this arsehole of the earth. What we need are Roman soldiers who are fluent in Aramaic, who have excellent Greek and can move amongst Aramaic speakers without their having an inkling that their words are understood. It was important to isolate you at once before you started spouting your head off in the language, ordering porters about and so on.'

'I was taken by surprise,' Marcus said. 'Our luggage was still on board, and my concubine's handmaidens. They will be running around like headless chickens.'

'All taken care of,' Pilatus said, 'thanks to my tribune Rabirius Regulus. Very well, then! Remember, not a word of Aramaic in Judæa from now on, except where strictly necessary. Tomorrow you leave for Jerusalem as a civilian.'

He got up, and Marcus leaped to attention again. Pilatus paused and looked at Marcus quizzically.

He said, 'You know some very distinguished people among the Jews.'

Marcus kept his face impassive in its military mask. He remembered what Asa had told him about this man. Marcus had been taken in by Pilatus' ease and informality, in danger of forgetting that the man was cruel and devious.

Marcus said, 'Only Nicodemus, sir. He was just a young official when I first met him; he connected the water to an apartment I had on my first tour of duty. But I've been in regular correspondence with him, and we are business associates with Joseph the Arimathean. It will be highly suspicious if we don't meet.'

Pilatus grunted. 'No problem; might be useful in fact.' He looked intently at Marcus, and went on, 'You don't need to ask whether I went very thoroughly into your background. Drusus Scipio. You signed on for twenty years plus four periods of vexillium. You have a gift for languages and horses, and you're a rich man with extensive lands and properties. Unlike most of the centurionate you have never taken bribes for sending men on furlough. You don't need the money. Yet here you are, still a centurion. Why?'

Marcus was silent for a moment. What could he say? He certainly could not confide in the Procurator of Judæa, but he could at least tell part of the truth.

So he said, 'It's my duty to serve. That's all, sir.'

'And a proper Roman sentiment,' the Procurator said with approval. Then he nodded to Marcus, who saluted again as the three men left the room. Marcus relaxed, thinking that in the end he had spent enough time at attention to satisfy the Camp Prefect.

He finished his beer, then went to the baths, returning to

find his luggage in the room, Kollura supervising while her girls unpacked twittering; Khosro was laying out weapons to make sure that nothing was missing.

Kollura ran to Marcus and hugged him.

'We thought something dreadful was happening. What's going on?'

Marcus stroked her hair and then detached himself from her.

'Only the Army,' he said. 'You know how it is by now: all at once they want me in Jerusalem. I'll arrange an escort for you to the villa. Khosro stays with me. Now put all that stuff back except for overnight gear and fresh clothing. We leave tomorrow.'

Marcus was in the Stygian regions of Solomon's Stables far below the Antonia and the Palace, and too distant from the torture chambers for the screams and yells of agony to be heard. He sat in a large, cool room where four oil lamps were burning; he was dressed in civilian clothes, and looked across a marble table at the tribune Rabirius Regulus, a cool, pale man with a straight nose and black hair arranged by his hairdresser in hyacinthine locks. So, Marcus thought, You are a vain man, Rabirius Regulus, but a clever one.

The tribune had been taking Marcus through the details of his military career, in good Latin. Marcus watched the man unwaveringly. Pilatus knew all this information, and Marcus believed that he was sitting opposite the man who had collated and supplied it. The only possible point of all this rigmarole was that sooner or later Marcus would be subjected to some kind of test. So he answered the tribune's questions, relaxed but watchful as a hungry kingfisher. He was ready when the tribune's eyes flickered briefly to a point above his shoulder and behind him, and a voice barked in Aramaic, 'Stand up!'

Marcus turned and saw a short, fat centurion with a squint.

Marcus said, 'What in Hades' name do you think you're doing, blundering in here with your gabble?'

The centurion grinned and looked over to Rabirius Regulus.

'That'll do to begin with,' he said. 'We can send him out on the streets.'

' . . . Jeshua,' the man in the wine-shop was saying. 'My cousin Eli from Nazareth told me. He preached a load of rubbish in the synagogue, he did, an' they chucked him out. I mean, the Law's the Law, ain't it? Have another drink, mate.'

The man and his companion were speaking in bad Galilean Aramaic. Marcus sat nearby, apparently taking no notice of the conversation and having ordered food and drink in perfect Greek. Khosro watched from twenty yards away.

The other man said, 'Same again then, mate. That's not much to write home about. I think they *need* a proper shake-up in some of them synagogues up there.'

'But that ain't all,' said the first man. 'Feller old Eli knows, name o' Simon. His mother-in-law took sick, like to die she was, an' this Jeshua put 'er right as rain. A bleedin' miracle some said, but Eli thinks it's Satan's work more like, an' I agree with him. If they won't let him preach the Law in the synagogue, I mean it stand to reason, don't it?'

'An omer of fresh oil, please,' said Marcus in Greek to the woman at the olive press.

She nodded and took the jar from him, continuing her Aramaic conversation with two other women.

' . . . His son Matathias was showing the first signs of leprosy.'

The other women clucked and hissed while Marcus looked away indifferently, and there was in truth nothing to interest him.

'That's right,' said the oil seller. 'Terrible for him, and the family.'

One of the other women said, 'So he got leprosy, and they slapped him into the nearest concentration camp for lepers.'

The oil seller tugged Marcus' sleeve and said in Aramaic, 'You did say a full omer?'

It's all good practice, Marcus thought.

'I'm sorry,' he said in Greek, and shrugged.

She smiled and handed him the jar; he gave her a silver

denarius, and while she went for change she carried on talking to her friends in their native tongue.

'I think it's exciting. The father hid Matathias away until this Jeshua came by — and healed him! Honest, my aunt Shushanna's seen the lad: not a blemish on him!'

'*Eukharistó*,' said Marcus as he took his change. 'I give thanks.'

Marcus found his duties boring, and ached for local leave and Kollura. He wanted to get on the track of the Sicarii, and so far had heard not a whisper of any interest. In due course he would be given names and contacts, but he wanted to find out something on his own, and was disappointed not to have done so. He sighed and sat down to write his first report. Idle gossip about some quack in the north — even in Galilee — was not worth mentioning.

LV

When Marcus' local leave came round he went first to
Cæsarea as a civilian, and after two days emerged in full
uniform. That was how it would be in future: a civilian in
Judæa, but he would always arrive home to his villa as a
soldier. This would help to maintain his cover.

Marcus had dismissed the two stories he had heard as
tittle-tattle, but as he penetrated into Galilee and stopped for
refreshment he began to revise his opinion. The name of
Jeshua was on too many tongues, for one thing. It appeared
that he had even found some followers from amongst the
fishermen of Capernaum, and as Marcus neared the Villa
Galathë he determined to see Asa and find out if the old man
knew anything.

As had become their custom, Marcus and Asa sat together
and took wine and fruit. After the courtesies had been exchanged Marcus said, 'Tell me, Asa, do you know anything
about some miracle-worker named Jeshua? I seem to be
hearing quite a lot about him in Galilee.'

Asa said, 'It isn't surprising, my friend. Let me try to sum
up what's been happening. This Jeshua bar Joseph got
himself some disciples. . . .'

'Fishermen?'

'Yes, from the lake.'

'I've heard about that,' Marcus said. 'What else do you
know?'

'He went into the synagogue at Capernaum and drove out
of a man an evil spirit that possessed him. The mother of
one of the fishermen was racked with fever, and Jeshua

simply took her by the hand. The fever vanished. Then in the evening when the word had run through Capernaum a whole crowd of sick people gathered round. I and others from Elon went there, and I saw this with my own eyes: Jeshua healed them all. Friend, can you think of some words of Isaiah which are apposite to these things?'

Marcus thought and then said slowly, ' "He took away our illnesses and lifted our diseases from us." '

'Exactly,' said Asa. 'Food for thought, isn't it?'

Marcus rode home to Kollura, and thought no more about the miracle-worker for some time. He took Kollura straight to bed, and for the time being she was miracle enough for him.

The under-stewards had run the estate efficiently, but Marcus found plenty to do; then, a week after he had begun his leave, Kradog came back from Britain.

He rode in on a scruffy little skewbald pony leading a string of five mules laden with presents, and accompanied by half a dozen hired spearmen. Joram's own men had seen him all the way from Britain to Cæsarea and then departed for Jerusalem. Kradog looked much fitter than when Marcus had last seen him. He was tanned and had lost weight, and there was something else about him that Marcus noticed when Kradog was bathed and refreshed: a deep inner peace which Kradog had always lacked before.

They went on a tour of the estate with the two under-stewards, and Kradog was happy, though he found fault over trivialities by way of reasserting his status above them. Dismissing the men Marcus walked back to the villa with Khosro and Kradog.

'Well, Kradog,' said Marcus. 'How was Britain this time?'

Kradog said, 'Beyond my wildest dreams, Marcus Drusus, for I found kinsfolk at Ynys Witrin: more than I would have thought possible. It was like a homecoming when I mentioned my mother's name and parentage. She dinned it all into me when I was a child, so that I could never forget my mother's line. I have aunts and uncles, cousins, nephews and nieces.'

Marcus said, 'You have always thought of yourself as a

Briton, and now it seems to me that you were right all along. But didn't it break your heart to come back here?'

They reached the peristyle and sat down; Marcus told Khosro to fetch wine, water and beer.

'I didn't know how I should find the strength to leave Britain,' said Kradog. 'But I had to come back. And not with empty hands, either. I have walked the swards of Avalonia beneath its apple trees, drunk the cold waters of its springs, and all thanks to you. I have brought you gifts, but one is bitter indeed. It is a letter from your son Aeron of the Trinovantes, in reply to your own. But I have to say this: the messenger who brought me the letter told me also that your son is dead.'

Marcus sat stone-faced while Kradog reached into his tunic and brought out a rolled piece of vellum sealed with a coarse blob of beeswax. Marcus broke the seal and unrolled the letter. Khosro came back with the drinks, but Marcus was gazing ahead without seeing, and Kradog motioned to the slave to leave them. Then Marcus read:

'To my Roman father M. Drusus Scipio from his son Aeron in the last days of his life, greeting. In the spring I caught a fever after a bear hunt. I began to cough soon after the fever had gone, and then to spit blood. I grow weaker day by day, short of breath and with pain in the chest. Of course there must be forgiveness between us, and between me and your man if he wills it as I do. I was young and hot-blooded, too ready with the knife, and seeing in him only the tool of your slighting. Put it behind us and let things past lie quiet, as I shall now that I send to you my farewell.'

Kradog said to Marcus, 'So, I forgive your son, and that golden afternoon here in Galilee is laid to rest at last. For I have to tell you that the Lady Cressida is dead also from natural causes, and perhaps the strangest thing of all is that she was a cousin of mine.' He poured out wine and beer, saying, 'Let us drink now and put it all behind us, as your son wished.'

Claudius and Geneura arrived to stay at the Villa Galathë.

Claudius said, 'Why don't we go to the festival at Sepphoris? Make a party of it: they're showing *The Frogs* as the high comedy. I can't remember what else they're performing, but that doesn't matter. Are you on?'

Marcus said, 'That's a splendid idea, Claudius. We haven't been to the theatre since we were in Alexandria.'

The games were in honour of Dionysos but the Promethean fire burned on the altar to Athenë at Sepphoris. Fifty rams had been slaughtered in sacrifice to the god at the beginning of the festival, and the wine flowed unwatered. Sepphoris was a Greek city, and its youth competed wholly naked after the Greek custom in the track and field events, and in the boxing and wrestling. There were musical competitions, singing and dancing, and the drama.

Five hundred years before in the days of the great tragedians the plays were held like the other events, in competition; but now they were non-competitive perform-ances. Marcus' party watched the *Antigone* of Sophocles, identifying with the luckless girl who buried her brother against her father's wishes and incurred the wrath of the gods, who drove her relentlessly to her martyrdom and the *katharsis* of the audience, purging the grosser elements in their natures:

'What law of heaven have I transgressed? What god
Can save me now? What help or hope have I,
In whom devotion is deemed sacrilege?
If this is God's will, I shall learn my lesson
In death; but if my enemies are wrong,
I wish them no worse punishment than mine.'

Marcus nodded sagely, full of wisdom and wine. Here was the good Greek truth. Do not offend God or the gods. He thought of the Jewish miracle-worker, who, Marcus now realized, was offending them by his every action. Marcus would write a report that very evening for the Jerusalem Intelligence office about that Jeshua. If people could work miracles the power of the gods would be suborned, and the established order of things, the fabric of human society and the power of Rome itself: it was unthinkable.

He sat in the tiered seat, Kollura's thigh warm against his own, looking down on the dancing floor where the blind

295

soothsayer Tiresias had made his entrance, larger than life in the short stilts under his costume, his face hidden by the stylized mask-amplifier. Marcus listened to the closing speeches of the play entranced, and feeling saved.

Next day they saw Aristophanes' *The Frogs*, and the mood was quite different. Dionysos was the god of drama and dramatists. The play shows him annoyed by the poor quality of contemporary tragedy, and he decides to do something about it by descending into Hades disguised as Herakles to bring back Euripides, his favourite tragedian. But Euripides and Æschylus have a contest, and Dionysos decides in favour of Æschylus, bringing him back to the world of the living instead.

Kharon the underworld ferryman makes Dionysos row the boat, to a chorus of dead frogs:

Frogs.   'Brekekekex, ko-ax, ko-ahx!'
Dionysos.   Oh dear! Oh dear! I do declare
    I've got a bump upon my rump.
Frogs.   Brekekekex, ko-ax, ko-ahx!
Dionysos.   But you don't seem to care.
Frogs.   Brekekekex, ko-ax, ko-ahx!
Dionysos.   There's nothing but 'ko-ax' from you. . . .
    My hands are blistered and they smart;
    My arse below it swelters so
    It's going to turn right up and fart
    Brekekekex, ko-ax, ko-ahx!

Marcus' joy was drowned in the joy of eight thousand others, secure and wrapped in the timeless legacy of Greece.

LVI

Marcus sat with the Tribune Rabirius Regulus in his office at the Prætorium in Cæsarea. The tribune was relaxed and easy, not a hair of his hyacinthine locks out of place as he faced Marcus across his standard issue marble table, officers, for the use of.

Rabirius Regulus said, 'The Procurator was impressed by your report. Not so much by the factual content: we have plenty of corroboration of the facts. Pontius Pilatus is an expert at infiltration; he always has been. After your report he'll infiltrate the followers of this Jeshua and find out just what tricks he gets up to in order to perform his so-called miracles.'

'Tricks?' said Marcus.

'The Jews want to believe in their Meshiah, Anointed One, Khristos. The King of the Jews. There are the facts and the interpretation of the facts. Let him paint the spots of some dread disease all over his shill's face, and with a pass of his hand – and sleeve – he'll wipe them away. Hosannah! A miracle! The common people *want* miracles, so they'll get them.'

'Are you sure there's no more to it than that?' said Marcus slowly.

'Nothing. But what impressed the Procurator about your report was your conclusion that this man could become a threat to public order.'

'I suppose that he'll just stamp on Jeshua now.'

Rabirius Regulus raised his eyebrows and said, 'Not a bit of it. He'll bide his time, until he finds some way in which he can profit. Then he'll take action. What he will want to gain is gold for Tiberius Cæsar, gold for Pontius Pilatus; praise from Cæsar or at least absence of blame.'

Marcus inclined his head, unwilling to risk a reply: any comment could be dangerous, for Rabirius Regulus might well have a secretary concealed somewhere within earshot and taking a verbatim record of the interview.

The tribune went on, 'Our Procurator is a wise man with much forethought, and will never act hastily. But there is another reason for which he commends you.'

'I can't think what that could be,' Marcus said, genuinely puzzled.

'There was a man who died of a stroke while you were on leave, and you couldn't have known that. His name was Joseph bar Jacob; he built that villa of yours up near Capernaum; and he was the father of this Jeshua, as of course you're well aware. That proves you're no soft touch, Drusus Scipio, and the Procurator was right to choose you for this work: you act without fear or favour.'

INTER SCRIPTUM (vii)

Potts met Doctor Waldegrave's San Francisco shuttle at the airport, then carried the old man's grip and ushered him to the car, Waldegrave coughing into a handkerchief.

'This air pollution is infernal,' said Potts. 'I'll soon have you out of it.'

Waldegrave was wearing his jeans, a red gingham shirt and a green foulard spotted with yellow; on his nose he had mirrored sunglasses. In the car Potts drove north on La Cienega past grasshopper oil pumps and sleazy buildings; but the cool filtered air conditioning was operating, and Waldegrave leaned back in his seat gratefully.

'That's better.' he said. 'How people can live and work in that atmosphere . . . !'

Potts asked 'What's the subject of your lectures?'

' "Diocletian – Saviour or Destroyer?" ' said Waldegrave, turning the insectile lenses to Potts, who stared straight ahead, keeping his eyes on the road as the car climbed out of the inferno.

When they reached Potts' home there was a TV repairman's panel truck in the drive.

'Go on in,' Potts told Waldegrave. 'Helen's waiting to fix you a drink. I'll just have a word with this chap and find out what's happening.'

Potts strolled past the panel truck, which was bright yellow, with red lettering: Red Dragon Repairs; there was a red dragon logo on the tailgate. The repairman held a coil of cable and looked up as Potts approached: he was in his late twenties, slight and dark, but alert and bright.

'Hi,' he greeted Potts. 'Your good lady rang and said her TV picture was acting up. There's nothing wrong with the set, so I came out here. That's where your trouble is, man, see?'

His accent was of the valleys of South Wales. Potts peered at the cable.

'I don't understand,' he said. 'Welsh, aren't you?'

'Glyn Neath,' the man said. 'Land of Max Boyce.'

Potts had no idea what the man was talking about. He stared at the cable and shrugged.

Patiently and in the tones used to one of limited intelligence the repairman said, 'This stuff is called co-axial cable, man, and it's got cracks and all-like-that-see? Your co-ax is shot to shit, your picture acts up. I'll renew the cable and you'll be fine.'

'That's good then,' Potts said. 'Better let you get on with it, hadn't I?'

He went through the house to the stoop, where Helen and Waldegrave were sitting with their drinks. Potts poured his finger of malt and clinked glasses with Waldegrave's cold fino and Helen's iced vodka martini.

'Cheers,' he said. 'Your co-ax is shot to shit, your picture acts up, Helen.'

'I'm sorry?'

'I quote the repairman working outside. The co-ax has cracks and all like that, see? Brekekekex, the co-ax has cracks.'

Waldegrave said in surprise, 'The repairman said *that*?'

'Only the first half of it.'

And Helen said, 'Then I think it's wrong of you to make fun of an honest American working man.'

'I didn't mean it that way,' said Potts. 'And he's a Welshman.'

Waldegrave said, 'Time was, a working Welshman would know his Aristophanes. In translation of course, but still. . . .'

'That one knows his max voice, whatever that is,' said Potts. 'And, presumably, his co-ax.'

Potts was dreaming that he sat somewhere in the Sinai Desert under a black sky with a few sunrays coming through like

300

searchlights. The tortured rock and sand danced in mirage; dust devils writhed over the ground, miniature tornadoes full of fleas and other insects together with the filth they had picked up.

Potts sat in front of a television set. A weather forecast was on, and the forecaster, a bearded man in a blue suit, was saying, 'So the prospect is distinctly eschatological, and if you want to know what that means take a fucking good look outside.'

The image changed: on a screen a Disney-type frog in a helmet with a centurion's transverse crest stared bug-eyed. With a deep bass croaking it said: 'Diocletian pegged the prices; lack of slaves shot him to shit. All he got was an energy crisis. Hard luck, tough tit. Brekekekex, co-ax, quarks; brekekekex, co-ax, quarks, *quarks!*'

Potts awoke, blinking and swallowing; he rubbed his eyes and reached for the water carafe, but it was empty. Helen lay at his side, warm and unmoving, fast asleep. They had been to a concert, then had a late supper, though Doctor Waldegrave had eaten very little. Potts eased himself out of bed and downstairs to the kitchen. The lights were on, and Waldegrave was sitting at the table in a parti-coloured dressing gown, silver and purple. He was gnawing a leg of chicken, a glass of iced coffee beside it. The clock showed just after 3.35.

'Well, Potts,' Waldegrave said indistinctly through a mouthful of chicken, 'you hungry too?'

Potts grunted and found a six-bottle pack of Löwenbräu dark. He opened a bottle and drank from it, then exhaled heavily.

'Mouth like a miner's jockstrap,' he said. 'That's better. I thought you were the one who wasn't hungry.'

'That was *then*,' said Waldegrave. 'This is *now*. I hope you've no objection.'

'No, no; forgive me. I'm scarcely awake.'

He looked at the small bottle, then went for a glass and poured the rest of the beer into it, sipped and said, 'Better every second. This'll help me get back to sleep. I had one of those dreams.'

'Tell me about it while it's still fresh in your memory.'

301

'Good idea,' Potts said, and recounted the dream.

Waldegrave waited until Potts had finished, then went to the sink, washed and dried his hands without speaking, and returned to his place.

'It seems mostly a mixture of the day's events,' he said, 'together with the continuation of the centurion theme.

'I'd submit that the rest stems from your television set and that repairman: even the phrasing echoes him, don't you think? Shot to – er, shit, and so on. You yourself provided the Aristophanes,'

Potts said, 'I suppose so.'

He finished his beer, then poured another, pensively, while Waldegrave sipped his iced coffee.

'I don't know,' Potts said suddenly. 'What about the eschatology? Where did *that* come from?'

Waldegrave asked, 'Do you still think we're ripe for the Apocalypse?'

'No idea,' said Potts. 'I've been thinking more about Marcus Drusus Scipio. But what could he have to do with Aristophanes?'

'If he spoke Greek, he could have seen *The Frogs*.'

'Exactly.' Potts paused, trying to make up his mind to commit himself to a confidence and then deciding in favour of it. 'It's almost as though something of the man were trying to get through to me: "through a glass darkly." '

Waldegrave frowned and said, 'I prefer the New English Bible rendering: "disturbing reflections in a mirror." '

'No,' Potts said. 'Think of Plato and his shadow-show. The word I want is *through*. Only in *Alice* can you go through a mirror. Reflections won't do.'

He drank his second beer and said, 'Drinking beer at four o'clock in the morning! And I never touch the stuff, nor does Helen: we keep it for guests. Would you like something after your coffee?'

'Thank you, no,' said Waldegrave.

Potts stifled a yawn and said, 'That beer's made me sleepy. I'm off back to bed.'

Potts was soon asleep, and when he woke up again at seven-thirty remembered a second dream. It had been of Marcus, in full centurion's uniform. One hand was slipping a dagger back into its sheath. Potts seemed to be watching through a glass screen. The centurion's other hand held a writing skin, new and unfolded. He spoke, and the words came through, but muffled.

'So. I live in Cairo.'

Potts sat up in bed, rubbing his stubbly chin; Helen stirred beside him, mumbling. She made more sense than that dream, thought Potts. 'I live in Cairo'! The place didn't even exist in Marcus' day. He would tell no one about it, and wished he hadn't mentioned the first to Waldegrave. It had been a night of absurdity.

Over coffee, Potts said to his wife, 'Helen, how'd you like to go away for Christmas?'

'Suits me,' she said. 'Where shall we go?'

'I think it might be pleasant to spend it in Jerusalem.'

LVII

The rest of the garrison were back under the chill sway of the Jerusalem Terror, but Marcus went about his duties in a state of automatism. He was saddened by Joseph the Builder's death, but the news that the man Jeshua was Joseph's son had – contrary to his tribune's assumption – came as a shattering surprise to him.

On a cold February morning under a grey sky, with a few snowflakes falling, Marcus was walking along the Valley of the Cheesemakers wrapped in a thick brown cloak and breathing in the dairying smells around him. The weather matched his mood. He had liked Joseph: the man had possessed an honesty and a forthright power which called to the same qualities in Marcus, though he himself could not have put it that way. Joseph had mentioned his doubts about one of his sons, and a possible connection with the Zealots; and only after his interview with Rabirius Regulus had Marcus realized that Joseph must have been speaking of Jeshua. It must have pained the father greatly to have had a charlatan for a son, and a charlatan with terrorist connections.

So Marcus stalked along in the middle of the Jewish city with scents around him which called up Virgilian pastoral eclogues and Arcadian milkmaids. He was thus quite unprepared for the ferocious attack which engulfed him. He was thinking that he would investigate the man Jeshua personally, when a weight fell on his shoulders. A man had dropped on him from above. Hampered by his cloak, Marcus tried to shrug away his attacker but he held the cloth round Marcus' body tightly, and tripped him to the ground. Twisting round Marcus saw a bearded face above him, the glint of a dagger, two more figures dropping beside him; the thud of the dagger again and again. Then Khosro was among the attackers. His habit was to shadow Marcus from a distance of about twenty yards, and this would have given him an adequate margin for defence had Marcus had his hands free to cope with the onslaught; but he had been wrapped in his cloak as well as his thoughts.

As it was, he was able to give a forceful double kick to the groin of his first assailant. Khosro was inside the second man's guard, hooking at his eyes, and from that position Khosro slipped his long knife through the third attacker's nostril into the brain. The action had taken no more than half a minute. Khosro was despatching the man whom he had blinded, and the first dagger-man was staggering about incapacitated by his mashed testicles.

Marcus finally got his hands free and pushed himself to his feet. He felt weak and uncomfortable. He was in time to see a Roman foot patrol running down the street, but then his vision darkened and Khosro jumped to his side, lowering him gently back to the ground.

Marcus had a deep puncture wound through the left deltoid, and an even more serious one in the right thigh: the femoral artery had been severed. Khosro knew nothing at all about first aid, and Marcus would have died soon but for the fact that the decurion in charge of the patrol had the skill to improvise a tourniquet. Then, when Khosro told him who Marcus was, he was rushed to the field hospital in the Antonia for immediate medical treatment.

The medical officer administered spirits of wine laced with opium after suturing the artery, then thoroughly cleaned the wounds with the same substance while Marcus was in a semi-comatose state; he felt no pain, and the shock was alleviated.

Marcus spent three weeks in the sick bay. Rabirius Regulus came to see him on the second day, bringing a clerk to take down Marcus' report. Marcus had never been seriously ill in his life before, and only suffered superficial wounds, so this was a new experience for him, and an unpleasant one. He had been whisked into Intelligence immediately he had begun his tour of duty, and knew only the Intelligence staff and the Procurator, who sent him fruit but did not visit him. He would have been bored out of his wits but for Khosro, who visited him twice a day, bringing him reading matter and luxuries, and another source of interest.

Marcus was bothered by flies, especially during his first days, when he was ordered to keep still. Khosro brought him a chameleon on a dead branch, which he placed at one side of Marcus' pallet, and a praying mantis in a square and open-topped earthenware container. They kept down the flies, and afforded Marcus a welcome relief from boredom. Khosro had furnished some strips of coloured cloth, and it amused Marcus to see the chameleon's colour changes, which took place slowly though not imperceptibly. Its hunting, too, was interesting. It moved very slowly, with precise move-ments, inching along pursuing a fly. Its turreted eyes could focus independently, so that its farther eye would circle in search of prey, while the nearer would remain fixed on Marcus. Then both eyes would suddenly focus together, the long sticky-tipped tongue would shoot out, and another fly would vanish.

The chameleon was amusing; the mantis anything but. She perched immobile with the two upper legs held out. They were bent in the opposite direction to a human arm, and the inner surfaces were toothed. The insect looked innocuous, but when a fly came within range she underwent a sudden transformation into an angel of terror, seeming to double in size, pale wings spread up and out while the legs snapped out and pinned the fly on their sawteeth. The mantis bit the head off the fly first, then consumed the rest of it.

After two more weeks Marcus was given twenty-seven days' sick leave. He travelled with Khosro in company with a detachment of troops bound for Antioch, leaving them at Capernaum. When they reached Elon and Asa rose from his seat outside his door to greet Marcus, he did not dismount.

They exchanged greetings and then Marcus said, 'Old friend, I'll hear your news some other time. If I get off this horse I don't think I'll be able to get on it again. I have been wounded, and I'm deathly weary, so please forgive me now.'

So he rode home to the surprise of all the household. Kollura and Kradog fussed over him, and when she heard the full story of the attack and Khosro's part in the defence Kollura gave him five aurei, which caused Marcus to grumble.

'He doesn't deserve *three*,' he said. 'One would have sufficed. If he'd been faster on the scene I mightn't even have been wounded.'

Kollura patted Khosro on the shoulder and said, 'That's why I gave him five aurei. You were wounded, and because of it you're home; and to me that's all that matters.'

For the first week Marcus rested and got up to date with Kradog on the affairs of the estate. Marcus sent him to accompany Kradog with a letter to Claudius, inviting him to come over on a visit. Claudius sent a tablet back with Kradog agreeing to come over the following week, and he also sent the gift of a quiet horse, a gelding named Abaster, 'Away from Starlight,' because it had not been judged fit for breeding; but for a convalescent it was an excellent mount.

Marcus had a marble bench installed in a pasture between the vineyard and the olive grove. He sat there on a sunny morning reading the tablet from Claudius while Abaster grazed in a head collar. Joram was on his travels and Nakdimon tied up with Sanhedrin business.

Marcus laid the tablet down in full sun, and the letters of Claudius' message dislimned on the wax. Marcus had been preoccupied, and had failed to notice that Abaster was behind him, and as he placed the tablet on the bench the horse put its head to his side, shoved him and the tablet sliding along the bench, and deposited him on the ground on top of the melting wax. At any other time Marcus would have been amused by this example of the equine sense of fun, but his healing wounds stabbed him in shoulder and thigh. He stood up wincing, the tablet stuck to the backside of his tunic, Khosro shaking with laughter in the shade of the vines, and clouted the horse's head in fury. Abaster shook its head snorting, curvetting away while Marcus detached the tablet and flung it to the ground. Then despite the pain of his wounds the humour of the situation struck him, and he went to Abaster's quarter, gentling it.

'You're right, horse,' he said, 'but a little early. A few more days, and then I'll get moving.'

Three days later Marcus went to visit Asa, and the two men sat outside the little house with nuts and posca. Khosro led Abaster into the shade while Marcus told Asa of the attack and his wounding, while the old man made sympathetic noises.

But then Asa said, 'It is to be expected. You have made a home here, and you are liked and respected, but there is no place in Jerusalem for the Romans. I am sorry for what happened to you as a person, but no Roman should be in our holy city.'

Marcus wanted a short ride. Over the next days he would gradually increase the distance ridden, but that day he decided to go no farther than Capernaum to order fresh supplies of his favourite Egyptian beer. Marcus spent half an hour with his supplier and placed his order, then rode back with Khosro at Abaster's side. As they approached a well on the outskirts of the town Khosro asked if he might drink some water, for he was thirsty.

Marcus said, 'I see. You mean *you* haven't spent the afternoon drinking posca and tasting beer. Drink a camel's draught if you want.'

Khosro went to the brimming well and began to drink while Marcus looked round about him, always alert now. He saw only innocent passers-by, including a veiled woman with jet-black hair escaping from her headdress. Her head turned towards Marcus. There were two women behind her leading three donkeys piled with bundles, all thrown into confusion as the woman stopped in her tracks, and threw back her veil.

She would have known him anywhere, at any time, and her action was immediate and involuntary. He sat a quiet gelding, but on the horse she saw Marcus watchful and yet not seeing what was in front of him. He was still a strong man, but a wreck of what he had been when he and Meriem had first met. Lined and scarred, his face had set into a grim mask. She could have wept. But instead, being always Meriem, always valiant for truth, she flung back the veil and stared him in the face.

Marcus stared back unbelieving at the fat, middle-aged Jewish woman with coarsely-dyed black hair – a widow by the looks of her – and those lustrous purple-blue eyes. Faltering he said, 'Meriem?' and turned the horse. She saw a man come from the well with dripping mouth, Marcus dismounting and tossing the reins to him. Marcus came to her and gripped her by the shoulders as the women behind her twittered with alarm. Meriem spat a word over her shoulder, and the women subsided, controlling the donkeys. Then Meriem turned, pliant in Marcus' grasp.

'Marcus,' she said. 'You again.'

Marcus said, 'May we talk together, you and I?'

'We can't just stand here talking in the street.'

Marcus smiled and let go of her.

'We can sit outside the house of an old Jewish friend of mine not far away, then the proprieties will be observed.'

Marcus walked with her to Asa's house, while Khosro and Meriem's women came behind with the equines and disappeared into the vineyard. Marcus called Asa out and introduced Meriem as the widow of an old friend. Asa looked at Meriem, whose veil was modestly in place again, and nodded, glancing over at the little synagogue.

He said to Meriem, 'The Adonai is a friend to Elon, and I am pleased to offer some small hospitality.'

Asa shooed away some curious children, then brought stools and some fruit and wine. After that he withdrew discreetly.

Marcus leaned forward on his stool, fists on knees, and looked at Meriem smiling.

'I'd never have known you,' he said, 'except for those eyes. Your hair's quite different. And the way you dress.'

Meriem said, 'We've grown older. Different people. I think I told you what I would do, and I did it. To the world I'm a respectable Jewish widow.'

'Yes,' said Marcus. 'I found out you'd gone to some great

house, but my leave was up.' He grinned. 'That was quite a day at the races!'

Meriem touched his hand briefly and said, 'We are told that the love of money is the root of all evil, but my winnings made me free. And what have you been doing?'

'I fight,' said Marcus. 'I married, but my wife and daughter are dead. I have two sons on my estate in Gaul, and a concubine at my villa and estate here.'

Meriem smiled, 'You keep busy as ever.'

As they ate and drank they brought each other up to date. Then they fell silent, a sudden constraint between them.

Marcus said, 'My slave is in the vineyard with your women, Meriem. Shall you and I go into the olive grove, and try whether some things remain the same, for old times' sake?'

He put a hand on her knee, and she let it rest there; he stroked her thigh tentatively.

'Marcus,' she breathed.

They looked at each other, held for the moment in the poignancy of the past, the young harlot and her soldier client. Despite all the years there was respect between them. Marcus removed his hand.

'You've come a long way,' he told her. 'Are you happy, Meriem?'

'Happier than I have any right to be. I am housekeeper to Mary of Magdala, and I serve Jeshua her husband.'

'You mean as well as Mary?'

'No, Marcus,' she said. 'This is different. He has forgiven my sins; I have wiped my tears from his feet with my hair and anointed those feet with spikenard.'

'The Prætorium thinks he's a trickster,' said Marcus.

'He is the Anointed and the Son of God,' Meriem told him; and there was little more to be said after that.

Marcus whistled for Khosro, and he came with the two women from the vineyard, bringing Abaster and the donkeys. Both women were tousled and flushed, and Khosro sheepish but quietly self-satisfied: there could be no doubt about how he had passed the time.

Meriem and Marcus kissed each other chastely on the cheek, and then the three women left, while Marcus stood and watched until they were out of sight, hoping that Meriem would look back, but she did not.

He stood in silence for a long moment, then called his thanks to Asa and mounted Abaster, riding back to Kollura. Marcus was lost in cogitation, based on two points. If Jeshua stated openly that he had the power to forgive sins, he would be in deep trouble with the Jews, and if he said that he was the Son of God, then he would be in equal trouble with the Romans. In a cleft stick. But one thing was certain: if Meriem was one of his followers, then Marcus would make no report. Much better to concentrate on the Sicarii when he was well again . . . He tried to put Jeshua out of his mind, but found it difficult. A piece of Isaiah kept on running through his brain, perhaps set in train by Meriem's words about the Anointed:

> 'Behold my servant, whom I uphold; mine elect, in whom my soul delighteth; I have put my spirit upon him: he shall bring forth judgment to the Gentiles.'

LVIII

When Claudius and Geneura came to visit the Villa Galathë they brought with them only the slave Gesmas and a tiring-woman as their servants, but they brought a verbal message from one of Joram's men to say that the Arimathean was in the district and that he hoped to call on Marcus; it had been too long since they had met.

Marcus and Claudius exchanged their news while Kollura took Claudius' wife to bathe and refresh herself.

Kradog came in with Khosro and a slave-girl carrying refreshments to the table by their seats in the peristyle. Khosro served Marcus and Kradog, while Gesmas attended Claudius; Gesmas kept an eye on Khosro and avoided going near the plunge bath.

Marcus looked at the company and thought, They're all fat, except for me and Khosro. Kradog had lost weight when he came back from Britain, but it's back again now; Claudius is fat too, and so is his slave.

Marcus said to Claudius, 'I think there is going to be trouble in this part of the world, and I need some good men here. I've sent for my horsemaster and for an ex-Prætorian.'

Kradog chuckled and said, 'Siegfrith had his nose permanently out of joint on the trip to Britain. Joram's men left him nothing to do, and when we were at sea he was sick all the time.'

'So much the worse for him,' said Marcus. 'They will bring my library and some other things I want to have here with me.'

Claudius and Kradog were guzzling unwatered wine

companionably. Marcus watched and sipped his beer; since his wound he had taken to drinking only sparingly. . . . He brought himself up short: not since his wound, but since his meeting with Meriem.

He asked Claudius, 'Have you heard anything about the miracle-worker these days?'

'Miracle-worker?' Claudius asked, puzzled as well as fuddled. 'Don't know what you're talking about.'

Marcus gave up. He left the pair to their drinking party and went with Khosro on the routine tour of inspection, enjoying the evening coolness. Afterwards he was about to go for his bath when he saw Kollura and Geneura sitting in the atrium drinking fruit juice. He went over to them and sat down after dismissing Khosro.

Marcus asked Geneura, 'Has Claudius taken to drinking unwatered wine in quantity?'

'Only with Kradog,' said Geneura. 'Kradog comes over to the villa Batanya and talks to me, and after that he and Claudius get drunk together; then Kradog stays the night.'

'How odd,' Marcus said frowning. 'They're as fat as porkers, too.'

Geneura said, 'Claudius' father never taught him a word of his own language, and he never asked me to teach him. But while they're drinking Kradog teaches him bawdy British songs. They enjoy themselves no end. You aren't thinking of stopping Kradog, are you, Marcus? They're cousins!'

'No,' said Marcus. 'Not now I know that my steward has not become a drunkard. A binge with Claudius once a month or so doesn't matter at all.'

Marcus was bored, watching Claudius and Kradog get paralytically drunk at dinner. Marcus told Gesmas to haul his master up to bed while Khosro attended to Kradog. When the two slaves came back through the peristyle Khosro shoved Gesmas into the cold plunge. From the dining room Marcus heard the splash, Gesmas' cry of rage, and Khosro's laughter.

In the years since Marcus had last seen him, Joram had become an old man, astonishingly transformed from the

313

super-energetic tycoon into a venerable patriarch, stooped and white-bearded, though his eyes were still bright.

His retinue set up Joram's palatial pavilion, and he invited Marcus to dinner. Marcus had thought that the meal would be taken outside, but the Arimathean ushered him in.

'Come inside, old friend and benefactor. If Nakdimon had been here we'd have had to stay in the open air. But as things are we can cosset ourselves.'

They ate the food which Joram's people served: steamed fish, cold roast lamb with boiled onions and greens, plenty of fruit and nuts, and an excellent wine served with the *entreé*. They sat with full glasses after the table had been cleared and they were alone.

Joram said, 'I heard you'd been wounded. Are you quite well again now?'

'Almost,' said Marcus, 'but I don't think I'll be taking on the Kenaïm single-handed.'

Joram smiled thinly and said, 'You could always ask for help from your friends at the Intelligence office in the Prætorium.'

He was looking at Marcus under raised eyebrows, and Marcus felt a twinge of shame.

Marcus said, 'There is a woman whom I've known for many years. She is very special and completely honest. She believes that Jeshua bar Joseph is the Christ. Can you tell me anything about him? I assure you that for her sake this would not go to the Prætorium.'

'Do you swear,' Joram said gravely, 'by all you hold sacred that what I tell you next will go no further?'

With equal gravity Marcus said, 'I do so swear.'

'Your Intelligence infiltrated a man among Jeshua's followers. He was converted on his first day; he sends in false reports. I am able to help Jeshua and find him safe houses, but I don't know how much longer I can do this. If I could obtain support within the Sanhedrin that would be useful; but Nakdimon is unconvinced. It's a pity.

'But the Anointed? I don't know. We are promised a King who will come in glory, not one who hobnobs with tax collectors, the lowest form of human life. People say, too,

314

that his wife was a whore, whereas she has always been of exemplary virtue, a woman of noble blood.'

Marcus nodded: people were evidently confusing Mary of Magdala with Meriem, who was now of Magdala also. But he kept silent.

Joram sighed and went on, 'I'm an old, old friend of his father's. I only wish I could bring Nakdimon round to my way of thinking.'

Marcus could not fault his own friend, Joram. He had said very little, except that the spy had been converted – and at the same time Joram had prevented Marcus from revealing the fact. Cunning old fox, thought Marcus, and changed the subject.

'I thought I'd be meeting Nakdimon soon after I began my tour of duty,' he said.

Joram spread his hands, his mouth downturned.

'Not in Jerusalem. Not as things are now: if a *Sanhedrin member* were seen socially with a Roman. . . . But there's no reason at all why we shouldn't all foregather again at the Villa Batanya. To inspect the stud!'

'Good idea,' said Marcus. 'And remember there are spies everywhere.'

Joram grinned at Marcus and said, 'Oh yes. We must remember that, mustn't we?'

Marcus grinned back, made his farewells with thanks for the dinner, then left the pavilion and walked back in darkness to the lights of the villa, Khosro like a wraith behind him. Kollura was in bed asleep. She murmured something unintelligible as Marcus slipped in naked beside her. But he did not reach for her. He lay on his back with his hands behind his head, appalled at the conflict of loyalties which had been set up within him.

LIX

On the third day before the Kalends of March, Year 785 after City Foundation, L. Pontius Pilatus from the Prætorium at Cæsarea by Imperial courier to Tiberius Claudius Nero Cæsar at Caprineum. Hail, Great Cæsar!

Your servant begs leave to remind omniscient Cæsar that this insignificant nation of Judæa possesses the greatest treasure known to the world: that of the Jerusalem Temple. It is vastly augmented every day. As I have reason to be aware – and suffered great Cæsar's just reprimand – the Jews will allow no graven images. This means that the common people buying sacrificial animals from sheep down to pigeons pay in their money, with images of gods like the Divine Augustus or men like Herod, to money-changers in the Temple forecourt, and receive a harsh rate of exchange. This has been going on for upwards of three thousand years, off and on, and the treasure accumulated is of staggering proportions. I do not think that this fact has come home to my superior the Governor of Syria, and for this reason I venture to recall it to Great Cæsar's attention directly.

It is a scandal that this treasure should not belong to Cæsar, Ruler of the World.

The Jews are riven by factions among themselves, and the country is occupied by people of other nations, notably Greeks, with Arabs, Samaritans and others, giving rise to a perpetual turbulence. Two factions exacerbate this: the Sicarii and the Léstai, both terrorists. There has also arisen another faction led by one Jeshua the Nazarene, a bare-faced charlatan of high charisma, who is hated by the Jewish establishment because his tricks are likely to stir up the mob.

Your servant has a suggestion to make. He has trained a claque of Syrian legionaries who can swing any crowd their way. I crave permission to execute three Jewish criminals without reference to Antioch, the executions to be carried out as the result of popular demand by the Jews: my Syrians will take care of this, so that I may order the death sentences while protesting the reluctance of Rome, which will be able to wash its hands of the business. I propose to take a man of the Sicarii and of the terrorist Léstai and this Jeshua, and put them to death. It may take a year or a little more to stage-manage or find the appropriate moment. But after the event there should be three factions in ferment and a generally confused revolt. Rome will act to restore order with the initial consent of the establishment. Having neutralized them and having reinforced the Jerusalem garrison, I shall capture the Temple and transfer its treasure to the Imperial Presence, where it rightfully belongs.

Farewell, Great Cæsar!

LX

South of the awesome Gorge of Arnon, which debouches
into the eastern side of the Dead Sea, lie the plateaux of
Moab, thick with sheep. And to the north, in Peræa and on
high ground lies Machærus, palace, stronghold and prison.
Herod Antipas had his soldiers arrest John the Baptizer and
throw him into the prison. Herod was in residence there with
his wife Herodias, whom he married illegally. The Herodian
relationships were something of a maze. Herod Philip first
married Herodias, who was the granddaughter of Herod the
Great; then Herod Antipas took her over while Philip
married the daughter of Philip and Herodias, the young
Salome. These alliances broke all manner of laws, which
troubled the Herodians not at all as they happily kept the
family traditions going: Herodias herself was the daughter
of Herod Agrippa I and Cypros.

Salome was one of those young women who exude sexual
magnetism almost palpably; and her mother, who hated John
for accusing her of incest, put her up to a simple strategem
on the occasion of Herod Antipas' name day. There was a
great deal of revelry, and during the feasting and drinking
Salome sat next to Herod Antipas and inflamed him with
lust by teasing body contact. It was an easy matter to
persuade him into asking her to dance the striptease for
which she was famous, though the performance had been
euphemized into the 'dance of the seven veils.' Salome agreed
provided that Herod Antipas in turn would agree to give her
what reward she asked. Drunkenly the Tetrarch told her she
could have anything if only she would dance; and dance she

318

did: an Arabian belly-dance punctuated by the shedding of her clothes. Then she asked for her reward. Herod Antipas, who by this time could only think of his engorged member and how he would get it into Salome, hoarsely asked her what she wanted. When she told him to bring her John's head on a platter his erection went down with a flop. But he could do nothing but nod stupidly. Salome dressed quickly and had a good drink of cold sherbet, while Herodias got what she had wanted all along: John's head.

The Syrian auxiliary, dressed in Jewish clothing, penetrated the estate of the villa Batanya as far as the upper sheep pastures and a shepherd boy, who blew a ram's horn. When the man protested that he wanted to call at the villa for a drink of water, two armed and mounted guards showed him politely to a spring and then escorted him off the estate, still treating him with courtesy. He was obliged to watch the activity from a distant point of high ground.

But it was all innocent, he concluded. There seemed to be some kind of in-hand inspection going on. Horse after horse was led out before the three men the spy had been ordered to keep under surveillance: the Jews Nicodemus and Joseph of Arimathea, and the centurion Marcus Drusus Scipio. The spy had been a cavalryman himself, and he flattered himself that he could reconstruct their conversation. People who were interested in horses talked of nothing but horses; and that was what the spy would report, omitting that he had failed to come within earshot, and so escaping the punishment which Rabirius Regulus would have meted out had he learned the truth.

They did indeed talk of horses, Marcus and Nakdimon and Joram, with Kradog and Shimmon adding occasional comments; but the horse-talk was limited to the periods when stable lads were present. Thus the spy in the pay of Herod Antipas heard only this conversation, and later Intelligence collation would provide cross-reference with the Roman spy's report: Marcus and his companions would be pronounced clean. It would have been a very different matter had either Intelligence organization been permitted to hear the private conversation which took place at the Villa

319

Batanya on that warm spring day with a cerulean sky plumed with mares' tails of high cloud, the ammoniac scent of horses in the air.

Joram said, 'It's quite extraordinary, the stories that are coming in. He has raised the daughter of a man named Jairus from the dead. I have impeccable witnesses to this. And there was a woman who suffered from a vaginal haemorrhage for years: it cleared up as soon as she touched Jeshua's robe.'

'He breaks the Law,' said Nakdimon darkly.

They broke off as a horse was led before them for inspection, Marcus running a hand over its withers and down a foreleg, picking up a hind hoof, watching as the lad walked the horse in a circle; talking horses. Then, before the next one:

'My teacher and I believe that this is the man foretold by Isaiah,' said Marcus. 'If he is to bring the light of God to the Gentiles as well as the Jews, how can he at the same time uphold laws which are for Jews only? I have had a great tussle with myself about Jeshua and Rome. And I think he is winning.'

Nakdimon looked sharply at Marcus and asked, 'Truly? I have known no one so unswerving in his duty than you, through all the years.'

Another horse came up with another stable lad, the spy of Herod Antipas. Again horse talk and an inspection. The horse departed, tail swishing and head tossing, almost lifting the lad off his feet.

Joram said, 'He has four brothers and two sisters, all younger than he is. He antagonized them when he preached in his home synagogue, and in some way which isn't clear to me he is estranged from his mother. His wife is with him, the women Meriem and Susannah, and an assorted group of disciples close to him. He has followers by the thousand now.'

'In Galilee,' said Nakdimon, 'not in Judæa. I shall have to go back to Jerusalem and stay there until this affair is over one way or another. I cannot miss a meeting of the Sanhedrin from now on.'

Joram said, 'I have a small house with a large walled garden surrounding it, on a hill outside the city limits, a place named Golgotha. You and Nakdimon could meet there if you want. And you could use it for rest and recreation while you're in Jerusalem, Marcus.'

'Thanks,' said Marcus. 'I think that may be too dangerous, but I'm grateful for the offer.'

Marcus kept his guard up. He was confident that Nakdimon would never betray him, but also had not committed himself: Nakdimon was keeping his options open, and Marcus would have no meetings with him in Jerusalem. So the secret conversation was closed, and then they really did concentrate on the horses.

Marcus left with Khosro in the late afternoon of the horse inspection, but Kradog stayed the night to talk with Geneura and get drunk with Claudius. On the following day he arrived at the Villa Galathë in the early afternoon. Kradog was in a bad way. He had not only a stupendous hangover, but also was jolted and shaken: half a mile from home his mount had bolted when a dead branch had fallen out of a tree at the roadside. Fat and out of condition, his head bursting, Kradog had been given a very rough ride.

He staggered into the atrium where Marcus was standing with Kollura.

Marcus asked, 'What's the matter with you? Still drunk?'

Kradog said weakly, 'Oh, I . . .'

His voice tailed off. He sawed at the air with one hand, then went completely rigid before collapsing in a heap at Marcus' feet. He and Kollura bent over Kradog, whose lips were blue; the whites of his eyes showed under half-closed lids. Marcus blew his whistle for Khosro and told him to fetch slaves, telling them to put Kradog to bed.

Kollura said, 'I think he's dying, Marcus.'

'Not yet,' said Marcus. 'Look after him as best you can. I'm going to set him to rights.'

He hurried to the stables, took Abaster and rode bareback to Asa's house.

After greetings Marcus said, 'Tell me, is Jeshua still at Capernaum?'

'Yes,' said Asa. 'Why do you ask?'

'Will you do me a favour? Take another elder with you

321

and find Jeshua. Tell him who I am. Say that my steward is struck down with sickness, and ask Jeshua to say the word that will make the man well again.'

'Why don't you come too?' asked Asa.

'It isn't necessary. I have military rank, and people come when I order them, and go when I tell them to go. Jeshua has but to give the order, and Kradog will be well.'

Two old men set off into Capernaum, and Marcus rode Abaster back to the villa, where he found Kollura in Kradog's quarters holding cold damp cloths to the man's branded brow; his breathing was uneven and stertorous, and he was still unconscious.

Marcus said to Kollura, 'Don't bother with those cloths. Find a girl and tell her to bring me some nuts and beer; I'm going to sit here until he gets better.'

Kollura said, 'Are you joking? Kradog's had a stroke or something like that. If he doesn't die he'll be paralyzed or unable to talk properly.'

'He's going to get better,' said Marcus.

'How can you say such a thing?' Kollura demanded.

Marcus smiled and said, 'He's having dinner with us this evening.'

Kollura turned with a flounce of her robe, clicking her tongue as she swept out of the room. But she had remembered Marcus' request, and he sat on, sipping beer and nibbling nuts. After an hour and a half Kradog suddenly stopped breathing and shook all over like a dog coming out of water. Then he was breathing normally. He sat up and opened eyes as clear as a child's, his colour restored, and spoke some words in his native language; then he saw Marcus.

'How do I come to be in bed?' he asked. 'What's been going on?'

Marcus grinned and said, 'You were sick, and now you're well again. That's all.'

Kradog duly dined that evening with Marcus and Kollura as their honoured guest, and on the following morning Asa came to see what had happened. Marcus whistled for Khosro and told him to bring Kradog, who looked fifteen years younger.

His beard wagging, Asa nodded his head and said, 'So the mission to the Gentiles begins.'

Marcus said, 'As Isaiah foretold?'

'Exactly,' said Asa. 'This is entirely appropriate. You Romans have perfected your system of roads and sea-crossings covering the known world. They are there to carry the message of a new covenant.'

He took a scroll from his robe and handed it to Marcus.

Asa went on, 'This I had from a friend in Capernaum. It's the translation of a sermon which Jeshua preached from a hilltop to a huge crowd. This copy is for you, in Greek.'

'Why, thank you,' said Marcus. 'I'm the one who ought to be making you and your friend a gift.'

Asa said, 'Not at all. When I told *him* about you and Kradog and what you had said, Jeshua called to all those present that he had never known a faith equal to yours in all the land. Keep the scroll and read it.'

Marcus told Khosro to go with Kradog, find two amphoræ of their best wine and carry them to Elon for Asa and his friend. Then Marcus went to his study and read the Sermon on the Mount, the Beatitudes and all the rest. He put down the long scroll at last and blew out his cheeks. Counsels of perfection, he thought. How could normal men and women follow those injunctions? One in particular. Marcus had thought that he understood love, even asexual love, for that was now his feeling for Meriem. But how could an *enemy* be loved? Marcus was troubled and shaken by the intimation that the horse-sense of Rome, the clear-cut military duty and morality, could be overtaken by something greater, no matter how difficult to live up to. He fingered the scroll, hearing the domestic sounds of the villa's daily life outside: a clatter of utensils, two slave-girls' voices suddenly raised in a quarrel, Kollura's sharp interjection quelling them. In that integrated centre of his being Marcus knew that what he had been reading was purely right, and sufficient to turn the world upside down.

LXI

Marcus stared down at the letter from his son in disbelief. His library had arrived at Cæsarea with only the letter to accompany it; Marcellus had written it as the better writer of the twins. Marcus had asked for Siegfrith and Akbar to join him, with Phalaris if he wanted to come. But the truth was that none of them wished to join him, and he felt betrayed and abandoned. Siegfrith and Phalaris went with the estate which Marcus has signed over to the twins. He could demand that Akbar come out to the villa Galathë, for Akbar was Marcus' own freedman; but what kind of service could he expect in that event?

'Dear Father,' Marcellus had written. 'Both Siegfrith and Akbar beg you to reconsider your request. Both say that they are too old to uproot themselves at this point in their lives and travel so far to a foreign country. Akbar adds that the land where you are has never known peace, nor in his view will it ever be peaceful; should you insist on your rights under the law he will open his veins. Appius and I believe him, and are loth that he be put to the test, for he is a good man. We have made provision for the continuation of Kradog's income from the estate as you requested, and we do this with great pleasure.'

The letter ended with expressions of filial love; Marcus crumpled it up, and hurled it to the floor.

He was in transit from the Villa Galathë to Jerusalem in September after a local leave. He had spent it immured on the estate. Capernaum was like a beehive, buzzing with the followers of Jeshua, and Marcus was still Roman enough to have his sense of decorum offended. He had accepted intellectually the truth of what Jeshua had to say in his sermon, and the validity of his miracles; but all the years of Roman military life and the Greek ethos of his background held him away from a final commitment. It was too much; and on top of all that his sons had rejected him. Marcus went to the horse lines after arranging for the delivery of his library to the villa.

He walked among the horses in a world which he understood. He found Abaster and spoke to the gelding, holding its neck and burying his face in its mane, remembering the boy who had once owned a young stallion named Smoke.

And at the same moment a voice said in his native vernacular, 'I expect he's in trouble. That's a sure sign.'

Marcus turned slowly, detaching himself from Abaster and peering at the two men who stood at the entrance to the stall. They were auxiliary cavalrymen wearing light chainmail over whitish tunics, leather trousers just below knee length, and boots. Presumably they had just come off duty, and had stacked shields and spears; both carried only long daggers and wore no helmets; they had long hair bound with headbands.

In the tongue of his youth Marcus said falteringly, 'I have . . . just about forgotten . . . my native language.'

One of the men was short and stocky, the other taller, with sloping shoulders and a slim waist. The taller man strode forward, sparing a contemptuous glance for Abaster.

'We have *horses*,' he said. 'Come.'

They went to the cavalry lines. Despite their appearance the two Illyrians had Roman names: the taller was named Rutilius and the shorter Horatius. Marcus introduced himself, then admired the auxiliaries' mounts; they each possessed eight.

'Can you ride?' asked Horatius in Latin. 'Not creatures like that armchair you were with. Could you ride one of these?'

Marcus said, 'I've ridden a bit from time to time.'

Marcus half-expected the auxiliaries to provide some evil-tempered firebrand for him, but instead he was offered any of the three which they brought. He settled for a bay stallion, spoke to him, patted him, then was up in the four-pommel saddle with a lithe movement, walking him on while his two companions mounted and caught up. They left the camp by the side gate used by the cavalry, and trotted on out of the town past its two great aqueducts and out onto the flat, green coastal plain with a forest visible to the north-west.

Marcus felt better already. He had spent a frustrating few months before his local leave. After being transferred from light duties in the Intelligence office he had been detailed to investigate Essene activities, but had got nowhere. The sect was so secret and exclusive that it could only have been penetrated by a genuine Pharisee seeking Essene enlightenment; and a person of that persuasion would consider himself eternally bound by the oaths required of him. So Marcus could only report in the same terms as many agents before him: that the Essenes kept themselves very much to themselves, but were peaceable and no apparent threat to civil order.

During his office duty Marcus had spent much of his time with the squinting senior centurion, Plinius Otho, collating routine reports which Plinius sifted, sending those he selected upward to Rabirius Regulus, who performed a similar creaming process. Other sections were working similarly, together with the cryptographic unit, and at Marcus' humble level nothing made any sort of sense; too much low-grade material obscured whatever coherent threads ended up on the Procurator's table, and eventually in Rome. To Marcus it had been all dull and bureaucratic boredom, assigning file numbers, making lists, arranging files in alphabetical order. No one below the rank of centurion was admitted even to this level of work, so Marcus had to do it all without the help of an amanuensis.

He had spent his local leave on the estate getting fit again, and now he was a match for any horse, enjoying himself as the three of them cantered into the Samaritan countryside, shouting pleasantries at one another in the Illyrian vernacular, which came back more and more easily to Marcus.

Neither Rutilius nor Horatius made any further reference

to trouble, and Marcus was grateful for this. As the afternoon passed with these two congenial horsemen Marcus lost his depression. The countryside was green, and whatever Jews might have thought of Samaritans, they were not hostile to the three riders. The last vintage was being taken in, while the figs had already been harvested. Dismounting at a wayside inn, Marcus and his companions ordered bread and olives, figs and wine. They ate well and drank deeply. Marcus sighed at last, leant back and patted his stomach.

'I feel better than I've done for months,' he said. 'Glad I met you two.'

Horatius emptied his third beaker of wine and said, 'Most Romans sit a horse like a dead sailor, but you're Illyrian-born. Explains a lot.'

Marcus nodded sagely. Not only had his depression gone, but now he was also feeling positively happy.

He said, 'Some Romans can ride well. I knew a Roman once, name of Piso. He wasn't interested in horses at all, but he could ride very well. How about a drop more wine?'

When they left the inn they were mellow. They walked the horses at first, Horatius carrying a wineskin and passing it round.

Rutilius said, 'I know what! Let's race. Back to the first milestone out of Cæsarea.'

With a whoop Horatius brought his mount up to a gallop, Marcus a couple of seconds behind him; then they were all racing neck and neck, wine sloshing up and down in Marcus' stomach until he was at a full gallop. He yelled with joy. He wanted to forget the king who was no king, all that stuff about God and good and evil and loving one's enemies. So he galloped, with a good horseman either side of him, and for a while he might have been back in the land of his youth, living the elemental life of the senses.

Marcus came last in the race, and Horatius second, beaten a length by Rutilius. Panting and gasping they slipped out of the saddle and led their horses back to Cæsarea and the grooms, supervising their work closely. Marcus thanked the two Illyrians and would have parted from them, but Horatius grasped him by the arm.

327

He said, 'What about making a night of it, out on the town?'

Rutilius said, 'Good idea. Are you on, Marcus? See what else you can ride.'

Marcus was roaring drunk, spouting Dionysian verse in Greek, howling bawdy songs in Latin and Aramaic in the atrium of the brothel behind the amphitheatre at the northern quarter of the town. He ended with one yelled quatrain which left the brothel in silence.

> 'On the Isle of Goats old goat Tiberius –
> Though his manner's still imperious –
> He can't get a girl to fuck him:
> *He has babes in arms to suck him!*'

Every head had turned Marcus' way, faces distorted in harsh and flickering light and shadow from the torches on the walls. About thirty people were carousing in the atrium, Marcus and the two Illyrians with four girls at a table near where the floor show had taken place: a conjurer, a jester, and then a small dance band with a belly dancer.

The moment of silence passed, giving way to applause and laughter, then the general babble of conversation resumed.

Rutilius said, 'That told 'em all, didn't it? I hope there's no security police in here yet.'

Marcus said, 'Security police? Show 'em to me, and I'll have the lot of them in the cooler. I don' give a female fig for s-selurity colice.'

'Well,' said Horatius, 'speaking of female figs, that's what we're here for, isn't it? Time to go upstairs with our dryads an' oreads.'

Marcus found himself lying down with one of the young whores at his side. He must have dozed off. He fumbled at the girl's breast while she chuckled and teased his penis. Marcus and Kollura had made love that morning before his parting from her in the inn at Dor, ten miles to the north. Kradog, Khosro and Kollura's two women had accompanied her, combining her seeing Marcus on his way with a jaunt to the seaside and a change of air. Now Marcus wanted to go to sleep, but the girl was working him up to some response even in his drunken state.

'What's your name?' he asked, turning to mount her.

'Meriem.'

Marcus should not have been surprised. This was the commonest name in the country: Meriem, Miriam, Maryam – Mary – were interchangeable. But Marcus had already felt overburdened by Fate. His outing with the Illyrians had afforded a temporary surcease, but at the mention of this name he shouted in rage, picked up the girl and flung her down again. She screamed. Marcus put on his tunic as a burly house guard put his head round the doorway, eyes gleaming in the light from the single oil lamp in the room. He came in and Marcus hit him in the face, mistiming the blow. Khosro was not at Cæsarea, having been ordered to escort Kollura's party back to the Villa Galathë before rejoining Marcus.

He fought the guard out into the corridor; the man was bellowing for reinforcements. Heads popped out of the adjoining rooms, and then Rutilius and Horatius were at Marcus' side. They battled their way downstairs to the atrium, overturning tables in a welter of smashed glasses and beakers, and a general brawl developed. Marcus floored the man in front of him, then dropped to his knees and crawled through the mêlée which he had started, collecting a leather bottle of wine on the way. He curled up in a corner behind a marble table lying on its side, drank some wine, and went to sleep while the uproar continued. He began to snore, and was still snoring when the military police patrol arrived to quell the disturbance. He never saw either Horatius or Rutilius again.

Marcus stood at attention in spotless uniform, his transverse crested helmet perfectly straight on his throbbing head, his face set and his eyes narrowed against the painful morning light. A civilian in his condition would have been swaying and moaning, but his years of military discipline kept Marcus immobile under the glare from the Camp Prefect sitting opposite him.

'Dead drunk; fast asleep in a brothel for private soldiers,' said the Camp Prefect. 'And a fight like the Battle of Carrhæ going on! All I can say is it's lucky for you that you weren't fighting, and you weren't in uniform. What've you got to say for yourself, eh?'

Marcus rapped out, 'In pursuance of duties known to the tribune Rabirius Regulus I followed a couple of Aramaic-speaking persons into the establishment and found an excuse to join them. They were hard drinkers, and – ' He let his voice tail off into lameness. 'I must have taken more than I could handle.'

The Camp Prefect snorted and said, 'You're getting old, and so am I. But *I* know I can't drink like a young soldier: *you* don't. Take more water with it, Drusus Scipio!'

'Yes, sir,' said Marcus.

'The Procurator's in residence, and so's your tribune. What's more, he wants to see you, so the matter's out of my hands. I'd have confined you to camp for a month. You can go now.'

Marcus went for a long drink of posca, and felt marginally better for it; then he made his way to the tribune's office. Before going on leave Marcus had become convinced that Pontius Pilatus had some grand design afoot, and that this had been the reason for the endless upward transmission of apparently discrete Intelligence material; but Marcus had no idea whether he was correct. And at his level he would find it impossible to find out any more except by a stroke of fortune. Perhaps that would come his way in the future.

He was to be disappointed. Rabirius Regulus sat at his table rubbing a smooth block of pumice over his face to keep down the growth of whisker-shadow. When Marcus came into the office the tribune jerked a thumb at the clerk sitting on a stool bent over a tablet, and the man left the room. Rabirius Regulus tapped his table twice with the pumice block, and Marcus snapped to attention; but the gesture was not meant for him: the tribune inclined his head and blew a small accumulation of dust from the marble, then put down the block and looked up at Marcus.

'Oh, stand easy and sit down, Drusus Scipio,' the tribune said. 'You made a fool of yourself last night, didn't you?'

Marcus sat down and nodded his agreement. The Army

story he had given to the Camp Prefect would not wash with the man Marcus was with now.

'I was an idiot,' Marcus confessed. 'I met two of my countrymen, the first I've seen for many years. They lent me a splendid horse, and we went for a ride: my duty doesn't begin until tomorrow. Well, we started drinking in the afternoon, then we had a horserace, and . . . well, I got very tired.'

Marcus had told part of the truth, but his stomach lurched at the tribune's next words.

Rabirius Regulus said, 'You were holding forth in Greek, Latin and Aramaic. You had something to say about Cæsar also, I believe?'

Marcus moistened his lips. Unless he could find a way out of the trap which he had dug with his own words he could be in serious trouble. Quick! he thought. Aramaic. That song: what was it? As a Roman citizen Marcus could not be crucified, and he had the ironic right to be sent to Rome to be judged by the very man he had sung about. He would devise some very special punishments . . . Then Marcus remembered that he had sung one of the scurrilous marching songs of X Fretensis: to the legions any slander was permissible in a marching song.

He said, 'Well, sir, I was specifically ordered not to speak Aramaic in Judæa. But we are in Samaria. As for the song, I do dimly remember singing some marching songs, but I was too far gone by then to know what I was singing about, really.'

Rabirius Regulus paused, considering, then came to a decision.

'Very well,' he said. 'You get away with it, Drusus Scipio. On a technicality: two technicalities in fact. I won't bring any charges against you. Your work has been satisfactory, though you lack any real flair for Intelligence work apart from your languages. But you are seconded from Intelligence duties forthwith.'

Marcus must have shown his surprise, for the tribune leaned forward over his table and wagged a finger at him.

'You are growing old, Centurion,' he said, 'but in many ways you are like a child. Consider this place Cæsarea.

331

People are constantly on the move through here to the interior. Last night you drew a great deal of attention to yourself, yelling in three languages and in civilian dress. You have destroyed your cover, and believe me, it's very fortunate for you that I have accepted what you have told me. Appropriately enough I am transferring you to general duties at the transit camp until the Army decides what to do with you. Pick up the order from my secretary this afternoon. It's effective from tomorrow.'

Marcus went to his quarters and flopped on his bed with a great outrush of breath. Thanks to his knowledge of Army ways he had escaped punishment. He had disposed of the Camp Prefect with ease; but he shuddered at the thought of what Rabirius Regulus could have done to him. Then he brightened. There had evidently been an agent present at the brothel, but equally evidently that agent had stayed downstairs, and had not known that the fight had been started by Marcus. He whistled for Khosro, remembered that the man was still in Galilee, and went to the centurions' canteen. No more unwatered wine for him: in future he would stick to beer.

In the canteen he sat for over half an hour with a beaker.

On his way out he reached into his tunic for a coin to pay for the beer. His fingers encountered a smooth square shape. It was a small tile with a few words in Hebrew fired into it: a pass to Joram's garden outside Jerusalem, sent to Marcus while on leave. Marcus knew that he would never need it, but he had decided to keep it as a curio. He went back to his quarters and made life difficult for the batman assigned to him until Khosro put in an appearance. Soon Marcus felt cheerful again. Siegfrith could be something of a bore. Marcus liked Akbar very much, but he was a horsemaster and bloodstock trainer-manager. Claudius might have a use for him, but as far as Marcus was concerned he had to admit to himself that Akbar was better off in Gaul. And Phalaris? Marcus shrugged. He could stay with Siegfrith. So that was that. Marcus would write a graceful letter to the twins, then resume life in Galilee with those he had the strongest bonds with now: Kollura, Kradog and Claudius.

INTER SCRIPTUM (viii)

John Potts was up early, leaving Helen asleep; Waldegrave was nowhere to be seen, though that was no guarantee that the old man was asleep too. Potts visited the lavatory and then brushed his teeth, trotted to the pool and gave himself a cold plunge, immensely refreshing in the early morning. He dressed in light casual clothes and sat at the patio table with muesli and coffee. It would be an hour and a half before the daily help arrived. Only when he was almost finished with breakfast did Potts remember his dream.

He was in Glastonbury, in the Lady Chapel, looking at Saint Joseph's Well through a sheet of glass placed in front of the rough arch: he knew that the glass was there because, although it was perfectly clear, there were halations here and there on the surface from a light source behind him and to one side.

Sitting on the stone space to the left of the well was a baby, fat, pudgy, cuddly with a mere light down of hair on its head. It was apparently unaware of Potts as it gazed into the well. With surprising co-ordination the baby leaned and dipped an index finger into the limpid water, then turned, its movements those of an adult. It drew a downward line on the glass, smiling a baby's toothless smile as it looked past Potts to his right. The line was drawn, but it was not composed of the liquid, water, but of the colloid, blood. Potts was desperate to see who was the object of the baby's unblinking gaze, but he could not move his head. Then he was falling, into a close-up of the baby's face; eyes, mouth becoming paradoxically larger the farther he fell. Then he was awake, gasping, Helen warm by his side. She gave a small grunt and turned over. Potts drank some water and, to his later surprise, soon went back to sleep.

Potts pushed his breakfast bowl away and gulped his coffee, then stood up and walked to the patio wall, sunlight behind him, the scent of eucalypts rising with the sun. There was no smog, and he could see clear to the coast and its crawling white lines of surf. Then a movement closer by caught his eye. It was Doctor Waldegrave coming uphill, leading a borzoi, an unfashionable dog prized for that reason by its owner, a film director who lived in the next house down the drive. Waldegrave turned in there with the dog. Potts grinned and went back inside, woke Helen and gave her a cup of coffee.

By the time Waldegrave came in Helen had brewed a pot of Earl Grey tea, and cooked ham and eggs, serving them on the patio. Potts looked wistfully at the food, then patted his waistline with resignation; but he joined the old man in drinking tea.

Waldegrave said, 'The Americans are the Romans writ anew. Went for an early stroll before you were up, Potts, and there's this great fat man in a terry towel robe behind a military fortification. I used to have a borzoi many years ago, so I poked my nose in and said, "Splendid dog you have there," and the fellow told me I could take it for a walk if I wanted. I jumped at the chance, of course. Highly-strung dogs, borzois, but they *know* if you know them. Odd, all that wealth and fortification, and then total informality. Roman, purely Roman.'

'I thought it was all *dignitas, gravitas* and *maiestas*,' said Potts.

'Oh, they had all that as well. But great men unbent in total informality too from Cæsar down. And I suppose a film director is a Cæsar of sorts, these days.'

'What's that about Cæsar?' asked Helen, coming to the table with buttered toast and marmalade.

Potts said, 'It doesn't matter. If you'll just stop moving for a moment, love, I can tell you both about my latest dream.'

He recounted the dream, and when he finished there was a short silence. Helen shuddered.

'That's not at all funny,' she said.

'I agree with you,' Potts said, 'but that's not what I was thinking about. I once read an article in *The Times*. We are now aborting living, breathing, crying babies, strangling them, and burning them in *hospitals*.'

'Oh, no!' Helen cried.

Potts said, 'Yes. The nice, safe western democracies are sending babies to the ovens in droves. We haven't got a Hitler or a Stalin in charge, but we have the State: a morally relative State which gives itself the right to kill on the scale of a Hitler. So there's your baby and your blood. Personally I'd rather believe in Somebody Outside who says "Thou shalt do no murder".'

Helen said weakly, 'All those babies . . .'

'Yes,' said Potts. 'There aren't enough millstones to go round, are there? The babies, AIDS, Lebanon, Africa — almost anywhere you care to look: murder, disease, famine and war.'

Waldegrave said, 'Oh. Your Four Horsemen.'

Potts said, 'I think finally, however we interpret dreams, the facts matter, and they point to one conclusion: the twentieth century deserves the Apocalypse. Whether we get it or not is in the hands of God.'

The three fell silent; then Helen was the first to speak.

She said, 'I wonder if that *does* account for your dream . . . the baby drawing a line of blood on glass.'

'I believe so,' Potts told her. 'Doctor Waldegrave and I had been talking about disturbing reflections.'

Helen said, 'We've had enough disturbing reflections. After all that we need an anti-climax, and maybe I'm the one to bring it in. An alternative explanation. John, you didn't explain the location, that well at Glastonbury. Dedicated to Joseph of Arimathea. You got all uptight about him and Mary Magdalene when we were over in England. You were reading a book about the Holy Grail and the Blood Royal. Before I specialized in romance languages I had to do the German bit as well. A year or two back I bought a Penguin Classics translation of *Parzival*, just for Auld Lang Syne I guess. Anyway, I remember something. I'll fetch the book.'

She went into the house and came straight back. Helen

335

said, 'In the Foreword, by Professor Hatto.' She turned a couple of pages and then read, ' "Robert de Boron in his *Joseph d'Arimathie*, composed sometime between *Perceval* and 1199, not only has the Graal as a vessel – the chalice of the Last Supper – but also fills it with Blood from the Cross, anticipating if not already clinching the pious pun 'San greal (Holy Grail): Sang real (True Blood)'." How's that? The only thing is that Prof Hatto is a Germanist, and he's reading *true* for *royal*.'

Waldegrave said kindly, in contrast to what his tone would have been had Potts been speaking, 'Yes, my dear. I know you had an academic training before you went into publishing, but what precisely is the point of all that – beyond a twelfth-century attribution?'

Helen said, 'John dreamt of a baby before. Now the baby's at Glastonbury, drawing a line of blood. Do I have to spell it out? Don't you know what a bloodline is? A *royal* bloodline – at Glastonbury, taken by Joseph Arimathea?'

The two men looked at her in astonishment.

Potts said slowly, 'Of course there's the legend that Jesus visited Britain, but . . .'

Helen cut in with a gesture for silence.

She said, 'Just suppose it's true that Jesus was married to Mary Magdalene, since Jesus was a rabbi and rabbis had to marry. Don't you *see*, you men? Married couples tend to have babies!'

Waldegrave peered at Helen with swift alertness and said sharply, 'What you postulate is that the Blood Royal arrived at Glastonbury as a baby born of Mary Magdalene, and that Joseph of Arimathea was somehow involved?'

Helen simply inclined her head.

Potts exhaled heavily and said, 'Here have I been digging away, and then you just . . . And that's your idea of an anti-climax!'

LXII

MEMORANDUM
Date xvii before Kal. Mar., 786 after City foundn., xviii Tib.
From Procurator
To Sen. Trib. Gn. Rabirius Regulus
Subject M. Drusus Scipio, Cent. He is expendable. (For your information; no action your part.)

LXIII

Jordan's river is narrow and shallow. In no place is it wider than about one hundred feet nor deeper than about ten feet. It is also extremely serpentine, winding its length of two hundred miles into the sixty-five miles of crow flight from the Sea of Galilee to the Dead Sea, which has no outlet other than the evaporation of its water content.

Marcus had been detailed as an assistant transport officer at Cæsarea until his orders had come through posting him to the Jericho garrison far below sea-level. The eastern end of the Wadi Kelt debouches into the Jordan valley from a great gorge, and at this end Herod the Great built his winter palace on both banks of the wadi, with an assured water supply from one of the three springs which feed the Herodian city; the ancient city's ruins lie some distance to the north. East and south of the city the river passes through a lunar landscape of tortured rock, but the western side of the valley is kinder, and well settled all the way up to the Sea of Galilee; it was also an important north-south route.

Herod Antipas had a strong force of Judæan soldiers at the winter palace, but the Roman garrison in its fort consisted of only one maniple and support troops. The countryside was alive with people waiting to be baptized in the river by disciples of Jeshua, and the Procurator was confident that civil disorder would break out. Nothing of the sort happened, however. The mood of all the crowds during Marcus' service near Jericho was joyful and unquarrelsome: a state of affairs which was incredible to one who knew these turbulent people as Marcus did.

As senior centurion of the maniple Marcus was kept busy with administration, but he managed to get out as head of a patrol two or three times a week. One day he took his patrol to the river about six miles from Jericho when he saw a crowd of Jewish civilians some distance upstream. Marcus had twenty-four men and a decurion with him, and he led them quickly along the river bank, then halted them while he reassessed the scene. People were crowding round a man who was now and then revealed to Marcus. Jeshua. He was above average height with long black hair escaping from beneath his headdress, and a full beard. He was barrel-chested, a man of immense strength, stronger even than Marcus had been in his prime. Meriem and two other women were standing behind him, motionless in a kaleidoscope of movement: followers, worshippers – and others. As Marcus moved round the edge of the crowd, his eyes on Meriem, he caught the glint of a dagger and shouted, 'Look out!' as he leaped forward, knocking Meriem aside and gripping the assailant's wrist as he thrust past her at Jeshua's back. Marcus lifted his knee and broke the man's arm over it at the elbow. He was a short, squat man with hair in braids around a skullcap and a short, greasy robe; he screamed and then whimpered as Marcus rough-handed him over to the decurion with orders to take six men with him and deliver the would-be assassin to the nearest detachment of Jewish troops. Then Marcus looked at Jeshua.

He had turned during the commotion and was looking at Meriem, but then his gaze passed to Marcus, who felt himself summed up: everything he had ever done for good or ill counted and weighed in that instant.

And Jeshua said, 'Thank you.'

'I thank you for healing my servant,' said Marcus.

They were speaking Aramaic, but then Jeshua interjected one word in Latin.

'*Serviam*,' he said. ' "I will serve" is ever your watchword, man of decisive interventions.'

He bent and filled the palms of his hands with water from the Jordan, then cast the water at Marcus' face: coruscating jewelled drops under the sun's blaze; then Jeshua came and put a hand on the Roman's head.

339

And Jeshua said, 'I baptize you, Marcus Drusus Scipio, in my Father's Name. When your need of me is great, call and I will come to you.'

Marcus stood silent, the blessed water on his face. Jeshua turned away, and was lost among the press of followers, but Marcus caught Meriem's sleeve and detained her.

'Meriem,' he said. 'Did you . . . ?'

Meriem said, 'Yes. You are committed to the Christ, Marcus. Just you remember it.'

'I heard other words too,' said Marcus. 'His voice, speaking in my head. *Continue in good faith: the best is yet to come.*'

'I could not hear that,' Meriem said. 'The words were for you alone. Now I must go.'

Marcus took her hand, stroked it and then released it, watching her go and then turning to his troops; ribald comment died into silence.

He led the patrol in a curving line of about eight miles back to the fort, uneventfully, and after a bath sat in his office in the prætorium to complete his bumfodder: strength report, weapons report, daily situation report. In the last he made no mention of Jeshua, merely noting that an attack by an armed man upon an unarmed man – both Jewish civilians – had been intercepted, and the attacker delivered to soldiers of Herod Antipas. But he thought of the man Jeshua. Marcus had met plenty of people of strong presence: Targui for example, or Joram in his prime, and Marcus himself possessed it in full measure; but the impact of Jeshua on him had been extraordinary, to say nothing of his baptism of Marcus. The presence which Targui and Joram had projected was of aggressive and steely strength, but that of Jeshua transcended it and yet was peaceful, calming and complete. As for the message, Marcus puzzled over it and got nowhere. His attention slackened, for he was tired, and he found himself thinking of Meriem. He remembered her as she had been when young, and sighed, feeling melancholy over time past and opportunities lost.

Marcus went to the canteen, where he drank posca and chewed a locust pod, the curved black fruit of the carob tree, sickly-sweet and full of sustaining sugars. His junior centurion, Sergius Flaccus, came in and ordered red wine, then sat down by Marcus.

After a few minutes of general conversation the man suddenly asked Marcus, 'What did *you* do to get posted to the No-Hopers?'

Marcus said, 'I don't know what you're talking about.'

'I'm not saying where or when or why,' said Sergius, 'but all the old-stagers here belonged to a cohort that was decimated.'

Eyes wide, Marcus stared at the man. Decimation was one of the most severe of military punishments: selected by lot, one man out of every ten was then clubbed to death by his comrades, and the survivors forced to sleep outside the protection of their camp or fort. The punishment was only imposed for gross dereliction of duty.

Marcus said, 'I had no idea.'

Sergius finished his beaker of wine and called for another; Marcus sipped his posca.

Then Sergius said, 'All our replacements are expendables. That's why I asked what you'd done. But of course I won't ask you again. You don't want to tell me, so that's that, and forgive me for being nosy.'

Marcus grunted, put down his empty beaker and whistled for Khosro, then went to his quarters. Marcus had two rooms, bedroom and combined living room and office. Opening from the latter was a small storeroom, and Khosro had a pallet there, together with the chameleon, the mantis and a stick insect. A scorpion spider had been in residence to begin with, and it sat like a black egg with long and hairy legs in one corner of the ceiling in Khosro's little room.

Marcus asked him, 'Have you heard any rumours about this maniple?'

'Nothing at all, Dom'nus,' Khosro said. 'Except that it's a dead end.'

'What's that supposed to mean?'

'People get posted to this unit. But they never get posted *away*. That's what the supernumeraries say, but I don't know. They're a surly, unfriendly heap of camelshit.'

341

The chameleon was sitting on the back of Khosro's hand, holding his thumb and a finger, its turreted eyes searching independently, its colour settled into an indeterminate grey-brown. Marcus watched it, his mind elsewhere. By this time he had realized that his service in Intelligence precluded release from the Army. He was reconciled to that. Local leaves were generous, and his home now was in Galilee. He wrote to his sons every couple of months, and knew that they continued to prosper. But the thought that he might have been relegated to a unit from which there was no escape but death alarmed Marcus. Unknown to him a fly circled behind him and was about to land on his forearm: as it became motionless the chameleon got it, and Marcus jumped at the lash of the sticky tongue.

He said, 'Take that creature back to your hole. I'm going to dinner, and I don't need you to attend me. Do what you like, but stay in camp. And don't believe all you hear.'

Marcus walked to his dinner, pondering. He knew that his strength was declining with age, and hence that his chances of survival in close combat were decreasing, but unlike the majority of his comrades he had a good fighter to guard his back. Khosro must be soothed and kept in good spirits. But danger could also come to Marcus from his superiors. He decided that he would emulate Khosro's chameleon: blend in with his surroundings but remain capable of decisive action of a kind which he hoped circumstances would make plain. And at the same time he knew, after his encounter earlier in the day, that if Marcus had owned his freedom he would have dropped everything to follow the man Jeshua.

So the days went by, and one morning the crowds were gone. In a Jericho tavern Marcus, in uniform, listened to conversations in Aramaic for his own purposes. Jeshua had gone to Jerusalem. At the outskirts of the city he had selected an ass which had never been ridden before, for the reason that it was of the large dun breed reserved for the exclusive use of kings; and as a king he had been greeted by the crowds with the royal tribute of palm branches. That was all the

342

news that had come from Jerusalem so far, but Marcus would soon be able to get the latest tidings. The garrison was being disbanded, and the maniple was posted to reinforce the troops at the Antonia.

LXIV

The road from Jericho to Jerusalem was known as the Red
Ascent since the time of Joshua. Marcus slogged uphill at
the head of the maniple under a darkening sky, the junior
centurion bringing up the rear; they skirted the rim of the
Wadi Kelt gorge, and then trudged upward among the round-
topped hills of the wilderness. An earth tremor rumbled
through them, and Marcus glanced down over his shoulder
at the pewter surface of the Dead Sea. The Jews called it the
Salt Sea, salt having a wealth of associations both secular
and religious, and at the southern end salt floated in big cakes
for the taking. The Greeks, interested for worldly reasons in
another of its products, called it Asphaltitis: the Sea of
Asphalt. Everyone knew that one of the openings to the
underworld lay by its shores, and Marcus was glad to be
leaving its proximity. As though echoing the tremor, thunder
growled above.

They began climbing a steep stairway. Marcus moved
automatically, puzzling over a dream. He patted a fold of
his tunic below his body armour, and felt the little tile given
to him by Joram, and the gold box Marcus had bought in
Antioch. A very peculiar dream. In it he had been detached
from events, powerless to intervene. A pair of hands had
been holding the box, with a background similar to the
countryside he now saw. But on one wrist there had been
an ornament or jewel beyond his comprehension. It was
clasping the wrist with a band of metal of inconceivable
complexity, a miniature chain-mail such as no smith on earth
could have forged. The ornament, jewel, device or whatever

which was held on the wrist shone bright gold encasing a piece of glass, and below it symbols could be seen, changing even as Marcus watched: meaningless symbols. Then the hands were opening his box. But instead of the crisp clean parchment inside, a piece of ancient garbage was taken out and opened some way. A deep voice with an accent so barbarous that Marcus could scarcely recognize the Latin said, '*Ante diem undevicesimum Kalendas Januarias,*' and then Marcus was falling, falling towards the box, into a golden blur. And a cold sweat when he had shuddered awake, knowing that like Pylades he had been dreaming true; but quite unable to read his dream.

They walked through Bethany at ease; someone tried to strike up a marching song now that the going was easier, but the sky was black and doom-laden, and the song died. One of the soldiers snatched up a chicken and wrung its neck. Aramaic imprecations followed the marchers out of the village.

The earth groaned, bellowed and shook as the maniple entered Jerusalem. Marcus halted his troops as they staggered into one another in confusion, and then in a quiet spell he ran with them into the Antonia where he dismissed them and reported to the Camp Prefect, Attius Fimbria.

'I never thought we'd get here,' Marcus said. 'But now we have done, Longinus owes me thirty silver denarii. He bet me we'd lose at least ten men on garrison at Jericho, but we haven't lost even one. No casualties at all.'

'That's a coincidence,' said Attius.

'No casualties?'

Attius said, 'No: thirty denarii. Or more likely it's just the way money circulates. Pilatus turned one of the followers of that rabble-rouser Jeshua . . .'

Marcus interrupted: 'He's no rabble-rouser. Jeshua's a man of peace.'

Attius snorted and said, 'You haven't been here; you know nothing. When he rode in there was almost a riot. And there *was* a riot when he went to the Temple. He set about the money-changers for a start. Jupiter knows what else! But to come back to what I was saying before you broke in. The Jews want a king, and at first they proclaimed Jeshua King

345

of the Jews. Cæsar is the only king-maker, so Pilatus arrested Jeshua when this agent pointed him out publicly for a bounty of thirty denarii. Then Pilatus primed the crowd with his usual claque. The mob demanded the death penalty, and Jeshua's being crucified at this moment. What's more, Longinus is in charge of the execution squad.'

Black sky and shaking earth. A bolt of lightning showed Marcus three bodies on their T-barred crosses. Crucifixion was a routine event, but such a dreadful form of death that its terror never became blunted by custom. The three men whose corpses sagged behind Longinus had been scourged until the flesh of their backs lay in ribbons. They had then been compelled to carry the timber crosspieces almost half a mile from the Antonia to Golgotha. Eight-inch nails had been driven into the wrists beside the median nerves, causing violent contractions of thumbs across palms. The men had then been hoisted into position and an eight-inch nail had been driven through each pair of feet. The death agony had begun from that moment, the body raising itself on transfixed feet to take a breath until intolerable pain forced it to relax into a position where breathing was impossible, the up-and-down movements repeated until death supervened.

The mob was beginning to disperse as Marcus pushed his way through. The executions had taken place in the walled garden belonging to Joram, where the crowds could witness them without becoming a threat to security. At the entrance Marcus showed his tile pass, and went in past the guards. The soldiers' customary dicing for the victims' effects was over, and Longinus stood in front of Jeshua's body holding a spear. Beyond him Marcus saw Meriem with other women and two men. Longinus was ashen-faced and trembling, scarcely able to speak. The blade of the spear which he must have taken from one of the soldiers was smeared with bloody fluid, and a wound in the rib-cage of the corpse testified that Longinus had found out that the lungs had filled at death.

Marcus' immediate concern was for his comrade. He took the spear and handed it to a soldier.

'Give me your water-bottle,' he said to the man. 'What's in it?'

'Only posca.'

Marcus led Longinus to one side, sat him down and put the leather water-bottle to his lips. He drank thirstily and then wiped his mouth; Marcus gave the bottle back to its owner and waved him away.

'We . . . gave him . . . posca,' Longinus said shakily. 'Posca mixed with myrrh. It didn't help much.'

'Do you want me to take over?' asked Marcus.

'No. I'm better already. I'm glad you came, though.'

Longinus got to his feet and squared his back, calling the squad together while Marcus went over to Meriem and the people with her. There was no wailing or other lamentation as yet, and Marcus wanted to get away before it started when the bodies were taken down, washed and anointed before being conveyed to their tombs.

Marcus said, 'Meriem. There's nothing I can say, is there?'

The others were clustered together in a silent knot of kinship, numbed and bemused. Meriem shook her head.

'Have you seen Jor— Joseph of Ramathaim?' Marcus asked.

'He was here,' Meriem said in a dull voice. 'He has gone to ask Pilatus for Jeshua's body while Nakdimon prepares the tomb.'

Marcus was aware that anything he could say would be an anticlimax, but he spoke just the same.

'If I can be of help, let me know and I'll do what I can,' he said.

'Yes. Farewell, Marcus.'

Marcus leaned down and kissed her on the brow, then left the garden without looking back, scarcely noticing that the earth tremors and the storm had passed before he had met Longinus. Marcus never saw Meriem again.

LXV

Worldyear 3792, 17 Nísan, Joram to Nakd. by hand. You did well to carry the crosspiece. He is risen.

LXVI

Nothing came of Pilatus' plan to seize the treasure of the Jerusalem Temple. Even the most devious of people sometimes make a miscalculation. Apart from those who followed Jeshua the Jewish people were very satisfied to have secured the release of the freedom-fighter bar Abbas. They had been disappointed by Jeshua's failure to rise in the glory of earthly kingship and miraculously expel the Romans from the holy ground of Israel; and while bar Abbas was free they kept some options open. He might turn out to be their king, or might at least point the way to one. But there was no sign of a rebellion. Pilatus withdrew to Cæsarea and sulked.

There were three thousand Roman troops in the area, two thousand five hundred foot soldiers and five hundred cavalry. Units with ikonic standards could not be used in Jerusalem, so the garrison was maintained by a few anikonic maniples constantly shuttling between Jerusalem and Cæsarea, replaced at intervals by troops from Antioch. Marcus' maniple served for three weeks after Jeshua's execution before transferring to Cæsarea, and a week previously Marcus' periods of free time coincided with those of Longinus; one evening they sat in Marcus' quarters while Khosro served drinks and fruit, then went into his little room to his insectivorous pets.

The troops on duty were at drill. In the distance Marcus heard shouted commands, a trumpet call, feet stamping in unison as he watched Longinus, a tough and hard-bitten veteran like Marcus staring into his wine.

In fact Longinus was wondering whether he should confide in Marcus. He decided to do so, and looked up.

'There are wild rumours,' he said. 'People are saying that Jeshua came back from the dead, not as a shade but as living flesh, and showed himself to some of his followers.'

'But how can that be?' asked Marcus incredulously.

Longinus said, 'You believe that Jeshua cured your steward, I think you said.'

'Unquestionably.'

'Then anything is possible. We are not speaking about the reanimation of a dead body, but a fleshly statement of what the future holds for those who believe. Nothing less than that.'

Marcus thought this over, and said at last, 'I think all this is too much for me. Perhaps things will be clearer in a while.'

Things did not become at all clear for Marcus over the succeeding months. His maniple was employed on a series of garrisons in out-of-the-way places. This service was dull and boring, potentially extremely dangerous, even though the danger never materialized.

After the tour of garrison service the maniple was posted to Cæsarea for a refresher course to bring them up to date in liaison with specialist troops using improved siege machines: arrow firers, stone throwers and other heavy catapults. From time to time he met Longinus, but neither man referred to the event at Golgotha. The message of Jeshua seemed quite simply incompatible with the fact of the Roman Army, and both centurions had made a retreat. There was no one to guide them, to show them a form of worship. Marcus felt diminished in a sense, and when the maniple finished the training course Marcus snatched a few days' leave, and rode with Khosro to the Villa Galathë, hoping that the short break would refresh him. Kollura and Kradog were delighted to see him, and so was Claudius when Marcus rode over with Kradog on a visit; but he was merely going through the motions now: of love and personal relations as well as his life in the Army. Marcus felt beyond earthly refreshment.

Marcellus wrote from Gaul: 'Appius and I are well, but Phalaris has killed Siegfrith! It was an accident, of course.

Appius was practising with our grandfather's bow. Phalaris strolled up and slipped on wet grass, cannoned into Appius as he loosed the shaft, and the arrow went straight through Siegfrith. He died at once. Phalaris has gone to Massilia, half-mad with grief, and we've heard nothing from him since.' Marcellus added some general news, and then went on: 'I have decided to cease growing goosefoot, so Kradog's income will be cut off. But this crop has for years been uneconomic. We need the land for crops which pay better, and we hope that Kradog will not take it as a slight. He is assured of a welcome any time, or a home at need.'

Kradog took the news with good grace, and said to Marcus in reply to his question, 'No, I don't mind. I can only be grateful that a suggestion of mine made so many years ago has brought in so much. I have enough put by for life.'

And Marcus said, 'Strange: if Siegfrith had come out here when I asked him he'd be alive today.'

'He'd be alive if Phalaris hadn't slipped,' said Kradog, reasonably enough: but Marcus snapped at him.

'Don't chop logic with me! He'd be alive if my father's bow had not come back, or . . .' His temper subsided, and he went on, 'I'm sorry, Kradog old friend. I've not been myself lately. Do you know that I was there when Jeshua was crucified? At least, I was too late; he was dead when I got there.'

Kradog said, 'I didn't know. I knew that the Romans had crucified the Christ. We use the Greek letters that begin his name as his symbol: Khi and Rho. There are little groups of us who worship God through him; the people of Easter.'

Marcus asked, 'Is there a form of worship, then?'

'Yes,' said Kradog. 'It isn't much, but enough for us. There is a prayer followed by a meal in memory of the Christ, as he commanded.'

'What is the prayer?'

Kradog recited the Lord's Prayer, and rehearsed Marcus until he had it by heart, which did not take long. Afterwards Marcus went to his study and mulled over the words. He could find nothing at all incompatible with his duty as a soldier, and felt a great weight lifted from him. He spent the

351

next three days in happy domesticity with Kollura, then went back to garrison duty at the Jerusalem Antonia.

One winter's day Marcus met his former comrade, the centurion Plinius Otho. They had got on well together, and Marcus readily accepted Plinius' invitation to go out for a drink. They found a Gentile wine-bar. It was the same bar which Marcus had visited on his first tour of duty thirty-five years before, and although it had undergone many changes both of management and decoration, wine was still served there. It gave Marcus a feeling of continuity. He and Plinius sipped their drinks.

'Well, Plinius,' Marcus said, 'how is the great work of Intelligence getting along without me?'

Plinius grinned and squinted at his companion, saying, 'Oh, we're just about surviving. Rabirius Regulus has been posted to Rome, and we've got a new tribune trying to learn the ropes. Pilatus is in residence at Cæsarea, keeping very quiet. He's got wife trouble. Our lovely Claudia.'

'Has she found a lover?'

'No, nothing like that,' Plinius said. 'She's become a follower of the very man her husband crucified. Marvellous, isn't it? He could put away a lover, but as things are he's in a rare old mess.'

'Ironical,' said Marcus. 'And what are you doing in Jerusalem, or shouldn't I ask?'

'You're an old comrade. I'm getting on-the-spot reports. I keep hearing of Sicarii meeting the Essenes at Secacah. Something's cooking, and we'd like to know what it is.'

Marcus stood in the office of the Camp Prefect in the Antonia. He was a grizzled old man in his last year of service. He looked Marcus up and down. Marcus was excellently turned out: helmet straight, cuirass burnished with its medallions gleaming, tunic and kilt spotless and greaves shining. He wore his sword and carried his centurion's vine rod parallel with the ground.

His face was set in its impassive mask. The hair under his helmet was short and grey and his eyes unblinking as he stared straight ahead.

The Camp Prefect said, 'My opposite number at Cæsarea sent me a note about you, Drusus Scipio. Dead drunk in a private soldiers' whorehouse; fighting. You haven't been here a week and you cause a riot. What have you got to say?'

Two days after his meeting with Plinius Otho, Marcus had been walking in the crowded streets with Khosro close behind him, when he had chanced upon a group of people bustling one another about in aggressive postures. In the middle of the group were a couple, middle-aged and terrified. People were shouting in Aramaic. 'Call yourselves Jews!' 'Dirty Christers!' 'Teach 'em a lesson they won't forget!' 'Stone 'em to death!'

Marcus was off duty, but still in uniform. He beckoned to Khosro and the two men stepped in and whisked the couple out of harm's way and into protection, then escorted them to another street. There were howls and yells behind them; more people had joined the group, which was turning into a crowd, the members fighting among themselves. Marcus and Khosro went back to their quarters, where Marcus wrote a short report of the incident and handed it to a clerk in the Camp Prefect's office. That was why Marcus was here again.

He had been invited to speak, so he said, 'It wasn't a riot against Rome, sir. It's all down in my report. In the absence of the civil authority when that pair was under attack I decided to take them to a place of safety.'

'A whole howling mob,' said the Prefect. 'Thirty people killed!'

'Not by me, sir,' said Marcus. 'They began fighting among themselves. And I did bring that couple to safety.'

'That's the whole point. Will you never learn that it isn't your job to safeguard members of one idiot sect from another? These . . . what d'you call them?'

'I don't know whether they have a name for themselves. Some say Christers, others Easter people or Jeshua's folk.'

'Compounding blasphemy which the Procurator himself punished. Subversives, revolutionaries! Essenes, Sicarii, Samaritans, Christers, the lot! I had to turn out the whole duty maniple, and where were you? Sitting in your quarters writing a report.'

353

Marcus kept silent after this outburst. He knew that the Camp Prefect was being unfair, and that in the absence of a report Marcus would have been in even worse trouble; but this was very certainly not the time to point it out. The Prefect said, 'I'm sending you on an assignment tomorrow. I hope it pisses with rain all the time.'

He told Marcus about a spy's report that an escaped Roman slave was being sheltered at an Essene monastery above Jericho at Secacah. Marcus was to take sixteen men with their two decurions next day, apprehend the slave, stay overnight at the Jericho garrison and then bring the prisoner back to Jerusalem.

'Those Essenes are pacifists, so you should meet with no resistance. Just see if you can do the job without sparking civil war on the way. Pick up your orders at dawn tomorrow.'

Marcus had picked up his orders and, on an impulse, incised them with the marks of faith. Now nineteen Roman soldiers trudged along in the chill morning, Marcus at the head of the column, and the decurions each leading his section. It began to drizzle.

Two things had happened the previous evening. Marcus had gone to find Plinius Otho, having remembered what he had said about Secacah.

'I have to pick up some runaway slave there tomorrow.'

Plinius had grinned and said, 'One of our reports.'

'You said something about Sicarii meeting the Essenes.'

'Only in ones and twos. No need to worry about meeting them in strength.'

Marcus had been reassured, and had gone back to his quarters to find Khosro with a broken ankle, and a medical orderly binding him up. Khosro had slipped on a fruit skin in the street. So Marcus marched in the rain, without Khosro to guard him, and his thigh hurt from his old wound. The Camp Prefect at least would be feeling happy, Marcus reflected.

Towards the rear of the column a few men were singing one of the many bawdy songs about Tiberius: it was the one which Marcus had sung in the brothel at Cæsarea. The rank and file were adept at finding out information about their centurions, and Marcus knew that they were having a dig at him as well as their emperor, but it was without malice. Marcus' exploits would have been passed along with each tour of duty: his historic ride through Gaul, his being one of the four men to find the body of Varus and his lost legions, Marcus' lands and wealth in goods and horseflesh, his wild night at Cæsarea, his never once having taken a bribe – all these added up to a centurion who was held in awe tinged with some slight modicum of affection. And now he was credited with having started a riot in which thirty civilians had been killed! What was more, Marcus had promised the men a feast at his own expense. So for the most part they were marching in good humour despite the rain.

Marcus turned right, breaking away from the road, and beginning the ascent, gentle at first, to the plateau. The column followed and the men picked their way among boulders and smaller loose stones, slippery from the drizzle. The soldiers were fully armed, each carrying two spears, short sword at the left side, and a pack. But they were not carrying their entrenching tools or their share of palisade stakes. So for heavy infantry they travelled light, and this added to the generally cheerful mood.

Marcus concentrated on the climb and his twingeing thigh. The men behind him stopped singing as the ascent steepened. They reached the rim of the plateau after a long traverse. The drizzle cleared, and a watery winter sun shone over the desolation.

The value of an Intelligence report depends on its remaining valid. Plinius Otho's was out of date, and useless. During the previous day a hundred Sicarii had arrived in small groups at the monastery for a conference with the Essenes. Their leaders had become convinced that both Rome and the Jewish Establishment were getting ready to crush both groups: all their interests were being forced into the same channels.

That night ecumenical services were held in the Hall of Congregation, and the leaders preached to the effect that they must all work together for the common good. The

Essene Chief Priest produced the runaway Roman slave, who backed up all that the leaders had said.

It all went very well, and even better the following day, when an outpost of the Sicarii rushed in to report: a Roman unit of nineteen men was heading across the plateau towards the monastery. It was time for a show of solidarity. While the Essenes prayed with holy fervour, the Sicarii stripped to their loincloths and oiled their bodies, armed themselves, then faded away into the rocks of the landscape.

The Romans had no chance. In the ordinary way of things a superiority of five to one against them would have been regarded as the right sort of odds for heavy infantry in a prepared formation. But they had no time to form up. Surprise was complete.

Marcus was thinking about Kollura. He had bought her a bolt of azure-blue silk, intending to present it to her when he went home on local leave. Khosro's accident had altered things. Khosro was ordered to stay off his feet until he could travel, and then take Abaster, and the silk, to the Villa Galathë. Kollura would have a pleasant surprise.

Marcus and his men had a surprise which was anything but pleasant. His thoughts were interrupted by a sudden outcry. A storm of stones showered among the Romans, followed by the Sicarii. Marcus had a confused sight of scores of almost naked brown bodies in among his men, then his focus narrowed to just one of them in front of him, teeth gleaming in a blue-black beard, swinging a small but deadly hatchet with his left hand, while a long knife shone in his right.

As the man was in mid-leap Marcus sidestepped with a reflex action, swept away the man's axe with his short sword on the downstroke, then swung back-handed as the knife ripped grating down his cuirass and into his wallet. He despatched the man with the backhand stroke.

The air was filled with shouting. A few of the Romans were fighting desperately on their own: others were grouped in haphazard knots about their fallen comrades, battling on all sides against an enemy as ferocious as they had ever met.

Two more Sicarii came at Marcus, one to his front and one to the right. The first man had a dagger in each hand, while the second carried a three-pronged and barbed fish spear. Marcus rushed inside the daggers, planted the sword in the daggerman's belly and then swung the man round onto the other's lunging trident. A swift kick to the side of the spearman's knee stopped him.

Then the glint of gold caught the periphery of Marcus' vision. His box lay on the ground where it had dropped from his slashed wallet. He dived for it, grabbed it, then came upright to fend off a limping attack from the spearman. Marcus took a pace back to set himself, then his right leg betrayed him, giving way slightly. He took another pace back to transfer the weight, and fell off the cliff. There came a stunning shock. He felt no pain, but there was a sudden blackness.

When Marcus recovered consciousness he found that he was lying in a crevice of rock. His shoulders were jammed tight and he was staring up at something softly luminous. The moon? His vision began to clear, and he realized it was his gold box, resting on a little ledge.

He moved his head, and his helmet rolled off to one side. His right leg dangled below him, and the left was trapped, pulsing blood from a deep wound: a slash from the rock as he had fallen and deep as any swordstroke. In desperation he tried to free himself, but was too weak from loss of blood, and growing steadily weaker. He was in pain from a multitude of abrasions, but disregarded it as a Roman soldier should.

There was silence from above, the battle over and the bodies cleared away. Marcus knew that he was dying, but with that realization came another, ready to fly free the moment he made his commitment. Pylades had been right, all those years ago when he had asserted that Marcus and Kradog would be at the verge of great events. The Crucifixion; the miracles, including Kradog's cure. . . . Marcus was very weak now, but despite his weakness of body his mind was racing free. And words rang in his head like a bell: '*When your need of me is great, call and I will come to you.*'

'Lord!' he groaned.

And he was back on his first tour of duty in Judæa, drunk and almost incapable, holding onto the lintel of a door and peering in at the yokels inside; some were chattering and others were making the wailing sounds he had later learned were prayers.

In a corner were some women, among them one whose cool appraisal made him stumble in sudden shame at his condition. He turned his head to cover his discomfiture. There was a rough wrought-iron manger fixed to the wall and filled with hay, a baby lying on it in tight wrappings. Marcus stared at the baby, which was obviously the centre of attention. Its moving eyes stopped briefly and locked with those of Marcus before moving on, and he saw that the baby's eyes were those which had locked again with his thirty-three years later: child and man and God in one. And back in the fissure pain vanished as Marcus made that final pass to a higher authority than that of Roman arms, and stepped out into the radiance of his welcome.

LXVII

'What am I going to do, Claudius? I didn't know where to turn except to you.' Kradog said in despair.

His eyes were staring with worry and weariness, the blue smudge of his tattoo creased in the lines of his brow. He dropped Abaster's reins, and the gelding began to graze on the hay which a groom had brought from the stables at the Villa Batanya.

Claudius said, ' "Missing, presumed killed." '

'You were in the Army, cousin. Khosro says there's no hope. Jerusalem sent in a whole maniple, and Khosro tagged along. Everything had been cleared up when they got to Secacah. They found only peaceful and innocent-looking Essenes saying blessings on the Romans for having come to protect them from an incursion of Sicarii – but having come too late; the Sicarii had killed a small Roman unit and then vanished. There were no survivors, and no runaway slave. I've left Khosro to look after the Lady Kollura. He came in yesterday on Abaster, and brought the lady a bolt of silk from Marcus Drusus. It didn't do anything to console her, I can tell you.'

Claudius sighed and said, 'Look, Kradog, I want to talk with Khosro myself. You're in no fit state to go back today, so you'll stay the night and we'll both ride to the Villa Galathë early tomorrow. There'll be no end of things to be done, and I may as well give what help I can. He was a good friend of mine, and a good man.'

The leader of the Sicarii was the man bar Abbas, who had

359

been pardoned by Pontius Pilatus at the insistence of the Jerusalem mob spurred on by his claque. They were enormously elated by their victory over the Romans, not only because of its fact but also because of the propaganda value. As soon as the fight was over, they withdrew swiftly from the plateau and regrouped in the concealment of the Wadi Kelt. Out of a hundred men, twenty-three had been killed outright, and twelve wounded. Bar Abbas discarded the wounded to find what help they could, and with his remaining men swept north up the right bank of the Jordan after bypassing the two Jericho garrisons, of the Roman and Herodian troops. Where the Sicarii found Roman life and property they destroyed both, killing and looting their way up to the Sea of Galilee and skirting the large towns such as Tarikheæ and Capernaum.

When Kradog and Claudius reached Elon they found Asa and the menfolk of the village with torn garments, hair smeared by ashes, faces streaked and smudged, the air filled with lamentation. The two men listened briefly to Asa's sobbed and almost incoherent account, then rode grim-faced to the Villa Galathë, where smoke still rose curling from the ruin. The faint-hearted villagers had not dared to approach the villa.

Kollura and Khosro lay side by side in a welter of blood, the bodies of her two maids and the rest of the staff laid out behind them, their throats cut: presumably Khosro and Kollura had fought to defend them, and the staff had offered no resistance after the pair had gone down fighting; Kollura's bladed fan was still clutched in her hand. The building had been looted and the library set on fire, but Marcus' iron chest, set in concrete as it had been in Gaul, had resisted any attempt to open it. All the treasure which had belonged to Marcus and Kollura, together with gemstones and other valuables, were inside. Kradog's tears splashed on the iron surface.

Claudius said, 'I'll get some strong men from the village to break out that chest. It'll be a long job, which is why those murdering bastards must have left it. Now listen to me, Kradog.'

360

Kradog turned his desolate face to Claudius obediently.

He said, 'My master took me from nowhere years and years ago, outside a Celtic shrine when I spoke to the druid there on his behalf. He looked after me well, freed me and made me his steward. And now it has come to this, and there is nothing left.'

'I told you to listen to me,' Claudius said, 'not to give a funerary oration. There is a lot still to do, and you are to perform what Marcus would have wished. That chest and its contents belong now to Marcus' sons. I shall have it lifted into a cart and covered with firewood, and then you must take it to the Arimathean in Jerusalem. I'll write a letter which you must take with you. Joram will get that chest to Gaul of Narbo, and yourself along with it if that's what you want. I'll arrange all the other matters here.'

And so it was that in the morning Kradog set out on Abaster pulling a cart, a gelding riding a gelding on the road to Jerusalem. To a fruition.

Joram looked up from Claudius' letter and called for ewer and cloths. He washed and dried Kradog's feet himself, then ordered food and wine.

'You are a good and faithful servant,' he said, 'and your coming here is the answer to a prayer. I have here in seclusion the widow of the Lord Jeshua and her housekeeper Meriem, with others. The Magdalena is great with child. When it is born no one with servants will be able to keep this secret, and the child will not last five minutes here. But my best ship takes nineteen days to Ostia, and from there five days to Narbo. We go to Gaul, and the child will be born there.'

Kradog said, 'My master saw our Lord on the cross. Great one, we should go to the Villa Belinuncia, where I have to be at all events.'

The Arimathean inclined his head in agreement, and as Kradog ate and drank the old man went to a side table and brought back a small pot with some winter flowers: Kradog saw that Joram was holding a thorn plant.

'I struck this from the green thorns with which they cruelly crowned the Lord,' he said. 'We shall take this with us to

361

remind us that he died and rose again, even as these blossoms flower in the winter. It must be that we ourselves, somewhere and sometime after all our grief, will find our summer again.'

POST SCRIPTI

It was Christmas Eve, and John and Helen Potts were at Bethlehem, outside the Church of the Nativity in the commercialized little town. The doorposts of the church are incised with long, swordlike crosses, and Helen traced the outline of one with a finger.

'Who made these?' she asked.

Potts said, 'Crusaders, yelling "*Oli Cros!*" The early Christians would have found it all obscene.'

'Meaning?'

'Well, holy war, for one thing. The message was of peace. And the Cross itself, for another. It wasn't used until the memory of what crucifixion was really like had faded from people's minds. The early Christians used the Khi-Rho, the first two . . .'

Potts stopped short, staring up into the cold grey sky.

'What is it, John?'

'We're going back to Jerusalem.'

They stood in an office in the Department of Antiquities. An assistant had brought them the original documents which Potts had found in the gold box, the skins open and restored as far as possible. Potts was interested only in the later one, which had intrigued him in photocopy. He had told Helen about his absurd dream on the drive back from Bethlehem, and now he studied the document with a *loupe* at his right eye. He took out the magnifying lens and let out a deep breath.

'I was taken in by the Latin text,' he said. 'I read X for the Greek Khi, and P for Rho. But Marcus cut his orders in the literal sense with his dagger: χ at the beginning and ρ at the end. And that means that he was among the very first of the Gentile Christians.'

He looked at the document again and went on, 'How strange, after all our running around, it all comes back to this. It's dated the nineteenth Day before the Kalends of January. That is December fourteenth.'

Helen said, 'Well, so what?'

'It's been staring at me too. That's the Julian calendar. For modern western reckoning you have to add eleven days to the Julian dating. *Christmas Day*.' He put down the document on the desk where the other lay and came to his wife smiling. He hugged her and said, 'We'll go back to Bethlehem for the Watch Night service, and see the Day in. We live in Khi-Rho.'

(ii)

It was a hot August day, the shade temperature over a hundred degrees Fahrenheit in the San Fernando Valley, and even up on Mulholland it was over ninety. Potts lounged under a sun umbrella, the scent of the eucalypts in his nostrils. Any motorist caught smoking, even in a closed car, would be heavily fined on the spot. It was a Saturday, and for once Potts had nothing to do but sip a tall glass of iced pineapple juice. There was no smog, even though the conditions favoured its development: a light wind from the ocean. If he turned his head he could see the wavering white lines of the surf. A small earth tremor shook his glass on the side table and made the ice tinkle briefly. Potts ignored it.

Helen came out with a paperback and, native Californian as she was, sat in the sun. Potts wandered into the house and came back with a radio tuned to some music with the volume turned down, a Chopin nocturne of trickling tears.

'Listen to this,' said Potts. 'Maundering away about being

364

in love with George Sand. Bloody old Choppin from Boggart Hole Clough.'

'What's that?'

'Oh, nothing. Just some place in Lancashire. I'm having a mindless day.'

Helen said, 'John Potts, we've been married a long time and we're *supposed* to speak the same language, but there are times when I . . . Oh, my God, John, look there!'

She was pointing out and away, towards the ocean, or to where the ocean should have been. It was not there any longer.

'Tsunami,' Potts said tersely. 'There's going to be one hell of a tidal wave.'

Then the music died. The radio was a Worldmaster, and a voice began to speak excitedly in Dutch, which neither Helen nor Potts understood. And then the voice itself was cut off.

Potts said, 'Thank God we live up here.'

'Find a local station,' Helen told him. 'Be quick!'

But there was no time, for time was running out at last. The process began in the Great Rift Valley by the west shore of the Dead Sea with an earthquake that flattened every high-rise building in Israel; then the Rift sundered itself apart from Syria to East Africa. But that was only a local effect. Unprecedented transfers of heat energy were taking place deep within the Earth: changes of state. Molten crustal material welled up through every volcano in the world in a devastating series of eruptions and explosions. Simultaneously every earthquake focus was activated as the plate boundaries ruptured across the globe, decillions of tons of rock uplifted and fractured. The plates lost their form: Arabian, Antarctic, Indian, Nazca, African, Philippine, Caribbean, Eurasian, Pacific, South American, Cocos, North American. The energy transfers involved were enough to make global thermonuclear war look like a child's firework display. The skies conformed as the oceans of the world roared in tsunami, and billions of people died in the first minute.

The tidal wave which hit the Los Angeles Basin was three hundred and thirty feet high, travelling at five hundred and eighty miles an hour when it struck the Pacific Palisades. John and Helen Potts knew nothing of the wider happenings: like soldiers in a battle, they had only a confused and limited view of things. The P-wave of the first shock had thrown them to ground as it went through at five miles a second, rippling the earth and jolting the rocks as it went, bringing down the Playboy Club on Sunset Strip, the Century Plaza, taking total chaos through into downtown Los Angeles, while gigantic cracks were riven in a crazy-paving; the San Andreas could hold no longer, and half of California was on its way into collision with the tidal wave.

After the jolting shock of the P-wave came the wrenching, twisting shock of the S-wave, moving at only two and three-quarter miles a second, but still five times faster than a high velocity shell. John Potts was still able to raise his head and look with tortured eyes into a black and green sky. Running in panic on the open sandy ground with Helen, he had suddenly found his legs crossed, then had been hit by the ground, a trampoline of geology. When the S-wave struck he had been looking for Helen, had seen her moaning a few yards away, her mouth open and her face agonized. He crawled to her and put an arm round her. Something was broken, back or pelvis. Noise was in the air, the earth, inside himself. Fire and steam and thunder immeasurably multiplied, a mesh of red-hot wires screaming in his skull from high-frequency sound, the bellowing of a million bulls as a ground-bass. Fire was leap-frogging through the stands of eucalypts.

Potts thought he could hear a voice in his head or outside it − he could not tell which − that said, 'So things are concluding'; and one detached particle of his being assented: 'We don't deserve a Baby this time round.'

A chasm sixty feet wide opened up. John and Helen Potts were falling. Helen was in pain, only semi-conscious, and Potts as he fell still held her. He felt strangely removed, time and subjectivity altering as he fell. From the first millennium head cases had predicted the end of the world; he remembered them in London proclaiming its imminence on sandwich boards. But the world had turned upside-down and bade fair to turn inside-out now; and the time had come for the head cases to be right.

And the mountains broke like glass. The enclosing ranges shattered round the cities of the plain of eighteen hundred square miles: the Tehachapis, the San Gabriels, the Santa Monicas, the San Bernadinos, the Santa Anas. The Palos Verdes had already vanished. And still Potts fell.

He had time for thought. His eyes were open, but his mind was racing free in the darkening fissure. Sodom and Gomorrah were infant playschools compared to the world he had lived in.

The West. Take the money and run. Do as thou wilt shall be the whole of the Law. And the drugs internationals and the gambling internationals; environmental destruction in the name of progress; the sexual morality of the mole-rat with attendant plagues; the weapons of mass murder. And only a few men and women had paused to consider that certain behaviour patterns might be wrong.

The East. Genocide and the subjection of peoples; the Gulag; the perversion of medicine into the State drug racket that kept its dissidents in mental hospital prisons; lack of the basic freedoms and any sense of the value of the individual. Uncountable loss, the abomination of desolation: a system geared only to keeping an élite in power, making the Roman Empire seem avuncularly caring by comparison. The weapons of mass murder.

East and West conspiring to hold down the Third World, helped by its own massive corruption. It had all been *wrong*.

Still Potts fell, into total darkness. The world deserved to go: that was the only rational thought left now. But then images supervened. The houses he owned in London. A camel. The eye of a needle.

Hypocrite! he screamed at himself soundlessly in huge contrition. And heard in his head again words as high and thin as a gnat voice: 'Call . . . I will come to you.' He called, from the utter depth of desperation. And with millions of others passed through the event horizon of a Christian death, the flesh changing: molecules, atoms and quarks shifting over, for eternity.

He stood in subdued light, Helen at his side, her body

367

touching his warmly with thigh and upper arm. She was unhurt, healed. And opposite them the centurion was standing. He wore ankle-length sandals of soft leather, gleaming greaves, an immaculate kilt and a neat belt, but no weapons. His cuirass was burnished and his red cloak thrown back from his shoulders. Marcus was looking at them with eyes which held gentle compassion and perhaps a touch of amusement. The helmet he wore was shining under its white transverse crest. Everything was new, like himself: perfected.

Potts said in a faltering voice, 'But I know who you are.'

'That is why you see me like this,' the other said, taking him and Helen by the hand. 'Come with me now. There will be an examination, and then your children will be waiting.'

And he led them into the radiance.

STABIT CRUX DUM POSTEAQUE VOLVITUR ORBIS

GLOSSARY OF PLACE NAMES

Antibarum	Stari Bar
Arelate	Arles
Birziminium	Titograd
Brundisium	Brindisi
Butua	Budva
Carcaso	Carcassonne
Lugdunum	Lyons
Massilia	Marseille
Narbo	Narbonne
Remi	Rheims
Rhedæ	Rennes-le-Château
Rhegium	Reggio
Tingis	Tangier

Other place names will be self-evident from the text.

NOMENCLATURE

To supplement the place names above, a note on nomenclature may be useful. With a few exceptions I have used the ancient names for human habitations and the modern ones for rivers. The reason is that towns and cities are evanescent, but rivers are not, even though they may change course. But I have kept *Rome* and *Gaul*.

Targui, of the Tuareg, would have been a member of a

tribe then known as the Garamantes, totally unknown to the general reader; and I have given his people the modern appellation.

The tribes inhabiting what is now Germany I have called Teutons collectively. The German national language was originally *Tiutisc* (Teutish), and so I felt this extension was possible in a work of fiction.